PREPARED TO FIGHT

E.J. SHORTALL

This is a work of fiction. Names, characters, places, brands, media, and incidents are either the product of the author's imagination or are used fictitiously.

PREPARED TO FIGHT

ISBN: 978-0-9932979-0-8
ISBN-13: 0993297900

Cover art by E.J. Shortall. Photo courtesy of Depositphotos / stokkete & konradbak

DEDICATION

Karen, thank you for being you and for patiently listening to my whinging and moaning when my confidence evaporates. Without you I wouldn't be here doing this. Love ya loads!

Now, where's the wine?

ACKNOWLEDGMENTS

To my wonderful non-hubby, T. Thank you for making me watch all those UFC fights with you. Now I can see the benefit of it. Not so much at the time though. ;) Maybe this will be the one book of mine you'll actually read, huh?

Karen and Brandi, thank you for reading this probably as many times as I have, even in its bit part stages with horrendous typos and bad grammar. Nate and Liv thank you for your perseverance.

To my son, the child giant. As ever, I am so proud of you and what you are accomplishing. Thank you for bringing me back to reality when I get stuck in author mode for too long. Once again, sorry you're shirt wasn't ironed.

Huge love to my amazing beta team, Karen S, Brandi, Karen P, Kendra, Geraldine, Alison, Rhiannon and Kay. As ever, thank you for taking the time to read my baby and for being brutally honest with me.

There are two people I should have acknowledged way before now, like when I published my first book. These two authors have not only provided me with many great books to read, they also offered unwavering support, advice and have given me the confidence to pursue this dream. Kitty French and Jade C Jamison, thank you from the bottom of my heart!

To the ladies of Shortall's Sexy Sirens, thank you for the daily pimping and constant Facebook notifications. My phone battery really appreciates them. No, seriously! Each of those little comments, pictures, shares and likes means more to me that you can ever now.

Special thanks to Alison for joining me as my assistant for my first ever signing in Peterborough, UK. We first introduced Nate to the world that day and your enthusiasm for getting him out there made me smile, HUGE! The party in the evening was pretty epic too! Just for you— #NateIsHere ;-)

Thank you to each and every blogger out there. There are just too many to name individually, but please know how grateful I am that you are willing to share things for me without question, and without asking for anything in return. Please know this is a two way relationship and I am always happy to reciprocate in any way I can. All you need to do is ask.

Finally, to you, the reader. I can't believe I am now publishing my third full-length novel. I wouldn't be here doing that if it wasn't for you showing your support by doing the purchasing. When I started on this journey I could never have envisioned where it would take me. I still smile and squeal like a loon when I get an email or private message from someone saying how much they enjoyed my book. As a reader, I knew how I felt when an author responded to messages I sent them. To be the receiving those messages, well I don't think I will ever get used to that high. And I don't want to. Please feel free to contact me whenever. I'd love to hear from you!

~CHAPTER ONE~

"WORK, GODDAMN YOU. PLEASE DON'T do this to me, not today."

Staring at the screen on the desk in front of me, my hand desperately tugged on my ponytail nervously while I waited… and waited some more. The stillness of the usually blinking cursor, along with the persistent turn of the hourglass over my document told me that today my computer was standing up for itself and taking back control. It was mocking me, making me its bitch, and it knew it.

Why today?

With an accelerated heart rate and my breath rushing out of my lungs in short, sharp, frustrated pants, I battered my finger against the mouse, hammering out a frenzied tune.

Please work you piece of shit.

Nothing. Grabbing it by its plastic neck, I strangled

the life out the mouse, shaking and torturing it. Still nothing.

I cursed and slumped back into my leather office chair, scowling at the useless piece of machinery sitting in front of me. For over eight hours straight I'd been working on the plans for the new corporate headquarters of GO Leisure, an up and coming competitor in the British sports and leisure industry. Their account was my first big opportunity to make a name for myself and to prove my worthiness in the male-dominated field I'd chosen to pursue. With this project I was ready to go above and beyond to prove to everyone I could, and would, become the best. But to do that, I needed my computer. Trapped behind the dizzying spin of the hourglass were my flamboyant designs I was quickly becoming known for and the pitch perfect presentation that would get me noticed.

"Do not do this to me now," I growled through clenched teeth, once again wiggling my mouse furiously, hoping the movement would remind the PC who was boss. It didn't.

"If I lose everything, I swear to fucking God...." I continued staring at the screen and hitting keys on my keyboard with more force than was necessary. Nothing worked; it simply stared back at me in all its non-responding smugness.

"Problem, Liv?" Adam asked with an amused voice, as he sauntered into my office and dropped into the chair in front of my desk.

Without looking up, I continued glaring at my screen, hoping it would give in to my menacing look and relent, allowing me to put the final touches to the plans. I needed to print them off and prepare for tomorrow's meeting with the GO associates I'd met countless times before. "No," I snapped, making Adam chuckle. "No problem."

"Well, just for your information, beating the crap out of your machine won't do you, or it, any good. We have network issues and everyone's machines are locked. Gary is working on it as we speak. So, hopefully we should be back up and running soon."

I muttered a curse under my breath and finally gave up hitting my keyboard and looked up into the laughing eyes of my best friend. Having lived just two streets apart for most of our lives, Adam and I had attended the same schools, hung out at the same places and then, eventually, I'd followed him to Oxford to start my degree. Although he was a year older than me, from the moment he'd tripped me in the school playground and I'd punched him in the nose to say thanks, we had been inseparable. He must have liked my feisty, five-year-old attitude and in me saw a kindred spirit. I'd seen nothing but an annoying boy. Weren't they all at that age? After he'd begged and pleaded for my friendship, I eventually tagged along for the ride, giving him and his mates a run for their money in football matches and other 'boy' related games. Before long, my 'girl' status was being overlooked and I was one of the gang.

As we grew older, we spent more and more time with each other—playing football, studying together, watching movies. In fact, if we weren't being dragged along to our respective family gatherings, you could bet your life on us being together somewhere. Once we reached dating ages, people often commented on what a cute couple we were, always assuming we were together. Even the thought of that made me cringe. Adam and I were best friends, like brother and sister. He was my rock, the only person I could truly rely on. I would never risk our relationship by crossing that line - not that I'd ever considered it. I just didn't see Adam in that way. I didn't see anyone in that way. I was career focused through and through. Getting all emotional and mixed up over some guy was simply not on my radar.

Crossing my arms over my chest, I leaned back in my chair. "How long?" I asked, referring to the badly timed IT problems that were going to turn me grey at the tender age of just twenty-six.

"How long is a piece of string? Could be minutes, could be hours." He shrugged.

"For fuck's sake, I need to get this finished, Ad." I was all for living on the edge and thriving on pressure but not when both my job and reputation were at stake.

Adam chuckled in his deep baritone that was as familiar to me as my own voice and leaned in, crossing his forearms on the edge of the desk. "Someone's in a good mood today. Is it that time of the month or something? Do I need to duck for cover? Or should I go and raid the vending machine for whatever jelly bean packets you haven't already taken?"

"Ha, fucking ha. You're hilarious."

Adam's chuckle became a full on laugh as he took in my narrowed eyes and pouting lips.

"I just want to make sure everything is perfect for tomorrow. Is that too much to ask?"

Adam's smile faded into a look of concern. "Look, you've worked your arse off to get these plans ready.

My dad's out for the afternoon. Go take a break, chill out, and hopefully when you get back, everything will be up and running again and you can do whatever you were trying to do. You've got this Liv. You're going to blow them away."

I glanced back at my screen just as my stomach growled, reminding me I'd skipped lunch in favour of getting the GO presentation finished. A quick trip to the coffee shop for a caramel latte and a fully-loaded bacon and brie sandwich sounded divine. I might even totally indulge and go for a piece of their decadent Victoria sponge cake decorated with jelly beans. I wasn't going to be able to get anything more done until the computers were back up and running, so I grabbed my bag from my desk drawer. "You talked me into it. I'm going to walk down to Benito's on the high street; do you want anything?" I asked Adam as I walked past him.

Joining me at the door of my office, he said, "No, I'm fine. Don't be too long. You know Dad has his little snitches around the place." He gave me a wink, and then he was off, striding along the corridor with his usual confident gait.

I closed my office door and followed the path Adam had taken through the open plan area of the offices. He was standing off to the side with Ross and Carl, talking to them quietly. As I approached, he tilted his head to look at me, keeping his gaze locked on me until I'd passed by out into the main reception. He hadn't smiled or said anything and I couldn't help but worry that he didn't believe I could pull this off. The thought stung. Adam had always been my number one fan, my loudest advocate. I'd always been able to rely on his confidence in my abilities, even when others hadn't.

I forced a smile to my lips as I passed Tina in the main reception area of the small building that housed our company. Her grin at least showed me that she had belief in me. In fact, she was always gushing about how I needed to show these arrogant male egos that women deserved to be as successful in business as they were. Then she would go back to checking and filing her nails.

I pushed through the heavy glass front doors, stepping out into the heat of the late June afternoon. The humidity hit me with the force of a speeding articulated lorry and I soon began wishing I'd worn something lighter than the charcoal grey, wool mix trouser suit I had on. I carried around a few too many extra pounds and the hot summer days were proving to me that I really should do something about them. None of my lighter summer clothes fit properly, and in the heat, I often sweated like a pig, leaving me red and bloated.

The coolness of the air conditioned coffee shop was a welcome reprieve when I stepped inside. Normally, I would have grown irritated by the length of the queue in front of me. But today, I appreciated the chance to stand with the cool air blowing on my neck and back and that I was able to get out of the office for a short while. I loved my job. The fact that people trusted me with their ideas and visions and I turned them into reality was a buzz like no other. There was nothing more satisfying than seeing something begin as a rough sketch, or a vague idea jotted down on a piece of paper, and then see its completed form standing in front of you. Whether it was a small, single story extension to a two bedroom semi or an imposing skyscraper full of offices and restaurants, seeing the plans I'd been involved with come to life had my chest swelling with pride every time.

With every positive there was always a negative though, and in my case, the negative was Adam's father. Robert Ashworth was my boss's, boss's, boss and major shareholder of the company. He was as mean as they came and downright scary if you got on the wrong side of him. He was also a fantastic businessman, and his drawing skills and eye for detail constantly left me gaping in awe. But he had no people skills. I tried, wherever possible, to stay out of his way, not wanting to ever be on the receiving end of his wrath. That meant keeping my head down, working like a dog and never doing anything that might put me on his radar. I might be his son's best friend, but, as far as he was concerned, I was an employee like everyone else.

My stomach rumbled again as I studied the menu, trying to decide if maybe I should deviate from my normal food and beverage choice. As I perused the various coffee and smoothie options available, I heard sniggering from behind me. Not usually the type to get all paranoid at hearing the unmistakable cackle of girls giggling, I turned my head to see what was so funny. Sat around a table near the front window were three girls as skinny and fake looking as any Barbie doll, and they were looking directly at me. I swallowed down my natural urge to throw them a snarky comment and simply stared back with a raised brow. Whatever their problem was, they would either have the guts to tell me to my face or let it drop. Either way, I would not rise to their pettiness. I'd learned how to deal with bitchy girls like that during my teenage years when they would comment about my tom-boy ways and how I always hung around the guys. Of course I did; the guys were always so much more entertaining than dealing with the cattiness of some girls.

I was about to turn back to the barista and order my coffee when the tallest of the three—she also happened to be the skinniest, with the fakest boobs I'd ever seen—looked me up and down derisively and clucked her tongue. "You do know obesity is a growing epidemic and puts too much strain on our health service, don't you?"

Confused, I twisted around to see who she could possibly be talking to. Nobody stood near me, well apart from a long line of perfectly healthy and average looking people. Surely she wasn't referring to any of them? Realising her comments had been aimed at me, I turned back to look at the evil, Barbie-bitch. Her dull, lank hair had obviously been bleached far too many times and hung around her shoulders like a cheap, overly styled, synthetic wig. Excessive amounts of make-up were caked onto her scowling face. Yet beneath it all, I could still see the bags and dark circles under her eerily unnatural, lifeless blue eyes. And she'd been looking at me as though I'd offended her? Yes, I would be the first to admit that I carried around a few too many pounds that tended to accumulate on my backside and stomach. But at least I still looked healthy. This woman looked pale and gaunt.

"I'm sorry, are you talking to me?" I asked in an

overly sweet voice, as a burning rage coursed through me. What right did she have to publically humiliate me? I needed to rein in the anger and fire back with a suitably biting comment. What people failed to see when they looked at me was that I was no pushover.

"Hell yes, I'm talking to you. Do you see any other ugly, fat people in here?" She smirked and the two clones on either side of her giggled.

Sucking in a deep lungful of air, I tried to swallow the tirade I wanted to hurl at her. If I let myself explode here there would be many witnesses, and I didn't want the evil cow to have that satisfaction. As my abdomen expanded with the breath, the waistband of my trousers pulled tight, and then… *oh God no, please no, not that, not now…* I felt the thread holding the button in place snap. The little black disc popped off, clattering to the ground. To add insult to injury, it twirled at my feet a few times before skimming across the polished wood to land at the bimbo's feet. I closed my eyes for a moment, cursing every button and waistband god that ever existed and wondering what I had done to deserve the day from hell.

Barbie reached down and picked up the button, holding it between the tips of her thumb and forefinger as though it were vile and diseased. "Hmmm, looks like the garden salad—no dressing— and a bottle of water might be what you're looking for." She laughed and nodded towards the black chalkboards behind me.

Taking a few steps in her direction, with a glare, I snatched the button from her grasp. Leaning forward so I was almost nose to nose with her, I said, "The thing is, I may be ever so slightly overweight but I can do something about that *if* I choose to. A bitch is a bitch and always will be. Next time you want to comment on how someone looks, or think it's okay to bully someone because they aren't a flake like you, take a long hard look in the mirror first and redirect those comments."

Her startled expression left me with an element of triumph despite my blood boiling with pure fury at her comments.

I turned on my heel and strode out of the shop keeping my head held high, my left hand discreetly checking that my zipper wasn't slowly creeping downwards.

***

I FORCED MY way through the doors of the Ashworth-Moore building and stomped my way back towards my office. I was fuming. The short walk back had done nothing to ease my temper, and I was sure if anyone had so much as looked at me the wrong way, I would have ripped their head off. I was a bit like the Hulk, in that you wouldn't like me when I was angry. I might not turn green, but I certainly roared loud enough. People who knew me had learned that lesson the hard way. So, as I stormed through the open plan area, heads ducked and people quickly moved out of my way. It was for the best. I didn't fancy getting fired for slapping one of the admin juniors.

Back in the sanctuary of my office, I tossed my bag down beside my chair and heard the clattering of items spilling out onto the tiled floor. "Oh for God sake," I yelled into the stuffy humid air, staring down at the lip balm, mobile phone, bag of Jelly Beans and travel sewing kit scattered across the floor. *At least I'll be able to sew my button back on,* I thought snorting a sardonic laugh. I was so angry at the audacity of the airhead in the coffee shop that I'd probably need valium to calm me down, or at the very least a large, stiff drink.

I was crouched down, scooping up the strewn items and cursing ignorant bitches and crap computer systems, when Adam poked his head around my door.

"Liv?" he questioned apprehensively. Adam knew better than anyone to stay out of my way when I was clearly pissed off. He had suffered the backlash of my shorter than short fuse many times over the years. "Is everything okay?" He was also the only person alive who could calm me down with a couple of words and a gentle look.

All of a sudden, the anger and fight in me drained away and I fell onto my backside with a sigh and a gentle thud. "Why are people so nasty, Ad?" I asked, tipping my head back to look up at him as he walked into the room and towered over me.

He gave me a small sympathetic smile and reached his hands out to help me to my feet. "What happened?"

I allowed Adam to pull me up and then pinched at the extra skin around my waist. "This... and this!" I slapped my right arse cheek.

"What are you talking about?"

"I'm talking about the fact that my rolls and love handles seem to have offended the general population of London."

He frowned. "What love handles, and who is

offended by what?"

I sighed and stepped over to my desk, plopping my offending backside on the corner. "When I was in the coffee shop I had a run in with Barbie."

Adam paused for a moment, seeming to rake through his memory bank trying to place who I was talking about. "Who's Barbie?"

I rolled my eyes and shook my head. "Long blonde hair, plastic looking, perfect tits but no hoo-ha. You know… Barbie!"

The light bulb behind his eyes lit up and the corners of his lips twitched upwards. "Oh, that Barbie!"

"Yes, *that* Barbie! How many fucking Barbies do you know?" I slipped off my perch and walked around to my chair. "Anyway, Barbie-the-bitch pointed out rather rudely that my excess bulk is the sole reason the NHS is so overstretched right now." I sat down and tapped on my keyboard, hoping for signs of life that would distract me from the misery of my situation.

"She what?" Adam barked incredulously. "What the hell?"

I put a hand in the air to stop him from going off on one of his 'Adam-knows-best' rants. "She has a point, Ad. I think I ate far too many chocolate oranges at Christmas and they stuck to my tummy and arse like glue."

He rolled his eyes and looked me up and down. "There is nothing wrong with you, Liv. NOTHING!"

"Yeah, thanks for that, Mr. I-can-eat-whatever-I-like-and-never-put-on-an-ounce. I know I've put on a few pounds, but her comments were just cruel. She said I was obese," I whined. How was it that the remarks of one pathetic, ignorant individual and the sympathetic ear of my best friend could send me into petulant eleven-year-old territory? I slumped back in the chair and looked up at him with a pout.

Adam chuckled. "You are not obese, Liv. I wouldn't even say you were overweight. To me, you are perfect. However, if you are so worried about having put on a few extra pounds, why not come with me to the new gym I've just joined? I'll help you do something about it if you like."

I gasped and blinked rapidly at him. The gym? Was he fucking kidding me? Oh no, no, no, that was so not going to happen. Treadmills and I just did not get on. I still had the scar on my left knee to prove it.

"Yeah, like that is going to happen." I snorted.

"Oh come on. It will be fine. I can show you the ropes, get you started on a simple plan, and before you know it, that chocolate orange belly and butt will be well gone. Just think how hot you'll look for the Christmas party this year." He wiggled his eyebrows making me laugh. "Look, just think about it, Liv," he said, retreating to the doorway. "I usually get there at seven. Meet me there if you want to give it a try. Oh… and Gary said the network should be fully operational again very soon, so you should be able to get back on with your work."

As Adam walked out of my office, I shouted, "Hey, Ad?" He glanced over his shoulder. "Thanks! I knew I could count on my best friend to cheer me up." He gave me a slight nod of his head and left.

I slowly spun my chair around, pushing off the edge of my desk as it came around to keep me spinning, and mulled over the events of the past thirty minutes. What was it that had pissed me off the most?

Was it the way Barbie-bitch had called me out in public, embarrassing me in front of the coffee shop clientele? Or was it the fact that, deep down, I knew she was right? Okay, I wasn't as overweight as she made me out to be, but I wasn't your typical slim and beautiful book heroine either. I had curves. I knew I could do with losing some weight, or at least toning up and getting fitter.

I planted my feet firmly on the floor to stop spinning. Looking out of the small glass window into the comings and goings of the main office floor, I saw a tall, slim woman walk past. She was dressed immaculately in a navy blue shift dress with matching suit jacket and an elegant, ivory scarf. Her shoulder length, black hair framed her face perfectly. I could see from the way she was holding a stack of files that her nails were manicured and painted to perfection. She was stunning.

I sighed and looked down at my hands resting on the arms of the chair. My nails were not elegant; they were bitten to the quick and ugly. I caught my own reflection in the window as I peered up again. My dull, dark brown hair was pulled back into an untidy ponytail, my face looked plain without a hint of make-up and the puffiness and podginess from too many caramel lattes and chocolate oranges was evident in my slight double chin.

There was no denying it, I was Loathsome Liv and the lady in the office was Stunning Stranger. The question was, did I want to do something about it or was I happy being me regardless of a few extra pounds?

Barbie-bitch's words came back to me. *'Obesity is a*

growing epidemic and puts too much strain on our health service.' Whilst her bitchy words about weight were insensitive and uncalled for, she did get me thinking about my general health. I had lost members of my family due to heart disease and other illnesses associated with poor diet and lack of exercise. Did I want to continue the trend of putting on an extra pound here and there and risk illness? The answer was no. It was as simple as that. I needed to do something and I needed to do it now.

As my computer pinged back to life I made the decision to take Adam up on his offer and join him at the gym, starting tonight.

~CHAPTER TWO~

THE PARKING LOT WAS RAMMED when I arrived at the gym. I'd been driving around for a good five minutes looking for a space and had begun to think it might be midnight before I'd find one. Shaking my head, I cursed Barbie-bitch yet again. If it wasn't for her obnoxious comments, I would have been at home, happily munching on a pizza and enjoying a beer or two while I caught up on the latest episode of my favourite series.

I sighed again and continued edging forward at a snail's pace, hoping I'd spot someone leaving. A horn blasted from behind me ratcheting my ire up a notch further. Peering through my rear view mirror, my gaze settled on an idiot with a scowl so deeply ingrained on his forehead I was sure he must have a permanent scar there, a tell-tale sign to the world that he was a miserable bastard. He frantically waved his fists at me, like that was going to miraculously help me find a spot I could pull my car into. Extending my arm out of the open window, I gave him the one finger salute, which rewarded me with another blasting of his horn. *Whatever! Jackass!*

"Finally," I yelled, slamming my foot on the brake and hitting my turn signal. A skinny, middle aged lady in the pre-requisite Lycra yoga pants and tight t-shirt had walked past me and stopped by a fancy looking car. I looked down at my baggy, grey sweatpants and plain, white t-shirt that had seen better days. Not for the first time did I fear I would not fit in at this establishment. It looked too classy.

Miss or Mrs Lycra pulled out of her bay and my tyres screeched as I gunned the gas to make sure no one stole the spot. *It's mine, all mine.* I laughed to myself as the words played in my head like an evil exclamation that wouldn't have been out of place in a horror movie.

With my car safely parked and Mr. Impatient still driving around looking for somewhere, I wandered towards the imposing gym, taking in the expertly clipped hedges and well-kept flower borders.

"I was beginning to doubt if you would actually come," Adam said as I walked up to the front entrance, heaving my ridiculously heavy bag onto my shoulder.

"Don't start with me, Ad. I'm here, aren't I?" I grumbled, tilting my head back to take in the huge building in front of me. The place was enormous. From the outside, it looked as though it spanned two or three floors, and it was easily as wide as any major supermarket store. The front was constructed completely out of frosted glass, with a steel overhang covering the main entrance. Etched into the windows of the ground floor were the words 'Golden Oakes Sports and Leisure.' The place was clearly a high-end establishment and, even from outside, reeked of money.

I also recognised the logo. How had I missed the connection before? Golden Oakes just happened to be owned by one N. Oakes, owner of GO Sports & Leisure, the company I had been working with and would be submitting final design plans to tomorrow. I knew part of GO was a chain of gym and fitness facilities, but up until now, I hadn't realised Golden Oakes was a part of that conglomerate.

I let out a whistle. "This is some swank place. I bloody hope you're paying, Adam, because what's left in my bank account each month won't get me in."

Sure, I had a well-paid job, but when I had rent, student loans, credit cards, utility bills, car loans... I was barely left with enough each month to feed my daily caffeine fix. A posh gym membership was definitely out of the question.

Adam wrapped an arm around my shoulders and started walking us towards the sliding glass doors. "You're covered for the month. I managed to get you a free trial."

I snorted and elbowed him in the side. "Yeah? And how did you manage that? Am I going to be embarrassed when we walk in and the girl on the front desk looks at you like you're about to marry her because you let her suck your cock?"

Music pounded through speakers and the tell-tale sounds of weights clanking against each other drifted through the air as we entered the building. "You will be happy to know, I got you in the bona fide way."

"Oh yeah?" I eyed him suspiciously.

"Absolutely. What do you take me for?"

A player man-whore who wouldn't know the meaning of 'relationship' even if you were given nursery-style flashcards.

I shrugged. "It's just your usual MO."

Stopping mid-step, he turned to face me, clutching his chest and batting his lashes. "Olivia! You wound me deeply with your cruel words."

"Whatever." I rolled my eyes and began walking towards the large stainless steel reception desk behind which a large brushed-steel banner stating 'Welcome to Golden Oakes' was hanging proudly on the wall. "Are we going to do this or what?"

Adam signed me in with the blonde receptionist who was, sure enough, watching him like she wanted to eat him. With another roll of my eyes, I turned away to inspect the rest of the bright reception area. As I stared at the numerous pictures of some bloke who appeared to be a fighter of some sort, I couldn't help but think that this was probably a waste of time. I never managed to go back to the gym more than a couple of times in any fitness streak. There was never anything there to keep me interested long enough to want to go back.

***

I'D ENTERED THE building with no expectations and no idea of what I would do. My sole focus had been on getting through the front door—anything else would be a bonus. I stood in the middle of the first floor, looking around with wide eyes and a sense of panic. The large room was full of treadmills, cycles, cross-trainers, vibrating plate things that looked like they belonged in a BDSM club and God knows what else. I wanted to turn around and leave. Never in my life had I felt so intimidated. Nearly every machine was in use by men and women alike who were giving it their all but also barely looked like they were breaking a sweat. I had to fan the front of my t-shirt just to cool off from the anxious sweat dripping between my rather ample breasts.

Standing next to me, Adam asked, "Are you sure you're okay, Liv? You look a little pale. Maybe I should just take you around and show you how to work the machines today?"

"I'm fine. I think I can manage to press a start button and walk, don't you?" I twisted my head to look at him with an arched brow.

He raised his hands in an appeasing gesture. "Okay, I get it. Miss Independent strikes again. You're gonna do this your way, I get it. I'll be downstairs in the weight room if you need me." He backed away with a grin on his face until he rammed into a rather bulky and bald dude who didn't look too happy. At that point, Adam gave me one last wave and turned away.

Chuckling to myself, I skirted the outer edge of the room, trying to decide what to try first. As I passed a few rooms that were obviously studios for various classes that would no doubt kill me, I came to a stop in front of one with a 'Private' label plastered across the wooden door. Being a nosey bitch, I chanced a peek through the semi-frosted glass pane. The room looked like it was some kind of boxer's paradise with several punch bags and speed balls hanging from brackets lining the walls, along with racks of pads, skipping ropes and gloves. What caught my attention the most, though, was the imposing ring in the centre of the room. From my vantage point it appeared that the ring was almost circular in shape and wasn't edged with ropes but some sort of mesh. I was no expert, but I was almost positive that boxing rings were square and edged with three horizontally lined ropes.

Realising I was wasting my time looking into a lifeless room, I ambled over to a free treadmill. Luckily it was at the end of a row, against the wall, and, as if the treadmill gods were looking down on me, the one next to it was also vacant. Result! It meant I wouldn't embarrass myself in front of any treadmill pros.

It'd been at least two years since I'd last graced a gym with my presence, and it showed. I stepped on that evil black belt and froze. I was almost positive that all I'd done on the machines at the tiny university gym was press the button and away you went. As I looked down on the black touch screen in front of me, it was clear I needed a degree to get these machines started. I should have gone to NASA and learned astro-physics. The machine must have, at one point, doubled up as a flight deck for a shuttle. Tentatively, I hit the screen where it said 'START,' and I was amazed that the belt actually started moving. It was only when I started rolling backwards that I remembered I was also supposed to move my legs with it. Putting one foot in front of the other, I was soon congratulating myself on not falling off.

Okay, Liv, time to crank this bad boy up a notch.

Slowly, I increased the speed on the machine until I

was walking fast but not so fast that I would end up sprawled on my arse with everyone laughing at me.

You've got this, girlie.

After a few minutes of acclimatising myself to the new speed, I gathered up my courage and let go of the hand rail. I was on a roll. I was breathing heavily but not like I was about to keel over in cardiac arrest. Sweat lined my forehead and dripped down my back, but I felt good. I even managed to nudge the speed up just a little higher.

The TV monitors hanging from the ceiling near the cross-trainers were showing various sports, music and news channels. I made a mental note to make sure I brought headphones with me the next time so I could listen as well as watch. *If* there was a next time.

"Is this one taken?"

"Huh?"

"Can I use this machine? Is it taken?"

I twisted my head to look at the muscled giant stepping onto the machine next to me. "Help yourself," I mumbled through the breaths I was fighting to take.

"Thanks! Do you come here often?" he asked, tapping away at his screen.

I peered over at him incredulously, careful to keep my stride even. Was he serious? I thought that cheesy chat-up line had died with the dinosaurs.

Grabbing the small towel next to me, I wiped my forehead to prevent the sweat beads there from blinding me at any moment. "No. This is… my… first time…. I've got… a month's… trial." I wheezed, my exertions beginning to take their toll on my respiratory system.

"I thought I hadn't seen you around before." My eyes rolled of their own accord. Who was this guy, and what crappy school of pickup lines did he graduate from?

Mr. Cheesy Chat-up Lines started saying something else, but it got lost in the noise as his feet began pummelling the machine. I ignored him and diverted my attention back to the TVs I couldn't hear. There didn't appear to be anything interesting showing so I focused on the monitor in the middle, the one showing what looked like a martial arts fight. The guys were trapped in some sort of cage and were beating the crap out of each other. It looked like a modern day version of a gladiator fight in Ancient Rome.

The TV kept my attention for a while until I'd seen enough of their grappling. I couldn't work out if it was fighting or foreplay, and the thought turned my stomach.

Glancing down at the screen in front of me, I was impressed that I'd managed to power walk for over half an hour. *Take that Barbie-bitch*, I thought, pressing the screen to start a cool down.

When I lifted my eyes up again, my gaze locked straight ahead onto a bulging bicep, or rather the God who the bicep was attached to. He was standing sideways from me giving instructions to a slim brunette on a cross-trainer. *Holy Moly, the dude was hot!* She was giggling and batting her eyelashes at him. *Oh please! Can she be any more obvious?* Ignoring the woman, I trained my eyes back onto the guy. He really was a work of art, in a tall, brawny kind of way.

As my machine gradually slowed down, the guy running next to me said something but I didn't reply. I couldn't. My eyes were glued to the muscular stranger in front. Standing with his arms crossed over his chest and his legs spread wide, he oozed power and authority. He must have been about six feet tall, with dark hair that was cropped short at the back and sides but longer on top. He had broad shoulders and a muscular upper back that progressed down into a narrow waist. A nice firm arse was distinguishable through his black track bottoms.

I grabbed my water bottle to moisten my suddenly dry mouth. As I tilted my head back to drink, Mr. Sexy peered over his shoulder, looking right at me and piercing me with his electric gaze. The liquid trapped in my throat as I choked and spluttered, the motion causing me to lose my footing. I screamed an embarrassingly girly squeal as my arse hit the belt and I was catapulted off the machine, landing on the pristine wooden flooring with a loud thud which was quickly followed by the water from my bottle spilling all over me.

"Shit! Are you okay?"

Embarrassed by my less than graceful fall, I chanced a glance up at Mr. Cheesy Chat-up Lines. He'd jumped off his machine and was looking down at me, his lips curling at the corners as though he was trying to repress a smile. *Bastard!*

"I'm fine," I said curtly, dragging my sore, humiliated backside off the floor. The throbbing sensation radiating out from my lower spine proved I would no doubt end up with a lovely bruise as my souvenir of my visit. Reaching over the machine, I grabbed my towel with a huff and turned to leave, ignoring the idiot's sniggering.

As I limped off towards the changing rooms, I chanced a glance in the direction of the hottie. His focus was back on the brunette, and he was paying me no attention. I breathed out a deep 'thank fuck for that' sigh of relief and carried on into the ladies' changing rooms. For some bizarre reason, I was thankful he hadn't witnessed my elegant dismount of Satan, otherwise known as the treadmill. There had been something in his eyes in that one moment that he'd looked at me that left me hot and bothered in my most intimate places. I would have been absolutely mortified if he'd seen me fall.

***

THANKFULLY, THE CHANGING room was quiet and almost empty when I barrelled in through the heavy wooden door. For how busy the gym was, there were only a couple of women standing around chatting and one drying her hair. Relief swept through me that I might actually be able to shower and change without humiliation.

I grabbed my stuff from the locker and found the quietest corner. Away from scrutinising eyes, I performed the towel tango, quickly undressing without baring an inch more flesh than was essential. With my modesty protected by the burgundy towel wrapped tightly around me, I disappeared into the shower area. My eyes lit up when I discovered individual cubicles, each one made private, thanks to the white curtains hanging around them. Having to shower in front of others was not something I'd looked forward to doing.

My body felt fatigued, and there was a dull ache in

my lower back from my rather ungainly meeting with the floor. The heated water soothed and caressed my skin, easing the knots in my shoulders and soothing away the pain in my butt. With my eyes closed, I stood and savoured the feeling of warmth from the water as well as the heat that flooded into me when I remembered the hot trainer. Visions of his naked form joining me appeared unbidden behind my closed eyelids. Thoughts of his strong hands massaging shower gel into my flesh and aching muscles caused a shiver to run along my spine. I relished the feel of his hands skimming down my back, around my hips, up to my breasts… my eyes sprung open at the realisation that I'd been fantasising about a stranger and was about to fondle myself in a public shower. With wide eyes and a racing pulse, I quickly squeezed more soap into my hand and rushed through washing my body down. I needed out of the shower before my imagination ran wild again.

When the sweat and tension of my exertions—and the fantasies—was washed away, I dried off and walked into the main changing area. I'd finished up much earlier than expected and knew Adam wouldn't be anywhere near done with his routine, so I debated what to do. I could send him a text to say I'd left early and gone home. Or I could stick around and wait for him. We'd planned to stop in at a local bar when we finished so we could spend some time catching up. With how busy we were at work, we'd barely had the time to say hi and bye to each other in recent weeks. I missed him. I missed our chats and banter, but most importantly, I missed the calming influence he had on me. With the presentation looming before me, I needed that more than ever.

I remembered that the gym had a small café that served various healthy and nutritious meals, snacks and drinks. I vaguely wondered if they counted coffee as healthy and nutritious. I did, after all, take my coffee with milk so it was therefore part of my daily calcium intake surely? I figured I could sit in there and use my phone to catch up on emails while I waited for Adam. I also secretly hoped I might catch a glimpse of the hot trainer again.

I was brushing a piece of lint off my jumper, still lost in my indecent thoughts, as I walked out of the changing rooms, so I didn't notice the person casually leaning against the wall opposite.

"Good evening, Olivia."

Surprised, I jerked to a stop and lifted my gaze. The black track bottoms and white polo shirt, embroidered with the Golden Oakes logo, could have been filled out by anyone, but standing in front of me was my fantasy man himself. It was clear this guy was at the peak of physical fitness, each bunching muscle and pulsing vein evidence of the fact. After staring for far too long at the hint of a tattoo playing peek-a-boo from the sleeve of his shirt, I reluctantly dragged my gaze up to his face.

Holy Mother Mary, the guy was just... he just... he just was. He was perfection.

It took everything in me to not fall back against the wall and fan my face. It had suddenly become very hot in there.

"Are you all right?" he asked, pushing away from the wall. I blinked in confusion as I saw lips move and heard the words, but my brain obviously wasn't processing either fast enough for me to react. It was dull white noise muted by the whooshing of blood through my ears. "Did you hit your head when you fell?"

"What?" My voice was hoarse and quivered.

"I saw you take a tumble off the treadmill. I wanted to make sure you were all right."

I noted how his voice was deep and gritty, with a rasp that indicated he was either a smoker or someone who had at some point put his vocal chords through the wringer. Either that or he was just pure alpha male. It was sexy as hell and made my stomach and thigh muscles clench.

He stepped closer, looking at me with concerned eyes. "You seemed to land quite heavily. Are you hurt?"

The cavern of my mouth suddenly felt parched, and I wished I hadn't wasted my water earlier by tipping it all over me. Although, with how hot I suddenly felt, it would have been likely I might have just poured it over me anyway just to cool down. Licking my lips, I looked him in the eye and managed to say, "I'm fine."

He scrutinised me for a moment, his gaze flicking up and down my body before nodding and walking away. His confident swagger only highlighted his slim waist, firm backside and muscular thighs.

"Wait," I yelled after him as my senses slowly returned.

He turned around and stared at me expectantly. His brow arched emphasising a large scar that ran through it.

"How did you know my name?" I mumbled.

"Your membership form. I hadn't seen you around

before, so I checked what your deal was."

"Oh." I was annoyed with myself for barely managing one syllable words around this guy. I was usually well known for not being able to keep my mouth closed, but for some reason, this guy completely dazzled me.

"Are you sure you're all right? Can I get you a drink or something?" His long legs ate up the distance between us as he walked back along the corridor towards me. When he stopped, he stepped in closer and I caught a whiff of his cologne, or deodorant, or maybe it was just him. Whatever it was, it was sexy, powerful and deeply provocative. I drew in a slow, deep lungful of air and closed my eyes, intoxicated by him. I wanted to savour the moment and commit his scent to memory…

"Shit." Hands were suddenly circling my waist, tugging me against a firm chest.

"What are you doing?" My eyes darted open, and I craned my neck to look up into silver-grey eyes. I re-estimated his height; he must have been nearer six-two, towering over my five foot seven inch body. The guy was a mountain. A sexy, lean, man-mountain.

I used our closeness to get a sneaky grope of his body. My hands subtly pressed to his abdomen and I skimmed them up, memorising every dip and plane of his toned torso. He was definitely packing a mighty set of abs under his top. Moving my hands higher, they eventually came to rest on his rock solid pectorals. If the gym was going to be full of men like him, maybe coming back wasn't such a bad thing after all.

Nathan. That was the name embroidered on the material beneath my fingers. It suited him. It was a strong name, one that oozed power but not arrogance. I liked it. A lot.

"I thought you were going to faint. I didn't want you to fall again," he said, looking down at me, concern back on his beautiful features.

I pushed away from his chest, getting one last grope as I did so. "Thank you, *Nathan*, but I'm fine."

He chuckled and I looked away, embarrassed that he'd picked up on my subtle fondle. I caught sight of Adam through the glass wall partition. He was standing near a pillar chatting with a leggy brunette. It was obvious they were discussing more than the correct posture when lifting weights. His arm was resting on the pillar, and he had one leg crossed over the other. She was leaning towards him with a smile on her face. Her stupid fake lashes looked like spiders crawling over her face and I shuddered. The sight made my skin crawl. Adam lifted his free hand and caressed the black widow's arm, a move I'd seen him pull on countless other women. There was no way we would be meeting up now. Adam would be entertaining only one person that night and it wasn't going to be me.

I returned my gaze to Nathan, deciding I needed to get out of there as quick as possible. I was now more determined than ever to get home and wallow in my humiliation with a cold beer or two.

Keeping his eyes locked on mine, Nathan reached down for the bag I'd previously dropped. I snatched it from him and heaved it on to my shoulder. "Thanks," I mumbled, wincing when I twisted awkwardly, the movement tugging on my bruised backside.

"Olivia, I don't think you are all right. Did you hurt

your back when you fell?" Shame washed over me again, his words reminding me that he'd witnessed my epic tumble. "I can get someone from the spa to loosen you up if you'd like."

Outraged, I narrowed my eyes on him. "Loosen me up? You know nothing about me. How dare you insinuate I need loosening up? I'm perfectly calm and relaxed. If anyone needs loosening up it's… it's..." I couldn't get my mouth to articulate the words I wanted it to, so I gestured up and down his body.

Nathan grinned. "I'm not insinuating anything. I can see you definitely don't need to loosen up. You are obviously the epitome of tranquillity. But I was suggesting a gentle massage to help relax your back muscles and reduce your discomfort." *Oh.* "So what do you say? Would you like a massage to help you feel more comfortable?"

Only if it's you giving it to me.

"No, no need. I'll be fine. I'm just going to…" With blazing cheeks, I pointed towards the front entrance and side stepped around him.

"You really should get it looked at, Olivia." He said it with such a firm tone that I stopped walking again.

"Why's that, Nathan? So I can help line the already bulging pockets of the gym's owner? Or maybe you earn commission on the number of referrals to the spa you make? Do you walk around out there watching and waiting for dunces like me to make fools of themselves so you can refer them to the spa? Do you—"

Nathan glared at me, a smouldering dark look that made me take a step backward. "You are not a dunce," he said through gritted teeth. "And no, I don't get

31

commission. I'm offering you a massage on the house to try to ease the pain caused by falling from our equipment. If you don't want it…" He shrugged and turned to walk away.

"Wait!" I found myself shouting out for the second time, somewhat taken aback by his obvious anger. He swung back around and although his dark glare had gone, the tight lines around his eyes suggested he was still pissed off. "If there really is no catch, then I would love a massage. Thank you."

Five minutes later, I found myself in a room decorated in earthy and neutral tones. The lighting was dimmed, and soothing Tibetan flute music drifted through the air from carefully hidden speakers. The subtle scent of lavender and chamomile permeated the air, and I felt myself relaxing as I drew in deep calming breaths. Easing myself face down on to the massage table, I draped a soft towel across my semi naked body and waited.

I jumped when warm hands began to gently knead around my neck and shoulder blades. "Sorry," I mumbled, "I must have fallen asleep."

"No problem. I'll take it as a compliment that we can calm and relax you even before the massage." I twisted my head to see whose hands I was allowing to touch me. A petite Asian girl smiled back at me. "Hi, I'm Cassie. So, you've made a bit of an impression on the big guy, huh?"

I sighed and returned my face into the cut out, groaning in pleasured pain when Cassie dug into a particularly tense muscle. "If by 'big guy' you mean Nathan, then I wouldn't say that. He saw me make an arse out of myself when I fell off the treadmill. I think he felt sorry for me."

"Yeah, I'm sure that's what it is." She giggled and continued kneading and rubbing my tense and sensitive flesh.

***

AN HOUR LATER, I rounded my shoulders and neck feeling how loose and relaxed my muscles now were. Even the dull ache in my lower back had disappeared. "Thanks, Cassie," I said with a smile as I pulled on my denim jacket.

"You're welcome. Come back anytime. Try to stay upright on the equipment next time though," she replied with a friendly laugh as I left the room.

I walked down a short corridor also lined with various pictures of boxers or fighters. I tried to study them a little closer but they were all action shots, obscuring the view of most facial features. I scrunched my nose at the brutality of the images and carried on towards the main entrance.

Nathan was standing alone behind the reception desk flipping through paperwork. I couldn't decide if I should go over and thank him for the massage or whether I should just sneak past. I still felt like a total idiot for my incident on the treadmill and didn't want to have to acknowledge it again by speaking to him.

"Olivia!" So much for hoping I'd be able to sneak past. "How was the massage?"

Plastering a smile on my face I strolled over to the desk. "It was wonderful. Thank you so much."

"And how is the back?"

"Never felt better. Cassie has magic hands."

Nathan leaned onto the desk, propping himself on crossed arms. "I'm glad to hear it. Will I be seeing you again? It's just I'm a bit concerned about your treatment of our equipment." The twinkle in his eyes was the only sign he was messing with me.

"I'll definitely be back. I need to sort out this big, fat butt of mine," I said with a wink and took a step towards the doors, surprised to find that I actually meant what I was saying. "I hope to see you around some more, Nathan."

With a smile on my face and a spring in my step, I walked to my car and checked my phone. There were no missed calls or text messages from Adam. I took a quick look at the now half empty parking lot and couldn't see his car. I guessed he really had left with the brunette after all. I was saddened that I wouldn't get time with him, but I couldn't deny the thrill that I got from being able to spend the evening on my lonesome, picturing a certain fit, toned and handsome personal trainer. For the first time in a long time, I had been affected by a man. I wanted to soak in a long, soothing bath and remember every exquisite detail of him.

~CHAPTER THREE~

BACK AT MY APARTMENT BLOCK, I took the elevator to the fourth floor. When the doors slid open, I stepped out, rifling through my bag for my keys. Glancing up when I had them in my grasp, my step faltered.

Adam was sat on the floor, leaning against my door.

"What are you doing down there?" Tugging my bag further onto my shoulder, I stared down at Adam who'd made no attempt to stand.

"Where were you?"

"Where were you? When I came out of the gym you were nowhere to be found." Stepping over his legs, I unlocked the door and made my way inside.

"You didn't answer my question, Liv. Where were you? I couldn't find you in the gym but your car was still there." Adam jumped to his feet and followed me inside closing the door behind him.

I laughed and patted his cheek. He hadn't looked

worried about me when he was pulling his too-hot-for-you-to-handle routine with the brunette. "Aww was my Addy all worried about me?" I crooned.

He scowled. "Yes, I was worried about you. Where did you disappear to?"

I had cold beers in the fridge and they were calling my name. After a stressful day at work, and then having that interaction with Nathan, all I wanted to do was have a long soak in the bath and then a drink—or several. I thought for about a millisecond that maybe I shouldn't be drinking after my exertions on the treadmill, but that thought soon disappeared. I dropped my bag to the floor and turned towards the kitchen.

Pulling two bottles from the fridge, I handed one to Adam which he took without hesitation, twisting the top off but keeping his eyes on me.

"I was happily doing my thing, running flat out on the treadmill," I eventually replied after a taking a long gulp of the cool beverage, looking Adam square in the eyes. His lips twitched as his brow rose in amusement. "Okay, all right, so I was walking on the treadmill... fast. Anyway, I was watching some love fest, fighty thing on the screens when I saw… him." I'd wandered into the living room and dropped over the arm and back onto the couch with a sigh.

"Saw who?" Adam asked as he lowered himself gracefully onto the opposite end.

"Him, Adam, *him*," I said with far too much enthusiasm. "Mr. Hot Dude. Mr. I-should-come-with-my-very-own-warning-label-because-come-too-close-and-you're-gonna-get-burned." I peered over my shoulder and Adam was listening to me intently but he didn't look happy. "I was so engrossed in what I was looking at I wasn't concentrating. I choked on my water, stumbled on the treadmill and arse planted onto the floor."

Adam re-enacted the very sound I'd made when he choked on the mouthful of beer he'd just swallowed. "You fell off?" he asked through a laughter filled coughing fit.

"Yes, dumb arse, I fell off. It fucking hurt!"

"I'm sorry, Liv, but oh how I wish I would've been there to witness it."

"Yeah, thanks," I mumbled under my breath and took another swig from my bottle.

"That still doesn't explain where you were. I checked the cardio suite, you weren't there. I asked some girl to see if you were in the changing rooms and you weren't."

I smiled at the memories of my interactions with Nathan and how he made me feel. I sighed remembering the bliss of the massage. "Well, you see, after I got changed, he was waiting for me. He'd seen me take the dive and was worried I'd hurt myself. When he saw I was in pain, he offered me a massage—"

"He what?" Adam shouted, sitting bolt upright. "Some strange guy offered you a massage? You said no, right?" I turned further in my seat to face him and pulled my legs up underneath me. Adam had his gaze locked on me, his eyes wide. His knees were bouncing slightly in agitation.

"No, I said yes." Adam's lips parted as if he were about to say something then he slammed them shut and gestured with his hand for me to continue. "The guy works there, Adam. He's some sort of personal trainer. It was a no strings attached offer of a free massage in the spa. I would have been crazy to turn it down."

I closed my eyes and wiggled my shoulders, feeling the looseness of my now tension free neck and back. The massage had also left me feeling relaxed and therefore sleepy. A yawn escaped me as I rested my head against the plump cushions of my couch. "Besides," I continued without opening my eyes, "with the worry of this bloody presentation tomorrow, I needed it. Hopefully now I'll be relaxed and stress free so I can go in there and smash it."

"You'd smash it anyway. You always do. It's about time you got some recognition for the amazing work you do."

I peeled an eye open and took another swig from my bottle. I'd always had a flair for design. Even from a young age, I would be found doodling buildings while everyone else was drawing unrecognisable stick figures of mummy and daddy. By the time I was a teenager, I was hooked on simulation games—not for the fun of playing a character through their life, but so I could design their homes. That transferred into drawing and design programmes I found online. I couldn't get enough of it. If I wasn't in front of my computer working on something, I would be out with a sketch book immortalising buildings, statues, scenes... anything... for reference at a later date. My parents hadn't been overly keen on me going into architecture, mainly because they were worried about me joining a male dominated field and being taken advantage of. But I used to laugh and say, 'Have you looked at me recently?' And besides, more and more women were taking up the profession. Eventually, they accepted my choices, knowing I was as strong minded as any man and could handle myself. Studying buildings and design was in my blood. It was the path that had been set out for me. I couldn't imagine doing anything else, so I'd worked bloody hard to get to where I was.

This project for GO, though, was my first solo assignment and one I was extremely privileged to have been handed, considering my fairly recent graduation and accreditation as a chartered architect. I hadn't undertaken the job lightly and had put everything into making the plans eco-friendly and sympathetic to the lay of the land surrounding the site but still keeping in tune with the client's expectations.

"This job is a huge stepping stone for me, Ad. I want your dad to see all I've put into this project, and I hope it lives up to his exacting standards."

Adam settled back on the couch and began rubbing across the light stubble on his chin. It was a sign of his nerves. "You know my dad, nothing will ever be good enough. He lives by the motto that your best is never enough and perfect doesn't exist. As far as the grumpy old bastard is concerned there is always something that can be improved in everything. You show him a Van Gogh, and he'll show you a brush stroke that could have been better. People travel thousands of miles to visit some of the most beautiful buildings in the world, he'll take one look and tell you how he would have done it differently. That's just Dad." He sucked down the last of his beer and placed the bottle on the coffee table.

Our conversation stalled for a moment as Adam seemed to get lost in thought. I didn't want to disturb him so I grabbed his empty bottle and walked through to the kitchen.

The sky was inky black as I looked out of my kitchen window and across the roofs of nearby houses. Being in a busy suburb of London with lots of street lighting we didn't often get to see stars. Tonight, though, I spotted something moving and twinkling in the darkness. I wasn't sure if it was a star or not, but right at that moment I needed to place some of my burden on something or someone beyond me. I needed to believe there was a power out there bigger than me that would help me through. Closing my eyes, I made a wish. I wished that the meeting with GO Sport and Leisure would go well and we would get the final approval for the plans. I wished for the courage to go back to the gym so I could work on making me a fitter and healthier person. But mostly, I wished that while I was there, I would run into Nathan again. Seeing him would certainly make gym visits a lot more bearable.

"What are you thinking about out here by yourself?" Adam said from somewhere behind me.

"Oh, just this and that." The star, or whatever it had been, had disappeared from view, so I closed the blind and turned to face my best friend.

"What else happened at the gym? I'm sure there was more to that story than you're letting on." He had kicked his trainers and socks off and was leaning against the door frame, his legs crossed at the ankles. That was Adam's thing. He hated shoes and would end up going barefoot whenever he could, preferring the feel of fresh air around his toes to the confines of leather. I joked with him constantly that he had been born into the wrong family. With his golden skin, shaggy dark blond hair, deep blue eyes and lean body, he looked more like a surf bum than the well-respected, second-generation architect he was becoming.

As I looked down, I couldn't help but notice that Adam had sexy feet. They were long and masculine with neatly trimmed nails and a hint of dark hair dusting the top. Why had I never noticed his feet before? That got me thinking about Nathan and whether he had sexy feet. With his height, he was sure to have long, lean feet, maybe with a smattering of dark hair covering the top. And if his feet were big he was sure to have a big…

"Liv?"

Snapping my gaze up into Adam's deep, Mediterranean blue eyes I thought I saw something I'd never seen from him before. Longing maybe? For me? I narrowed my eyes and cocked my head to the side, trying to decipher his look. As soon as I did Adam closed his eyes for a brief moment. When he reopened them, the look had gone.

Beer, I needed another beer. This whole fascination with Nathan was getting to me. He had roused feelings in me I'd not had in a long time, and now I'd begun to project those on to my dear friend. I shook my head to clear it and reached into the fridge for another couple of bottles. I continued with my tale of the gym, how Nathan had made me feel, how good the massage was, and finally our jokey interaction before I left.

Adam pulled his bottle to his lips. "Do you like

him… you know like, *like* him?"

"Despite popular belief, Adam, I am a girl, and when a hot guy like that is presented to a girl, she cannot help but admire him. What was there not to admire? He's tall, muscular, obviously fit beyond belief and has a deep voice that makes your undies wet. Quite frankly, I was kind of relieved when you weren't at the gym when I left. I was hoping to get home and play make believe with my vibrator." Adam choked on his beer and looked as though I'd just kicked him in the gut.

"Jesus, Liv," he sputtered, "I really didn't need to know that." I grinned sheepishly and pulled my beer to my lips.

***

THE NEXT MORNING I woke before the alarm went off. Two hours before the alarm was due to go off in fact. Still, I rushed through my morning shower and then dug around in my wardrobe for something super smart to wear. Thanks to my slowly expanding waistline, my choices were restricted so it didn't take long. I pulled out a grey and white skater dress and yanked it over my head. The dress had always been a favourite of mine, flirty and fun but still all business. I twirled in front of the mirror a couple of times, checking my appearance from different angles before deciding it made me look like a rhino and yanking it off again. Maybe it wasn't a favourite after all. In the end, I settled for yet another unassuming trouser suit. Teamed with a plain white blouse, pale pink and grey scarf, black pumps and subtle silver jewellery, I felt strong and powerful. I looked like the respected professional I was striving to become.

An hour before I was due to start work, I dropped my bag into the drawer of my desk and tried to think. Everything I had planned on saying, everything I had planned on showing, the direction I wanted to give, it was gone. I was as blank as one of my father's unwritten cheques.

"Olivia!"

I looked up from my blank computer screen and into the stern face of Robert Ashworth, my boss's, boss's, boss, and Adam's overbearing, perfectionist father. "Good morning," I said with a forced smile.

"It will be when you finalise those plans with GO today. Need I remind you that we have taken a huge risk giving you such a high profile project at this stage of your career? Don't let me down."

"No, sir." I projected my voice, hoping to sound strong and in control even though inside I was a frightened little girl and wanted to run home to mummy and tell her the bad man was upsetting me.

With a nod of his head—no smile—he turned and left me to resume staring at my blank screen.

I felt better after grabbing a coffee and actually managed to work through the morning and into early afternoon. If everything went well with the GO account, I was hoping to land another large project for a famous toy retailer who was looking to expand their current research headquarters. I spent the morning researching the location, company, local architecture and building regulations, basically anything that would help me build a case for Mr. Ashworth awarding the contract to me. To succeed I needed to be organised, and to be organised I needed to be prepared.

At two thirty, I began packing everything I would need to take into the boardroom for the presentation. A wave of nervous nausea washed over me, and I had to grab the edge of the table to stabilise myself when I felt lightheaded. With my head bowed, I closed my eyes and took a few deep breaths, trying to draw on the meditation classes I'd taken for about two weeks a few years before.

"Hey, Liv. You need a hand?" I'd never been so grateful to hear Adam's voice. He'd been mysteriously absent all morning when all I'd wanted was his strong shoulder to lean on and for him to reassure me that everything would be okay.

"Thank you!" I sighed. "I'm so nervous, Ad. What if I totally mess this up? What if they hate the plans? What if your dad thinks I did a shit job and he fires me?"

Adam sauntered into the room, looking his usual cool, calm and collected self. Wearing his professional uniform of a deep navy three-piece suit, pale blue shirt, navy tie and dark rimmed glasses, he looked every bit the high-flyer. In that moment, I looked and felt anything but. I'd never been one to feel nervous; usually I thrived on the butterflies, using them to push me and centre me on my task. For some reason though, this meeting had me all flustered.

Adam stopped in front of me, bending his knees slightly so he could look me in the eye. "Firstly, what's this all about, Liv? You have to be the most confident person I know. You never get flustered like this. You will not muck up the presentation. You know it inside and out. Besides, all the tough work was done during previous visits. This is just a formality to approve the final plans. Cross the T's and dot the I's as it were." He tapped the papers rolled up in my arms. "Secondly, my dad will not fire you. Despite what you think of yourself, you are already well respected in this place, so don't worry about that."

I dropped the plans on the table and wrapped my arms around Adam's waist, snuggling my head into the crook of his neck and inhaling his familiar and calming scent. "Thanks, Ad, what would I do without you?"

It was a moment before Adam spoke but when he did, his voice cracked with emotion. "One for all and all for one, right?"

"Isn't that supposed to be The Three Musketeers?" I heard his chuckle rumble deep in his chest.

"Well, yeah, but it's still appropriate. Even for the dangerous duo." This time it was my turn to chuckle at the name given to us as children by our parents. Tentative hands snaked around my back and rested there with just enough pressure that I could tell Adam was pulling me into him. He inhaled deeply and held the breath.

"Ad?"

"Hm-mm?"

"You might want to let that breath out now before you pass out on me." His chest deflated as air whooshed out of his semi parted lips over the top of my head. "And thanks, Ad, I really do mean it when I say I don't know what I would do without you."

"I know, princess," he replied with a grin. I growled. I hated that name. In fact I hated any pet names. My parents had given me a name for a reason and I happened to love my name. I could just about tolerate people calling me Liv; after all, it was a shortened version of Olivia. Princess, though, that was a complete no, no and he knew it. He'd called me it once when we were younger when I'd been whining like a brat about something. Of course, when I got on my high horse and bitched him out about it, he'd continued using it just to piss me off. I had never been able to get him to stop after that.

Reluctantly, Adam disentangled himself and took a step back, suddenly looking nervous. "You know I know you've got this, right?" I nodded. "Well… um… Dad wants me to sit in there with you, just to make sure everything goes okay." He winced when I scowled at him. I couldn't believe that after Adam's ego boosting words of encouragement I was back to feeling edgy again. In that simple gesture, Mr. Ashworth had clearly shown he had no faith in me. Not for the first time did I attribute that lack of belief to the fact that I was not male. I'm sure the only reason he gave me a job in the first place was because of Adam.

"Fine," I said, grabbing the plans. "But this is my baby, Adam. I've put blood, sweat and tears into getting this just right to try to please your father and please him I will, if it's the last thing I do."

I stomped out of my office with a pounding heart and absolute focus. Angry was good. Angry meant I wasn't curled up in a corner sucking my thumb and crying for my mum. Angry meant I had fire, and I was going to need that to deliver the presentation of my life.

***

IN THE MEETING room, everything was set up and ready to go. I had everything set up and chosen where I wanted the clients to sit. All that was left was to wait for them to show up. The nerves were really starting to kick in and my mouth was parched. Jugs of iced water enticed me from their position in the middle of the large table. I was debating whether or not to pour a glass when there was a knock on the boardroom door. Trish, the receptionist, poked her head in with a smile. "The representatives from GO Sport and Leisure are here. Shall I send them in or do you need a few?"

I sucked in a deep breath and looked over to Adam who was sitting quietly at the end of the table. He gave me a full smile and nodded his encouragement. I could hear his voice in my head saying I could do this, even though he didn't utter a word.

"Send them in, Trish. We're good to go." It was show time.

A minute later, the two gentlemen from GO that I'd met on previous visits walked in. We shook hands and passed pleasantries, talking about irrelevant crap that just amped up my edginess. I was about to gesture for them to take a seat when the door opened. Twisting around, I came face to face with an impeccable charcoal grey suit, crisp white shirt, silk silver tie and a set of penetrating, deep grey eyes.

What is he doing here?

"Hello again, Ms Buchanan."

Nathan's deep gravelly voice rumbled through me, causing every nerve ending to become highly attuned to every movement he made. Even the swing of his arm as he raised it to shake my hand caused me to shiver. When we touched, my hand pulsed, not from his firm grip but from the spark of sensation I'd been zapped with. It wasn't like the bolt of electricity that knocks you on your arse and leaves your hair frizzy that you read about in romance novels, it was more a thud of awareness—a taser shock that belts you once, leaves you paralysed with the after effects rippling through you and leaving the hairs on your arms standing on end.

"Beautiful," I mumbled, looking down at his perfect, beautiful, large hand resting in mine. It was just as I'd imagined his feet would be; large, with long, lean fingers, a hint of a tan and dark hairs peeking out from under his cuff. I was pleased—although I tried to ignore the fact—that there was no ring or tan line on his left hand. In my haze at the gym I hadn't taken in any specifics about him, other than he was deliciously good looking and had a body that made me squirm with desire, and a voice that left me panting.

"Excuse me?"

I suddenly remembered where I was and what I was about to deliver. I needed answers as to why he was there, and I needed them now. Regaining my composure, I cleared my throat and lifted my eyes to his, determined to act the consummate professional. "Hello, I don't believe we've met officially."

He grinned down on me as he withdrew his hand. He'd heard me. He'd heard me loud and clear telling him I thought he was beautiful. I wanted the ground to open up and swallow me whole. "Do forgive me. I'm Nathan…" *yeah, I already know that,* "Oakes. I'm the owner of GO Sport and Leisure. I apologise I've been unavailable to meet with you until today."

Oh. My. God!

For the second time in less than twenty four hours I'd been left speechless and knocked on my arse, only this time it was metaphorically. Nathan, the beautiful personal trainer dude, the one who had witnessed my total mortification just the night before, was my client?

"It's nice to meet you again, Mr. Oakes. I hope you don't mind but I'll be in here today supporting Olivia. Please take a seat." I watched on in stunned silence as Adam shook Nathan's hand then showed him to a seat. Adam knew who Nathan was? Why didn't I know who Nathan was? I'd done my research when I first took on the GO account. Or at least I thought I had.

I stood motionless. Nathan was here. He was the N. Oakes, owner of GO Sports and Leisure, the person I was about to deliver my presentation to.

Oh. My. Fucking. God!

I felt my eyes getting wider as I realised the ramifications of his presence before me. I'd been a quivering wreck before imagining him naked, squirming at the sound of his voice, dreaming about him supporting himself above me with his thick, strong arms as he thrust inside me…

"Are you all right, Liv? Do you want me to take over or something?" Adam whispered against my ear, startling me.

I looked up at him and blinked several times, trying to regain my composure. I felt hot and needy. My pulse was racing, and my heart thudded a tribal beat in my chest. This couldn't be happening. Not today.

Adam's eyes continued searching mine, looking for answers or maybe just some sort of response, when the sound of a throat being cleared drew my attention back to our clients. I looked at Nathan as Adam steered me towards the corner of the room with his hand resting on my lower back. Nathan's eyes narrowed as they centred on the point of contact between Adam and me.

"What has gotten into you?" Adam said in a harsh whisper looking over at our clients and offering them an encouraging smile. "Are you not well? Do you want me to do this for you?"

With a shake of my head, I closed my eyes for a moment and sucked in a deep breath. I was a professional. I had a job to do, and Nathan Oakes was just another client... a beautifully sexy client. I gave myself a discreet pinch to encourage me to pull myself together and opened my eyes. I had to do this. This was my moment, my time to prove my worth. I had to forget him and concentrate on the presentation. With a deep inhalation I nodded at Adam and slowly turned to face the three gentlemen watching me expectantly.

"I'm fine. Let's do this."

***

FORTY-FIVE MINUTES later, I'd delivered my speech, showed off the plans and answered questions. So many questions. The presentation had gone well and Nathan seemed impressed. I felt like I was floating as I gathered in the drawings and began to roll them up.

"Well, Olivia. Is it okay to call you Olivia?" My gaze rose to connect with Nathan's and I nodded. "I'm impressed. You've come up with exactly what I visualised. In fact, you've exceeded my expectations." I ducked my head and grinned behind the cascade of my brown hair that was actually behaving for once. He liked the plans, he was impressed. I closed my eyes briefly and basked in the joy of praise. I doubted I would get any from Mr. Ashworth.

"Unless there is anything else you need to go through, are we done here?" Nathan continued.

I took a quick mental inventory, checking off everything that had to be finalised and settled. "That's everything, Mr. Oakes. If you—"

"Please, call me Nathan," he interrupted.

Adam made his way to my side, resting a polite hand on my lower back once again. The proud smile he was trying to contain was clearly evident as he looked between Nathan and his colleagues.

"Okay, Nathan. I think we have everything finalised. If you need anything more, please don't hesitate…" I trailed off when he suddenly pushed his chair back and stood abruptly, his two companions following suit.

"I won't," he said brusquely looking between Adam and me and then down to where Adam's hand touched me. "So are we done here?" I nodded, stunned into silence. What was with the sudden arrogance?

"I, um, we, um…" Sensing my sudden unease, Adam whispered in my ear that he would see them out and stepped towards the three gentlemen. Feeling bad for not concluding our meeting appropriately, but grateful to Adam for taking away the added pressure of Nathan's sudden mood swing, I turned my back and allowed him to show them out. Their polite small talk faded away as they left the room with the unmistakable sound of the door clicking closed behind them. I let out a deep breath, exhaling all my tension and worries in one big whoosh.

"You did it, Liv," I muttered, busying myself with gathering everything. "Despite Mr. Hot-as-sin's rather rude farewell, you did well. You should be proud." I smiled, balancing the rolled up plans across my arms.

"I agree. You should."

Startled by the deep, husky voice, I stumbled and pivoted around. The items in my arms fell, scattering across the floor in a mess of disorderly white papers. My eyes widened as my hand flew to my racing heart. "Mr. Oakes… Nathan, what are you still doing here?"

~CHAPTER FOUR~

AS AN ACT OF PROTEST against the suddenly warm air in the room, my lungs decided to cease operation for a brief moment. A strange gasping sound escaped my throat as my breath caught. Despite the air conditioning system blasting out arctic like air, my flesh heated as I stood gazing at the man standing across the room. My nipples pebbled in the tight confines of my bra, creating proud little turrets pushing against the lace. Aware that Nathan's gaze was sweeping my body, I pulled my jacket tight across my chest, in the vain hope he wouldn't see the little peaks pointing their way up through my blouse. Why was he still here? And why was he looking at me with such dark, scrutinising eyes? Had he heard what I'd called him? Pulling his eyes up to meet mine, he moved across the room, making his way towards me with strong and commanding strides.

"I wanted to talk to you," he said, his deep voice melting into me in a way no double shot caramel latte could. Leaning against the table, he curled his fingers around the edge of the polished mahogany surface, stopping their restless dance. His elbows angled out in a way that emphasised his large, firm biceps under the sleeves of his jacket.

Without realising what I was doing, I licked my lips and dropped my gaze to his mouth. His lips were a deep pink and plump. So plump. Kissably plump.

"About what?" I asked, finding my voice breathy and betraying my desire to stay professional. My gaze wandered to his thick neck where the knot of his tie rested just underneath the slight bulge of his Adam's apple. It rose and fell as he swallowed, causing a rippling effect around the collar of his shirt. "I thought we'd concluded the meeting," I added, finally dragging my eyes away from the small appendage I suddenly wanted to run my tongue over. I continued my inspection of every inch of Nathan's upper body. Every slight crinkle or ripple in the fabric of his jacket helped to define the hard muscles hidden beneath. Whether in an expensive, tailored suit or casual track pants and t-shirt, I couldn't deny he was a fine specimen of a man. So masculine and powerful.

"We did."

"So what did you want to discuss with me then?" My brow furrowed in confusion as my gaze finally made it back to his handsome face. His chiselled, square jaw line was dusted with a light growth of hair that had me wanting to run my fingers along it to see if it was soft or rough. He had a slightly crooked nose that had obviously been broken at some point, maybe more than once. Finally, I made it up to his large, almond shaped eyes that were studying me with a knowing glint. Today they seemed more charcoal in colour, a deeper tone that expressed his power.

"Here. Take a seat." He kicked the rolling desk chair near him and sent it gliding across the short pile carpet until it stopped just in front of me. I looked down at the chair and then back to Nathan, impressed he'd managed to kick with just enough force. Surprised that I so easily relented to his command and hadn't argued, I lowered myself into the seat.

"Let me ask you a question, Olivia. Are you happy?" Nathan finally asked, removing his hands from the table and resting them, clasped together, against his thick thighs.

"What kind of question is that? And what business is it of yours anyway?" I asked, frowning. He knew nothing about me, didn't need to know anything about me. My happiness was of no concern to him. We'd met only once. And while I was grateful for the massage, we were total strangers. I had every intention of keeping it that way.

"Do you always answer a question with a question?"

Finally pulling myself out of the fog and rediscovering my sass, I raised a questioning brow, to which he shot me a stony glare then sighed. "Just answer the question, Olivia. Are you happy?"

"I'm sat here talking to you, so of course I am. I'm ecstatic," I replied sarcastically and sank back into the seat, twisting it from side to side. "What's this all about, *Mr. Oakes*? What do you want from me?"

Nathan disentangled his hands then once again

gripped the edge of the table. "I want to know if you, as a person, are happy... I'm not just talking about merely existing. I'm talking about being comfortable and content. Are you happy with who you are? What you are?" His gaze bore deep into mine, seeking answers I wasn't sure I knew.

His tone and probing expression let me know he was deadly serious. He was genuinely interested. I thought about it for a moment. It was a bit of a deep question for a Thursday afternoon, especially coming straight after my brain cells had been fried trying so hard to impress both him and his companions during the presentation.

"Put it this way," he continued when I'd made no attempt to speak, "if something happened to you tomorrow, could you look down from up high and be content that you'd lived a happy and fulfilled life?"

"Absolutely! I'm living the dream," I fired back immediately.

Of course I could. *Couldn't I?*

"Yes. Sort of..." My shoulders slumped when it dawned on me that yes, I had a fantastic job, great friendships and wonderful but eccentric parents, but I had to admit my life was missing something. It was lacking a real purpose, something that could be added to my eulogy that would forever carve out my place on this earth, letting the world know that Olivia Buchanan had very much been somebody. And as confident and carefree as I came across to others, I had my insecurities. Who didn't? It couldn't be denied that I wanted more. An adventure. Something to take me away from the lonely hum drum, nine-to-five existence I'd found myself in since graduating.

For a while, I'd been having a few niggling worries about being alone. Whilst I wasn't looking for love and for someone to immediately settle down with and start a family, I couldn't deny I craved those special intimate moments that only happened with someone you cared for. But I let my career come first. It had to. I'd worked too hard to not become the best I could be. The only way I would be able to accomplish that was to forgo relationships. It didn't stop me dreaming though.

"Um no, not really, something's missing." I admitted with a sigh.

Nathan nodded as though my answer hadn't come as a surprise to him. "Why were you at the gym yesterday? What made you decide to walk through those doors?"

Heat extended across my chest, slowly creeping along my neck and into my cheeks. My reaction to Barbie-bitch hadn't been a typical one for me. Usually, I brushed off idiotic and ignorant comments. The way I saw it, people who made fun of others or felt the need to comment on how somebody else looked or acted usually did so to cover up their own feelings of inadequacy. So why had I taken her comments to heart and not just brushed them off? Maybe she'd hit a nerve I hadn't even realised was exposed.

Nathan was watching intently, waiting patiently for something I wasn't comfortable admitting to him. I didn't want to come across as a pathetic shrinking violet. I was far from it, usually.

"I'm waiting, Olivia. I need to know why you came to Golden Oakes yesterday. What were you hoping to get out of your visit?"

"A sore backside and bruised ego," I fired back, crossing my arms over my chest and staring straight at him.

Narrowing his eyes, Nathan pushed away from the table and moved in front of me. Leaning forward, he gripped both arms of the chair, abruptly halting my swinging motion. "Sarcasm doesn't look good on you, Olivia. Perhaps you want to try that again," he said, his already deep voice dropping an octave as he kept his deep, brooding gaze locked on mine.

I flicked my eyes to the window, needing a distraction from his close proximity and the intense way he looked at me. Why was he so concerned about my motives? I was pretty sure he didn't stalk every person who walked into his gym, asking them their innermost secrets.

"If you must know, Mr. Oakes," I eventually conceded, turning my face to his once again, "much to my mortification, I was offended by a remark made by somebody who really had no business poisoning the air with her breath."

"What was said?"

I sighed and rubbed at the back of my neck, feeling the onset of a tension headache. "It doesn't matter. I let it get to me when it shouldn't have. It also made me think a few things… about myself."

There was a brief moment of silence where Nathan seemed thoughtful and I just felt uncomfortable. Looking him in the eye, I said, "Excuse me," and began to push myself from the chair. I needed a drink, something, anything to distract me from his close scrutiny. Thankfully, Nathan stepped back giving me space to walk to the table.

"What things?" he asked settling himself against the table again as I poured a glass of water. "What were you thinking?"

"Why are you so interested, Nathan? Surely my boring little life is of no interest to you."

"Firstly, I get the impression you are anything but boring. Secondly, as a gym owner I make it my business to be interested in what motivates people to sign up. I watched you yesterday, Olivia. You didn't seem much like you wanted to be there."

I grinned as I turned and rested back against the edge of the table, mirroring his pose. The bottles of beer in my fridge and endless supply of chocolate and sweets in my cupboards were evidence enough that I definitely had not *wanted* to be there.

My smile diminished as I recalled the insulting words that spewed from Barbie-bitch's toxic mouth. "Let's just say that those words, as hurtful as they were, got me thinking about my health and fitness. I came to the conclusion that I needed to do something before my future looked bleak. Adam—Mr. Ashworth—suggested I join him at the gym, your gym. With nothing left to lose, I decided to tag along. I mean, what's the worst that would happen? It wasn't like I'd end up on my arse, embarrassed by a less than graceful treadmill exit." I snorted a mirthless laugh and tipped the glass to my lips, needing the chilled liquid to cool my shamed, heated flesh and parched throat.

"Is he your boyfriend?" he asked, moving to stand directly in front of me.

Shocked, I choked on the water and spluttered a mouthful all over his crisp Armani – or whatever it was – suit.

"Oh my God, Nathan, I'm so sorry." Frantically, I dropped the glass on to the table, the remaining contents spilling across the wooden surface, and reached out to touch the wet spot on Nathan's shirt, rubbing it as though that would remove the dampness. His hand came up to rest over mine, holding me still.

"Answer me, Olivia. Is Adam your boyfriend?" he repeated in a firm, yet deep and husky, voice.

"What? Why would you think that? Why would you ask that? What does it have to do with you? And why do you even care?" I tugged on my hand, needing to free myself from him. His touch was doing strange things to me, things I didn't want to acknowledge.

His hand pressed down firmer, keeping my palm locked over the steady rhythm of his heartbeat. "There you go again, answering a question with a question… or several."

Hearing the slight humour in his voice, I glanced away from our joined hands and up into his face. His scarred eyebrow was raised and the corner of his lips had pulled up infinitesimally, other than that, his features were still expressionless. "Is he or is he not your boyfriend?" he demanded.

"It doesn't matter if he is or isn't. It really has nothing to do with you." I flexed my fingers again, and this time he let me go. I grabbed a few napkins from the side and began mopping up the spilled water, feeling confused by the direction of our conversation.

"In some ways you're right. It really is no concern of mine who you might be involved with." I nodded and continued blotting up the water. "However, I need to know if I'll be stepping on someone else's toes—on Adam's toes."

"WHAT?" I dropped the napkins and spun around to find him standing extremely close to me. "What do you mean stepping on toes? Stepping on toes how?"

"There you go with the questions again."

"Mr. Oakes… *Nathan*, are we talking here as client-architect or gym patron-arrogant gym owner? I take it from the fact that we concluded our business meeting – rather abruptly might I add—that it is the latter, therefore, if I want to reply to you with questions, I will bloody well reply to you with questions." My tone was getting louder as my exasperation increased. "Who the hell do you think you are? You come waltzing in here, for the first time ever, making me feel more nervous than was necessary. You ask me bullshit questions that have nothing to do with your project, and then you have the audacity to chastise me for asking a few questions. So, I repeat, what do you mean stepping on toes?"

Sighing, I stepped back to rest my bum on the edge of the table again, exhausted from my emotional outburst.

"I want to help you train, Olivia. I watched you yesterday and saw your reactions in the gym. It was obvious you had motive for being there but weren't confident enough about using the equipment or pushing yourself. I want to put that right."

He was watching me?

Shame surrounded me as I thought back to what I must have looked like wandering around, looking lost and more than a little overwhelmed. And then the hiking on a treadmill at not much more than a snail's pace, red and out of breath through pure lack of fitness. *Oh. God!* It was no wonder he saw me, I must have stood out like a bright 'loser' beacon flashing in a dark night sky.

But what was in this for him? Maybe it was just another sales ploy. Pick the most out of shape people to venture into the gym and push personal training sessions on them. Make them see that they needed the encouragement of coaching to help them achieve their fitness goals. In most cases, that was probably true, but I was the type who rebelled against instructions and orders. How I made it through my education with the grades I did confounded my parents for years. So, there was no way I would stand for some fitness freak shouting orders at me to push my big, fat arse that bit further or work that bit harder.

Not to mention, after paying my rent, household bills and student loans, I barely had enough money left for my daily latte, never mind an expensive gym membership. Putting myself through university had amassed a mountain of debt, and I was determined to pay it off before I splurged on anything else for myself.

"Thank you for the offer, Nathan, but I'm not in a position to pay for expensive gym memberships and personal training at the moment."

"Who said anything about paying? I like you, Olivia, you're bolshie, charismatic and obviously challenging. And I enjoy a good challenge." He smirked.

"I am perfectly capable of working out on my own, thank you very much. I do not want, nor do I need, you to order me around like some sergeant major, pushing me to do things I am not comfortable with and making me puke everywhere. I have a Jillian Michaels DVD I could dust off for that." He grunted in disgust.

Ignoring him, I continued. "I'm NOT a challenge, Nathan, yours or anyone's. You can't come in here parading your hot self in front of me and just expect me to throw myself at you, begging you to show me your machismo ways like the floozies you usually deal with. It won't happen."

With arms crossed over his chest, Nathan stepped back far enough that he could lean against the wall, smiling. "Oh believe me you are definitely not my usual type." Nathan threw his hands up to stop me before I released a full-scale verbal assault on him. "What I mean by that is you are different to many of the women I come across at the gym. I see something in you, Olivia. I want to help you unleash whatever that is. I'll help you with your fitness and whatever else you want to achieve, and you can help me rediscover something I lost a while back. It will be refreshing— for both of us. But first, I need to know if someone else might have a problem with that. If you have some arrangement with Adam, then I'll back away."

I wanted to laugh. In the midst of the craziness unfurling around me all Nathan was concerned about was if Adam and I were in a relationship?

"He's my best friend—has been since we were small children. He's the one that suggested I join him yesterday and got me the trial. Adam knows me, too well sometimes. He could tell how much those comments I mentioned had gotten to me and encouraged me to do something about it. So if I dare show my face in that place again after yesterday, I will continue joining Adam until my trial ends. Then I'll have to think of another option."

Nathan pushed away from the wall and took the few steps to the table, settling down beside me. "If you join me, I'll give you a lifetime membership. You'll be free to use the facilities whenever and however you want."

My head hurt with the breakneck speed of our conversation. "It's a really kind offer, Nathan, but I couldn't do that. Thank you, though."

I stood and began gathering up the scattered paperwork on the floor.

"Olivia," he said with softness in his voice that totally knocked me off guard. "Please don't refuse this because of your sense of pride. Just think about it."

I paused. "Why, Nathan? I don't understand what you can possibly get out of doing this. I'm sure your time is precious. You don't want to waste it on someone like me." Grabbing the last of the papers, I slowly rose to face him.

"You really have no idea, do you?"

My brow furrowed in confusion. "Any idea about what?"

Shaking his head, he replied, "It doesn't matter. I want to train you, Olivia. I won't take no for an answer.

I could see I was getting nowhere fast with brushing him off. So despite my better judgement, I found myself telling him I would give it a try.

For the next few minutes, we discussed when we might both be available and what I might expect from my sessions. I had to admit the thought of seeing him in his workout gear a couple of times a week was a definite plus. So when he eventually left, telling me he would see me at eight the next evening, I couldn't help but smile. Maybe working out wouldn't be such a chore after all.

***

"WHAT WAS THAT all about?" Adam asked, walking up behind me as I was making my way back to my office. "I turned to say goodbye and he'd disappeared. Or rather he'd not left in the first place."

I stopped and waited for Adam to catch up.

Nathan had left the boardroom alone, insisting he could see himself out. That had given me the time to compose myself and try to comprehend what had taken place after our official meeting. In the short time I'd had with him, as brief as it was, Nathan had lit something inside me. Excitement? Joy? Lust? I wasn't sure. A mix of all three seemed more likely. The one thing I was sure about was that I wanted more time with Nathan Oakes.

But I was still confounded by what had happened and not even sure where to start explaining it all to Adam. Taking the rolled up plans from my arms, he looked down at me with concern as we continued walking back towards my office. "Is everything okay? What did Mr. Oakes want? Are there issues with the project? Did he upset you?"

I chuckled to myself thinking how Nathan would be throwing a hissy fit right about now if he'd heard all those questions spewing in a deluge. If one thing was clear, it was that Nathan Oakes was certainly a straight to the point person.

"Everything's fine. He was impressed with the plans, said I'd exceeded his expectations." I grinned and tamped down the overwhelming urge I had to jump up and down, squealing in excitement.

We reached my office door, and I pushed my way through, Adam following close behind me. He placed the plans down on my small table. "Well that was a given, the drawings are brilliant. If I weren't my father's son and the lucky bastard who will be running this magnificent place one day..." I watched as the blue of his eyes darkened. Adam was good, damn good, at building designs and drawing, but it wasn't his passion. He'd been forced into the field by overbearing parents laying guilt trips on him about keeping the family business going. Growing up, all he'd wanted to do was study people. He found the diversity of every individual deeply fascinating and had wanted to study psychology and what makes us humans tick. Instead, his father forced him into architecture and figuring out what makes buildings tick instead.

"... I'd be shit scared of losing my job to you right about now. The two guys I escorted out couldn't praise you highly enough. I think it's safe to say you blasted this project right out the park." He grinned, the pride I knew he felt for me lighting him up like a neon lamp.

"Thanks, Ad, that means a lot coming from you." I walked to him and wrapped my arms around his waist. He reciprocated, tugging me in close. The weight of the day dropped away, and I sucked in the first deep, relaxing lungful of air I'd had in days. I finally felt like I could breathe properly again.

We stood like that for several minutes until Adam broke the silence. "You still haven't explained why he stayed back, Liv. What did he want?"

Pulling away from Adam's embrace, I hoisted myself up to sit on my desk. "He offered me a lifetime membership to Golden Oakes," I replied nonchalantly, like it was an everyday occurrence to be offered such a thing.

"He did *what*? Why?"

Shrugging, I proceeded to explain my rather bizarre conversation with Nathan and what he'd offered me.

Adam looked horrified. "You're not taking him up on the offer are you?"

"At first, I said no. I wanted to tell him where he could shove his challenge. But then he got me thinking. After what happened yesterday with Barbie, I realised I really should start taking better care of myself. He was offering me the facilities and the expertise to help me do just that—at a price I couldn't argue with."

"But I can help you, Liv. Whatever he says he can help you with I can do it too. I'll nag you, push you, praise you. I'll even pay for your gym membership if I have to."

I lifted my gaze from the floor to meet Adam's sad looking eyes. "I appreciate that, Ad. And I know you would do that for me and more, but the simple fact is he is the expert and he's offering that expertise to me for free. I couldn't say no."

Adam began pacing the floor, shoving his hands deep into his trouser pockets. "I don't get it, and I don't like it. Nobody ever gets anything for free these days, Liv. He must be after something."

And therein lay my only real fear. What was he getting out of it? He had absolutely no reason to be helping me out. There must have been a wealth of loaded people out there happy to pay for extortionate membership fees and personal training sessions. All he would get from me would be an earache when he started pushing me to do more than I was comfortable with and exasperation when I could do no more than a bit of brisk walking on the treadmill.

"Honestly, I don't know. But I don't want to be another statistic, Ad. Just another person who keeled over and died from a massive heart attack due to blocked arteries and a diseased heart." I slid off my desk and stood looking up into Adam's eyes again, pleading with him to try to see this from my perspective. "I would be crazy to turn down this offer. The fact he's hot is an added bonus too." I winked and walked over to grab the plans to file away.

A distinctive growl vibrated from Adam, clearly demonstrating his dislike of my choices. But he was just going to have to live with it. I'd made my decision. Being the stubborn mule that I was, I would not back down. I needed to prove to myself, as well as Adam and Nathan that I could and would do this.

"Liv, I—"

"Olivia!" The deep voice echoing from my doorway had my smile dropping immediately.

"Mr. Ashworth, I was just going to—"

"Well done. You did a great job."

For the first time I could remember, a minute smile tugged at the corners of Robert Ashworth's thin lips. Then with a slight nod, he was gone. Adam and I both looked at each other, shocked. A compliment from Robert Ashworth? Would wonders never cease?

This had ended up being a great day after all.

~CHAPTER FIVE~

FRIDAY MORNING I WAS A bundle of nervous energy. I'd woken up bright and early and momentarily panicked when I remembered what I'd agreed to. Thoughts about Nathan's ulterior motives also still plagued me. Who in their right mind would offer to train and support an unfit, slightly overweight, self-confessed gym-phobe? *And* not get paid a penny for doing so. It made no sense. Still, I concluded that he'd made the offer and all I'd done was accepted. I just needed to roll with it and see how things played out. There was every possibility he might give me one day and then decide I was beyond helping. Either that or he would set me up with a workout plan and leave me to my own devices from then on. I was shocked to realise that neither option was acceptable to me. Despite my nerves, I wanted to do this… with Nathan.

My distinct lack of appropriate work-out attire had

been another source of worry. Having witnessed first-hand the Lycra clad die-hards at Golden Oakes, I knew my baggy sweatpants, oversized t-shirt and discoloured old trainers would make me stand out from the crowd. I needed to look the part. So, with that in mind, I'd decided that after work I would grace my local sports store with my presence and hopefully purchase something that flattered rather than shamed. I tried to ignore the fact that I also wanted to look nice and possibly even vaguely attractive for Nathan.

Looking at the time display on my PC, I saw it was just past noon. Lunchtime. I debated whether to walk down to the coffee shop for my usual latte and Panini or go to the cafeteria on the top floor and just order a standard salad. After all, I should make a start on the new me now, not just in the gym.

I'd convinced myself that starting as I meant to go on was the way to go when my desk phone rang. "Olivia speaking," I greeted the caller.

"Hello, pumpkin. How did the presentation go?"

"Hi, Mum. How are you?" I replied, smiling into my monitor and ignoring her infuriating pet name for me.

"Oh, I'm great, just great." Telephone conversations with my mother required absolute focus at all times, purely to make sense of her ramblings. She already sounded distracted and I had visions of her petting and pruning her poor house plants as she talked. I swear she'd had more conversations over the years with her plants than she'd had with my dad. She also mollycoddled them, overwatering, over feeding and over pruning them until they eventually wilted and died. Thankfully she hadn't done *that* to my dad… yet!

Of course it was never *her* fault if they died. She would swear they had draught problems, had been given contaminated water, and sometimes even blamed it on my dad when he knew better than to go anywhere near her beloved plants. The way she looked after those plants was cute in an eccentric kind of way.

"Mum?" I questioned when she hadn't said any more. "What do you need?"

I heard the unmistakable sound of her water spritzer and shook my head, wondering how long that poor plant had before it would be sent to horticulture heaven. "Oh, right. You didn't phone last night to tell me how the presentation went. So, how did the presentation go? Did you present everything okay?"

I chuckled. That was Mum, always multiplying her point, several times. Always asking lots of questions. Suddenly, visions of deep grey eyes penetrating into me as a deep sultry voice demanded why I asked so many questions overtook my mind. A tremor ricocheted down my spine as I remembered the sexy, ripped athlete looking suave and sophisticated in his suit, watching me intently whilst he waited for answers to his questions. "Sorry I didn't call. The presentation went great and yes, I went through everything professionally. The clients loved it."

"That's wonderful sweetheart." I heard the pride in her voice and sensed her smile. Despite my parents' initial wariness about my career choice, they had always shown me how proud they were of my achievements.

The sound of the spritzer echoed down the line again, and I had to prompt Mum to speak again. "Oh right, sorry, darling." I sighed at her persistent use of pet names. "I was wondering if you would like to come over for dinner tonight so you can tell us all about it."

My eyes widened and I unconsciously began shaking my head no. As much as I adored my eccentric parents, I could only take them in small doses. Meals could consist of anything and everything thrown on the table together, and trying to have an intelligible conversation with them was like pulling teeth. Besides, I had somewhere to be.

"That's kind of you, Mum, but I'm going out tonight. Maybe another time, okay?"

"Oh my goodness, you have a man!" she yelled down the line.

"What? No. There is no man."

"Olivia Buchanan, do not try to pull the cotton over my eyes. You have a date."

I rubbed my forehead and closed my eyes, feeling the throb of a major headache coming on. I was getting a lot of them recently. "It's wool, Mum."

"What is?"

"The saying. It's pull the wool over my eyes."

"Whatever. There's no need to be flippant, Olivia. Cotton… wool, it's the same thing. And there is no need to keep things from your mother. You know I want you settled down and giving me grandbabies."

Oh here we go.

"There is no man, Mum. Well not in the way you're hoping. I'm just going to the gym."

I could hear the bottle she was holding clatter onto the table. "You… the gym? As in, weights and stuff? Are you sure?"

I didn't know whether to be cross or embarrassed

that she found the idea of me going to the gym so shocking.

I spent the next few minutes giving her a brief outline of what had happened at the coffee shop and how I'd ended up with Nathan's offer.

"So you *are* going out with a man tonight," she said knowingly.

"No," I sighed, feeling drained. "I am going to meet up with a personal trainer who is going to help me lose some weight and become a fitter, healthier person."

By the time we'd ended our conversation, I felt like I'd been through a few rounds with the fighters I'd watched on the screens at the gym. Feeling like I needed a lunch of some substance to get through the rest of the day, I decided to ditch the salad and go for one last blow out down at the coffee shop. I just prayed Barbie-bitch and her clones weren't going to be there.

***

AFTER WORK, I walked into the brightly lit sports shop and very nearly turned on my heels and walked straight back out again. Loud music rang in my ears, an overwhelming amount of rails and racks were strategically laid out in front of me and I could tell store assistants were waiting in the shadows, ready to pounce. I scoped out the area and judged my safest path through to avoid being accosted.

"Hello, can I help you with anything this afternoon?"

I stiffened, having been nabbed no more than five

paces in, and turned to face the over friendly assistant. *Fuck!* My eyes closed, and I sucked in a deep breath as I wondered what I had done in a past life that I was now face to face again with the evil cow that had caused me to be in this position in the first place. When my eyes snapped open, I caught the recognition as her own eyes widened and her mouth transformed into a perfect O. The last thing I needed was for her to get the satisfaction of knowing her rude remarks had gotten to me so much. I'd hoped my parting shot in the coffee shop would have been my last impression on her.

"I'm just browsing, thank you," I said, turning to continue over to ladies wear.

"Is there anything in particular you are looking for? We have a good selection of plus-sized garments over in the back corner," she stated with a caustic tone, following behind me.

"No," I growled through gritted teeth. *Don't let her get to you, Liv.* "I am perfectly capable of finding what I need. Thank you!"

I swerved around a rail of hoodies and ducked behind a rack of golf umbrellas. After counting to five, I peered over the top and was thankful that a broad chested bald guy had caught her attention. I couldn't help gagging in repulsion as she stuck out an overly long, brightly painted, acrylic claw and touched his arm. Her smile appeared to be friendly and welcoming, however, the batting of her eyelashes indicated it wasn't Nike's she was trying to sell him. At least she was no longer following me.

Refocusing on my mission, I continued over to the ladies section and sagged in exasperation, faced with far too many choices. What had happened to the good old days of baggy sweats and T-shirts to work out in? Browsing through the rails, I immediately eliminated the ultra-tight, almost indecent, short shorts. I wasn't going clubbing—not that I would ever be able to get away with hot pants, even if I were—and needed something comfortable and forgiving. In the end, I picked up a few items to try on and wandered over to the changing rooms.

Twenty minutes later, with shaky hands, I pushed my debit card into the reader. A cold sweat beaded on my forehead as I punched in the PIN to confirm the painful amount that would be ripped from my bank account. New clothes were an expense I could have done without, and I could only hope that the expense would all be worth it in the end.

***

ROCKING BACK ONTO the heels of my new pink and whiter than white trainers, I stared once again at the imposing building in front of me. Despite knowing what—or rather who—was inside, the place still intimidated me. There were fewer people entering and leaving, and I could only guess that was because most saw the significance of TGIF and were therefore down the pub drowning out another long week.

The sliding glass doors opened and two giggling brunettes walked out, laughing over some mishap in their Zumba class. As the doors slid closed again, I caught my reflection in them. Who was this person staring back at me? I'd pulled my long, dark waves back into a tight ponytail and was wearing some of the clothes I'd purchased earlier. Black capri pants that were gathered and tied just below my knees actually made my legs look longer and more slender than I would ever have imagined. The white zip up hoodie over a tank top that also had gentle ruching along the sides completed the look. But I didn't look like me. I would even go so far as to say I looked... sporty, like I might just fit in. I laughed and shook my head as I walked towards the entrance. I doubted my lazy arse would ever truly fit in at a gym, especially one like Golden Oakes.

"Liv, wait up."

I heard quick paced steps pounding over the decorative concrete walkway behind me and slowed my pace.

"What are you doing here, Ad?"

"The same thing you are. I'm here for a workout." Adam never worked out Fridays or Saturdays. Those were his rest days he always said. 'An awesome body like this needs time to recover' would be his usual excuse. It was more like those were his trolling days. I'd been out clubbing with him far too often and seen him sloping off with far too many women to believe any different.

"You don't work out on Fridays," I replied, tightening my ponytail.

"I do..."

I glared at him, daring him to lie to me.

"...occasionally."

"You're only here for one thing tonight, Ad, and we both know what it is. But I don't need a chaperone." I hiked my bag onto my shoulder and started walking towards the doors again.

Adam sighed behind me. "Okay, okay, I'll admit I came to keep an eye on you." I caught his reflection in the doors when they slid open as I approached. He had his hands up in a placating gesture. "This whole 'let me train you for free' bullshit doesn't wash with me. I just want to make sure you're not being taken advantage of."

I snorted. "Who the hell would want to take advantage of me?"

He grabbed my elbow as we stepped into the cool, brightly lit lobby. "Princess, you have no idea," he whispered against my ear, and then he was off, striding through the lobby like he owned the place. It was then that I noticed Nathan leaning against the reception counter. He looked cool and casual, with his arms folded across his chest and his feet crossed at the ankles. Despite his relaxed pose, I couldn't help but notice the sharp look in his eyes and the subtle twist of his head as Adam walked past. I took a brief moment to enjoy the sight of him. I'd never really been into sporty guys before, preferring the thrill and mystery of your typical bad boy. Still, I couldn't deny the draw of those bulging biceps and the tattoos that were still playing peek-a-boo along the cuff of his sleeve. I decided to make it my mission to uncover the secrets that his white polo shirt was hiding. If I got nothing else out of these sessions, discovering his artwork would make it worthwhile.

***

"HARDER, OLIVIA. YOU aren't pushing hard enough."

I grunted and swiped a towel across the

perspiration dripping down my forehead. We'd only been at it for thirty minutes, and I was already conjuring up ways to kill Nathan Oakes. Any fantasies I'd had of him starting me off gently had been blown away by a force ten gale when almost immediately he had placed me on a treadmill. Not only did he get me facing my arch nemesis straight away, he wouldn't allow me to take it easy and walk. No, after a very short warm up, he had me running. Or attempting to run. It was more like a gangly jog because I wouldn't let go of the bar. When he'd leaned over the touchscreen and notched the speed up, my eyes had nearly bugged out of my head. My verbal cursing also got me nowhere. With Nathan watching on, I either pushed myself or fell flat on my arse again. There were no half measures. Nathan was ruthless.

"I... can't," I growled through laboured breaths, trying to alleviate the pressure on my burning lungs.

"You can and you will. It's all about mind over matter. Focus. Control the breathing and ignore the burn." *Easy for you to say*, I thought. My leg muscles and chest felt like they were being incinerated.

I managed a deep lungful of air that gave me only a millisecond of respite before I gasped and wheezed, my knees buckling beneath me. Sensing my growing panic, Nathan pounded the stop button and was around the back of the machine before I could blink. Just as it had done a few days before, the treadmill tried to expel me unceremoniously, but this time, thankfully, Nathan was there to catch me. Wrapping his arms around my waist before I crumpled to the floor, he hauled me to my feet and held me steady. My eyes closed, and I tried to catch my breath. I couldn't remember the last time, if ever, that I'd felt so lightheaded. The trouble was, I couldn't be sure if it was because of my exertions on the treadmill or because of the strong arms banded around my body and the heady masculine scent caressing my nostrils.

"Are you okay?"

I opened my eyes at the sound of his deep, concerned voice that was close—too close—to my ear. My sight refocused and landed straight on Adam who was staring at me from across the room. Or rather, he was staring at my middle, where Nathan still held his arms tight around me.

Reluctantly pulling away from his hold, I inhaled deeply, feeling the tightness of my oxygen deprived chest. "What are you trying to do to me," I rasped in a breathy voice that could not have been my own.

"I'm pushing you. No pain no gain, Olivia. I need to test your limits and your abilities so we can work on a regular schedule for you." He arched a dark eyebrow as he spoke.

I couldn't help the tremor that zapped through me at the thought of having my limits tested by Nathan. Though I wasn't thinking about the gym kind.

"But you're going to kill me before you're even half way to discovering my limits. Go easy on me, Nathan, please," I begged.

He shook his head and started backing up towards the stairs leading down to the badminton courts and weight rooms. "I don't think so. I'm kind of looking forward to pushing you as far as you can go." He said just before he disappeared down the stairs.

I glanced over at Adam who was sat stationary on a rowing machine, watching me. Grabbing my water bottle and towel, I smiled, wiggled my fingers at him and went after Nathan. Whatever he had planned for me next, I knew it wasn't going to be good.

***

"SIT STILL WITH your back straight. Pull it slow and steady," Nathan barked, standing behind me.

Having abandoned the cardio machines, Nathan led me into the weights room. Well it wasn't so much a room as a huge, open plan space that was filled with various machines and a dedicated space for free weights. The moment I'd set foot in the area and realised what was coming next, I'd spun around and started walking back out. Nathan had simply taken a firm grip on my elbow and tugged me further into the room with a determined stride. Weights really were not my thing.

"My back is fucking straight," I snapped, getting more frustrated by the minute.

"No, it's not. You're arching. You'll do yourself an injury," he replied calmly as though I hadn't just been cursing at him, loudly.

He'd tortured me with arm curls, leg presses, kettle bells, some sort of ball thing—medicine, I think—and the list went on. The more we did, the crankier I became. So, as I sat—with my back straight—pulling a metal bar down in front of my chin, with him shouting and nagging me, my resolve broke. It not only broke, it shattered into a million pieces, each piece flying through the air and heading straight for Nathan.

I let go of the bar and jumped to my feet, turning to face him. The weight plates crashed back into place earning me a few curious, and some annoyed, glances from the people nearby. "No, I won't. You know why? Because I'm done. I knew this was a stupid idea." I grabbed my stuff and began walking away.

"Olivia, don't—"

Spinning around, I glared at him. "No, Nathan. You've pushed and pushed, and I can't take it anymore. I'm on the verge of passing out or vomiting all over your precious gym. This is too much for my unfit body. It was a stupid idea. I'm out."

"You're giving up already? I didn't take you for a quitter. I guess you really can't take it," he shouted after me when I started walking off again. "Maybe I didn't see the *real* you after all."

Stopping abruptly, I turned to face him again, stomping my way across the wooden floor. I was not quitting. I would never quit. My pride wouldn't allow it. "All right, hot shot," I countered, standing tall in front of him with my finger pressed to his chest. "Just this once, I'll prove you wrong. Do your worst."

"This isn't about me or trying to break you, Olivia. It's about determining how far I can push you when we work together. The fact you're still standing here tells me you have so much more to give me."

His smug expression riled me further. "Oh, I have plenty to give all right, just not to you."

"Prove it to me. Keep—"

"I don't need to prove—"

Nathan placed a single finger over my lips. "Shh, keep the sass zipped for a minute and let me finish. You have guts, Olivia. I can see it in your eyes. That burning hunger to prove yourself, to show the world what you're made of, I see it. You had it during our meeting too, daring us to even contemplate thinking that the plans were not up to expectations. Which they were, by the way." He offered a genuine smile that had my gaze focussing on his lips. "You can do this. It's always tough starting out, and lots of hard work. But the reward far outweighs the effort. So, I'm going to ask you, Liv, are you prepared to fight for it?"

That was the million dollar question, and one I'd never answered before.

Lifting my eyes to his, I nodded. "Bring it on."

***

FRESHLY SHOWERED, AND smelling all the sweeter for it, I pushed through the changing room doors and felt a moment of sadness when Nathan wasn't there to greet me. I'd taken much longer than I'd needed to get ready, lost in my own thoughts. As I'd lathered my hair, I'd replayed our conversations and interactions over in my mind. He was a master of fitness, of that I had no doubt. And nobody could argue how attractive he was with his rough, chiselled looks, massive arms, broad shoulders, slim waist and sexy backside you couldn't resist wanting to nibble on. But what I seemed to really latch on to, and couldn't let go of, was his demeanour, his command. He had this presence about him that demanded respect. It was very alluring. And that was not good. He was my client, my trainer, and a nice bit of eye-candy. There was no way I could think of him as anything else.

I couldn't help but look for him as I walked through the gym towards the entrance. Although we'd ended my session with me agreeing that I would continue coming and working on the plan he'd set me, he hadn't actually confirmed if he would be around. He had simply goaded me into rising to his challenge of perseverance and pushing myself. I rubbed my sore and aching muscles with a wince and wondered how much perseverance I actually had.

"Was it all you thought it would be?" Adam asked, startling me as he emerged from the shadows beside the front entrance as I exited. The evening had turned into darkness, and the magnificent frontage of the gym looked even more impressive lit by only a few strategically placed spotlights. Old fashioned lanterns dotted the pathways back to the car park, leaving the area with a serene and calming aura.

I pulled my hoodie around me tighter as the cool evening breeze whipped past me. "It was… different.

"Did he give you everything you were looking for?"

I shot Adam a look, not liking the contempt dripping from his voice. "He gave me more than I bargained for."

Adam followed beside me as I made my way back to my car. "Look," he blurted, placing his hand on my door before I could open it. "I don't understand why you feel you need to do this with him when I'm here for you. I'll always be here for you."

"Adam, I… I can't explain it, I just need—" I cut off at the hurt look in his eyes.

He stood motionless and silent for a moment, staring into my eyes. Then, he released his hand from the car door and stepped back. "If this is what you want then I'll try to understand. Enjoy the rest of your night, princess." With a sad smile and slouched shoulders, he pressed a kiss to my forehead and walked off towards his own car.

Confused, I watched him walk away.

"Ad!"

He turned to look at me, stopping under the glow of a nearby lamp. The artificial rays reflected off his golden hair and seemed to backlight his deep blue eyes, highlighting his handsome yet sombre face. "Yeah?"

"Thanks."

With a nod he backed up, keeping his eyes locked on mine until he reached his car.

I sucked in a deep breath and turned to open my car door. Nathan stood off to the side watching our interaction. His body posture looked stiff and tense but his face was an impossible to read mask.

With a smile, I waved and jumped into my car. Guys were so difficult to understand.

~CHAPTER SIX~

THERE WAS A LOT TO be said about heavy gym sessions. None of it was good.

Groaning in agony, I attempted to stretch out in my bed only to snap back into a curled up position. No amount of moving or stretching could ease the persistent ache of every limb and muscle in my body. Why had nobody bothered warning me that exercising would kill me? I'd thought it was supposed to be good for you.

'No pain, no gain, Olivia.'

I shivered at the memory of Nathan's deep, gravelly voice barking instructions at me. And when he'd had his hands on me, manoeuvring me into positions he wanted me in, I hadn't been able to keep myself from ogling him through the mirrors and thinking wicked and dirty thoughts. There was no harm in thinking, right? As long as it was only thinking and not acting.

I groaned again, twisting around to check the time. The face of my alarm clock indicated it was just past seven, an ungodly hour for a Saturday morning. Weekends were my luxury, and being able to sleep in late for two days was my indulgence. So, ignoring my protesting muscles, I grabbed my pillow and covered my head, wanting to block out the world. I hoped the pillow might also shut up the voices in my head who were persistently reminding me of Nathan's existence.

But try as I might, I could not fall back asleep.

At eight o'clock, I gave up and crawled out of bed. I could not believe how much pain I was in. Nathan truly had given me a good working over and in that moment I could not possibly see how this was benefiting me. My arms felt like lead weights dangling at my sides. My legs were tight and protested with every step I took. I could barely move.

Yet I felt alive, full of something I couldn't describe.

Hot water began soothing away the aches and pains the moment I stepped under my showerhead. I stood there for a few minutes, allowing the heated water to work its magic on my body and the sounds of the droplets hitting the cast iron bath to soothe my senses.

'Reward outweighs the effort' I scoffed at that idea. I'd put in the effort and ended up in so much pain I wasn't sure I'd ever be able to walk properly again. Where was the reward in that?

'Are you prepared to fight for it?' I stood still remembering Nathan staring down at me so earnestly. The look of challenge mixed with compassion and sincerity in his eyes had left me feeling somewhat off balance. In the cold light of day, away from his

provoking ways, I wasn't so sure I could fight. Not when it hurt so much. It had been easy to get riled up by Nathan and accept his challenges when he was in front of me, goading me. But standing there in the shower, with my arms wrapped around my waist, feeling alone, I wasn't so sure I was strong enough after all.

***

"DAMN IT! SATURDAY afternoon TV is crap," I grumbled as I channel surfed, looking for something remotely interesting to watch. Even the overly made-up people on QVC looked bored, and re-runs of everything I'd ever watched just didn't seem appealing.

I punched the standby button with my finger and threw the remote onto the coffee table. Why did I feel so restless? After my shower, I'd dried off and dressed in my comfy stonewashed jeans and a black hoodie. I'd had every intention of vegging on the couch all day, nursing my poor aching body, but the longer I sat there, the more restless I became.

The cream and duck egg blue walls of my living room were closing in on me and I didn't know why. I never felt restless at home. Ever. It was my haven. I grabbed the magazine from the coffee table and aimlessly flicked through the pages of the latest celebrity gossip. With each page I turned, my frustration increased. My knees began bouncing with the agitation crawling its way through me.

"What is fucking wrong with you?" I flung the magazine across the room where it landed in a mess of crumpled pages next to my trainers. I stared at them for long minutes, feeling an inexplicable draw to them. Eventually, I pushed to my feet and ambled over to my music dock and hit shuffle. I needed something heavy blasting in my ear drums to drown out the niggling, indecipherable voice that was getting louder by the minute.

"Radioactive" came pounding through the speakers but it wasn't loud enough. I cranked the volume, not caring what my neighbours would think, and walked into the kitchen. Not caring what the time was, I grabbed a beer from the fridge. I flicked off the top and rested back against the counter. Through the archway, my gaze once again caught on my trainers, sitting there so innocently yet somehow mocking me.

"Stop fucking looking at me." I scowled at the inanimate objects and trudged into my bedroom, slamming the door closed behind me. Falling back onto my bed, I stared up at the ceiling. I debated calling my mum but knew that a conversation with her would most likely frustrate me further. Adam was out of the question because I couldn't work out what was going on with him and needed a bit of distance to try to figure it out.

The longer I lay there, the more my mind wandered. The more it wandered, the more it kept ending right back at the same place. Golden Oakes. Or rather, Mr. Oakes himself. In the short, unbelievably annoying, time we'd spent together he'd opened up something in me. Maybe it was a desire to beat back my own weaknesses and fight for a new me. Maybe it was just his incredibly hot body that I could not deny being attracted to. Whatever it was, it was calling me.

Reaching over, I left my untouched beer on the

nightstand. I knew what I needed to do and where I should be.

***

"STUPID, STUPID, STUPID," I scolded myself quietly, pulling the bar down in front of my chin and wincing as my still-sore muscles protested. As soon as it had become glaringly obvious why I'd been so restless, I'd pulled on another pair of black, three quarter length running bottoms, a pale pink tank top and my trainers. Twenty minutes later, I'd been warming up on a treadmill before moving on to complete the exercises Nathan had given me to do. Despite the aches and pains, I soon began to feel rejuvenated, almost intoxicated, by the feeling of my muscles stretching and yielding to my movements.

"You're a glutton for punishment, eh?" The female voice sounded vaguely familiar. "He didn't completely kick your butt and put you off coming back then?" I released the bar slowly until the rack of weights quietly lowered back into place and then turned to face whoever was talking to me.

It took a moment to recognise Cassie without her black spa uniform, but her smiling almond eyes and dark, sharp bob soon gave her away. She was standing nearby with a huge dumbbell in each hand, performing bicep curls with enviable grace and ease.

"Hi, Cassie. It's nice to see you again. I didn't recognise you there for a minute." I gestured to the short black figure hugging shorts and white sports bra top she was wearing. She was petite, but certainly not weak. The swell on her biceps and her super flat tummy clearly demonstrated her commitment to taking care of her body. That thought had me feeling self-conscious and out of place. It was a feeling I'd not had since walking through the front doors.

Cassie smiled knowingly but didn't say anything. "I thought Nathan would have scared you off by now." She completed her set and placed the weights on the ground.

"Ha. I would not give him the satisfaction of knowing he could do that to me." Something occurred to me. "How do you know? About Nathan training me, I mean."

"Nathan and I go way back. We talk to each other about everything." Oh. For some reason I hated the thought of that. "I was also in here training last night and saw him putting you through your paces. It was good to see someone giving him shit for a change," she laughed.

"Is he around?" I asked, looking out across the room. I'd been looking for him since I'd arrived, but it appeared he wasn't around on weekends.

Shaking her head no, Cassie gulped down some water from her bottle. "Not yet. He trains with Wes during the day. He usually comes down later on." She swiped at a dribble of water on her chin with the back of her hand.

I nodded, feeling disappointed and then annoyed with myself for being so. "I guess I should…" I gestured out to the room, indicating I should return to my workout.

"I'm sure you're aching something chronic, especially as you're inflicting more pain today." She winked playfully. "I'll be back down in the spa shortly.

Fancy another massage?"

Yes! "No, you're good. I'm sure you've got clients, plus I didn't bring any money out with me. Thanks though."

"You don't need money. Nate said you have full use of the facilities. That includes all spa treatments."

I gaped. "But, I…" Having Nathan allow me to use the gym facilities free of charge was more than I could have expected. In fact I had planned on trying to find a way of paying for the membership myself. But full use? How much would that even cost?

"I'll see you downstairs in a bit." With a beaming smile and bright eyes, Cassie slung her towel over her shoulder and strolled across the room, leaving me standing alone staring after her.

***

HAVING FINISHED WHAT I could remember of the workout plan Nathan had given me, I debated whether I should take Cassie up on her offer or not. It all seemed to be too good to be true, and in my experience that usually meant it was. In the end, my body fought with my brain… and won. I showered quickly and made my way down to Cassie's treatment room, hoping she didn't have a client.

"Are you sure about this? It feels all kinds of wrong," I asked, pulling myself onto the end of her padded treatment table.

"There is nothing wrong with a bit of pampering, Liv. Do you mind me calling you Liv?" I shook my head. "Besides, Nate gave us all explicit instructions that we are to give you whatever you need when you're here." My cheeks flushed at the thought that he'd spoken about me with his staff.

"What did he…" I couldn't bring myself to continue the sentence as I settled face down on the massage table.

"Don't worry, he was very discreet. I don't know what the deal is, he just said you have been given a special lifetime membership and you are free to use all the facilities as you please." Cassie draped a towel over my back. "I'll be back in a minute. I just need to get more oil."

The door clicked closed on the latch. Alone with my thoughts, my forehead crinkled in as I thought about why Nathan was doing this. I felt like some kind of elaborate science experiment for him. Or worse still, he was playing with me. Allow the poor, fat girl into your gym and see if you can break her, all while saying you are doing your bit for humanity.

"You're not fat," a deep rumbling voice growled from behind me. "And you certainly are not some science experiment." *Shit, had I really said all that out loud? And what was he doing in here?*

"I've already told you why I'm doing this," Nathan continued. With my head planted in the hole on the table and my muscles so tight I could barely move, I couldn't see him but I could certainly feel him. The hairs on my arms and the back of my neck stood on end when he stepped closer and I was very aware that I was undressed. "I don't like being second guessed, Olivia. This is the last time I'll be explaining myself, so listen closely. There is something about you that I am drawn to, something different to all the others—"

I wriggled, trying to move to sit up without

embarrassing myself by exposing too much flesh. "By the others, you mean all the bimbos that like salivating all over you."

"Shut up, Olivia!"

The brusqueness of his reply stopped me in my tracks.

"You needed help and I offered it. You can sass and fight me all you like, but I committed to help you achieve your goals. I'm not a man to go back on my word."

"Nathan, I…" I finally managed to manoeuvre myself so I could look at him. Every inch of my skin heated when I found his eyes raking over my exposed flesh, my modesty barely protected by the small towel now wrapped around me. He looked delicious in a pair of grey sweatpants that fell in a sexy way from his hips and a plain, white t-shirt, emphasising the fine physique underneath. He was in workout attire, ready to put his own body through its paces. My stomach muscles clenched at the thought of his large muscles rippling and stretching with his exertions.

His eyes met mine. "Stop overthinking and questioning this, Liv." I swallowed hard, unsure what to say.

"Oh my God, get out. Shoo!" Cassie flounced back into the room snapping a towel in Nathan's direction. I couldn't stop the giggle that bubbled up at seeing her petite frame pushing on his much taller, much stronger body. "You can't come in here when we have clients. You know the rules. You made them."

Nathan's heated gaze remained locked on mine until Cassie had him at the door. And then he was gone.

I collapsed back onto my front wondering how my orderly world had suddenly become a circus.

"I'm sorry about that. He hardly ever comes down here, and he's *never* come in to an occupied room before." I heard the confusion in her voice. "Anyway…" She warmed oil between her palms and began massaging life back into my dead muscles whilst telling me all the gossip of Golden Oakes and GO.

***

AFTER ONLY AN hour sprawled out on her table, Cassie had poked, prodded, rubbed and dug into my tired muscles reviving them to the point of being almost pain free and relaxed. She'd then proceeded to demand I go for the full works and slathered gunk on my face whilst waxing and buffing every inch of flesh from the armpit downward. Well, almost every inch. I'd refused point blank when she'd suggested a Brazilian.

Despite the torture, I came away feeling like a princess and on top of the world.

After a quick shower to remove the sticky wax remnants, I stood at my wardrobe wrapped in only a fluffy white towel and debated what to wear for the evening. I had no plans and didn't fancy making any. I'd just pulled a tan-coloured jumper off its hanger when my doorbell rang through my living space. Wrapping the towel tighter around me, I went to the door, pulling it open only enough that I could hide behind it and peer around it to greet my visitor.

In hindsight, it would have been wiser to have checked through the spyhole first because standing there, looking cool, calm and gorgeous, was Nathan.

"Um, hi," I greeted him sheepishly.

His lips twitched and his eyes sparkled, a sign I was beginning to recognise as a smile, even when his mouth didn't cooperate. "Hi."

"What are you doing here?"

"Can I come in?"

"Who's answering questions with questions now?"

"Do we have to go through that again?"

I quirked a newly shaped eyebrow.

He sighed. "May I?"

Nathan gestured at the door, and before I realised what he was doing, Nathan was stepping over the threshold.

"Nice view," he smirked as he pushed the door closed.

Realising I was still only in my skimpy towel, I desperately tried to cover myself further with my arms. "Let me ask you again, what are you doing here and how do you know where I live?" I kept my chin up in a vain act of confidence. In reality, I felt naked and abashed beneath his roving eyes.

"Form," was his reply, directed to the upper swell of my breasts.

As much as I wanted to know why Nathan was there, I couldn't continue talking to him while I was practically naked. It totally screwed with the sass and inner diva I seemed to need when dealing with Nathan Oakes.

"Just give me a minute." I ran off to the safety of my bedroom. Before fully closing the door, I took a minute to watch him through the crack. He looked edible in dark jeans that hung on his hips in the same sexy way that his sweatpants had. An untucked, long sleeved, white shirt covered the hard muscles of his chest and the tattoos I knew decorated his arms. The longer lengths of his hair were tousled and untamed. I sighed in appreciation of his fine form and shut the door. What on earth was he doing in my home?

Having quickly thrown on some underwear, I took more care in revising my clothing choice. Being faced with the fact that I needed something nice, yet sexy, yet I-haven't-made-an-effort-for-you—and I needed it to fit properly—it took me longer than it should have to decide. By the time I'd settled on a long, black and white patterned maxi dress, there were clothes strewn everywhere.

I yanked a brush through my hair and pulled it back, securing it with a large silver clip, and quickly applied some lip gloss and mascara to try to at least make me look semi presentable. With one final glance in my floor standing mirror, I nodded my approval and exited my room… into hell.

***

"WHAT THE FUCK do you think you are doing?" I yelled, rushing over to the kitchen.

In the relatively short amount of time I'd been in my bedroom, Nathan had ransacked my kitchen. Every cupboard door was open; bottles, tins, cartons, packet mixes and boxes of this and that littered every work surface. And he was filling my bin.

"Nathan, what the hell?" I screeched again, grabbing the six-pack of beers in his hands that were about to be discarded into the brushed chrome garbage bin. He wouldn't let go.

"A healthier lifestyle doesn't just happen from a bit of training at the gym," he replied, with a soft, yet commanding, voice. "If you're committed to doing this, then you are going to have to make changes in every area of your life. That includes what you eat and drink."

"But…" I looked around at all the convenience foods scattered around the place.

"These," he said lifting up a packet of sweet, sugared waffles, "are of absolutely no use to you nutritionally."

"But…"

He continued as if I wasn't there. "They are pure sugar, salt and wasted calories. They have no nutritional value to them whatsoever."

"But…"

I looked at him, blinking. Who was this man?

"Your whole attitude to eating, exercising and resting needs to change if you are going to succeed in your goals."

I slumped back onto a stool, bewildered beyond all belief. In short order, I had gone from a happy, content, albeit unhealthy lifestyle, to one full of demanding trainers and food dictators.

"Nathan, this is ridiculous. It's too much too fast." I understood changes needed to happen but I hadn't signed up for a total take-over of my life.

He placed the beers on the counter and moved in front of me, placing his warm, slightly calloused hands on my shoulders, his thumbs rubbing in soothing circles. "I know it all seems daunting at the moment, but it will all be worth it. Just think of the rewards," he said tenderly.

I laughed. My rewards were the very things he was trying to throw out.

"Just trust me, okay?" His hands began stroking along my upper arms.

"But if you throw all of that stuff away, I'll have nothing left to eat. Even you can't tell me eating nothing is acceptable." I suddenly felt so very tired. Joining up with a fitness freak like Nathan Oakes was a bad idea for someone like me. I was in over my head with him.

With a genuine smile, Nathan stepped back, extending a hand. "We'll go grocery shopping and stock you up with healthy alternatives."

At that moment I had no fight in me to argue. In a daze, I left him to it and went back to my room to tidy my clothes. I needed a few minutes alone.

When I re-emerged a short while later, the kitchen was mostly clear and tidy. I'd entered just in time to stop him from dropping one last thing into the bin.

"No," I cried, rushing to him and ripping the bag from his grasp. "I will give up anything but those." I held the giant bag of jelly beans against my chest.

Nathan chuckled. "Do you know—"

My eyes slammed shut. "Don't. Don't say it. I don't care what they do or don't contain. They are my guilty pleasure and I absolutely will not give them up."

"Well, okay then," he replied with a smile and a shake of his head. "We'll see."

~CHAPTER SEVEN~

IF YOU WOULD HAVE TOLD me a month ago that I'd be going to the gym pretty much every day for a solid sixty minute workout, I would have laughed in your face… and then gone to the fridge for a beer.

As it was, I'd spent nearly every evening of that month at Golden Oakes. If I wasn't kicking my own butt with Nathan's workout plan, I could usually be found in one of the studios attempting to look like I knew what I was doing in one of the many classes. It wasn't easy, and I'd been tempted to throw in the towel on more than one occasion. Each time that happened, Nathan would crawl out of the woodwork and rile me up. He got to me every time, talking about me being a quitter and not having the strength to see this thing through. I would always throw him a witty retort with a shit ton of sass and get straight back to my workout. He would laugh and return to whatever hole he'd crawled out from. It became a mutual understanding between us and I soon found myself eagerly anticipating those exchanges. Although as time went on, he seemed to be away from the gym more and more.

After emptying my kitchen cupboards of anything worth eating—minus the jelly beans, which I absolutely refused to budge on—Nathan had kept to his promise and taken me grocery shopping. That had been a rather bizarre event. Rocking up to my nearest supermarket in his graphite grey Porsche Cayenne had been weird enough. But when he literally tugged me down each aisle, throwing things in the trolley, all I got to do was look on in bemusement. What he had failed to realise was that there was a reason for my stash of convenience foods. I couldn't cook. What point was there in preparing a lavish meal for one? It was so much easier throwing a pizza in the oven or nuking a ready meal in the microwave. It was simple, quick, delicious and left me hardly any cleaning up to do. It was also apparently really bad for me.

'You carry on eating that shit," Nathan had said when I'd tried to sneak a double pepperoni pizza into the trolley, 'and you'll never truly change. As soon as you hit a hurdle, the old ways will come back. You have to break this cycle, Olivia.' And regardless of the thoughts that went through my head at the time, it must have worked because I did find myself being much more conscious about what I was putting into my mouth. It was like he'd hypnotized me at some point in our blossoming friendship. The words 'bacon double cheeseburger'—or similar—soon became triggers and in my mind I would see Nathan's face looking at me with determined tenderness. His voice would be soft and encouraging as he reminded me I needed to focus on my health.

I was still a liability in the kitchen. Nothing short of going back to college to study food tech would help me with that. Most of the foods Nathan had bought me—yes bought, he wouldn't let me pay, saying he'd left my kitchen empty so it was only fair he restocked for me—had gone in the freezer. I didn't have a clue what to do with it all, so I decided to store it and eat elsewhere. It was easier than burning my flat down trying to cook something edible. I ended up spending far too much money—money I didn't really have— buying meals from the Golden Oakes café each evening.

All that time at the gym inevitably meant I also got to know Cassie more. On the evenings that Nathan wasn't there to watch over me, she would join me and we'd work out together—of course her sessions were much tougher than mine. She was a good laugh and kept me focused. I learned a lot from her. I felt that in time we could become really good friends. With Adam still being weird I felt I needed a friend more than ever.

'Three… two… one, and you're done,' I said to myself, dropping my arms from the cool down stretch I'd had them in. It was Friday night, and I'd just completed another training session in which I'd managed longer on the treadmill, increased the weight on the machines and didn't feel like I would pass out on the cross trainer. I felt fantastic. The hard work was definitely starting to pay off. I could already see improvement in my fitness levels.

"Are you busy tonight?"

I looked over my shoulder. "Why if it isn't the Scarlett Pimpernel. To what do I owe the pleasure this evening?"

"Cut the crap, Olivia. Are you busy tonight?"

Twisting around so I could see him properly, I came face to chest with Nathan. My voice dripping in sarcasm, I said, "Nice to see you, Nathan. Long-time no see. How are you doing?" I hadn't seen or heard from him all week, and it had pissed me off more than I cared to admit. Every day I would walk in with eager anticipation that today I'd get to see him, talk to him. If was really lucky, maybe I'd get to feel his hands on me as he helped me correct my posture when I was pushing weights.

"I've been busy," he said, grabbing my elbow and pulling me towards the wall and out of the way of some girls heading towards the changing rooms. A relieved smile tugged at my lips when he ignored their blatant attempts at attracting his attention and kept his steely gaze on mine. "So, are you doing anything now?"

I swatted his arm away then immediately missed its warmth when it was gone. "No. I'm going home to curl up on my couch with a book."

I began walking away. "I want you to come home with me."

My eyes widened and my legs refused to move another step. "What?"

Moving to my side, Nathan placed his fingers under my chin and lifted so I had to look at him, his eyes searching mine with an sense of hope. "Liv, I would like you to come home with me so I can cook for you?"

"But…"

His lips pulled into a cautious grin. "As grateful as I am for you keeping the gym's café afloat, you eating there every day gives me the impression you might need a few culinary tips so you can use what you have at home. Am I wrong?"

I wondered how he knew I'd been eating there. "I want you to come home with me so I can cook you a proper meal and give you a few tips about preparing healthy meals." Was he serious?

I tried protesting, I really did. But when he fired back an argument for every excuse I made, it became apparent he wasn't going to accept no for an answer. I was also kind of intrigued about where he might live and what his place would be like. Did he live in the flamboyant, city bachelor pad I imagined him to have? Or was his home a more sedate, suburban affair? Did he even live alone? What if he had a girlfriend? I inwardly chastised myself for even caring. But I couldn't deny that the thought of some lucky bitch having the monopoly on his time stung—hard. Still, I'd only caught a glimpse of Nathan the business man at my office. The Nathan I knew only marginally more, the personal trainer, was focused, to the point and sometimes scary. But all of that was only a small part of the whole. Deep down I knew there were so many more layers to him. He had secrets, I was sure of it and for some reason I wanted to uncover them all.

Before I could think on it anymore, I agreed to his offer. With a huge smile on my face, I tugged on the changing room door. "Just so you know, Mr. Oakes," I said over my shoulder, "I will be expecting haute couture dining from you this evening." And I disappeared inside.

***

WEIRDER AND WEIRDER. That's what my world was becoming. I'd somehow managed to walk through a time-space continuum, black hole thing and was living a strange parallel life. It was the only logical explanation, because nothing around me felt real anymore.

Staring out the window of Nathan's car, the buzz of London passed by in a blur. I'd assumed that he lived close to the gym, or even near the headquarters for GO. But we were driving into the city, into the buzz of central London. The roads became congested, more pedestrians lined the pathways and there was an undeniable energy in the air.

"Where is it you live, exactly?" I asked, turning in my seat to face Nathan. He glanced over quickly before refocusing on the road ahead.

"I have a new apartment in Bayswater." He flicked the indicator and smoothly made a right turn into a road of Edwardian houses. That led to a row of Victorian houses. This was why I loved London so much—the mix of old and new blending together seamlessly. Architecture of different eras mingled so perfectly, creating a unique and interesting backdrop at every turn. As we drove along the road, I felt my excitement growing. I wondered what Nathan's place was like. Was his apartment a Victorian conversion that he'd retained all the classic fixtures in? Or had he opted to take a place in one of the few, newer built blocks that crept in every so often? My curiosity was answered a minute or so later when he rounded a corner and indicated before turning onto a ramp that would take us into an underground car park below a newly built, mostly glass, multi-storey block.

Under the bright fluorescent lights of the car park, Nathan drove around with confidence and ease, seeming comfortable and in control. He pulled the car into an empty space and killed the engine. I sat there staring forward feeling suddenly awkward. Nathan had hardly spoken to me on the drive over, and suddenly I was acutely aware that I was going to be walking into his personal space.

When he opened his car door, I followed. Taking a discreet look around the other vehicles parked nearby, I determined that the people who lived there must have money. All the cars filling the nearby spaces were expensive looking, with everything from big SUV's like Nathan's, to small sporty things. There was also a fancy looking superbike parked next to the Cayenne. I'd never been on the back of a motorbike before, but the thought of sitting behind someone, clutching hold of them tight, as they sped down quiet country roads, or weaved in and out of busy traffic, gave me a thrill.

"Do you like bikes?" Nathan asked, moving to stand beside me.

"I've never been on one," I admitted. Placing a hand to my lower back, he gestured towards a bank of elevators. "It's on my bucket list, though."

He smiled down at me. "We'll have to see what we can do for you then, won't we? I would hate for you to not achieve all your dreams and goals, JB." Just then the lift door opened and he encouraged me in with a little pressure on my back.

"JB?" I asked, turning to face him when the elevator began ascending.

He smirked. "Hmmm."

"What the hell is JB? Is that a pet name? Because I have to tell you now, I don't do the pet name thing. Nu uh." I shook my head almost violently. "And have you forgotten my name already? Because JB is nowhere near OB if you're going for my initials."

His grin widened. "Yes, it's a pet name, and I will be using it. No, it's not your initials. Well, not your real ones anyway," he said cryptically.

"What the hell does that mean?"

The elevator stopped on the eleventh floor and the doors opened. Nathan placed an arm around my shoulder and began walking us out. "All in good time, JB, all in good time."

***

"SO, WHAT AMAZING culinary secrets are you going to share with me tonight then?" I asked. I was perched on a stool on the living room side of his kitchen island, watching him curiously. He stood on the other side, looking comfortable resting against a counter. His kitchen was bright and modern with white walls, white gloss and frosted glass cupboards, granite worktops, stainless steel appliances and rustic wooden flooring. The kitchen opened out into an open-plan living and dining room that had floor to ceiling windows on two walls offering a perfect view over London.

He shot me a grin that was so unlike him it stole my breath. "None actually. I just want you to sit back, relax and enjoy a home cooked meal. I want to do this for you. I'm sure you're sick of the café food by now." Turning his back on me, he opened the tall, built in fridge and started rummaging.

My brows crinkled as strange, conflicting thoughts raced around my mind. Choosing to ignore my hammering heart at the fact that this could easily be seen as a date, I asked, "How did you know I've been eating at the gym anyway? I've hardly seen you there this week."

A mountain of meat and various vegetables and herbs appeared in front of me. "That doesn't mean I haven't been around. I've just been really busy with a lot going on at the moment. But I see *you*, Olivia. At first, I wondered why you weren't using the food we'd picked up." He swiped up the carrots, courgettes and aubergines and took them to the sink to wash. "Then I thought even you wouldn't be so stubborn as to let food go to waste. Finally I came to the conclusion that maybe you'd been living on that crap before because it was easy. You can't cook." It wasn't a question. He knew. He placed the washed vegetables down on a chopping board and began to chop them.

"Of course I can bloody cook," I replied defensively.

He shot me a look, and then returned his attention to chopping. "So, anyway, I figured if I cooked you something nice, it might just help you out a little bit. You know, give you an idea on what's healthy and how to go about cooking it."

My eyes rolled. I was sure it would but I wasn't going to admit that to him. "Don't you think you're taking this whole helping the hopeless charade a little too far?" I watched, mesmerized, transfixed as he sliced through the carrots with surprising ease and grace. His hands, strong and powerful, and dusted with a smattering of dark hair and redness covering his knuckles, flexed with each fluid motion.

His movements stopped abruptly, causing me to drag my gaze upward. He was watching me knowingly, those all-seeing, stormy eyes of his piercing me with their sharpness. "There is nothing fake about my willingness to help you, Olivia. The sooner you accept that the better."

"I just… I don't get it okay? None of this makes any sense to me, and I'm struggling with that. I'm an independent gal, Nathan. I do what I want, when I want, because I want. Not because someone else wants or tells me to."

"If you look back, I think you'll find everything you've done so far has been of your own choosing."

My brows lifted and I coughed a laugh, thinking back to his rather rude clearing out of my kitchen. "Um, my kitchen?"

"Okay, maybe I was a little out of line with the food thing—"

"A little?"

"But I'd seen what you'd left out on the counter," he continued, as if I hadn't spoken. "It made me curious about what other unhealthy things you might be hoarding. I just went through and got rid of the worst of it."

"You left me with nothing!" I shrieked.

"Wrong. I just moved things around a bit. Tell me, have you actually been through all your cabinets since my visit?"

"Other than those you put the new stuff in, no." My head dropped in embarrassment. I felt stupid. I'd just assumed he'd been a totally arrogant, dictatorial arse and had literally thrown everything away that had any reasonable calorie content to it.

"It's all about moderation. I'm not saying you can't have those items you love, but you need to learn that they are occasional luxuries, not every day indulgences. We can't always have what we'd like, Liv. Despite how much we really want them." His voice carried a hint of regret, and I found myself trying to gauge his thoughts. Was there a double meaning to his statement? As usual, he was a closed book, concentrating on his task.

I left Nathan chopping veg and preparing meat so I could take a look around his living room. I needed a moment away. Whenever I was around him, I felt flustered, frustrated and more than a little hot around the collar. I knew my feelings for him were growing beyond mere attraction and that scared me. Olivia Buchanan didn't usually do relationships. I wasn't interested in giving up my careers goals and dreams only to live someone else's. It wasn't who I was. Yet I stupidly found myself constantly wanting to impress Nathan, craving that little bit of praise or intimate attention he would occasionally offer.

"Can I use your bathroom?" I shouted, whilst looking around his fairly minimalist living room. I'd not known what to expect from his home, but the distinct lack of anything personal led me to believe he didn't spend much time here. The place seemed cold and unloved, not a happy place to retreat to after a long day at the gym. I felt a rush of relief sweep through me when I realised there were no indications of anything female being there either. It would appear he lived alone.

"Down the hall, first door on the left."

***

NATHAN OAKES WAS a mystery. There was no getting away from it. Standing at the basin in his bathroom, I noted the room was just as bare and cold looking as his living room. Were all the rooms like this? My flat might not have been the biggest, or in the nicest of areas, but it was home. I'd decorated and furnished it with warm, welcoming colours and didn't give a shit about something being out of its place. It was my sanctuary, not a catalogue show home like Nathan's place felt.

As I left the room, my inquisitive nature got the better of me. I wondered what the other rooms were like. After all, he hadn't given me a tour. I wanted to know what his bedroom looked like. Did that have colour? Had he made that his one decadent room, where he could chill out after a long day doing whatever it was he did? Or maybe he had it kitted out, warm and welcoming for all his female companions. My gut churned at the thought.

Peeking round the corner to make sure he wasn't looking, I opened the door next to the bathroom. It was just another white, cold and unloved room, a bedroom. I guessed it was probably a guestroom going by the size of it and the fact that it was furnished with nothing but a double bed and an oak wardrobe.

Closing the door quietly behind me, I stepped across the hall to the room opposite, expecting either another plain guestroom or Nathan's bedroom. I gasped when the door swung open and found myself looking at… a museum.

Stepping further into the room, my eyes darted from left to right, up and down and then around again when I'd done a full three-sixty turn and was still trying to work out what I was seeing.

Every wall, shelf and bookcase was covered in posters, trophies and news articles. There didn't appear to be an inch of wall space that wasn't somehow decorated with memorabilia. This room was such a stark contrast to the emptiness of the rest of the apartment.

I walked to a large, glass frame adjacent to another floor to ceiling window. With the room bathed in darkness, I had to rely on the gentle glow of moonlight filtering through the tinted glass to help illuminate the picture. Only it wasn't a picture. Inside the frame was what appeared to be a large, wide belt, the front of it being a huge circle of gold. It wasn't the only one. Lined up alongside were another three frames, all with similar belts proudly displayed inside.

I ran my fingers along the edge of a table littered with small picture frames and magazines. Picking up one of the magazines, I swivelled it into the light filtering in from the hallway to read the headline.

Golden Boy retires after controversial Sanchez KO

I dropped the magazine and scoured the table for more photos, articles, anything. Was this all for real? My shaking hands knocked over a small frame and I pulled that into the light. In the picture stood a smiling, shorter teenager who shared the same dark hair and stormy grey eyes as the slightly older guy next to him, the guy I thought I was getting to know. The taller of the two was shirtless, his exposed torso shining from bright lights hitting obviously sweat soaked skin. His arms were raised above his head with his hands wrapped in some sort of blue bandage. It was a pose of triumph.

There was photo after photo after photo, article after article, all showing the same thing, a shirtless Nathan.

Nathan *'Golden Boy'* Oakes, MMA legend.

~CHAPTER EIGHT~

SUDDENLY IT ALL MADE SENSE. The closed off studio at the gym – the one with the bags and funny looking boxing ring—the constant fights being shown on the screens around the place, his fitness and health freakery. He wasn't just a gym owner and personal trainer, he was a world famous mixed martial artist. A hugely successful mixed martial artist, going by the numbers of trophies and belts displayed around the room.

I felt his presence watching me before I knew for sure he was there.

"Why didn't you tell me," I whispered.

"Would it have made a difference if I had?"

I returned the photo to the table and ran my finger along the rim of a giant silver cup. "I don't know, maybe. Probably."

"Why?"

I finally looked up at the same time that he stepped into the room, flipping the light switch as he did. The shock of bright lights had me closing my eyes for a second. When I reopened them, Nathan was standing right in front of me, looking cool, calm and collected. He was every bit the Nathan I had begun to care for. Except now he wasn't. Now he was this superstar, this highly respected athlete who I knew nothing about.

"Because you're famous, Nate," I replied softly. Despite his eyes searching mine, looking concerned and unsure, his lips tipped into a small smile. I realised it was because it was the first time I'd called him anything other than his full name. That fact made me think that somewhere along the line our relationship had changed. It had morphed from just being trainer and trainee, helper and helpee, to something more. Was it friendship? Had we become friends? No, it felt different to that. Adam was my friend; I now classed Cassie a friend. With Nate, things felt different... more powerful.

But had he not thought that at some point in the beginning it would have been useful to say 'Keep that fucking back straight, oh and by the way, I'm Nathan Oakes, world famous MMA star. Thought you should know.'

"I thought you were just an ordinary guy—"

"I am."

"—feeling sorry for the ugly, fat butted burden on society."

"You are not ugly or fat and certainly no burden on anyone," he growled.

I smiled courteously but knew he was only being polite. "But you're not are you? You're not some ordinary guy. Why waste your time helping out someone like me?"

Making my way back over to the framed belts, I studied each one. Those things weren't easy to win. I'd heard Adam and the guys ranting about enough boxing matches over the years to understand that only the best of the best won them.

"I didn't tell you because I didn't want this. I didn't want it to have any bearing on how you saw me. Women throw themselves at me on a daily basis, Liv. They are willing to pay extortionate amounts for my time but they don't focus. It isn't personal training they are really after. They come to me for one reason only. To bed a famous MMA star."

I barked out a laugh. "You have no worries there with me. I could care less what your status is. I don't even get the sport. To me it seems like a bunch of guys rolling around together using the 'manly' sport as an excuse to feel each other up... no thanks. Not for me."

He smiled, his eyes twinkling under the inset spotlights. "I can assure you, no touching up takes place in the octagon."

I scoffed. "The octagon? What, four sides isn't enough for you, you need eight?" I stood tall and crossed my arms over my chest. I needed to show him I hadn't been affected by this news, yet in reality, it had rocked me to the very core. I was standing in front of someone famous, someone women across the globe probably lusted over. Women he could easily have and probably did. My eyes closed and my lips pulled into a flat line as I imagined some blonde bimbo on his arm, accompanying him to his fights and seeing him rip into his opponent with feral power. Afterwards, they would be together as she helped him come down from his fight high. I shook my head and opened my eyes, trying to rid myself of the unwelcome images.

Nate started laughing. The sight of it was so unexpected and beautiful that I found myself completely forgetting my unpleasant thoughts. My scowl was soon replaced by a quirk of my lips.

"You are a breath of fresh air, you know that, JB?" he said, drawing me against his firm body and placing a kiss to my forehead.

***

NATE COULD COOK. I mean *really* cook. Having pulled me out of his hall of fame, he led me to his dining table where he'd pulled out my chair for me. That had made me giggle. I couldn't ever remember a guy being so... gentlemanly. He'd wowed me with a delightful main meal of succulent steak with sautéd potatoes and roasted vegetables. It was all very healthy, apparently. And delicious.

"Tell me about your family," Nate said, lifting his glass of water to his lips. During the meal, any tension between us had slowly dispersed and we slowly began opening up, getting to know each other a little more. Not deep and meaningful things, just little tidbits of information that helped us understand each other more. It hadn't escaped my notice that I was more forthcoming with information than he was, but I shrugged it off and hoped he would loosen up eventually.

"There isn't much to tell," I replied with a shrug.

"My mum is a housewife and plant murderer… Don't ask," I said quickly when he opened his mouth at my ridiculous statement. "My dad is a neurotic accountant and wannabe Scrooge. I love them both dearly but they are eccentric. How about you?"

I lifted my fork to my lips and took a bite of the succulent strawberry I'd speared from the fruit salad in front of me. Juice burst from the plump berry and trickled down my lip.

"Here, let me." Nate leaned across the table and ran his thumb along my lower lip, wiping away the juice. I watched in awe, and maybe a lot of heat, as he sucked his thumb into his mouth and licked it away.

"Do you… was that… I…"

Nate laughed at my inability to string more than two words together and scooped up a strawberry of his own.

"Delicious, right?"

Words could not describe the thoughts that ran through my mind when he bit into the fruit and then slowly licked the juice from his lips. It was like a slow motion scene from a hot romance novel or blockbuster movie. I was transfixed. Unable to process thoughts as his tongue slowly drew across the plush pink of his…

"You're staring, JB," he chuckled.

"And you're hot," I mumbled under my breath, fiddling with my napkin. His eyes shot to mine and I realised I'd not mumbled that quietly at all.

Shit, shit, shit. Why did he have the ability to make me act like a bumbling idiot around him?

"Well I'm glad you think so. And you're beautiful," he replied with a smile.

My cheeks burned and my hands shook. I knew he was only being polite and friendly, but still. This was Nathan Oakes telling me I was beautiful. Nathan Oakes, MMA God. He was famous.

"Oh my God!" I shrieked and bolted out of my chair.

He was by my side in a second, gripping my upper arms and staring concern into my eyes. "What is it? What's wrong?"

"You're famous. You're fucking famous, Nate. People all around the world know who you are. You must have millions of people who want a piece of you and I'm sitting here dribbling strawberry juice everywhere and talking crap." I was breathing hard, on the verge of hysteria.

His eyes grew soft as his smile returned. "You weren't talking crap." His arms circled around my waist and pulled me close again. I didn't fight it. In fact I was beginning to really like the feeling of being wrapped in his arms. "And everyone dribbles strawberry juice, JB."

I sighed and snuggled in. It really did feel good to be cocooned in his strong arms.

I savoured the comforting feeling for a moment before tilting my head and asked, "What's with the JB thing? Spill it, Oakes."

His whole body vibrated with his chuckle. "JB... As in *Jelly Bean*."

Trying to pull back, I slapped him on the chest. "That's just…"

Nate laughed harder. "You. It's *you,* JB. My sweet little jelly bean."

Narrowing my eyes, I tried to be angry with him. I

tried to show my displeasure at the ridiculous pet name. But it was difficult with happiness zipping through me. *'My jelly bean'*. I actually *really* liked the sound of that.

After a moment or two of total serenity, Nate let me go and returned to his seat. The playfulness and softness in his eyes had disappeared. It was replaced with the same blank—maybe determined—expression I was usually greeted with.

"We, um… we kind of went off track there," I declared, wanting to try to break the sudden, unexplained tension between us. "Tell me about your family."

"There's nothing to tell." He scooped up more fruit and shovelled it into his mouth.

"Oh come on, I'm sure you have plenty of stories. How about relationships? Are you involved with anyone?" A cold sweat broke out across my back, wanting but not wanting his answer.

"No. I don't have the time or desire to be tied down." The relief of knowing he wasn't seeing someone was immense.

"How about brothers or sisters? Do you have any?"

"One younger brother," he replied bluntly.

"Okay, how about your mum and dad? What do they do?"

"Nothing. They're dead."

The clipped tone of his voice told me he didn't want to discuss it.

I pushed the fruit around in my bowl using the tip of my fork. "I'm sorry," I replied quietly. Sorry for bringing it up. Sorry for souring the mood, and sorry for him, for something that clearly still hurt.

Peering up from under my eyelashes with my head still bowed down, I quietly watched him. Here was a man who seemed to have everything going for him. On the face of it, he was successful, popular, wealthy and handsome. He had it all. The storm brewing in the depths of his eyes told me otherwise. There was a sadness to him that pulled at my heart strings. It made me want to cuddle him and protect him. I inwardly laughed at the irony. I was sure he was perfectly capable of protecting himself, at least on a physical level.

My eyes followed him when he scraped his chair back along the wooden floor and took his bowl into the kitchen. Placing it in the sink, he stood there for a moment, his head bowed and his shoulders rising and falling sharply. I wished I could see his face, wished I knew what was going through his mind.

"Nate, are you okay? Do you want me to go?" I asked quietly, coming up beside him with my own half-full bowl. My appetite had vanished.

He turned his head and regarded me with his gorgeous grey eyes that had softened slightly. "No. Please don't go yet." His grip on the edge of the counter increased, the knuckles on his hands turning white. It was almost as if he were trying to rein in the temptation to touch me.

I nodded with a smile and rubbed along his arm as I passed by. He needed a minute to himself, and I wanted to give it to him. I'd pretty much give him anything he wanted.

***

NATE PULLED HIMSELF out of his momentary funk and joined me on one of the white leather couches in the living room as I tried to think of ways to rescue our evening. He shocked the hell out of me by handing me a chilled bottle of my favourite beer.

"All in moderation," he'd replied, in answer to my confused expression. "If you want something, sometimes you just need to give in and indulge." His gaze had been blazing as he looked me straight in the eye when he said it. I wondered if we were talking about more than just the beer.

Needing distraction from the several conflicting thoughts running rampant through my head, I thought maybe bringing the conversation round to his true profession would help me understand him a little better.

"So, how come you haven't shown me any of your fancy MMA moves yet then, huh?" I asked, taking a sip from the bottle.

"I've thought about it," he admitted smoothly. "I was going to wait until you were ready. And until you, well, knew who I was." He shrugged and looked away abashed.

This could be interesting.

The thought of rolling around on the floor with Nate had me practically bouncing with excitement. "Show me something now."

"Now?"

I nodded. "Yup."

Shaking his head, Nate stood and looked around the room. Then, with purposeful strides and steely determination, he dragged the coffee table out of the way and pushed the opposite couch back against the wall. When he turned back and pushed back the couch I was sitting on, I squealed in surprise. His eyes shot up to meet mine, and he winked with a beaming smile. It was such a playful gesture that I could not help but return it. I loved this side of him.

"Come here," he commanded when the furniture was out of the way and we had plenty of space to move about.

Placing my bottle to the side of the couch, I grabbed his outstretched hand, using him as an anchor to pull me to standing. I felt awkward, yet energised, waiting for his next instructions. It felt different somehow being with him like this, in his home. It was more intimate, more personal. We didn't have the hustle and bustle of the gym to distract us, or the unease of being watched on my part. Despite trying hard at the gym to concentrate on me and what I was doing, the little insecure voice in my head that sometimes reared its ugly head, would occasionally tap me on the shoulder and tell me that people were watching and laughing. Here, in his apartment, everything was just him and me. He wasn't the master trainer or MMA star. He wasn't even the highly successful business man. He was Nate.

"Are you sure you want to do this now?" he asked, watching me carefully.

I bounced on the balls of my feet like I'd seen boxers do and grinned. "Bring it on, hot shot."

Shaking his head, he knelt in front of me and tapped my shoe. "You won't need these. We'll do this bare-foot." I tilted my head down and my breath caught at the sight of Nate in that position, smiling up at me. He looked so young and carefree... and gorgeous.

"Lift." Using his shoulder for balance... and a chance for a cheeky grope, I steadied myself while Nate took hold of my foot and pulled off my converse and sock. My gaze was fixed firmly on every movement he made as he shifted to my left foot and then stroked his hand along my calf and upwards as he slowly returned to standing. Even under thick denim, the sensation of his touch ignited my skin, sending shock waves through my body. I wanted him to move those hands everywhere. He was so strong, so graceful. Everything he did seemed effortless.

You can't be thinking this way, Liv.

I felt a sudden sting on my arm and jerked back.

"Ouch! What the fuck was that for?" I rubbed at the sudden burning on my upper arm.

"Lesson number one. Never let your guard down," he smirked.

"You bastard. That fucking hurt. You could have warned me."

Nate crossed his muscular arms over his chest grinning. "Do you think an attacker is going to warn you when they come at you with a knife."

I scowled. "No. But you're not an attacker."

He narrowed his eyes trying to look menacing as he stepped from side to side his arms moving almost faster than I could see.

"Ouch. For fucks sake, Nate. Stop it! That hurts!" I rubbed along the opposite arm which was now also going numb from another sharp slap.

Nate chuckled. "Stop being a girl. That doesn't hurt, I'm barely touching you. And keep your guard up. Be prepared, Olivia!"

"I thought you were going to show me some fancy flying kicks or something," I said petulantly, watching him closely with my hands raised in the same defensive pose he carried. I began moving with him as he slowly started to circle me.

"Not my thing."

"No? What is your thing then?" My arm instinctively moved away when his twitched.

"My first discipline is Ju-jitsu. I'm more dangerous on the ground grappling and holding."

"Ha, so you do enjoy a good fumble and roll around on the floor then." He shot me a look of heat before he quickly refocused.

"There is only one time I *enjoy* rolling around, and it isn't in a fighting arena." I jumped back when he lunged forward.

His eyes got a mischievous glint to them, and he stepped back, dropping his arms.

"What are you doing?" I asked with a frown, disappointed. Surely we weren't done already? I hadn't even managed to sneak in a slap of my own. I dropped my arms to my side, waiting for his next move.

Suddenly his left hand flashed in my peripheral vision and my arm instinctively came up to block it. At the same time he swept his leg out, catching my calf and knocking me off balance. With a screech and a thud, I landed on my back on the thick, deep red rug.

"Ooof!" Air jolted from my lungs, leaving me winded and fighting hard for a deep breath.

"Shit! Fuck! Liv, I'm sorry." Nate was on his knees straddling my prone form before I could blink. His eyes were wide and fearful staring down into mine. "Are you okay?"

All I could do was nod and swallow hard when he looked at me with such regret. My eyes closed at the feel of his hands smoothing my hair back and then trailing a hot path down my cheek. It was such a gentle, almost reverent touch.

"God, do you know how beautiful you are?" he asked tenderly, his body lowering towards mine.

I sucked in a deep breath, my heart pounding a frantic beat in my chest. He was so close, our lips only inches apart. His words and his slow, precise movements had my head spinning, but in this moment I knew I wanted him to kiss me. I was desperate for it.

No I don't want him to kiss me. That will just complicate things.

The moment his lips lightly pressed against mine, his tongue tracing along the seam, I was lost. The feeling was too much and not enough. It was heaven. As if feeding off my acceptance of his actions, Nate deepened the kiss, coaxing my lips apart so he could explore the cavern of my mouth. Tentatively, I touched my tongue to his and let him lead us in a slow waltz. I was lost.

I held my breath, soaking in the feel of Nate's hand gently stroking along my side to the outer swell of my boob, his body pressing into mine, the heat and hardness of his erection resting against my thigh... My eyes snapped open in shock. What were we doing? My startled moan had Nate pulling back, watching me with his own surprised expression. Gulping, he shook his head infinitesimally. Then, as if a spell had been broken, he jumped to his feet in one easy, fluid movement and ran shaky hands through his hair. "You need to keep your guard up at all times, Olivia. Always be prepared to fight and protect yourself."

As I lay out on the ground trying to catch my breath—which no longer had anything to do with my tumble—Nate strode to the windows keeping his hands in his hair.

"Self defence is built around a person's natural instincts. You need to be aware of your own body at all times. Watch your opponent or a perpetrator closely, anticipate their next move, but trust what your body is telling you. If you learn to read their body language and trust your own instincts, you're one step ahead."

Climbing to my feet, I smoothed down my t-shirt and ran a hand through my mussed up waves. I wasn't sure exactly what had just happened, or what it meant for us, but I knew it was time for me to leave. Something big had shifted between the two of us during those few seconds. I couldn't pinpoint what exactly, but if I was listening to my own instincts and acting on my body's natural reactions to Nate, it was clear I was falling into something deeper than I'd ever anticipated.

'Keep your guard up at all times.' Those words had never had a truer meaning.

I took one last look at Nate, his sombre face clearly reflecting back through the glass and darkness beyond it. He'd felt whatever that had been too and seemed to be in as much turmoil as me.

"Thanks for the lovely meal, Golden Boy." I tried to sound jovial, not wanting to end the evening on a sad note, but it sounded forced, even to my own ears.

I'd reached the hallway and was slipping my converse back on before Nate turned round. "What are you doing?"

I picked my bag up and pulled the strap over my shoulder. "I'm going home. It's getting late, and I'm tired. I had a great time tonight, Nate. Thank you."

He was at my side before I'd pulled the door open. "I'll take you."

"It's fine. Don't worry about it. I can just grab a cab or walk up to the station." He was pulling his trainers on with one hand when he reached out and grabbed my elbow with the other, stopping me from moving any further.

"I said, I'll take you. Don't fight me on this, Liv."

I sighed but knew I couldn't even if I'd wanted to. At that moment sassy, Liv had deserted me, leaving me exhausted, confused and needing my bed. I nodded and waited for him to finish getting ready.

***

"THIS IS YOURS?" I cast an appreciative gaze over the red and white bike I'd been eyeing up earlier in the evening.

"It is. Are you ready to cross another item off your bucket list?" As soon as we'd left the confines of Nate's apartment behind us, he'd loosened up. We both had. It was almost as if in there, together, we were a sexual, ticking time bomb. But outside, we were once again Olivia and Nate. Friends.

I gaped at the sexy machine in front of me. "You want to take me home on that?"

"Yes. Give me your bag." I handed my sports bag over, wondering where on earth he was going to put it. There hardly seemed like enough room on the seat for

Nate, let alone my fat arse and a bag. The Cayenne bleeped and he opened the door, throwing my bag inside.

"I need that," I protested.

"I'll drop it off to you tomorrow. You'll need your arms free so you can enjoy the ride."

I shrugged, admitting that made sense. "Okay then, let's go."

A minute later, he was securing a helmet to my head before pulling one of his own on and then straddling the bike. "Are you sure I'm going to fit?" I shouted over the load roar of the engine.

"You'll fit. Climb on." He gestured with his head for me to climb on behind him.

Taking a moment, I stared with female appreciation at the fine form before me. Nate looked mouth-watering wearing faded jeans with a black leather jacket and a black helmet. Knowing now that he was a bad boy fighter, that visual just added to the appeal that would make him every woman's dream guy.

"Get on, Liv," he shouted again as he dropped his visor.

Moving quickly, I stood beside the bike trying to work out how to get on. I was pleasantly surprised when I managed to easily swing my leg over and settle in behind Nate. The padded seat felt strange below my backside, as did the fact the seat was raised slightly at the rear, lining my body up perfectly with Nate's. A thrill coursed through me when he gunned the throttle and the bike vibrated beneath me.

"Ready?" he yelled.

"As I'll ever be," I shouted back, hoping he could hear me.

"Hold me tight, Liv, and don't let go. Stay relaxed and move with me."

Before I had a chance to respond, he'd kicked up the kickstand and we started moving. I shrieked with the alien feeling, even though Nate only walked us backward.

"Hold me, Liv."

Gripping my arms as tight as I could around his chest, I rested my head against his shoulder. Looking out to the side, I settled in for the ride.

Nate handled the bike pretty much like he did everything else, with ease, grace and control. As we drove along Bayswater Road, with Hyde Park on our left, I settled further into Nate's back, thinking I may have just found my new favourite mode of transport.

Being later in the evening, the roads were quieter, although not empty, so Nate could open the throttle when we had clear runs. Cold wind washed over us, and I shivered. I kept my eyes open, watching the world fly by, lights blurring into one long line as we sped by.

For the first few minutes, my nerves and tense muscles made it more difficult to move with Nate when we rounded corners. He shouted, "Relax, Liv," more than once, and as soon as I did, I found I was moving fluidly with him, melding to him as though we were one.

It became apparent Nate was in no hurry for the journey to end either when we hit the banks of the river Thames. The bike slowed slightly, and I felt the tell-tale sign of a deep sigh through the sharp rise and fall of the chest I had a tight hold of.

All too soon, we were pulling up outside my block

and Nate was killing the engine.

"You okay?" Nate asked softly when he'd removed his helmet.

I nodded but wasn't sure I was. The night had been full of strange and intense emotions and discoveries. I felt different somehow, yet the same. Stronger, yet weaker. One thing was for certain, Nathan Oakes had gotten under my skin. There was no ignoring it.

~CHAPTER NINE~

"YOU HAVE GOT TO BE fucking kidding me!" I groaned, looking at the illuminated numbers on my alarm clock. Each little digit glowed and mocked me as they grouped together to form 07:00. What was with my wacky weekend body clock these days? I'd been tossing and turning all night, dreaming and thinking, and then dreaming again. I couldn't remember the last time I'd had such a restless night.

Punching my pillow over and over in frustration, I muttered a few choice words and then dragged myself out of bed. With no motivation to do anything or go anywhere, I had no clue what I would do with myself for the day. Even the thought of going to the gym didn't sound appealing, and since getting into a routine with it, I'd been eager to go almost every day. The only times I hadn't gone were when I'd had to work late or go to my parents' place for dinner. It wasn't that I didn't want to work out, because I did. It was slowing becoming my addiction. It was more the case that I didn't want to run into the gym owner.

My evening with Nate had been strange, to say the least. I needed to deal with the feelings and emotions that had edged their way in and then pack them away in a box so I could continue with my usual happy and content life.

I thought about maybe doing something different. Not every workout had to be in the gym. I could enjoy the local park and attempt a proper run. Nodding approval at my plan I walked into the kitchen. I needed coffee and sustenance first.

I filled the kettle and then stopped, the appliance resting in mid-air in my hands. The conversation I'd had with Nate the previous night came back to me. *'Have you actually been through all your cabinets since my visit?'* It was an innocent comment, a simple question, yet it was loaded with so much meaning. In the past few weeks, things had changed… I had changed. Nate's control of my kitchen might have appeared absurd and downright weird on the face of it, but I now realised that in his actions he had been showing me he cared. To what extent, I wasn't sure. Was it just a desire to impart his expertise in all things health and fitness on someone who really needed it? Was it that he saw me as a friend? Or was there more? I knew I felt more. Last night's unexpected make-out session proved there was more.

Tentatively, I tugged open one of the wall-hung units. My eyes widened in surprise at the neat and tidy space. Herbs and spices were organised and evenly spaced out along with other bottles and packets of seasonings. I closed the cupboard and moved on to the next, and then the next. Each one was as tidy as the first, and just as he'd told me, I wasn't left with nothing, just products that he deemed to be healthy and nutritious for me and, of course, the items we'd purchased together.

His caring touches were there for me to see, as clear as if he'd been standing with me and whispering his innermost thoughts to me.

Deciding I didn't want to disappoint Nate by polluting my body with caffeine, I returned the kettle to its cradle and stood leaning against the counter. The radio played softly in the background as I stared at a small piece of plastic resting on the opposite counter. My membership card to Golden Oakes. My green light into a part of Nate's world. Yet another symbol of the generous and caring man I was beginning to fall for. The front doorbell rang loudly over the hum of the music. It startled me from my wayward thoughts, pulling me back to reality with a jolt.

At the door, I peered through the spyhole. My heart instinctively began pounding out a sensual, slightly irregular beat as I grinned at the handsome face that greeted me. *Why is he here?*

An eye appeared in my vision and the laughing cadence of Nate's deep voice tantalised me through the wooden door. "I know you're there, Liv. You can stop staring now." His laughter grew louder when I gasped and jumped back. Had he really been able to tell I was ogling him… through a tiny spyhole?

"Good morning, JB," he said brightly when I'd unhooked the safety chain and opened the door for him to walk in. "I've gotta say, I like the dogs but the towel was definitely my favourite." I frowned in confusion until I realised he was talking about my white, flannel pyjamas that had little brown puppies scattered over them. I winced in embarrassment as heat rapidly scorched along my throat and up into my cheeks. He continued chuckling as he walked past me into the living room. He seemed to be in a jolly mood.

"What brings you here this morning?" I asked, following behind.

"I brought your bag back." He shoved my sports bag at me, the one he'd thrown in his car the night before. "You might want to check your phone. The fucking thing was ringing non-stop on the journey over."

I mumbled my thanks and took the bag from his hands. Ripping the zip open, I felt about in the bag for my phone. There was a missed call from my mum, eight from Adam and two text messages. I quickly opened the message app and read the texts.

Where are you? The first one read.

Do you ever answer your phone? Call me. I need to speak to you, said the second.

Okay, someone was pissy.

"Do you want a drink?" I asked Nate, walking back into the kitchen needing something, anything, liquid to help rescue my suddenly dry throat.

"No, I'm fine thanks." His sexy smile dropped and his expression grew serious. "Look, there is another reason I came over. I need to ask you something. I meant to talk to you about it last night, but... well, things didn't quite work out how I'd planned."

Pausing halfway into the kitchen, I turned and gave him my undivided attention.

"Okay."

Nate bit on his lip for a minute as he seemed to contemplate his words. "I'm going away… out of the country… for a while." My heart felt like it had combusted in my chest and then fallen to the floor as nothing more than a fine mess of grey ashes. We were only just getting to know each other, and, like it or not, things were changing between us. I didn't want him to go away.

"For how long?" I asked, quietly.

"A couple of months. I'm coming out of retirement for a rematch with Sanchez." He replied, a frown appearing on his brow as he searched my face. It must have been showing the disappointment I felt because he looked away and kept talking. "He's bitter over our last fight and has been talking crap. I ignored it for a while, but eventually it became impossible to leave alone. I decided the best way to shut him up was to rise to his challenge and knock him out again."

I kept my eyes locked on his but pulled my trembling hands behind me, hoping he couldn't see how much his words were affecting me. "I've been training here, but I need to step it up now. I have a place in France I go to."

"France?" I yelled in surprise.

Nodding, he continued. "I have a house down in the south. It's where I go… went… to prepare. It's secluded and offers me the peace to focus. I can't do that here, not properly. There is always so much going on. Plus, I have the added advantage that the fight is being held in Monaco this time."

"When are you going?" I asked, wanting to slap myself when my voice quivered.

"Monday," he replied, almost apologetically.

I stopped breathing. He was leaving me already? Who was going to train me? Who was going to nag me to be good and rifle through my cupboards? It had only been a couple of weeks, but I enjoyed what we had together, well, when we were together. I didn't want that to come to an end so soon.

"I want you to come with me," he continued with a strong, determined edge to his voice.

"Excuse me?" I spluttered.

"I want you to come with me… No wait, before you start arguing, I have an ulterior motive. I need your services. My property there needs renovating, and I also want to build a new training facility on the land. It has always been my intention to offer training and rehabilitation for people with sports injuries when I retired. I want you to do the designs for me."

My jaw dropped. Was he for real?

"Your designs for the GO headquarters were outstanding, and I want to use your talent for this new project. Please, Liv. I want you to come and join me out there."

I shook my head. "I can't just up and leave. I have a job, a home. I have commitments."

"Take a sabbatical."

I gripped the edge of the worktop behind my back. It was easy for him to say that. He was rolling in money and had everything he could possibly ever need. It wasn't as easy for me to just drop everything on a whim.

"I can't do that," I said. "I've not been with the company that long, and I love my job and the people I work with. They've taken huge risks on me, giving me accounts… like your account… that someone with my lack of experience wouldn't normally get. I can't throw that back in their faces. I won't. I need more experience under my belt, and I want to get that with Ashworth-Moore. I'm not going to risk losing a job that means so much to me." I hoped my pleading tone was enough to convince him I meant every word.

He stepped in front of me and stared into my eyes. "What better project to have in your portfolio than plans for GO *and* Nathan Oakes' passion project. Think about it, Liv. I'm well known, influential. When the facilities open, people from around the world will want to use the buildings purely because of who I am. That's a prestigious string to add to your bow."

"It's just not a good idea. I'm sorry, but I can't," I whispered sadly. I wasn't only thinking of my career, I was also thinking about my heart. Things had already tipped on a weird axis between the two of us. Spending any length of time together like that in a foreign country, away from the hustle and bustle of normal life, was just a recipe for disaster.

Nate seemed to understand my meaning but didn't look happy. His shoulders dropped and any hopefulness that had been there drained away. I hated being the one to cause that defeated look on his handsome face.

"Please, just think about it. That's all I'm asking," he pleaded, reaching out to place a warm, large hand on my shoulder and squeezing gently.

I looked at his hand on me, the darkness of his light tan and the smattering of dark hair a contrast against the white of my nightwear. I'd think about it. Hell, I'd dream about it, but I knew it wouldn't do much good.

As appealing as it sounded, my long term future was far more important. I couldn't jeopardise it all for one job. Or for one person.

***

I IGNORED ADAM'S missed calls and sent him a simple text saying, **Sorry, busy. Will see you on Monday.** I did the same with Mum, telling her I would call her in the week. Nate's proposition had taken me by surprise so much that after he'd left, I'd collapsed on my couch and done… nothing. I felt torn. One part of me was screaming that it would be a fantastic opportunity. The other, more sensible, part was calmly listing all the things wrong with taking him up on his crazy offer.

Saturday afternoon was spent curled up watching on demand movies—which somehow all seemed to be fight related—and cheesy reality shows. I asked myself time and time again, were they truly real? Because surely nobody's lives could be that filled with drama. I'd even caved in and ordered pizza. That then led to the guilt. What would Nate say? He would no doubt be disappointed in me. Then again, after Monday, what would he care? He would go off to wherever for however long he would be there, and by the time he came back, he would have forgotten who I was.

I reminded myself that I wasn't doing any of this for him. It was all for me. Still, he had shown faith in me, and I didn't want to let him down. I ended up throwing the pizza, untouched, in the bin and actually cooked some pasta with a fresh tomato and herb sauce. I was so proud of myself.

Sunday was spent in much the same way. This time,

I defrosted some meat and made my version of what Nate had cooked for me. It wasn't as tasty as his cooking, but it was edible, and I didn't keel over and die afterwards. I missed being at Golden Oakes though. I just wasn't sure if I was still welcome to use the facilities if Nate wasn't going to be around and after I had pretty much turned down his offer.

I'd kind of expected him to maybe push things more, try to persuade me to change my mind. But there had been nothing. No phone call, text message or email. I tried damping down my disappointment by saying it was okay. I'd said no, and he'd respected that decision. The other part of me, the side I didn't want to admit had growing feelings for Nate, let me believe that by saying no, I'd also said no to any future contact with him. It was a depressing thought.

**

MONDAY MORNING I was in my wardrobe rifling through my clothes, trying to decide what to wear for another day in the office. I still felt emotionally drained by Nate's proposition and the fact I wouldn't be seeing him anymore. A dark mist had descended on my mood and I wanted that displayed through my attire. Pulling down my trusty black trousers and a black, ruffle neck blouse, I held them up to my body and looked in the mirror, nodding my approval. All black, just like my mood.

I grabbed a black lace underwear set out of the top drawer of my dresser and flung the lot on my bed. Having dried my hair, I pulled on my knickers and wiggled into my bra. Then I wiggled some more. It didn't feel right. Stepping over to the mirror again, I checked my reflection and, for the first time, I noticed a difference. My bra was gaping a little on the cups. My knickers didn't pull tight across my pelvis, and my stomach was definitely flatter. I smiled briefly thinking all my hard work at the gym was starting to pay off. It wasn't a huge difference, but as I twisted this way and that checking my body from different angles, I could definitely see toned areas that had previously been a little 'loose'.

When I finally felt comfortable in my underwear, I tugged on my trousers and blouse. I again looked in the mirror and blinked at the sight in front of me. Trousers that not so long ago had been a snug fit, now gaped along the waist. The blouse that had previously been a perfect fit now hung in all the wrong places. I yanked them off and rushed back to my wardrobe needing something else. A dress caught my eye. A very professional, very elegant looking, cream-coloured shift dress with a thin red belt. I'd only ever worn it once, several years earlier, during my first year's placement. I'd been younger and slimmer then.

I pulled the dress off the hanger and held it up to me, looking in the mirror. This was who I wanted to be. The powerful, smart, beautiful woman everyone respected. I knew they were only clothes, but clothes talked. Clothes gave you confidence. They were like a costume... or a mask. If you had on the right outfit, you could be whoever you wanted to be.

Suddenly, my black mood was behind me. I was eager to get my day started, to see if I could slip into the role of a high roller. I lowered the zipper and pulled the dress over my head. When it easily fell into place and I could zip it up, I sang a little happy chant, bouncing on my feet in glee.

'Ha, take that Barbie-bitch,' I thought as I slipped on some red, peep-toe heels. Liv was back and feeling phenomenal.

***

DESPITE KNOWING THAt turning down Nate's offer was the best thing for me to do, I couldn't seem to get it out of my mind. All morning I'd been distracted, wondering where he was, what he was doing. I couldn't help but question what we would have been doing at that moment if I had gone with him. The thoughts were getting me nowhere fast.

"Liv, do you have a few minutes? Mr. Ashworth would like to see you in his office," Trish said smoothly into my phone when I answered it just before eleven.

"Sure, no problem. I'll be there in a minute." Rising onto shaking legs, I smoothed the skirt of my dress down and took a steadying breath. Mr. Ashworth never called for somebody at my level unless they'd seriously fucked up somehow.

"Good morning, Olivia. Please come in. Take a seat. Can I get you anything?" Robert Ashworth asked brightly a couple of minutes later, gesturing with an outstretched arm to a seat opposite his.

"Um, no. I'm fine, thank you." I sat in the black leather chair and placed my hands in my lap, discreetly rubbing my sweaty palms along my thighs. What was going on? His friendly, welcoming approach was somewhat of a surprise and had caught me completely off guard. When you spoke to Robert Ashworth you needed to be sharp, quick and to the point. He had no patience for time wasters and drove home his points straight away.

"I'm sure you are wondering why I've called you in here." I nodded.

"I have wonderful news for you. I would like you to go home and pack your bags because you're going to France." He pushed an envelope across the desk towards me as I blinked rapidly. *What did he just say?*

"A wonderful opportunity has arisen for you to study European architecture whilst working on a prestigious account that will benefit both the company and you individually, Olivia. Mr. Oakes was so impressed with the way you handled things for GO Sports & Leisure that he has personally asked that you accompany him to his property to design his new training facilities in the South of France."

I continued staring at Mr. Ashworth, absently blinking. I'd heard him, but I couldn't comprehend what he was saying.

"Olivia!"

"Um, sorry. Could you repeat that please?"

Mr. Ashworth looked irritated for a brief moment but then a touch of a smile tugged at his lips. "I'm sure this is all a bit of a shock." The France bit, no, not really. The fact I was being sent out there, yeah, a huge fucking shock. "But I want you to know, you have our total backing. Don't let us down, Olivia."

That was is it? No, would you like to go? No, how would you feel about going? Apparently it was a done deal. Apparently, I was on my way to France whether I liked it or not.

I walked back to my office in a bit of a daze. I'd turned Nate down because I didn't want it affecting my job. He was obviously not good at accepting no for an answer and had gone behind my back and straight to my boss. When I dropped into my chair, I was furious. How dare he? I'd said no, he should have accepted my decision and moved on. What gave him the right to force my hand like this? I could still turn it down. But the way Mr. Ashworth had spoken, it sounded like I was expected to do this. If I didn't, would I still have a job?

"Liv, what the fuck is going on?" Adam came barrelling into my office and straight to my desk, bracing himself with rigid arms on the edge. "Everyone's saying you're leaving."

"Oh, for the love of God," I shrieked, throwing my hands into the air in exasperation. "I am not leaving!"

Without even looking inside, I passed Adam the envelope that had been given to me and proceeded to tell him about the rather unsavoury way Nate had gone about hiring my services.

"So, let me get this straight. You join him in France, all expenses paid, for however long it takes you to complete this project?" Adam's face looked grim as he handed me back the envelope.

"That about sums it up," I replied, sagging back into my chair.

"You can't do it, Liv."

"Why not? Don't you think I'm good enough?" Hearing that from my best friend hurt.

"No, it's not that." He sighed and rounded the desk. Crouching down in front of me, he continued. "I'm worried that he'll take advantage of you. It's all kind of weird don't you think? Let me go. I'll tell dad that it's better for the company if I do it. I'll spin some PR bullshit or something to get him to change his mind. I don't want you doing this, Liv."

I pushed back in my seat and walked over to my window. "You don't want me doing it? This whole thing is bullshit, Ad. Why can't people leave me to make up my own mind?"

"I just want what's best for you."

I shot round. "Do you? Do you really? Or are you just trying to get your hands on a big, prestigious project? What if I want to do this? What if I want to go but I'm just worried?"

My head throbbed with the pressure of everything. I felt like I was being pulled towards fifty different paths, and I wasn't sure which was the right one to take.

"I don't want you to go." Adam moved to my side and touched my arm tenderly. Swallowing hard, he stared at my face with pained, deep blue eyes. "I don't want you to go because… I love you, Liv. The thought of you being out there alone with him, it kills me."

My eyes widened. "What?"

"I love you. I've loved you for a very long time."

"No, no, no." I broke away from his touch and rushed to the other side of the room. I needed space, needed room to breathe. "Why are you saying this now, Adam? You're just trying to confuse me so I don't go." Unshed tears stung the backs of my eyes.

"No! I've wanted to tell you. I've needed to tell you. But, fuck, Liv, I needed to know there was even the smallest chance you might have felt the same way." His voice trembled but he kept his eyes locked to

144

mine, pleading for what… understanding? Acceptance? Reciprocation? He knew I didn't feel that way about him.

"Why? Why now, huh? I've just been handed what could possibly be the biggest career maker and you land this on me." I buried my face in my hands. I would not cry. I never cried. I was stronger than that. Sucking in a deep breath, I lifted my head and looked Adam in the eyes. "Why are you trying to ruin our friendship?"

He took tentative steps across the room until he was standing before me again. "It's not like that, Liv. I would never risk our friendship. I just can't let you go off to another country with another man and not let you know how I feel. It'll drive me fucking crazy every day you're gone, not knowing what you're doing, if you're okay. If you're *with* him." He closed his eyes, trying to hide the pain in them.

I couldn't deal with this, not now. Balling my hands into fists, I struck Adam's chest over and over, hammering my hurt and frustrations into him "You can't do this to me, Adam, not now. It's bullshit. You're my best friend, my rock. It can't be any other way between us."

"Says who?" he yelled, grabbing my fists and holding them against his pounding heart.

"Says me."

Our gazes remained locked, our breathing rapid. There was nothing more to be said. I couldn't be who Adam wanted me to be. That was a line in our relationship I would never cross. But by declaring his feelings, had Adam crossed it anyway?

Finally he dropped my hands and stepped back.

"Fine, go play with your famous, rich boy but don't come crying back to me when he breaks your fucking heart." And then he was gone, storming out of the room and slamming the door behind him.

"Arrgh!" I screamed, sliding down the wall until I sat with my knees drawn into my chest, my face buried in my hands.

I was still sitting there, in shocked outrage, five minutes later when Trish gently knocked and poked her head around the door. She'd heard everything and told me to go home. I had a lot to think about and needed space and a clear head to do it.

There was no way I could go home feeling the way I did. I'd go stir crazy. So instead, I decided to take a walk to the coffee shop. The fresh air and time away from everything would give me a chance to think, uninterrupted.

***

I SIPPED ON my flat black coffee, grimacing at the bitterness—oh how times had changed. Weeks of abstinence from my favourite energy pick me up had turned me against the stuff. Still, I continued sipping and listened to my mum drone on about another plant that was wilting. I'd called her hoping to get some words of wisdom. I should have known better.

"What's wrong sweetheart? You're quiet."

I sighed. Did I really want to burden my mother with my problems? Did I even really have any problems, or was I just blowing everything out of proportion?

"I've been asked to go and work in France and

Adam says he loves me," I blurted out.

"What!" I heard a crash and a curse and then she was back. "Say that again."

I recapped what Nate had offered me, and how he'd gone behind my back by contacting Mr. Ashworth when I'd turned him down. I then told her miserably about my run in with Adam.

"Wow! Sweetheart, no wonder you sound so down."

"What should I do, Mum? I'm so confused right now."

"What do you want to do?"

"I don't know. Part of me is really excited about the project. I mean I could learn so much whilst I'm out there. It's a great opportunity. But I feel I need to stay here and prove myself with Ashworth-Moore."

The door opened and a group of teenage girls walked in giggling, distracting me momentarily. "And what about Adam?" Mum asked.

"God, he's a completely different problem. I love Adam, you know that. He's my rock. But I don't love him *that* way. I don't have romantic feelings for him. He's more like my brother."

"Do you want my advice, sweetheart?"

"God, yes," I breathed. I needed someone's because my own voice of reason had deserted me.

"Do it, go to France. Unless you have concerns about this Nathan's motives, this is a once in a lifetime opportunity for you. You will get so much more out of it than just the architecture. And who knows, maybe some time away from each other will be just what you and Adam need. They say absence makes the heart grow fonder. If you're not seeing Adam every day, there's a possibility that maybe your feelings towards him might change. Or for him, not being around you might help him see the love he has for you is still only of the friendship kind. Maybe he just needs to meet someone new."

I closed my eyes. "When did you get so wise, Mum?"

"I have my moments," she laughed.

We chatted for a few more minutes before she had to go and replant 'Harry' who had apparently outgrown his pot.

Everything had been thrown at me so quickly, I honestly didn't know which way was up anymore. But the more I thought about it, as I quietly sipped on my coffee, the more appealing going to France became. I had one main concern, however, and that was about my feelings for Nate. I knew I was starting to feel more for him and that something had definitely shifted between us Friday night. I wasn't sure I would be able to bury that so I could remain professional about the job. If I said yes, I would have to be Olivia, the architect. Anything else was unacceptable.

I absentmindedly looked over the table-top coffee menu, lost in my thoughts, when I felt a presence beside me. "Everything is fine in moderation, Olivia." I knew that voice.

"Hi," Nate said when I looked up, his eyes bright.

"What... what are you doing here?" I sounded far too excited as I stood to greet him.

"I'm just on my way to the airport. I was hoping to talk to you before I left."

"Nate I—"

"No, please, let me say this. I'm sorry I went behind

your back. I know it was a bastard thing to do and you have every right to hate me for it. But I want you to join me over there. This training centre means a lot to me, and I trust you to come up with the best plans for it." His smile faded. "I know things got a little weird between us the other night, and for my part in that, I'm sorry. I want you to know that this is purely a business proposal, just in case you were worried about my intentions."

"Okay."

"Okay?"

"Okay, Nathan. I accept your proposal. This will be good for me as an architect. I'll join you in France."

His lips pulled up into a rare, dazzling smile. "Thank you, Olivia. I promise you won't regret it. Can I give you a lift home so we can discuss the logistics?"

On our way out, we bumped into Barbie-bitch and her clones. The feeling of satisfaction I got when she preened in front of Nate and he totally ignored her was better than any revenge I could have planned for her. Then she trained her eyes on me and the look of startled recognition on her face had me grinning widely. As we passed, I couldn't help but toss out a mouthed 'thank you' in her direction. Her bitchy comments had been the catalyst to everything, and she deserved recognition for it. Yanking my bag higher on my shoulder, I lifted my head high and walked out, proud, and ready to see where this adventure was going to take me.

~CHAPTER TEN~

Two weeks later

I TOOK A DEEP CALMING breath as the plane jolted to a stop and the fasten seat belt sign blinked off. Everybody around me began frantically jumping from their seats and fumbling around in the overhead lockers to extract their belongings. I sat still and looked down at my shaking hands. I'd arrived in Nice and had no idea what to expect from this point on.

Two weeks had passed since I'd agreed to join Nate to work on the plans for his new training facilities. In those two weeks, I'd had very little contact with him other than a couple of brief phone conversations and the barest of information via email on what I could expect whilst I was there. During those two weeks, I realised I'd missed him and couldn't wait to see him again.

Despite my head telling me I was going there to work, that crushing on someone was the very last thing I should have been thinking about, I'd found myself thinking about him. A lot. I missed seeing his face around the gym. I even missed his abrupt bossiness when he pushed me further than I felt comfortable with. Mostly, I just missed him being around.

I shook my head and tried to convince myself that the shaking hands were because of the flight. It didn't work. I'd never had a problem with flying before. In fact, I loved flying. I reasoned that maybe it was due to the fact I'd not eaten lunch before I boarded the plane. Again, it was a feeble excuse. No, my hands were shaking because within thirty minutes—depending on baggage reclaim and passport control—I would be seeing Nate again.

'He's a client,' I kept telling myself, over and over again. *'He's hired you to come and do a job. Be the professional you claim to be.'*

Outside, on the tarmac, little trucks began whizzing around preparing to refuel the plane and remove our luggage. It was chaotic but orderly, all done to precision timing. I wished I could get my brain to work in the same way. My thoughts were running rampant through my head, causing a whirlwind of confusion and unease.

My nerves had not been helped by a lack of contact from Adam. After our heated exchange in my office, he'd been staying out of my way. I'd catch the odd glimpse of him at work, but for the most part, he was out when he could be, or he stayed locked in his own office. He didn't call or text, and he hadn't been to the gym. It killed me that he'd distanced himself. In a world of crazy, he'd always been my constant, my shoulder to lean on or my voice of reason when I screwed things up. But for two weeks, I'd had nobody. I missed him. I needed him… as my best friend.

People started moving down the narrow aisle and I noticed the plane's door had been opened. When the crush had passed, I grabbed my bags from the locker and made my way towards the exit. I had no idea what the next few weeks were going to have in store for me, but one thing was for sure, no matter what, I was going to have a good time—with or without Nate. I would make damn well sure I did. I was, after all, on the Cote d'Azur, playground for the rich and famous. I smiled to the cabin crew as I passed. Yes, whatever happened, I was going to enjoy myself.

***

THERE WERE PEOPLE everywhere as I pulled my belongings through into the arrivals hall. I looked around for Nate but couldn't see him anywhere. Mindful of the goings on around me, I hauled my stuff off to the side and fumbled in my bag for my phone. I needed to double check our emails to make sure I was in the right place or see if he'd sent a message to say he'd been delayed somewhere. I powered it on, and while I waited for it to readjust to a new network location, I watched the people around me. There were business men and women arriving in their sharp suits with briefcases and phones attached to their ears. Holiday makers filed through the doors in their skimpy summer wear looking happy and excited, while tired-looking people sauntered through, having obviously just returned from their own vacations. I smiled as a group swarmed a boy—he couldn't have been any older than eighteen—clapping and cheering for him. He was obviously returning to a hero's welcome. But still there was no sign of Nate.

When my phone settled on a network, I checked my messages. There was just one new text message. It was from Nate and had been sent just before I'd boarded the plane in London.

Hope you have a smooth flight. See you later. N

"Hey, hey, it's JB," a bright, cheery voice sung to me from behind just before an arm wrapped tightly around my shoulders, scaring me half to death.

"Get off me, you creep. Who the hell do you think you are?" I fought off the arm and glared into unfamiliar, yet familiar eyes as I prepared to knee the man where I knew it would bloody hurt.

The stranger chuckled before bowing in a grand gesture. "Do forgive me. The name's Wes, Wes Oakes," he said in the worst Sean Connery, James Bond accent I'd ever heard. His eyes sparkled in amusement when he righted himself and stuck out his hand. "And you must be the lovely Olivia. Nate was wrong about you, you know? You aren't just beautiful, you're sensational." I flushed at the compliment and despite the bizarre situation, my lips curled up at the corners. *Nate said I was beautiful?*

"Come on, let's get you to the car." He grabbed the handles of my cases and started walking off.

"Wait! What the hell?" I yelled and ran after him.

"Who exactly are you, and where is Nathan?"

"I just told you, I'm Wesley and Nathan is… somewhere." He grinned sheepishly and winked.

Whoever this guy was, and whatever he was doing, he was doing it too fast. Struggling to keep up with his fast pace in my flip flops, I cursed myself for not wearing a pair of jeans and my converse.

"Where is somewhere? I thought he was supposed to be meeting me." He had been forced to slow down to allow a group of people to walk by which let me catch up enough to try to talk.

"He's got things to do, places to go, people to see. So, you get the pleasure of my company instead. He'll be around later." With the area clear, he walked off again with long purposeful strides.

"So I'm just supposed to go off with you, a complete stranger, to God knows where? I don't think so." I practically had to run to keep up with him.

Wesley stopped again and sighed. "Here!" He shoved something in my hand. "See. Wesley Oakes, born June 27th 1992. Now I'm not a stranger." I looked down at the driver's license in my hand.

"So you are…"

He smiled, his bright grey eyes so like Nate's and dancing with humour. "Nathan's much sexier, younger brother. It's nice to finally meet you, JB. Can we go now?" I bit my tongue at his use of *that* name as he grabbed my hand and gently pushed me along towards the exit.

We had just left the airport boundary behind us and were speeding along a French motorway heading north when I asked, "Where exactly are we going?" I was seated next to Wesley in the plush leather passenger seat of another Porsche Cayenne, a white one. I vaguely wondered if Nate had shares in Porsche, and then I remembered who he was. The cars were probably all part of a major sponsorship deal. That was still something I hadn't been able to comprehend. Nathan Oakes, personal trainer and gym owner, was actually a highly successful, well respected and famous mixed martial arts star.

"That's for me to know and you to find out," Wesley said. He peered over at me and wiggled his eyebrows. I rolled my eyes and turned to look out the window, wondering where Nate was and what he was doing. Why hadn't he been there for me?

***

"WE'RE STAYING HERE?" My eyes bugged out of my head and my jaw fell to somewhere around my ankles as Wesley stopped the car in front of a huge palatial hotel from the Belle Époque period, sitting in the heart of Monaco. "I thought Nathan had a secluded property in France," I whispered, fearing normal voice levels would spoil the aura of the luxury building.

A valet approached and opened the car door for me with a courteous smile. I was seriously impressed. Never in my life had I seen such extravagance. "Merci," I replied with about the only French I could remember from school.

"Nate does have property not too far away. It's an old vineyard about forty-five minutes from here." Wesley came around the car and joined me as my bags were being unloaded from the back. "We have to be here for a few days for press conferences and shit. He hates it but it's all part of the game." He shrugged and grabbed my hand, tugging me into the reception area that was brightly decorated in rich tones of cream and gold. An elegant chandelier hung from the ceiling, shedding a golden glow over a central table with a large floral display of pink and white wildflowers.

Well-dressed men and women stood around talking, whilst others lounged elegantly in the low, cream and gold-coloured armchairs scattered around the place. I allowed Wesley to continue pulling me as my eyes took everything in. I was in awe; no, it was more than awe. Words could not describe how I felt as I devoured everything with my eyes, itching to get my sketch-books out. I wanted to document it all and commit it to memory so I could use the inspiration at a later date.

Wesley still had a hold of my hand as we stood at the reception desk to check into my room. I didn't question it. I didn't even feel his hand in mine as mesmerised as I was with my surroundings. I looked up from studying the intricate scroll pattern in the flooring and met Nate's searing stare from across the room. I smiled brightly, happy to see him. But my smile dropped when I noticed his tight jaw and eyes so stormy I expected to hear thunder at any moment. He didn't look happy.

Nate kept his gaze locked on mine as he continued his conversation with a well-dressed guy and a blonde lady who were standing beside him. The guy said something and Nate nodded tightly in response. Turning slightly, Nate's companions followed the path of his laser beam stare and found me on the other end being burned by the pure heat and power of it. I squirmed as the man's hands flew into the air and gestured wildly and the woman simply glared. Their conversation continued. It was clear the guy was exasperated with Nate. Finally, Nate broke the hold he had on my sight and turned abruptly, moving to get into the face of his male companion. I watched as they faced off until Nate had clearly lost his temper. The woman placed a hand on his arm, appearing to calm him. It was obvious she was familiar with him. Just how familiar was not something I wanted to consider. Nate pulled his arm away and walked off, leaving the pair staring after him. The suit called out something that I couldn't hear.

"Leave it, Mal. This has fuck all to do with you," Nate bellowed as he approached Wesley and I. "Olivia." He greeted me tightly and stood to my side.

"Nathan." I replied in the same tight tone.

Wesley turned from the desk and, for the first time, noticed his brother's presence. "Oh, you're here. I was just asking for the keys." His boyish grin dropped when Nate glowered at him.

"No need," Nate snapped. "I have them. Are you coming Olivia?" He scowled at my hand still resting in Wesley's and strode away with purpose towards the elevators. *Holy shit, what is his problem?*

"He has been a fucking prick since the minute we left the UK," Wesley announced as I tugged my hand free and started following Nate. "If I didn't know better, I'd say he had woman problems. Only, he isn't one to get flustered over a bit of skirt. No offence."

"None taken," I replied automatically.

Nate stopped at the elevators and hit the call button before turning around. If I wasn't mistaken, there was a hint of relief across his handsome face when he saw I was standing close to him and Wesley was a few paces back. He looked down and finally gave me one of his rare genuine smiles. After two weeks of not seeing it, it took my breath away.

"How was your flight?" he asked softly.

"Uneventful."

The elevator doors slid open, and Nate stepped aside, gesturing for me to precede him in. When Wesley approached, Nate lifted his hand to stop him. "I'll take it from here and get JB settled," I pursed my lips, still loathing his general use of that pet name. "Besides, Mal needs to talk to you. There's a problem with Bennett he needs to discuss with you."

Wesley's shoulders lifted into a shrug and he nodded. "Sorry, Liv, duty calls. I'll catch up with you later. Don't let this dick boss you around." He pointed his thumb in Nate's direction. And then he was strolling off across the lobby with the same powerful grace as his brother.

"So, it's just you and me then," Nate murmured, following me into the mirrored cube.

"Just you and me," I replied settling into the corner. I almost whimpered when he stepped in beside me, standing so close I could feel the warmth of his flesh burning against my bare arms. Taking a deep breath, I savoured his scent as it floated through my nostrils, awakening senses in me that had been dormant for the previous two weeks.

We remained silent as the elevator ascended a few floors and then smoothly came to a stop. Nate steered me out, with his hand resting almost indecently low on my back. We stopped beside a set of large, decorative, white double doors. "This is where you'll be staying for the next few days."

"And where will you be?" I asked glancing along the corridor. There weren't many other doors.

"Right here. With you." His grin was devilish as he stepped forward and swiped a key card into the reader. As soon as the handle mechanism beeped and the small light changed to green, he was pushing the doors open and disappearing inside.

"Holy shit! Are you fucking kidding me?" If I thought the rest of the hotel had shocked the bejesus out of me, this room—no it wasn't a room, it was a fucking mansion—had me on the verge of hysteria. Shouldering past him, I stepped further inside.

Laid out before me was a large lounge area that was easily as big as my entire flat. It was decorated in shades of cream and taupe with a large Aubusson rug covering the wooden floor. Elaborate ornate mouldings edged the ceiling and walls, and strategically placed wooden furniture sat proudly in prominent positions. Several grand, white lamps occupied side tables while tribal pictures and statues were both out of place and somehow fitting.

I walked over to the large, floor-to-ceiling windows that followed the curved contour of the outer edge of the room. As I got closer, I realised the windows were in fact three sets of French doors leading out onto a large balcony. The doors were framed with taupe and mocha drapes while white voiles blew gently in the breeze. It was a room of extreme opulence, yet it felt comfortable and homey.

"I take it you like it then?" Nate asked.

"It's amazing."

A large gust of wind had the voile panels billowing wildly and I got my first proper glimpse at what was beyond the doors. I gasped and stepped out onto the balcony, keeping my eyes glued to the vista before me. From where we stood, we had a perfect view of numerous boats and yachts of all sizes gently bobbing in the clear waters of the harbour.

"Oh my God," The words tumbled from my lips in a rush as my hand lifted to my mouth. I'd seen it all on TV before when I'd been sipping on a beer whilst watching the grand prix. But to actually be there, witnessing those things first hand, it was unbelievable. And absolutely stunning.

"Impressive, huh?" I felt Nate move up close behind me.

I closed my eyes and breathed in the warm, salty sea air. My head spun with so many emotions, so many mixed feelings. Since stepping off of the plane, everything had been a whirlwind, a crazy concoction of events that had left me bemused yet happy. I just needed to take a moment to soak it all in and centre on the here and now.

"I missed you, you know?" Warm breath laced with the scent of mint whispered past my ear as demanding fingers grazed along my flesh as they smoothed my hair over my left shoulder. "I'm so glad you're finally here."

My body sagged and my breath hitched when Nate placed a gentle kiss to my bare shoulder and wrapped his strong, muscular arms around me. Trying to sound unaffected, I asked, "Um, what are you doing?" My soft, breathy response betrayed me and was more of a plea to not stop than it was a question why. It felt nice being in his arms, but I couldn't understand why he was doing it. It wasn't just a friendly gesture; that would have been a quick hug and then move on. It also wasn't exactly the act of a lover. A lover would have been more demanding, wanting to push the moment on to something else. There was something in the gentle way he held me just then that was almost reverent, like he didn't want to cling too hard in case he squeezed me clear away.

Nate sighed and pulled away. Leaning back onto the balcony railing, he placed both hands on the decorative stone edge and bit on the inside of his lip. A storm of thoughts and emotions swirled behind his beautiful, yet tormented, eyes.

"I'm sorry," he said after a minute. "It's just…" he sighed again. "Fuck! Look, I swore to myself I wouldn't do this. I shouldn't do this. But shit, seeing you again, here with me… you do something to me, Liv. I've been agitated and looking forward to your arrival ever since I left the UK. Now you're here… I feel… fuck, I don't know. I'm glad you're here. I want you here, but… I also have to stay away. I have to focus and train and…" His eyes closed briefly, and when they reopened, they were full of resolve. "You're here to do a job for me. *I* need to remember that. We're stuck here for a few days and then we'll travel up to my property so you can start doing your thing. In the meantime make yourself at home here." With a nod of his head, like he was trying to convince himself of something, he strode off back into the room, the white curtains fluttering around him as he passed.

Staring after Nate, I was left reeling. What the fuck was that all about? I dropped down into a patio chair and stared at the empty doorway. I felt both exhilarated and appalled all at once. Exhilarated because I had clearly heard him say he was happy I was there, and it wasn't just because of my design capabilities. I felt appalled because he had basically confirmed I was there as his employee and nothing else. He was paying me to be there, and I needed to remember that. It would be easy to get caught up in the romanticism of my surroundings, to dream up fairy tales of princes in rich French splendour. But Nate was no prince, and I was certainly no princess.

When I ventured back inside, I found my cases and bags had been placed in a bedroom off of the large main room. Nate was nowhere to be seen. Taking a seat on the padded bench at the foot of the extravagant queen sized bed, I stared through another set of French doors leading on to another smaller, private balcony, remembering Nate's lips lightly pressing into my skin, his hands sinking into my hair as he moved it back.

"Get a grip, Liv," I said to myself, shaking my head and dragging myself back to my feet. Whatever this attraction between Nate and me was, it couldn't go anywhere.

***

THE SETTING SUN began casting a picture-perfect glow of oranges and pinks across the harbour. Using my thumb to smudge a shadow onto my sketch, I studied the paper in front of me and nodded. Perfect. I'd spent at least two hours sitting on my private balcony drawing and sketching and jotting down observations

I'd already made of local architecture. The place was a wealth of ideas and inspiration.

A knock on the main suite door startled me as I packed my things away. Nate still wasn't back from wherever he'd disappeared to and I hadn't heard from him either. Dropping my sketchbook on the bed as I walked through my room, I continued over to the gilded mirror on the wall. I needed to make sure I looked presentable before greeting our visitor – I wouldn't want to answer the door looking like I didn't belong in a place like this. I was wiping a smudge of charcoal off my face when I heard raised voices filtering in through the slightly cracked open bedroom door. And they were getting louder. I hadn't realised I wasn't alone.

"I told you earlier, Mal, this has nothing to do with you." The distinct sound of Nate's deep voice followed by the quieter yet strong sound of another male filtered through the air. Not knowing if I should interrupt, yet curious about the obviously heated discussion, I stood at my door and watched. Nate was talking to the gentleman he'd been with in the lobby when I'd arrived. He was a middle aged man, tall and slim, with greying hair and a slick, black pinstripe suit. He looked smart and put together, but there was an air of arrogance surrounding him that made him look hard and moody.

"And I'm telling you, you cannot fuck this up. You don't have time to be worrying your pretty little head over a piece of skirt. She will distract you, Nate. She already has. If you take your eye off the prize for just one minute, Sanchez will be all over you. If you need to blow your load in her, do it now. Get her out of your system, because your dick will not be going anywhere near her after tomorrow. If this is why you've brought her here, fine, fuck her all you want tonight, use her tight little cunt to burn off whatever fucking mood you're in, but tomorrow, she goes."

Nate's hands clenched into tight fists by his sides, his whole body vibrating with barely contained fury as he stood chest to chest with Mal. "Don't you fucking talk about her like that. Why she is here has nothing to do with you," he seethed.

I gasped. Were they talking about me?

Nate's head snapped around at the sound. He looked at me with wide, deep grey eyes, eyes darker and deadlier than I had ever seen them as I opened the bedroom door a little wider. His companion glanced over, clearly unaffected by Nate's tone. A menacing grin spread across his face. "Ah, speak of the devil."

"Shut the fuck up, Mal," Nate growled.

When Nate began walking towards me, I backed up. I couldn't face him, not like this. I hadn't seen this side of him before and it scared me. I'd known he was dangerous, known what he must be capable of, but he'd always been so controlled around me. This other side of him took me by surprise.

There was also the matter of what they had been talking about. Despite how he had reacted to Mal's remarks, I wondered if that had been Nate's intention all along. No, I couldn't believe that. I wouldn't. I was there to work for him. Maybe that was the point, though; maybe he'd wanted me for a different kind of work. My head shook as Nate inched closer.

"Olivia, please," he pleaded. "Don't listen to him. He doesn't know what he's talking about. Let me explain."

"Is that why I'm here, Nathan? You thought poor Olivia would be an easy lay for you?" Looking into his face, the scene I'd just witnessed replayed in my head. Anger began washing away the fear, hurt and humiliation. "I'm sorry to disappoint you, Mr. Oakes, but I'm here for one reason and that doesn't involve spreading my legs for you. Now if you'll excuse me, I'd like to be alone."

Turning my back on Nate, I closed my eyes and willed back the tears that seemed ready to spill out. I was stronger than that. I'd never let a guy make me cry before, and I was damn well not going to let one do it to me now.

"It's not like that, JB—"

I pivoted around so quickly my head went giddy for a split second. "Stop calling me that," I yelled. "I'm here as your employee, you said so yourself. Employers don't give their workers cute little pet names. I'm here to do a job for you, Nathan, nothing more, nothing less."

Before I could spew any other infuriated words at him, I found myself pushed further into the room and pinned against the wall by Nate's rock hard body. He had both my hands clasped in one of his and captured between our bodies. His other hand cupped my jaw and tilted my face up to look at him.

"You are not just my employee," he growled. "And no, I don't think you are an easy lay. Far from it." I felt my anger melt away when soft, yet firm, lips crashed against mine, seeking forgiveness and demanding understanding. He licked along the seam and dragged my lower lip between his teeth before melding his mouth back over mine and staying there. The kiss wasn't deepened, he didn't push for more. He simply stood with his pounding heartbeat vibrating against my chest and his thumb gently caressing my chin. When he finally broke contact, he said, "You are so much more to me than that, Olivia. So much more."

~CHAPTER ELEVEN~

WITH CLOSED EYES, NATE RESTED his forehead against mine and slowly shook his head. "Christ! I can't do this, Liv. Not with you. Not now," he said softly.

If he had attacked me full force with one of his expert martial art moves it could not have hurt as much as those words did right then. Yet again, he'd reeled me in, seducing me with a look or a touch, taking what he wanted, and then pushed me away. I hadn't asked for this. I hadn't asked for any of it. Yet here I was, in a foreign country, being emotionally tossed about with no care for my feelings.

I pushed him away, putting all my strength into the movement. "Fuck you, Nathan," I yelled. "I don't understand you. You come on to me, kissing me, touching me, and then act like it's my fault, like I won't leave you alone? What the hell is that all about? I'm glad you don't want to do *this*, whatever *this* is, because I don't want it either." *Liar.*

My heart pounded heavily in my chest, and with each word, my irritation grew. Was this how things would be while I was there? If so, I feared I had made the biggest mistake of my life in accepting the job.

"Get out. Please. I need to be alone."

He stood still, his jaw tight as he watched me for a moment before backing away slowly. "You have it all wrong, JB. I *can't* do this," he said firmly, keeping his sad, haunted eyes on mine until he was out of my room, punching the wall as he left. The door slammed closed, leaving me alone once again.

Falling onto the bed, I screamed into a pillow. I had never felt as alone and out of my depth as I did at that moment. I'd only been in Monaco for a few hours and I was already wishing I was done so I could go home.

Running back to London wasn't an option though. Despite Nate's mood swings, I knew working on his project was a fantastic opportunity for me. My credibility at Ashworth-Moore was on the line. If I completed the project well, Mr. Ashworth and the others would have to give me greater respect. If I failed, all they would see was the fact I hadn't been good enough to complete the job. I would be seen as the silly little girl that couldn't hack it when the going got tough.

I would see this through, no matter what. I would just have to make sure I kept my guard up around Nate. Any feelings for him that had crept in would have to be buried, and we'd have to go back to being the strangers we were before I'd stupidly taken him up on his offer of training.

Turning on to my back, I felt the weight of the day's events catch up with me. I was exhausted, both emotionally and physically. I threw my arm across my eyes, and just before my eyes drooped and sleep claimed me, I heard the unmistakable sound of Nate's raised and angry voice in the other room.

***

THE SOUND OF laughter carrying on the wind slowly brought me out of my slumber. I was cosy, curled on my side and enjoying the feel of luxury bedding beneath me. Groaning, I fought with myself to remain asleep. I wanted to stay in the pleasant realm of happy dreams, where I didn't have to worry about mood shifting sex gods blowing hot and cold. Or best friends who were MIA.

Reluctantly I opened my eyes just as a sudden breeze blew warm air into the room, fluttering the white voile panels covering the open French doors. The remnants of early evening sun had disappeared, replaced by the inky darkness of night time. From my position on the bed, all I could see through the doors was a faint golden glow on the balcony and the silvery rays of moonlight that were peering through intermittent gaps in the clouds. Other than the sounds of laughter drifting up from somewhere below, the suite was quiet. I wondered where Nate was and what he was doing. If he was okay.

"Good, you're awake. I was debating setting the fire alarm off or something."

Blinking into the dark room, I tried to focus on the dark shadow in the corner. "Nathan? What time is it?"

I asked sleepily.

"Nine thirty. You've been out cold for a couple of hours." The chair he was sitting on creaked as he stood. His silhouette came into view in front of the doors, lit only by the soft glow behind him. He was a sight to behold, his fine physique outlined by nothing more than the gentle light behind him.

"Are you hungry? I presumed you probably would be so I ordered room service." He sounded apprehensive.

With a yawn, I stretched then climbed off the bed. "Actually, I'm starving. Thank you."

Walking slowly across the room, Nate's profile became more visible the closer I got. He looked wary, standing stiff and awkward. "You're welcome. It's all set up out on the balcony."

I offered him a tentative smile as I walked past. Things were strained between us, and I didn't know how to act around him anymore. I came to an abrupt halt on the balcony when I saw what was before me. The large, round, iron and glass table was sitting in the middle of the terrace, set with a large pillar candle burning slowly in a hurricane vase. Around it, several tea lights flickered in the balmy evening breeze. The table was set for two with silver cutlery, crystal wine glasses and fine linen napkins. Along the outer edges of the area were tall hedges affording us privacy from any onlookers. Fairy lights were strung through the greenery giving the space a romantic, soft feel. None of that had been there when I went to sleep.

"Very romantic, Mr. Oakes," I said lightly, not understanding the meaning behind the grand gesture. This wasn't just a meal between two colleagues. We could have eaten down in the restaurant or at the small dining table in the living room for that. The candles, the lights, the atmosphere he'd created, it all screamed of a deeper meaning that confused me.

He laughed, and if I wasn't mistaken, there was a hint of relief in his tone. "Yeah, it's not my usual style." He pulled out a chair and indicated for me to sit. I tried to contain my grin at his gentlemanly gesture.

"Would you like some wine?" He pulled a bottle out of a wine cooler.

"What? You're allowing me alcohol?"

"All in moderation, Liv." He raised the bottle and I nodded, lifting my glass to him. Once it was full, he pulled out his own chair and sat. I noted he didn't pour himself any wine.

"So," we both said in unison after a brief, yet uncomfortable silence had descended.

"Go on," I urged, taking a sip of the crisp, fruity liquid in my glass. I was pleasantly surprised. Wine wasn't usually my thing; I would much prefer a cold beer over the stuff any day.

Nate looked out over the harbour for a moment before bringing his gaze back to me. There was a fierce resilience and determination in the depths of his grey eyes.

"Look, I want to apologise for earlier. And I need to explain a few things."

I wanted to tell him he had nothing to apologise for, but the truth was he had pissed me off and his friend had been beyond rude. An apology and explanation were the least I deserved. With my lips pressed to my glass, I watched him over the top for a moment.

"Who was that guy you were talking to earlier? He seemed like a total bundle of laughs," I said wryly when he didn't seem to know where to start.

He had the good grace to look embarrassed. "That was Malcolm, my agent. He seems to think that he owns my arse and can therefore dictate my life beyond the cage. I'm sorry about what you overheard."

I swirled the wine around in my glass. "Was he right? About me I mean."

"Fuck, no. He's pissed off that I didn't act the part of the obnoxious fighter during the press conference. Mal is all about putting on a show for the press, playing mind games with your opponent and that sort of thing. When I don't play his games, he tends to throw his toys out of his pram. None of that was aimed at you. He was just trying to use an old school rule to make a point."

"Rule?" I asked, intrigued.

Nate scratched his head and looked away, embarrassed. "Yeah. During the lead up to the fight, I'm not supposed to have sex."

"Are you serious?" I spluttered and choked on a mouthful of wine. "That shit really happens?"

"With some, yes." He glanced over, his eyes burning into mine. "Some see sex as either a help or a hindrance. But abstinence before a fight has never bothered me before now."

"What's that supposed to mean?"

My question was interrupted by the sound of Nate's phone ringing. He apologised and excused himself from the table, wandering over to the railing to answer his call in private. I sat there, watching him, and witnessed the change from the almost relaxed Nate that I'd known in London, to a raging bull... again.

"No, Mal, this is fucking bullshit," he bellowed making me flinch in my seat. He was clutching the railing with white-knuckled ferocity and shaking in rage. "Stop trying to dictate what I do and do your own job. You are my agent not my fucking coach." He punched the screen of his phone to end the call and stood looking out to sea, his shoulders still hunched and tense with rage.

I moved up next to him and placed a tentative hand on his arm. "Nathan... is everything okay?"

He turned abruptly. "I'm really sorry, Liv, but I've got to get out of here. I'm so sorry." Without a backward glance, he stormed into the suite and a moment later I heard a door slam.

Walking back to my seat, I wondered what his conversation had been about to have made him so angry.

"Welcome to Monaco," I murmured to myself with a barked laugh. The day had certainly not gone how I'd expected it to. I could only hope that things would get better. Taking my glass, I abandoned our untouched meals—my appetite having vanished—and returned to the relative comfort of my room to call my mum. I needed to hear a friendly voice.

***

NATE HADN'T RETURNED to our suite by the time I'd finally given in and fallen asleep. When I finally caught up with him eating breakfast the next morning, he was quiet and brooding. It became apparent I would need to keep myself occupied during the day while he was training, so I decided to take a stroll down to the harbour. The peace and tranquillity of the lapping water and the elegance of the yachts soothed me. I sat there for hours, just watching the world go by. Eventually, I made my way back to the suite, hoping to find Nate. We had things we needed to discuss if I was going to be able to get on with the job I'd been hired to do, but all that greeted me when I'd walked through the doors was a note written on the hotel branded notepad. He simply said he was training and then had a meeting to go to. I vowed then to get his plans done as soon as possible so I could return home.

***

TWO DAYS LATER, I was sitting in a sweaty gym watching grown men beat the shit out of each other. I could have been wandering the streets of Monaco again, taking in the sights and culture and maybe doing a drawing or two. Even relaxing on a sun lounger by the pool would have been preferable to the gut wrenching stench of sweat and… *what is that God awful smell?* My nose crinkled at the thought.

But Nate had been around that morning demanding that I go along to his training sessions. He said he wanted me to get an idea of what his training was like. "You need to see what goes on so you can visualise it for your plans," he'd said. I got the impression there was more to it than that. The gym was a short drive away from the main streets of Monaco and was about as far removed from the comforts of Golden Oakes as you could possibly get. It was clear as soon as I'd walked in that it wasn't an everyday, run of the mill gym. Instead of rows upon rows of cardio equipment and weight machines, the place was full of hanging punch bags, free weights, racks of gloves and pads, and matted areas. What dominated the space was the huge mesh-covered cage in the centre of the room. The octagon as Nate had called it. It was the place where he currently rolled around with some poor innocent Monegasque man who'd been stupid enough to volunteer to be his sparring partner.

Watching on in horror and, alarmingly, more than a little bit of awe, I winced as Nate landed a sharp hook to his opponent's chin. An older guy with short, grey hair stood off to the side of the cage yelling instructions and expletives at Nate, who had followed the hook immediately with a knee to the chest. The other guy, having lost his balance, dropped to the canvas with a thud. Nate was on him in a second, throwing punches then rocking and twisting and wrapping solid arms around him, locking him to the floor in a choke hold. I gulped and reached for my own throat as the poor guy slapped the canvas over and over, gasping for breath.

I was supposed to be making notes and getting a feel for the place, all in the name of research, but I had abandoned my note book to the side. The scene playing out in front of me was far more interesting than jotting down words and doodling a few images.

Nate lithely jumped to his feet and took the water bottle handed to him. I couldn't take my eyes off him. It was the first time I'd seen him bare-chested and he looked amazing. I squinted, trying to focus on the tattoo that formed a ring around his right bicep and another that started on his shoulder and snaked around to his back. On his right pec was another image and on the left there appeared to be some sort of text, but from my position seated in a dark corner, it was difficult to distinguish what they were. I made a mental note to google him because I was sure there must have been hundreds of images of him in all his semi-naked, tatted up glory. Keeping my eyes on him, I stared down at the sexy V I wanted to run my fingertips along and wondered exactly what it led to. What was he like below the waistband of his black shorts?

"Enjoying the show?" Wesley appeared in my peripheral vision, pulling up a chair and straddling it with his front to the chair's back. He crossed his arms along the top edge of the seat and grinned. It was a look of pure mischief, and it was aimed at me.

"It's okay," I replied casually. I knew he'd caught me ogling Nate but I wasn't going to admit to it. "I really don't understand this need to beat each other up. It's barbaric."

He laughed. "Most people don't. Until you've tried it and felt it, it's difficult to appreciate the power of any martial art." I glanced over for the first time since Wesley had taken a seat. He was also dressed like Nate in red and black shorts with a bare torso. His hands, like Nate's, were wrapped in blue bandages.

"Do you fight too?" I couldn't keep the shock out of my voice.

"Why does that surprise you?"

I shrugged. "I don't know. I guess you don't come across as a dedicated-to-the-cause type of guy. But then, I don't know you. Maybe you are."

"That's right, JB, you don't know me," he replied seductively and shifted his chair closer. "But I'm sure we could do something about that. I can be dedicated to the cause."

"Back off, Wesley." Nate's expression was hard as he strode over, ripping the blue bandages from his hands along the way.

Wesley smirked as he stood. "Seems big bro doesn't think that's such a good idea," he whispered into my ear before backing away. A look passed between the brothers as Wesley walked by Nate.

"What did he say to you?" Nate lowered himself onto the chair, sitting in the same back-to-front position Wesley had.

"Nothing, I was just surprised he fights, that's all." He looked a little suspicious of my reply but didn't say anything.

He nodded. "Listen, I have to attend a function tonight, and I'd like for you to come with me."

"What kind of function?" I asked nervously. Any kind of gathering Nathan Oakes attended here would be full of glitz and glamour. I knew it would be way out of my league.

"It's a party at a nightclub. I have to go. It's for Mal's daughter's birthday. I can't get out of it." He seemed regretful.

There were two problems with that, the first was that he had barely said more than a few words to me since our aborted dinner and now he wanted me to attend a social function with him? There was also the issue of clothing. When I'd packed for the trip, I hadn't been expecting to go clubbing with Nate. I didn't have anything suitable to wear.

He appraised me for a moment. "What are you thinking, Liv? What's going through that head of yours?"

Tapping nervously on the back of the seat Nate was straddling, my gaze darted everywhere but at him. "I, um..." I cleared my throat. "I don't have anything to wear for something like that."

He chuckled. "It's just a club, Liv, we're not eating with royalty." When I glared at him, he reached over and stroked a tender finger down my cheek. My breath caught. "You could wear anything, Olivia Buchanan, and you'd look beautiful. Have a little faith in yourself."

Before I could process his touch and his words, he'd pulled me to my feet. With a wicked smirk, he pushed me forward, nudging me further into the gym. "It's time for me to put you through your paces," he whispered in my ear.

~CHAPTER TWELVE~

MY BODY ACHED ALL OVER. I felt like I could barely move a muscle. Having had two weeks away from Nate, he'd said I must have been slacking with my work-outs. What the hell did he know? To make up for lost time, he decided to up the ante. Every lunge, punch, lift of a weight or sit up was done with a dragon master breathing fire over me, pushing me on. Even my time on the treadmill was lengthened by two miles and an additional incline. When I'd glared at him, breathless and fearing I would pass out, he simply shrugged and increased the speed. It was as though he were forcing his own strict pre-fight workout disciplines on to me. Either that, or he was using his tough trainer mask to block out what had been happening between us. By the time we were finished, I felt exhausted. I stumbled out of the gym with one thought in mind… I needed a long, hot soak in the bath.

Back in the comfort of our suite, I left Nate in the living area talking quietly on his phone and headed into my room. I'd been thinking about the only semi-suitable dress I'd brought with me, a very simple, lilac maxi dress. I wasn't sure it was truly appropriate for clubbing in Monaco, but it would have to do.

Having laid the dress out on the bed, I rifled through the dresser for underwear. I settled on a set of white lace and placed the bra and knickers with the dress. There were a few hours until a car would pick us up and drop us off at the club, so I had plenty of time to soak my weary muscles and get ready.

The bathroom in the suite was huge and had a stunning, cast iron roll top tub that was large enough for me to be able to stretch out and relax in. Pouring some of the complimentary bath product under the hot water, I left the tub to slowly fill. The air around me filled with the scent of sandalwood and jasmine and my tension immediately began to ease away. I kicked off my clothes into a pile in the corner and stepped into the water. Easing in gently, I soon became engulfed in a blanket of calming bubbles, delighting in the peace and serenity of the room. With my eyes closed, I sighed in bliss. A girl could get used to this.

Suddenly, my little slice of heaven was ripped from me. The bathroom door swung open, spilling bright light into the dimly lit bathroom and momentarily blinding me. Nate appeared in the doorway looking delicious in his sweatpants and tight fitting t-shirt, but no matter how hot he looked, and how much I wanted to scan and lick every inch of his firm body, he shouldn't be in my bathroom, especially when I was naked. With a shriek, I screamed at him to get out and desperately fumbled to cover whatever flesh of my ample boobage was on display above the bubbles. His eyes widened and remained on me, or rather my boobs, for much longer than was appropriate.

"Don't you knock?" I huffed, wrapping my arms tighter over my breasts and sinking further into the water. I hoped the bubbles wouldn't sell me out and disperse too soon.

"Sorry. I didn't realise you were in the bath yet." He had the good grace to at least look a little embarrassed and finally lifted his gaze to my eyes.

"What do you want, Nathan?"

"I was thinking about what you said, you know, about clothes." He leaned back against the countertop of the vanity and crossed his arms over his chest. There was me all naked and shivering—not sure if that was because of the rapidly cooling water temperature or something else—and there was Nate settling in for a conversation. Perfect!

"And?" I snapped, shifting in the water. The bubbles were disappearing and it wouldn't be long before he'd end up getting more than an eyeful. He'd end up with the full 3D, IMAX experience.

"I don't want you to feel uncomfortable or out of place."

I snorted a bitter laugh and quickly flicked my eyes in the general direction of my nakedness. "It's a bit late for that, don't you think?"

His silver-grey eyes darkened as his gaze wandered to my boobs again. "I don't want to step over any boundaries…" *Unbelievable!* "But I asked someone to bring a few dresses over from a local boutique for you to choose from. Take your pick, it's on me." He strode out of the room and closed the door as if he hadn't just been standing inches from my naked body.

"Nathan, what the fuck?" I yelled after him, thumping the water. Bubbles blew into the air, floating around and taunting me. Some landed on the floor while others glided and came to rest on the marble countertop... and my nose.

I was blowing short puffs of air, trying to shift stubborn bubbles from my nose and fringe when he poked his head around the door again. With the bubbles in the bath now all but dispersed I barely had anything covering my modesty

"By the way," he said to my now mostly bare breasts. "There's a change of plan. I've made dinner reservations before the party. The car will pick us up at seven."

"What time is it now?"

"Six," he replied simply.

"Shit! Nate! Why didn't you say? That only gives me an hour." Shooing him out of the room, I quickly climbed out of the bath and grabbed hold of a fluffy white towel from the warmer. Wrapping it around myself, I made my way into the bedroom.

I stopped abruptly just outside the bathroom doorway where Nate still stood. My über sexy and glam dress—not—had been discarded, and laid out on the bed were four dresses, two black, one cherry red and one ivory. Next to them was an array of various undergarments and accessories.

"Nathan, I can't take any of those," I said sadly. They were all stunning but were so obviously out of my non-existent clothing budget. I continued to stare in awe at the decadent fabrics in front of me.

"You can and you will. I want to treat you, Liv. Please accept this stuff as my gift to you," he murmured softly. Urging me toward the bed, he moved up behind me and placed his hands on my hips, giving them a gentle squeeze. His chin rested on my shoulder as he joined me in looking at the stunning dresses.

All of my insecurities, no matter how deep I'd tried to bury them, suddenly resurfaced. I was standing in a room with a very wealthy, very sexy, very famous MMA superstar. No doubt he was used to the glitz and glamour of society events. He often must have any number of slender, stunning women on his arm. They would have fit in without the need for Nate to rush out and buy them last-minute dresses. They would have had closets full of glamorous dresses they could choose from and a team of beauticians to help pretty them up.

Without one of those dresses, I would stand out as the poor girl Nate brought along. I would attract attention to me, and to Nate, but for the wrong reasons. It occurred to me that the dresses weren't just about making me feel comfortable. I was attending with Nathan Oakes, public figure. He didn't want me embarrassing him by looking dowdy in my plain, cheap clothing. As sensible as it was, the thought still stung.

I stepped over to the bed and gently stroked the silk of the red dress. "How do you know any of these will fit me? I'm sure the shops around these parts only cater for super skinny ladies."

He shrugged, watching me closely. "I don't know.

We had to guess."

"We?"

"Cassandra helped. Seven, Liv. Don't be long." He gave me a hint of his beautiful smile, the one that tugged at something in my chest and then left, closing the door behind him.

I continued running my fingers along the fabric of the dresses wondering who Cassandra was. The irrational side of me thought she must be an old flame. Maybe she was his go-to girl when he was in the area. I battled back the bile that rose in my throat at the thought, trying to convince myself that it didn't matter who had selected the dresses. Each one was stunning and, apparently, now all mine.

A few minutes later, realising I was running out of time, I dropped my towel and went about seeing if any of the dresses would fit. If they didn't, I would just have to stay in the suite and see what English subtitled films were on TV. I couldn't be around Nate at a public event if there was any chance he might be ashamed of me.

***

"LIV, WE'VE GOT to go," Nate said, knocking gently on the bedroom door.

I'd been standing in front of the mirror for several minutes, staring. The woman looking back at me was hot. I mean, really hot. She looked sexy in an ivory satin dress that clung to her perfectly. The dress skimmed her curves and accentuated her assets as though it had been made for her. The neckline sloped just along the upper swell of her breasts and scooped lower in the centre showing cleavage without being trampy. Two thin straps over the shoulders held the dress in place. The bodice was fitted until eventually it flared out into a billowing skirt that rested just above the knee. The vixen, looking a little shocked and bewildered, leaned further towards the mirror, blinking her eyes in rapid succession. Her hair had been blow-dried straight and, thanks to the luxurious hotel's complimentary products, for once it shimmered with a brilliant shine. Her eyes looked bright and alluring thanks to smokey eye make-up and two coats of mascara. Her lips looked plump, covered with a dusky pink lip gloss.

"Damn, Liv!" I whispered to myself as I added the finishing touch, a pair of simple, diamond stud earrings my parents had given me for my twenty-first birthday.

"Liv, come on. We're going to be late." Nate knocked again, a little more forcefully.

With a final look in the mirror to double check it wasn't really a potato sack I had covered my body with, I grabbed my small, silver clutch bag and made my way through to the living room.

Nate stood on the balcony with his back to me. He was once again talking to someone on his phone so hadn't heard me approach. "I said *we'll* be there," he snapped, emphasising 'we'll' and abruptly ending the call. He turned with closed eyes, his breathing deep and erratic. His jaw was set and his face pinched, as though he were trying to contain his anger or frustration.

I took a cautious step closer. In the relatively short amount of time I'd know him, I'd learned that when

Nate was angry you were best leaving him alone to calm down. I'd seen him unleash the power of his fury on more than one occasion when he'd taken it out on a punch bag at the gym. *Better the bag than someone's face,* I'd mused at the time. Out there on the balcony it was just him and me.

The sound of my heels scraping on the decorative concrete floor alerted him to my presence. His eyes sprung open and drank me in. Slowly, he dragged his gaze from my silver sandals, over my body until his eyes met mine.

"Wow, Liv," he said breathlessly. "You look amazing."

My lips pulled up into a shy smile as heat crept onto my cheeks. I wasn't used to such compliments, especially not ones I thought could actually be true. "Thanks, I guess."

We remained in a weird sort of silence for a moment as he continued gazing at me. It was hard to decipher what he was thinking or what he was feeling. His face was impassive, masked by his usual set features. Occasionally his jaw would clench or his hand would twitch by his side. But he remained still, watching, assessing, contemplating. Eventually, he turned and walked towards the door, holding out his elbow for me to take. "We need to go, the car's waiting."

***

WITH MY HANDS clasped in my lap, I stared out the window as we made our way through the streets of Monaco. Beyond the blacked out windows of the sleek

Mercedes, the sun was disappearing along the horizon, leaving a sky full of pinks, lilacs and fiery golds that were disturbed only by the occasional opal-coloured cloud. It had been a beautiful day: warm and sunny with a gentle breeze. It was a stark contrast to the icy chill of the atmosphere inside the car.

Nate had been quiet since we'd left the hotel, speaking only to Marc, our driver, when he'd greeted us at the entrance. An occasional glimpse out of the corner of my eye showed me he was still lost in his own thoughts, brooding over his telephone conversation I supposed. I might as well have not been there.

"Damn moody athletes," I mumbled to myself.

The silence in the car was oppressive. I felt like, yet again, Nate was erecting an invisible barricade to keep me away. Every time he showed a glimmer of anything more than a friendly or professional relationship between us, I thought the wall was coming down. But then he would build it up and pack it out, making it thicker and more impenetrable than ever. Eventually it would crush me.

"Marc, can we have some music on please?" I asked, leaning forward in my seat to speak to our driver.

"Certainly, Miss," Marc replied in his heavy French accent. I'd always loved the French accent; it was so sensual and seductive. He pressed a button on his steering wheel and the car immediately filled with the soothing sounds of an orchestra. Sitting back, I smiled, dropping my head back against the head rest and letting the music soothe me.

Nate shifted in his seat, the leather creaking as he

did so. The weight of his gaze felt like a boring machine tunnelling into the side of my face as he watched me.

"What are you doing, Liv?"

"Enjoying the silence," I replied, trying to sound bored.

His gaze remained level as he observed me from across the seats. Watching, contemplating.

"Oh for goodness sake," I snapped a moment later. "This is ridiculous. What's the deal here, Nathan? Am I going to be facing your cold shoulder all evening? I just need the heads up so I know to take myself off into a dark corner and have a party for one. The conversation might be a little more riveting then. If you really didn't want me here, you shouldn't have invited me. I would have been more than happy to slouch around in the hotel. You don't have to feel obligated to bring me along with you to these things."

His eyes narrowed as he watched me. "Why do you do that?"

"Do what?" I huffed, inspecting my nail polish for any chips.

He shifted in his seat so he was facing me head on. "Why do you insist on calling me Nathan?"

I threw my hands in the air in exasperation. "Seriously? All you took from that is me calling you *your* name?"

He shrugged. "It's important. Only strangers and business acquaintances call me by my full name."

"I *am* a business acquaintance."

He shook his head and turned to stare out the window again. "No, Liv, you are so much more."

"And there you go again with the silent treatment.

Honestly, *Nathan*, I can't keep up with your mood swings. Maybe you should just drop me off back at the hotel."

"This is me, Olivia. This is who I am."

"What, moody, cold and boring? Nathan, you don't need me around to be those things."

I'd thought I'd known who Nathan Oakes was, but in reality I knew nothing about him. He had shared so little about himself. And other than the occasional glimpse at a more gentle side, he had always been quiet, reserved and brooding. I'd just been blind to it.

When the car stopped in front of a fancy looking restaurant, Marc opened the car door and I stepped out into the balmy air, wondering how the evening would progress from there. With Nate in such an introspective mood, I feared the elegant clothing had all been for nothing.

***

MY FINGER RUNNING around and around the rim of my glass made a high-pitched, ear-splitting, squeaking sound. It was awesome. I'd looked over the wine menu… several times, listened to the conversation of the American couple sitting behind me—apparently they were visiting their granddaughter who was managing one of the local hotels. It was all very interesting. I'd memorised where each and every lamp was located on the outdoor terrace we'd been seated on. But what I hadn't done was share more than a handful of sentences of conversation with Nate. I was beyond pissed off.

Dipping my fingertip in my Martini again, I began

another revolution of the glass' rim. I jumped when, out of nowhere a hand came crashing down on mine, halting my movements.

"Will you stop doing that?" Nate grumbled.

My eyes shot to his and I tried yanking my hand from his, but he just tightened his grip.

"Oh, I'm sorry, was that annoying you? Was it spoiling the *silence*?" My voice was saccharine sweet as I hissed at him through my teeth and continued trying to yank my hand away.

Nate sighed and slouched back in his seat. Clearly irritated, his hands ploughed into the longer tresses of his hair while his head fell backward. I'm sure the view of the stars was amazing and all, but what the hell? He needed to talk to me, not Andromeda or Orion. Suddenly, he shifted in his seat, moving forward once again so he could cross his arms on the edge of the table. He levelled his gaze on me, surprising me with the sincerity that glowed from the depths of the steel grey of his eyes.

"Liv, I'm sorry okay? I know things have been... awkward for you since you arrived and for my part in that I apologise. I should have maybe warned you that I become withdrawn right before a fight. I zone out. Everything has to be about the training, about the preparations. If I'm not in the right mind-set I might as well just throw in the towel now and hand the fight to Sanchez. Whilst we're here, things will be more hectic. People will constantly want something from me and I can't escape. I promise, when we're at my place, things will get better."

I nodded briefly. What he said made perfect sense to a certain extent. I wasn't a famous sports personality trying to juggle training and PR obligations. I didn't know all of the pressures he put on himself to ensure he was in tip top condition. However, whatever it was he was going through it didn't excuse his silence, or constantly shifting moods towards me. I deserved more than that.

"Nathan—"

"Please, call me Nate, like you were before. My friends call me Nate." He gave a small, almost timid smile and shrugged.

Friends, right.

"Okay, *Nate*. I understand this is serious business and you have to focus but… oh I don't know, maybe I'm just being overdramatic and pathetic. Either way, I don't appreciate being ignored." I raised the glass to my lips and downed the last of my drink. A waiter walked past and I caught his eye, indicating I needed a refill. I had a feeling I was going to need a lot of liquid courage to get through the evening.

"No, you're not pathetic. I've been neglecting you." I watched as he stared down at the pristine white table cloth. He looked weary, not like the pumped up athlete I would expect to see just before a fight. Something was troubling him.

"Nate, what's really going on?" I asked softly.

He lifted his eyes, his head still bowed. "Everything just feels… wrong," he admitted.

"Wrong? How?"

"I don't know. I can't pinpoint it. Mal is tightening the screws but there's something going on with him. He's acting an even bigger prick than usual. Bernie is getting pissed off with him, adding further tension. It all feels like an impossible situation." He shook his head with a sharp laugh.

The waiter chose that moment to return with my drink. He placed it on the table, his eyes meeting mine and lingering there for a while. They were dark, almost black, and spoke of a sensual threat that was both intriguing and scary. Swallowing hard, I reached for the fresh drink; my gaze was frozen to his. As I reached for the glass the waiter moved to take the empty one. For the briefest of moments, our hands touched. "Pardon, Mademoiselle," he rasped, grinning at me wickedly.

"That'll be all, thanks" Nate growled, glaring at the waiter. I blinked in surprise as the waiter bowed and meandered off. I didn't fail to notice his sly look back at me as he moved to clear a nearby table.

"Fucking prick," Nate growled under his breath and suddenly the whole situation seemed absolutely absurd. I started laughing. It started off as a chuckle, and then, when Nate looked at me with a raised brow, I couldn't hold it back. Before I knew it, I'd grabbed the napkin from my lap and had covered my face with it, trying in vain to control the hysterics and wipe away the tears at the same time. From across the table I heard the unmistakable sound of Nate's deep chortle and dropped the napkin to see him shaking his head and laughing with me.

"That's a lovely sound," he said.

Lowering the napkin to my lap, I saw him smiling fondly at me.

With the awkwardness between us broken, Nate spent the next several minutes telling me about his gruelling training schedule and strict diet. I nearly spewed Martini all over him when he explained how much he had to eat every day. I knew he trained like an animal, but really? How was it fair he could shovel so much into one amazingly perfect body, while I only had to say 'pizza' and I put on four pounds? It was mind blowing what he put himself through on a daily basis all in the name of a sport, a sport he was so passionate about.

"If things are that strict for you, why are we eating out? Why don't you have a personal chef or something?" I asked, genuinely curious.

He threw his head back and laughed. "It's not that strict, Liv. I just need to watch what I eat closely. I need to make sure I eat the right amount of calories, have the right things, get the right amount of protein and steer clear of fat and sugars, that sort of thing."

The waiter appeared from nowhere carrying a tray. Nate and I watched in silence as he placed two plates on the table and then elegantly removed the shiny silver cloches. His arm brushed along mine when he passed by, heading back to the kitchens. I heard a strange sound from the opposite side of the table and looked up to see Nate glaring at the guy's retreating back. It was then I realised we hadn't actually placed a food order.

"What's this," I asked, staring down at the plate in front of me.

Nate brought his attention back to me. "I pre-ordered the food. I knew we wouldn't have a great deal of time before we'd have to leave for the party," he explained. "I didn't have a clue what you liked though, other than pizza, ready meals and Jelly beans that is. So I hope you like it." Nate nodded for me to go ahead and try what was on my plate before dabbing his fork into the food in front of him.

"I'll have you know, I can be sophisticated when I want to be, Mr. Oakes." I peered down at my plate again, my face screwing up with trepidation. I had no clue what I was looking at.

"Scallops with parsnip mousse," Nate said, answering my unspoken question.

"I knew that."

Despite how it looked—all small and posh looking—the food was delicious, and I devoured it in record time. Nate watched me with a smile playing on his lips.

"Am I amusing you somehow?" I swiped a finger through a splodge of mousse left on my plate and then sucked it into my mouth, licking off the deliciousness. It really was tasty.

"Amusing, not exactly. Distracting, yes, very much so."

"Oh? How so?" I swiped my finger on my plate again and looked up to see Nate's heated stare glued on my finger as it slipped between my lips again.

The waiter reappeared, spoiling my enjoyment by removing the plate. I could only hope that the main course was just as delicious.

"Can I get you anything else, Mademoiselle?" The waiter asked. He was beginning to annoy me. The touches, the looks, they were bordering on creepy.

"No, I'm fine, thank—"

"Just bring the main," Nate barked over me. "And stop flirting with my date." My eyes widened and darted to his.

"Date?" I asked in astonishment. That would have indicated a certain level of intimacy that Nate and I certainly didn't have.

"I was just trying to make a point," he said, looking kind of embarrassed as he rested back in his chair. His features sobered. "Liv, the reason I brought you here is because we need to talk. We don't have long and I need to explain. You need to understand a few things. What happened between us back in the UK, what happened in the hotel the other day, this attraction simmering between us, it can't go anywhere… And before you shoot me with one of your smart comments, I know you feel it too." I sucked in my lower lip to stop myself from speaking. I did feel it, boy did I feel it. There was no way I could deny it. He was a hot guy and I was an appreciative female. But I was also a hurt, confused and angry one after the events of the previous few days.

"With everything going on in my life, I have neither the time, nor the inclination to get involved in a relationship. I can't offer a woman what she needs. Women want commitment. They want romance and all that fluffy shit. That just isn't me. I burn off my energy and frustrations in the ring—occasionally in a bed—and I get satisfaction from seeing my businesses grow and thrive." He closed his eyes for a brief moment. "But I need you to be my calm place. I need you to stay grounded when everything else around me is mayhem."

I frowned. "What are you saying, Nate?"

He ran a hand through his hair to rest on the back of his neck. "What I'm saying is I need you here for more than your drawing skills. I don't have a fucking clue what it is about you, but I feel calmer when you're around, more focused. I need that. On the flip side,

I'm aware there are feelings brewing beneath the surface." I gulped down my drink as the weight of his words registered.

"We have to stop them now, Liv. A lot is riding on this fight for me, and I need to devote everything to my training schedule. I need to be prepared to fight for my life in that cage. Damián Sanchez has a point to prove and he will stop at nothing to win. I have to be one hundred and fifty percent focused to deal with whatever he fires my way. I won't lose, Olivia. I can't. Not against him."

Holy shit! I had not been expecting that. I pressed the rim of my glass against my lip, replaying his words in my head. He wanted me there for more than just my design skills. What did that mean exactly? '*I burn off my energy and frustrations in the ring—occasionally in a bed,*' I narrowed my eyes at him over my glass. It occurred to me that maybe he did think I would be an easy, uncomplicated lay for him. That maybe I'd give him my designs with a side helping of stress relief. That thought, antagonising as it was, did strange things to my lady parts.

"What are you thinking about?" Nate's sexy rasp pulled me from my wayward thoughts.

"I'm trying to work out what it is you want from me."

"I want you to be you, Olivia. I want you to be the innocent, yet challenging, woman from the gym and the talented architect who blew me away with her design skills. But mostly, I want you to be my JB, my shining light in an otherwise bleak and dull world. I just need *you*, Liv."

Gaping at him, I couldn't seem to formulate words.

"But there can't be anything between us, not romantically. I have too much to lose if I take my eye off the prize even for a split second."

"So you just want me to be around?"

"Yes."

"And do what?"

Nate shrugged. "I'll be training a lot of the time, so do what you want to do then. I'd like it if you joined me at the gym sometimes too. You've done so well these past few weeks, I'd hate for that to slip because you're out here with me." I caught his appreciative glance at my newly toned body. I flushed. "You look amazing, Liv. You must not let being here stop you from continuing and progressing further. I want to see you achieve your dreams and goals."

"You think I look amazing?" I asked softly, staring down at the meal in front of me.

He nodded as he chewed through the bite of fillet of beef he'd just taken. "Of course I do. I'm going to have to keep you close tonight. I can't risk being thrown in a French jail."

"Why on earth would you be thrown in jail?"

He leaned in, pinning me with darkened eyes. "Liv, looking like that you're going to have men coming on to you all night. I'm protective of those close to me. I can't guarantee I'd maintain my control."

I laughed. An image of Nate grappling with someone on the floor while dressed all dapper in his black suit and white shirt entered my head.

"I'm serious," he continued, ignoring my chuckles. "If I see anyone being inappropriate with you, I'm liable to lose my shit. That can't happen, not this close to the fight."

"Oh please. You've already made it clear this place will be packed with classy, beautiful people tonight. Who's going to be interested in me?"

"You know, for someone so intelligent and sassy, you're pretty self-deprecating." He leaned over the table and tilted my head back. "You were a beautiful woman when I first met you, Olivia. But now I know that beauty isn't just on the surface. You're strong, capable, determined... Any guy would be proud to have you on his arm, and tonight I'm the one with that privilege. Tonight you're mine."

A cool breeze blew across the terrace, mercifully cooling my overheated skin. His words, and his touch, hit me deep, reigniting those foreign feelings I'd been experiencing since Nathan Oakes came into my life. I feared it was going to be a long night.

~CHAPTER THIRTEEN~

I RECOUNTED OUR CONVERSATION OVER and over throughout the rest of the meal. Nate had said he was attracted to me, which was a major turn on. He'd also said nothing could happen between us. That had been a major turn off. The confusion swirled around my mind, ripping up a vortex of uncertainly and… hurt. In my mind, I knew he was right, nothing could happen between us. He couldn't jeopardise his fight like that. That didn't stop my body from wanting things it would never get. I hadn't been looking for a relationship, yet the thought of getting into one with Nate filled me with feelings I wasn't accustomed to. Maybe it was just desire, after all, with a face and body like his, who could not want more from him? But I'd felt desire before, in the distant past of my uni days, when beer goggles led to far too many lust-filled one night stands. Whatever this attraction was that simmered between us, it felt like something more. It was more than desire, more than lust and so much more than friendship.

Marc pulled up outside a modern, glass fronted building with people milling around in groups and forming a queue that stretched along the street. I tried to take it all in as the door of the Mercedes opened and Marc stretched out a hand to assist me out. The nameless club looked small from the outside, but I could tell the façade was all just an illusion. The black glass windows stretched up for two, maybe three, floors and were topped with an elaborate steel overhang. Above that, laser lights shot moving beams of alternating colours high into the dark night sky.

Nate joined me on the pavement and snaked an arm behind me to rest a hand on my lower back. "Are you ready?" he whispered against my ear.

There were people everywhere, each of them dressed as though they had just stepped out of the pages of Vogue or GQ magazine. Feeling out of my element, I fiddled with the fabric of my dress as we walked towards the entrance.

We were a few meters from the entrance when a flash of white light momentarily blinded me. I stumbled on my heels and twisted, knocking into Nate's firm chest. His arms immediately enveloped me protectively, holding me tight. "Jesus, Liv. Are you okay?" he asked softly.

From the crowd of people someone shouted, "Look, it's Nathan Oakes!" More lights began flashing, blinding me with their persistent intensity. I closed my eyes and burrowed my face instinctively into Nate's crisp white shirt. "Nathan! Nate! Over here. Will you sign this for me?"

"Oh my god, it is him."

"Nate, you're the best. Please sign this for me."

"I love you, Nate."

The shouts and calls became louder and more tireless with each step we took towards the door. It hadn't occurred to me that we might come across Nate's fans. To me he was still just Nate, my personal trainer, not someone who would create a frenzy of attention from hordes of screaming fans. Yet that's what he got.

"Who's the lovely lady, Nathan? Needing a little pre-fight tension release are you?"

Next to me, Nate stiffened and murmured something under his breath, his hold on me intensified. I risked opening an eye and saw a man rushing towards us flanked by a guy pointing a massive Nikon in our direction.

"Phillips, from Fight Club Monthly," the reporter exclaimed with a smirk, sticking his hand out. Nate ignored it.

"What are your thoughts on Sanchez's allegations?" Phillip's asked.

"No comment," Nate growled and started walking towards the entrance again, gripping my hand in his and tugging me along with him.

"He claims this is a grudge match that goes beyond losing the previous fight. Is he right, Nate?"

"No comment."

With the pace Nate was striding across the concrete, I struggled to keep up with him in my heels. My vision was still blurry from the flashing lights and my head spun from the breakneck speed of events. I wasn't sure what Phillips knew, or thought he knew, but whatever it was, Nate seemed unwilling to discuss it.

Around us the hollers and catcalls of fans grew louder and more relentless as Nate's fans closed in on us. I had the overwhelming urge to yell, 'Shut the fuck up!' and storm off into the club. But as the person on Nate's arm, I realised it wouldn't look good for him, especially with a reporter sniffing around for a story. So, I kept my expression passive and tried my best to keep up with him without tripping and falling flat on my arse.

As we neared the entrance, security finally realised that chaos was breaking out around them and came rushing out, pushing people back and stopping them from getting any closer.

"Young lady, how do you feel about being connected to *the* Nathan Oakes?"

Realising that question had been aimed at me, my mouth opened but Nate's brusque voice stopped me from responding. He turned murderous eyes on the reporter. "Leave her alone. Any questions you have should be to me, you hear me?" Then, without another word, he grabbed my hand and steered us towards the entrance.

"Scared you'll lose another one, Nate?" The reporter shouted out. Nate stiffened and cursed under his breath but kept us walking.

"I can answer for myself you know," I seethed.

"You need to fucking stay away from the press, Olivia." I stumbled, taken aback by the iciness of his tone.

"Nate!" the reporter called out over the shoulder of

a burly bouncer with a shaved head and mean face. "Sanchez is claiming this is a grudge match, something to do with the death of his father in Brazil?" Nate dropped my hand and spun round.

"Note this down," he snarled, his voice dark, dangerous, and dripping in venom. The doorman stepped to the side allowing Nate to move to stand toe to toe with Phillips. "Sanchez is a fucking pussy. He will come out with whatever bullshit he thinks will help him. He's lost to me before, he will lose again!"

The guy smirked, clearly pleased with Nate's reaction. "And his father?" he asked raising a brow.

"No comment!" Nate hissed pushing his face close to the other guy's. "No fucking comment."

A moment later, Nate was back at my side, pulling me into the darkness of the club. I glanced at him out of the corner of my eye as he walked with angry purpose towards the bar, never once looking at me.

***

THE GLASS TUMBLER crashed down on to the bar making me flinch. With a wave of his hand, Nate gestured towards the barman for a refill. He hadn't spoken a word since his altercation with the journalist, other than to order me a glass of champagne and a whiskey for him. I opened my mouth to deliver some smart comment about feeding his body with unnecessary calories and toxins but the menace in his eyes told me I needed to keep my thoughts to myself.

With one hand supporting his weight as he leaned on the bar, Nate gulped back the entire contents of his second glass and groaned. His eyes were pinched tightly closed and his jaw was tense. Standing with his head slung back, he appeared tortured and distant. The man in front of me wasn't the Nathan Oakes, I knew. That cool, calm and controlled man was gone.

"Do you want to talk about it?" I asked, shouting over the pounding beat of the music. There were so many thoughts racing around my mind. I was curious about the reporter's questions, concerned over Nate's reaction and confused by our meal together. But the overriding feeling I had was the need to comfort and support him. Reaching for his arm, I stroked my fingertips softly across the skin, exposed because he'd ditched his suit jacket and rolled up the sleeves of his shirt. Under my touch, I felt rather than heard his deep inhalation of breath before he shook his head. His lips moved, a visual indication of the words I couldn't hear, but what really spoke to me, telling me he wasn't prepared to discuss things, was the tension radiating off him.

Taking a step back, my hand fell limply to my side. I was unsure what I could do or say to rescue the evening, *if* I could rescue the evening. The situation only emphasised the fact I knew so little about Nathan Oakes. He'd always been such a private, self-contained person around me. I didn't know how to deal with him, or how to help him.

I maintained my gaze on Nate's stiff, unrelenting posture for several minutes, hoping and praying with each change of song that he would come back to me, that he would let his fury go enough that he could enjoy his evening.

"Nate, this is stupid, let it go," I eventually yelled into his ear, moving in close.

Nate twisted his head so we were almost nose-to-nose and speared me with his vivid grey eyes that appeared even more moody and dark in the gloom of the club.

"Stay out of this, Liv," he growled through clenched teeth.

My back straightened and my shoulders arched back as nervous instincts took over. I didn't fear Nate, not really, but this new side of him had all my internal warning bells ringing out loudly. One thing he'd taught me during our training sessions was to never show your aggressor any weakness, to never let them know they had won. I had no intentions of letting this side of Nate win.

"Nate, you—"

I jerked away when a pair of hands covered my eyes from behind and with a racing pulse, I swung around and gasped, my eyes widening.

"Surprise!"

"Cassie? What are you doing here?" I shrieked, beaming at my new friend. It was so good to see a familiar face.

Cassie eyed Nate leaning against the bar and frowned. "What's eating him?"

"We got hounded by a reporter on the way in. He didn't take it well." I looked over my shoulder to see Nate gesturing towards the barman again, ordering yet another drink.

"Fucking reporters," he said.

"Woah, Nate, what the hell are you doing? You never drink this close to a fight." Cassie shot past me and grabbed the glass as the barman was handing it over.

"This has nothing to do with you, Cass. Give me the fucking drink." Nate reached around but Cassie pushed on his chest.

"No. What has gotten into you? The press never bother you this much?"

I stood back, watching the interaction between the two, wondering what their relationship was. How had I never noticed something between them before? I also wondered what she was doing there.

"Yeah well the press don't usually come at me with the shit this guy did." Nate frowned.

I tuned them out as Cassie probed Nate for more information and grabbed the attention of the barman for a drink of my own. With Nate and Cassie still talking, I backed up against a wall and sipped on my champagne, staring out over the wave of people enjoying their evening.

"Looking hot there, JB!" A body moved in close to my side and mirrored my pose, leaning back against the wall.

"Wesley." I greeted Nate's brother in a bored tone. "Are you two like a package deal or something? Where he goes, you go?"

He grinned. "Haven't you figured it out yet? I'm his burly bodyguard, here to serve and protect him."

I chuckled and looked him up and down. Wesley was lean and toned but he was no Nate. "I can see why he keeps you around," I replied sarcastically.

Wesley turned so he was leaning his shoulder against the wall facing me. "What's with him anyway? I would have thought being here with a gorgeous woman such as yourself he'd keep you close. Instead he looks like he wants to rip someone's head off. What gives?"

I recounted everything that happened outside the club and Nate's reaction to it.

"I've never seen him so mad, Wes. Why would he get so mad?" I asked.

"I have no idea. He usually shrugs the words of the press off." Wesley's brows pulled in tight as he shot a glance at Nate and Cassie. "Excuse me. I better go and see what's going on," he mumbled, marching over to his brother.

No longer prepared to hover on the edges of whatever was going on, I quickly gulped down my drink, wincing at the burn of bitterness and bubbles, and joined the others at the bar. Whatever the conversation I'd walked into, it was heated.

Nate glanced in my direction, his eyes meeting mine and holding them captive.

"…focus. It's all mind games, Nate. They are just trying to get a reaction out of you. Just man the fuck up and get on with it," Wesley snarled, finishing his berating.

Nate quickly shifted, moving into Wes's space and standing chest to chest with his brother. "This is not your concern," he seethed.

Cassie grabbed my arm and tugged me away towards the dancefloor.

"It's best to leave them to it," she said when I stalled. "Wes knows how to deal with Nate. He'll pull him round."

"That didn't look like friendly brother banter to me." I frowned, glancing back over my shoulder. "They don't seem very close. What if it gets out of hand and they end up fighting? We should get back there." I yanked my arm trying to free it from Cassie's grip.

She sighed. "Liv, they are close, as close as two brothers can be. Wes is the only one who can calm Nate down when he flies into a rage. You should see them in the cage together... fireworks!" She smirked and waved her arms like exploding rockets.

On the dancefloor, Cassie pulled us straight into the mass of moving bodies and immediately found her groove, swinging her hips wildly and waving her arms in the air. I danced a little more sedately, preferring to rock and sway to the beat of the music. Chancing a glance back in the direction of the men, I saw Wes resting his hands on Nate's shoulders whilst saying something to him. Nate nodded, acknowledging Wes, but his eyes were trained on me. I offered him a smile and continued dancing. Wes had clearly worked his charm.

"How are you enjoying it here?" Cassie asked, dancing in close and nudging her hip against mine.

"It has been... interesting," I replied. "So, are you going to tell me what you're doing here?"

She grinned and sashayed into a twirl. "Nate didn't tell you?"

"Didn't tell me what?" I shouted over my shoulder as a handsome, dark haired guy with dark framed glasses grabbed my hips and began moving with me.

"He didn't tell you that I would be out here too, did he?" She narrowed her eyes on my new dance partner and glided in so we were dancing as a group. "I always come away with him as his masseuse. Someone has to keep him in top shape." She winked.

I pulled away from glasses guy and wrapped my

arms around her shoulders. The bottle of wine I'd sipped on with my dinner along with the champagne I'd consumed in the club had left me lightheaded, giggly and carefree. "I'm so happy you're here," I gushed.

A strange shiver passed through my body as the hairs along my arms stood on end just before a large pair of possessive hands gripped my waist from behind.

"I've come to steal her from you, Cass." Tilting my head back I drunkenly found Nate glaring over my shoulder at the guy dancing with us. I giggled.

"What's so funny?" Nate asked, finally pinning me with his electric grey eyes. His lips pulled up at the edges into the semblance of a smile.

"You are," I said, resting my head back on his shoulder. "My Mr. Mean-and-moody has come to fight off the enemy. What a hero!" I laughed harder and tried to wriggle away when Nate's grip tightened and caught me where I was most ticklish.

"Yours huh?" he whispered into my ear.

I shivered again and nodded.

"Hmmm," he murmured, running his nose down my cheek and along my neck. "I like the sound of that."

"Wait!" I yelled, as something dawned on me. Pulling free of Nate's arms and stumbling over my heels in the process, I twisted around. "Cass? As in Cassandra? As in the one who picked these clothes?" I pinched the material at the front of my dress. Nate's eyes wandered to my chest and widened. I was still pinching the fabric away from my body, exposing to him more cleavage than was appropriate.

"That's me," Cassie yelled over my shoulder. "And I did a fine job, even if I do say so myself. You look amazing, Liv." She pushed on the chest of the glasses guy, who'd been standing, bemused, watching our interaction, and they moved off into the crowd with Cassie speaking into his ear.

Nate wove his arms around my waist again and pulled me in close. "I'm sorry!" he said against my hair, moving us to the music. His hips were swaying against mine as he tugged me in closer and trapped my hands between our chests.

"Did I tell you how sexy you look tonight?" My head shook as the bass pulsed around us, and I soon found myself in a fog, lost to the rhythm and everything Nate. "Well you do. Every guy in the room wants to be where I am right now." His hands trailed down my back coming to rest over my backside. He pulled me in close and soon our pelvises were grinding together. To anyone watching we probably looked like any other couple enjoying a passionate dance. It was a nice thought, and I wanted to savour it because if the last few days had taught me anything it was that soon the bubble would burst. With the buzz of alcohol racing through my veins and the heat of Nate's close proximity, I closed my eyes, allowed my head to fall back and gave myself over to the moment, letting myself be guided by Nate to the sensual dance track.

All too abruptly, my musical trance was broken, spoiled by the sudden disappearance of the warm body pressed to mine. My eyes sprang open as my body stilled. Nate stood, breathing heavy with hooded eyes and a tense jaw, staring straight at me, through me, as though he were reaching into the depths of my soul.

Captured by his silver gaze, I stood rooted to the spot, barely breathing, neither of us moving.

Wes's arms were suddenly wrapping around each of our shoulders, breaking the spell. "I hate to break things up, but Mal's looking for you, Nate."

"Tell him to wait," Nate instructed firmly, keeping his gaze on me.

"He said now. Honey's pouting because she wants to see you. What the princess wants the Princess gets, right Nate?" Wes rolled his eyes.

"I said she can wait."

"Who's Honey?" I asked uneasily, breaking our stare and looking between the brothers.

"Honey is the sickly sweet, slimy product of an irritating insect." Wes's description made Nate scoff.

"She's Mal's daughter. But yeah, she does live up to her name," Nate said. "Where are they?" Wes pointed to a VIP area at the rear of the room.

Grabbing Nate's elbow before he could step away, I cried, "Are you? Is she?"

Feeling a hundred kinds of foolish, I dropped my hand and took a step back. I had no right to feel jealous, to want to have any proprietary over Nate. Even knowing it was ridiculous, the competitive woman in me fired to life harnessing her green eyed monster. Despite the feelings I had for Nate and knowing nothing would ever come of them, I hated the thought of anybody else having him.

Understanding flared in Nate's eyes as he took a gently took hold of my elbow and began walking us toward the roped off VIP area.

"It's not what you think, Liv," he said, his warm breath teasing my ear. "She means nothing to me.

Absolutely nothing."

Cassie re-joined us then as we crossed the dancefloor, telling us about her dance with Philippe. I giggled drunkenly, thankful for the distraction, and then held my head when the room began to spin and everything started appearing in double.

"Let me get this over with and then we'll leave," Nate whispered, wrapping an arm around me to keep me standing upright.

In the VIP area, Nate sat me on a bar stool telling me he would quickly go and greet Honey and then we could get out of there. I agreed with relief and pulled myself onto the stool, resting my throbbing head on my crossed arms on the counter.

"Olivia, right?"

Wearily I lifted my head from my arms. "That's me."

"Let me introduce myself properly. I'm Mal, Nate's agent."

"Hello, Mal." I bobbed my head and offered a weak smile.

"Look, I'm not going to beat around the bush here. I don't know what your game is but you can't be here. You have to go back to London."

I blinked.

"Excuse me?"

Mal moved closer, piercing me with hard menacing eyes. "Nate doesn't need you around. You're distracting him. He's losing focus... Too much rides on him winning this fight, Olivia. You *have* to go home. I've arranged it all. A car will pick you up tomorrow morning to take you to the airport. Nate will move on to his vineyard and you will return home. After tonight, you are to have no more contact with him."

My drunken haze vanished immediately.

"Who the hell do you think you are?" I protested, pushing to my feet. "I am here to do a job for Nate. He's the one paying me, not you. If anyone decides I'm no longer needed here, it will be him.

Unfazed by my outburst, Mal continued, "If you stay, you will be risking everything. Do you want Nate to get hurt?"

"No, of course I don't. What are you talking about?"

"It's quite simple." He pointed toward Nate. "If you stay around, he won't focus. If he doesn't focus, he won't be ready for the fight. If he's not ready, Sanchez will slaughter him. I can't afford for that to happen." He brushed at his suit jacket as though bored with the whole conversation.

"With all due respect, *Mal*, Nate is doing just fine with me here. I'm here to do a job, and I intend to see it through."

"Now listen here, you bitch." I stumbled back as though I'd been struck by the malicious tone of Mal's voice. "You really think he gives a shit about you? You're just another pussy, another piece of skirt he can fuck for a good time and then move on from. You mean nothing to him," he spat.

I fell back on to the stool in stunned silence.

"Ah, Nate, there you are. I was just introducing myself to Olivia here. It was nice to meet you, Olivia." Mal patted Nate's shoulder as he passed and then shot me a look before walking to a stunning woman with long, waist length, dark blonde, wavy hair. I recognised her as the woman Nate had been talking with when I first arrived in Monaco. She stood with her arms crossed, glowering at Nate's back.

"Let's get out of here," he said, sounding irritated as he held out a hand.

"Is that her? Honey?" I asked, hating the jealous way it sounded.

"Yes," he replied sharply, leading us away.

If she was nobody, why was she looking at Nate like she wanted to maim his manhood, and why was Nate so desperate to get away from her? There was history there, there had to be. I wondered how recent and I hated that I wondered that.

"If she means nothing to you," I asked breathlessly, trying to keep up with Nate's strong and powerful stride, "why are you so pissed off and why is she looking at you like she wants to eat you alive?"

His grip on my hand tightened. "Because she's just another bitch who can't take no for an answer. She won't accept I'm not interested."

As we made our way out of the club, I chanced a glance back. Honey stood watching us, stony faced, while Mal mouthed, 'Tomorrow, Olivia.'

~CHAPTER FOURTEEN~

"WELL THAT WAS A FUN evening," I said sarcastically, climbing into the back of the Mercedes. Settling in to the quiet vehicle, my head began to throb with the onset of a wicked headache. I hadn't had time to process my dance with Nate, his relationship or non-relationship with Honey or consider Mal's veiled threats so, as the car pulled out into the traffic, I rested my head back and replayed his words. I wondered whether it was true that my presence was having a detrimental impact on Nate's training. He'd been so different from the man I'd trained and dined with in London the whole time I had been in Monaco. Although he'd always been blunt and had a take-no-crap attitude, I'd always felt comfortable around him before. Now, he seemed more on edge, unpredictable and secretive. And then there was the bubbling electricity crackling between us threatening to send sparks flying.

Closing my eyes, I took a moment to try to clear the haze so I could focus on one thing at a time.

"What are you thinking about?" Nate asked softly.

"You... us... tonight. There's so much." I cracked an eye open, my head tilting to the side. "Are you going to tell me what that was all about with the reporter?"

Any gentleness in his features dropped away. "The guy was an idiot. There's nothing more to say."

"Nate, he sent you into a tailspin. That's not *nothing*."

He sighed. "Liv, just leave it."

I watched his grim expression as he stared out of the window into the darkness.

"Nate, talk to me."

"I said leave it, Liv." His tone was clipped, his body suddenly vibrating with tension again.

"No!" Fumbling with my seatbelt, I slid across the seat and climbed onto my knees. With my palm resting against his cheek, I encouraged him to look at me. "Tell me what's going on."

His eyes met mine, searching. Once again, they were tortured. Whatever it was that had caused this intense pain and fear in him, I wanted to take it all away.

"Tell me," I whispered.

The car remained silent, save for the occasional rush of air when another vehicle passed in the opposite direction. Eventually, he shut his eyes then opened and closed his mouth a few times before finally speaking. "I have demons, Liv. A past I don't like to talk about."

"Will you tell me about it?" I asked, rubbing my thumb soothingly along his cheek.

He shook his head. "There's no point. The past doesn't change anything. It doesn't impact my future."

I laughed once and dropped my hand. "Bullshit! Look at you now. If whatever it is isn't impacting on your future by messing with your mind right now, I don't know what is. You're living behind those demons, Nate. You're letting them control you."

He twisted abruptly so we were nose to nose. "You don't know anything about me or my past—"

"That's right. I don't. Because you won't tell me," I replied, exasperated, my voice rising by an octave.

I heard a deep growly sound before strong hands were easing me onto my back. Firm, warm lips covered mine, silencing me. My body went rigid, my eyes widening from the surprise attack. A few seconds passed with neither of us moving, both breathing heavily. When Nate eventually dropped onto his elbow and began tracing his lips back and forth across mine, I found myself succumbing to his power. Allowing my eyes to flutter closed, I parted my lips and wrapped my arms around his back, pulling him in closer. He groaned and used the opportunity to deepen the kiss. His tongue slid into my mouth, curving and tangling with my own until we were both moaning. His hand stroked along my body until he grasped my knee and pulled it up around his thigh so he could settle his firm body between my legs. I shifted, giving him more room, and wrapped my arms around his neck, pulling him closer. My dress rode up indecently, but I was too lost in the moment to care.

When his fingers smoothed up my thigh and traced

217

along the edge of my underwear I gasped, my core clenching in need. I'd never felt as hot or desired as I did at that moment. Nate pushed his groin against my core. He was as turned on as I was, his erection pressing against me through the fabric of his trousers.

"Nate," I gasped, shifting and twisting my fingers into his hair. I needed more, the pressure building was immense.

Suddenly, I felt the car pull to a stop. A door up front opened and closed. We were alone. Nate pulled back, breathing heavily, and looked down into my eyes, blinking in bewilderment. I scrambled up, pushing him away before desperately yanking the hem of my dress back into place. Mortification and shame engulfed me when I realised Marc, the driver, had just witnessed the whole show. What had I done?

"Liv?"

When my door opened, I scooped up my bag and quickly stepped out. Rushing as fast as I could into the lobby, I headed for the bank of elevators and tapped furiously on the call button, willing one to arrive. I couldn't believe I'd allowed Nate to embarrass me like that. I'd never allowed a man to overwhelm me before, yet all Nate had to do was look at me, or touch me in some way, and I became putty in his hands, time and place be damned.

"Come on, come on." I cursed and hit the button again.

"Why are you running from me, Liv?" Nate approached me from behind, the heat of his body scorching my back through the satin of my dress.

"I'm not running."

"Like hell you're not." I felt his breath on my ear

and closed my eyes. "We need to talk about what happened back there."

"You don't like talking. You've made that perfectly clear on a number of occasions over the last few days." I feigned indifference to him and his closeness, but inside I was still a quivering wreck. Nate cursed and spun me around to face him.

"Stop doing that. This isn't about you and your fucking curiosity. That stuff is personal. It's in my past, where it needs to stay. It doesn't define who I am, just who I was."

The elevator bell pinged, announcing its arrival. I stepped inside muttering, "But it does." Everybody's pasts had some bearing on their future or who they had become. It was human nature. Something in Nate's past had affected him, causing him to withdraw into himself and keep those that cared about him away. Telling me that it didn't affect him now was just silly.

Nate followed me into the enclosed space, pinning me face first against the mirrored wall as the doors slid closed. "Nate, let me go," I berated, trying to push myself away from the wall.

"Do you know how fucking sexy you are when you get mad?" he breathed against my ear. Grasping my hands, he entwined our fingers before sliding my arms above my head. "I swore I'd stay away from you. The right thing to do would be to stay away from you. But I can't. Why is that, Liv?"

I shook my head. "I don't know."

Nate nuzzled my hair and wrapped an arm around my middle, pulling my highly aroused body against him. The hard column of his obvious interest pressed against my backside. "I don't think I can trust myself around you anymore, Liv. I want you. I need to be inside you," he murmured huskily against my ear.

His nose ran up the heated flesh of my neck before he nipped on my earlobe. My head lolled to the side, allowing him room to continue his sweet torture.

"Come with me."

I'd been so caught up in the moment, I'd been oblivious to the fact that the elevator had arrived on our floor and the doors had opened. Keeping his arms around me, Nate manoeuvred us to our suite. Every touch of his skin against mine felt like a spark shooting through my body. The flutters of his warm breath against my ear heightened the sensation of every nerve ending. I felt that at any moment my blood would ignite into a raging inferno that I would have no control over. All I could do was sit back and allow it to consume me until it burnt itself out.

Nate fumbled with the lock and then pushed me inside the room, twirling me around to press me against the closed door. He scanned my face while bracing his body off mine with his palms pressed flat against the door.

"I want you, Liv."

"I want you too." I fisted my hands in his shirt.

His eyes blazed. "Fuck, Liv."

I didn't know if it was the alcohol or the weeks of trying to ignore my attraction to Nate, but in that moment, all rational thoughts of what was right or wrong vanished. All that remained was a racing pulse and an unbearable need to be consumed by him. Wrapping my arms around his neck, I whispered, "Take me to bed, Nate."

Growling a deep animalistic sound, he pulled me through the suite into my bedroom. I wrapped my arms around his neck while he tugged down the side zip on my dress. He pulled on the thin straps of material covering my shoulders, allowing the ivory satin to fall to the floor, before taking a step back to appraise my body that in just a few short weeks had changed subtly. His eyes closed for a moment, his face pinched as if he was fighting to hold onto his control.

"Get on the bed," he said, opening his eyes. His smouldering look had me retreating, backing up to the bed. When the back of my knees hit the mattress, I lowered myself down and scooted back. Nate followed, bracing himself over me before crashing his lips to mine, hungry and possessive. He trailed a hand along my body, stroking and kneading, touching me everywhere.

"You know I'm not a 'take it slow and savour the moment' kind of guy, right?" he murmured, breaking the kiss.

"Yes."

"Good, I just wanted to make sure we were on the same page before I ram myself so deep inside you that you beg for mercy."

Trying to remain cool as yet another fire ignited between my thighs, I rolled my eyes. "Nate, do I look like the kind of girl to lie back demurely so my gentleman friend can politely slip his penis inside my vagina? I think not."

He leaned over me again. "No, I don't think you're like that at all. I think you're feisty and can give as good as you get, but I needed to make sure."

I was done talking. My woman parts were about to

leave home in search of the attention they required. Utilising a move Nate himself had taught me during our recent training sessions, I flipped us over so he was on his back. Straddling him, I pinned his arms with my knees and stared down into his heated eyes. "Nate, for a physical man you sure do talk too much." His eyes glimmered in amusement as he chuckled. "And seeing as you can't seem to show me what you are capable of, I thought maybe I better teach you what I can do instead."

"Is that right?"

I nodded. "Yes, I—"

He twisted quickly, so I once again found myself on my back with the man-mountain pinning me down. Reaching up, Nate trailed a fingertip along my lower lip. "This might work better if you'd stop running your mouth..." He shook his head and pinched my lips together when I tried to tell him what I wanted to do with my mouth, "...and allow me to do the things to you I've been fantasising about for weeks."

He'd been fantasising about me? "Oh God, Nate, you can't say stuff like that. Christ, this is taking far too fucking long... Why are you still dressed?" I began writhing on the mattress, jerking and wriggling to try to free my arms so I could grab him and relieve him of his clothes.

His eyes turned a deep smokey grey and the corners of his lips pulled up into a mischievous grin. "Because, oh sweet JB." He kissed my nipple through the fabric of my bra and dragged it between his teeth for a brief moment making me cry out. The pleasurable pain was exquisite and set every nerve ending on fire. Then the heat and moisture were gone, leaving my sensitive points erect, cold and screaming for more attention.

He pulled back and stared down at me with hungry eyes. With one hand, he traced a slow path from my breasts, down over the sensitive flesh of my ribs and, finally stopped over my underwear. My hips bucked of their own volition. I gasped and he groaned at the feel of his fingers rubbing against my most private parts. I felt torn, confused. Part of me was embarrassed about the way I was laid out on display for him, writhing and desperate for his touch. The other part didn't care. I needed him, and he had shown me he was just as anxious for wherever this was going. Gripping the sheet beneath me, I anchored myself, preparing for the storm ahead.

Lowering his head, Nate kissed me once again. It started off gently, a light sweep over my lips, a soft peck on my nose, eyelids and across my cheeks. But all too soon the passion increased along with the pressure of his hands stroking over my thigh and along the edge of my silk and lace panties. My sex clenched in need, wanting more. I whimpered a desperate, tortured sound.

"Nate, I need..." His fingers moved beneath the fabric as his tongue moved over the sensitive flesh of my neck. I shivered with the wonderful sensation, but needed more.

"Nate, please," I begged, rocking against his fingers.

He brought his lips back to mine, stealing my breath and my gasp as he slid a finger inside me. The feel of his thumb rubbing against my needy clit as his finger circled within me had me wanting to scream to the heavens. It felt so good.

When he added a second finger, I whimpered and

pulled my head back, desperately sucking in air, trying to breathe through the overwhelming sensations Nate was eliciting in my body. His mouth trailed down my neck and over my breast. I couldn't remember a time when I'd felt so aroused and needy. My hands flew to his shoulders, my nails digging into his flesh when he gently bit on a nipple. He eased the sting with a lap of his warm tongue before sucking on the hardened peak.

Every nerve ending was on high alert. My breathing was laboured, coming in gasped spurts. Everything around me became hazy. It was just Nate and me and the pleasure he was bestowing on me.

My core clenched, my eyes closed and my body bucked as wave after wave of sensation zapped through my body. I came crying out his name, almost sobbing. It was too much. It wasn't enough.

When my breathing calmed, I opened my eyes to find Nate staring down at me with a pained look of regret.

"I'm so sorry, Liv." His eyes closed as he pulled in a deep breath. "That shouldn't have happened." Then he pulled himself off the bed and strode towards the bedroom door, leaving me hot, bewildered and frustrated, panting for more. Panting for him.

"Nathan Oakes, you get your arse back here right this second. You can't do this to me again," I screamed.

Stopping at the door, he was still breathing hard and looked tortured. Running unsteady hands through his hair, he said, "I'll see you in the morning, Jelly Bean. I'm gonna kick your arse in the gym. I have a shit-load of frustrations I need to work off." Then he walked out, closing the door softly behind him as though he hadn't just slammed the brakes on, leaving me a quivering mess of hormones.

Growling in frustration, I grabbed a floral patterned pillow and hurled it in the general direction of the door then slumped back, staring up at the ceiling. I couldn't believe that had just happened?

***

I STARED AT the closed door for a good five minutes, going over in my mind what had happened. I remembered Nate's body pressed against mine, the heat of his skin, the roughness of his stubble grazing my flesh when he joined his lips to mine and the hardness in his groin when he pressed it against my pelvis. What had made him stop? The residual post orgasm high disappeared and I sighed, struggling with the frustration still clinging to me. Throwing myself off the bed, I grabbed my robe, determined not to let this go. Not this time. Enough was enough, I needed answers.

"Nate, what the hell was that? What's going on with you?" I fumed, storming into the lounge, yanking the belt of my robe into a knot. He wasn't there. "Nate?"

The door to his room was closed, so I strolled over and knocked, hammering my fist against the wood.

"Nate? We need to talk, can I come in?"

"Now's not a good time, Liv."

"Don't give me that crap. I'm coming in."

I pushed the door open to find him sitting on the bed. His elbows were resting on his knees, his hands clasped together in front of him. He was staring at the floor between his legs.

"What the fuck was that in there?" I asked, stepping in front of him. He didn't answer. His clasped hands began to fidget, as though he was physically restraining himself from using them. "Talk to me, please. Because right now, I'm seriously confused, Nate."

He peered up, meeting my gaze. The heat in his eyes from earlier had disappeared; it had been replaced with a sadness I didn't like seeing. I stood with my arms crossed, waiting for him to saying something.

Eventually, he sighed and ran a hand through his hair. "Sit down."

I eased down next to him, making sure my robe covered as much of my bare flesh as possible, and waited.

Nate returned to staring at the floor, his hands fidgeting again. "Liv, I'm sorry," he sighed.

I barked a disgusted laugh. "You're sorry? That's it? You're sorry? Nate I wanted you... want you." I couldn't bear to be so close to him, so I wandered over to his window and looked out over the marina. It was dark, illuminated only by a few streetlights and the glow of the moonlight reflecting off the rippling water.

The bed creaked when Nate stood, and I felt him behind me.

"I thought you wanted me too. I guess I was wrong," I whispered.

"No, Liv, you aren't wrong." He took a deep breath. "I've wanted you laid out before me since that night in my apartment."

I watched his reflection in the window. He closed his eyes. "I got scared... I am scared."

"What?" I spun around to face him. "Scared? You

are the mighty Nathan Oakes. What on earth do you have to be scared of? That's pathetic."

He gestured towards the deep-red coloured, crushed velvet chaise lounge near the window. "I'm not doing a very good job of explaining myself. Take a seat."

I settled on the taupe-coloured cushioning with my legs stretched out in front of me. "Talk!"

Nate remained standing, leaning against the glass doors with his arm crossed over his chest. He looked pensive. "I'm afraid I'm going to hurt you."

I pulled in my lips, trying to contain the laughter threatening to spill out. "Excuse me?"

"You heard me."

I peered down at his crotch. "What, are you hung like a horse or something?"

"For fuck's sake, Liv, I'm serious."

I stood, moving to stand in front of him. "That's your problem, Nate. You're too serious. You won't hurt me. Trust me, I'm no virgin. I can handle whatever you've got to give me."

"I didn't mean hurt you that way, not physically. You have to understand, I'm not a relationship kind of guy, Liv. I don't do emotions. I can't, not anymore. Everything is purely physical with me. But you... you are so passionate, so emotional. I can't give you that."

Stepping in closer, I rested my hand on his abs and smirked when I felt them twitch under my touch. "I'm not looking for an emotional entanglement, Nate. You won't hurt me. Not in that way."

"What are you saying?" His breath caught when my hand travelled lower and skimmed across the bulge in his trousers.

"I want your body, Nate, not your mind. I'm not looking for a relationship either. Putting it simply, I'm desperate to have you inside me," I whispered, cupping my hand around his growing length.

Growling, he pushed away from the window making me step back.

"Are you sure? This will change things between us."

"Not if we don't let it," I replied, starting to undo the buttons of his shirt.

"You're here to do a job for me. I need those plans, Liv."

I peered up, my fingers stalling on the last button. "You'll get them."

"I can't risk you running off because I won't declare my undying love for you."

"I don't want you to."

"Then what are we waiting for?"

I licked across my bottom lip. "Nothing."

Nate's eyes blazed, the heat from them igniting a touch paper between my legs. All thoughts of Mal's threats, Nate's past, his fight... they all faded away, leaving me with only the desire to be consumed by him.

Quickly freeing the last button, I pulled the shirt down his arms and threw it to the floor. There was no time to ogle his tattoos or fine sculpted body, I needed him, desperately. Reaching for his belt, I fumbled with the clasp as Nate deftly unknotted the sash on my robe and slipped it off my shoulders. He pulled me into his embrace and began kissing me, his demanding lips and tongue showing me he was as desperate for this mating as I was. I pulled back long enough to suck in a deep breath and finish undoing his belt and zipper, and then his lips were on mine again, commanding my submission. I gave it willingly.

Within seconds, Nate had shed his trousers, leaving just a few pieces of fabric protecting us from what would undoubtedly alter things between us, how could it not? To what level, I wasn't sure, but the reward far outweighed the small possibility that things could become any more awkward between us. Nate backed me up until I was once again seated on the chaise. Leaning over me, he braced his weight on one knee positioned between my thighs, his other foot resting on the floor. I shivered and closed my eyes when he traced his slightly calloused hands along the outline of my body, barely skimming the edge of my breasts as he passed.

"On your knees, Liv," he breathed against my ear. "Face away from me."

My eyes fluttered open and found Nate's piercing me, heated and feral. Despite the sensuality of feeling his domination, I wasn't prepared to show him I would obey so easily. With a leisurely pace and a smirk on my face, I pulled myself up, deliberately rubbing against him as I moved. On my knees, I turned and faced the darkness beyond the windows, clutching the high back of the chaise.

"What are you going to do to me, Nate?" I whispered seductively, looking over my shoulder.

Nate moved in behind me, wrapping his arms around my middle. "First I want to feel you. All of you."

When he sucked on the sensitive area of skin between my shoulder and neck and flicked open my bra clasp with a practiced move, I moaned. My pulse quickened and my breathing faltered as I fought to not lose myself to him too quickly. He trailed his lips along my flesh, slowly pulling the straps of my bra off my shoulders. Pulling the satin along my arms, Nate allowed me to let go of the chaise only long enough to rid me of the garment completely. His hands once again began caressing my skin, slowly working up from my waist to my breasts. When his touch finally reached my sensitive nipples, we groaned in unison.

"Fucking perfect," he rasped.

"Nate—"

"No, Liv. No talking, just feel," he whispered, his voice hoarse with desire.

One of his hands remained on my breast while the other traced gentle circles along my flesh towards my core. When he rubbed over my needy clit through the material of my panties, I gasped and squirmed beneath him, shamelessly pushing my sex into his hand in an attempt to gain the pleasure I now craved from him.

He continued to torment me for several minutes, not allowing me to speak and teasing me with touches that worked me into a frenzy of need. When his breathing became deeper and his movements wilder I knew he was nearing the edge of his control. He gripped the sides of my underwear and pulled them off, leaving me totally bare and at his mercy.

The cushions of the chaise dipped as Nate stood. "Stay right where you are. Do not move a muscle. You look so sexy and fuckable right now." I heard him move around the room behind me. A drawer opened and closed, fabric swished as he removed his boxer briefs and the packaging of a condom crinkled as he opened it. I wanted to turn to see what he was doing, but he had me under his spell, hypnotised into following his will.

A moment later, he was behind me, wrapping his arms around my middle once again. One hand snaked up my front, stopping to gently grip my neck. His other hand moved down to stroke along my core. "Are you sure about this, Liv? Are you sure you want this."

"God, yes," I panted.

I felt him at my entrance for a brief moment before he retreated and then slammed into me in one powerful thrust. All air left my lungs. "Fuuuuck!" I yelled, gripping the back of the chaise for stability as Nate rocked into me over and over, mercilessly taking what he wanted whilst giving me what I needed.

He slowed briefly, and with a little pressure from the hand on my neck, he drew me up, pulling me tight against his body, with his other hand rubbing circles into my over sensitised skin. Concentrating on my breast for a moment, his fingers then moved lower, down my ribs, across my stomach, rubbing against the small patch of hair along my pubic bone until… finally, I gasped in pleasure overload when he flicked across my clit, sending a shockwave of spasms though my whole body. I was on fire, burning up with desire.

Resting back on his heels, the angle of penetration was shallower than before, but as Nate twisted his hips and drilled his cock into me over and over whilst rubbing my clit, I raced towards pleasure overload. It was too much. It wasn't enough. I couldn't breathe, couldn't think. All I could do was feel the wondrous sensations that began as a tightening in my core and grew into a flood of quivering and spasming muscles. Unable to hold it back, I screamed out his name, convulsing in ecstasy with the most intense orgasm I'd ever experienced.

"My turn now," he rasped against my ear, using the hand on my neck to turn my head so he could plunge his tongue into my mouth.

I groaned through the kiss while Nate pulled out and manoeuvred us so I was lying on my back. He braced himself over me. Once again, and without warning, he plunged into me with a demanding thrust. Our new position allowed maximum penetration, and soon we were both moaning and fighting for breath as the need for release became unbearable. I smacked my hands onto his biceps, my nails digging into his skin as pleasure engulfed me. I cried out, crying his name and pinching my eyes shut as another powerful orgasm shook me to the core, leaving me limp and powerless. Nate pushed into me once again and groaned long and loud through his own release.

"Fuck, Liv. I…" Nate fell to his back, drawing me over with him so we were still connected in the most intimate of ways. He closed his eyes and rested his head back, his breathing laboured as he came down from his pleasured high.

Sprawled across his chest, I moved my hands along his warm, sweaty skin. It occurred to me then that despite seeing him shirtless several times in the past; I'd never seen his tattoos up close. I stroked one finger along the pattern of the tribal mark that ringed his bicep and another across the planes of his shoulder. Then I moved to the marking over his left pec.

"What does this signify?" I asked tracing the outline of a fist punching through a heart.

"It's just a tattoo," he replied casually, but there was

an undertone of sadness in his voice.

Tilting my head, I rested my cheek and peered up. "Just a tattoo?"

Nate sighed. "Yes, Liv, just a tattoo… It's getting late, we should go to bed. We've got a busy day tomorrow."

Cool air hit my skin when Nate moved me off him and sauntered into the bathroom. With Nate closed off in the bathroom, I was left alone to my thoughts. The realisation of what we'd done hit me hard. It was just sex, absolutely amazing sex and I'd enjoyed every second of it. But Nate was right. I was still technically his employee. How could we have shared that together and go back to how things were as though nothing had happened?

I grimaced, looking down my body. Despite my hard work in the gym, I still carried a bit of extra padding. And Nate had seen me naked. Grabbing up my discarded robe, I ran through the suite into my room. For the first time in my life, I felt ashamed of my body and of my actions after sex. Despite knowing it was just sex, I couldn't help but feel used. We'd both agreed to the no-strings encounter, but what I'd felt during, and then the way I'd responded to how he'd left me alone had me questioning how honest I'd been when saying I didn't want more from him.

In the bathroom, I scrubbed my face clean of all the make-up and winced when I looked in the mirror. The overindulgence of food, alcohol and sex had taken its toll. I looked tired, drawn and puffy.

"Tomorrow is another day, Liv," I declared, determined I would put everything behind me. I would chalk our liaison up to out of this world sex that could never be repeated. Tomorrow, I would slide my professional mask back into place and get on with the job I was there to do. My only hope was that my poker face was a good one.

With a final look in the mirror, I pulled my robe on. I was more than ready to curl up in bed and allow sleep to consume me. Stepping into my room, I looked up into a pair of concerned grey eyes.

"You left," Nate murmured.

"I thought we were done."

"We're not done, Olivia. Not by a long shot."

~CHAPTER FIFTEEN~

THE SOUND OF A DOOR closing had me opening my eyes to the bright sunlight billowing through the large windows. Blinking several times, I tried to get my bearings. In my sleep muddled head, everything seemed back to front, the reverse of where I remembered it to be. An unfamiliar aching sensation pulled on certain muscles in my lower region when I yawned and stretched in the warm bed. I winced, immediately remembering the events of the previous evening and what Nate and I had done. These were aches I was going to savour. He hadn't been lying when he'd said we weren't done. Before I could protest, he had lifted me off my feet and marched us back into his bedroom. Without another word, he had removed my robe and laid me out on his bed. Just as it had been the first time, he'd been attentive but aggressive, savouring my body while sating his hunger for release. When we'd both collapsed from exhaustion, he'd pulled me against him and we'd both fallen asleep.

To my relief, when I turned onto my side, Nate was sleeping soundly beside me. My initial fear had been that he would have left me alone in his bed, making me feel that it all had been a mistake. Lifting onto my elbow, I took a moment to study him. This man, who by day was always so serious and in control, looked almost vulnerable in sleep. Careful that I didn't wake him, I traced my fingers over his tattoos, spending longer on the heart and fist image over his heart. I knew there had to be a story behind it but he was always so guarded. I wasn't sure I would ever find out what it was.

A quick look at the alarm clock showed me it was nearing nine in the morning and we were supposed to be checking out at ten to finally move on to Nate's property. Knowing I needed to shower and pack, I slipped out of Nate's bed and grabbed my robe. Tying the belt around me, I stepped into the main room of the suite and screamed. Somebody was standing by the balcony doors.

"Mal! Wh-what are you doing in here?" I stuttered, rubbing my hand over my pounding heart.

"I'm just checking you're packed and ready to go. There's a car downstairs waiting to take you to Nice International." He narrowed his eyes, looking me up and down. "I can only hope he fucked you out of his system so he regains his focus."

I gasped, appalled at his statement yet fearful that he might be right.

"That has nothing to do with you," Nate said from

behind me. The hairs on the back of my neck stood on end, sensing his anger. He was like a power source. When he was calm, everything around him was calm. When he was angry, the air became charged with static, causing everyone in the same room to feel it.

I twisted to see Nate standing in his doorway, wearing nothing but a pair of black boxer briefs. He was holding the doorframe with a white-knuckled grip and staring menacingly at Mal.

"You broke the rules, Oakes," Mal said unaffected.

"Again, that has fuck all to do with you. That's your rule, not mine. It's pathetic. What I chose to do in the privacy of my bedroom has no impact on how I perform in the cage, and you know it."

"You are delirious, Nate. You're thinking with your dick and not your head. She needs to go before you totally lose focus and get pummelled by Sanchez. I will not let you lose. I cannot let you lose." I stared between the two as they glowered at each other. The tension between them was palpable, and I feared it would overspill into something nasty.

"It's all arranged, she's on the next flight out of Nice."

Before I could process what was happening, Nate had rushed past me and was pinning Mal against the balcony door, his forearm restraining Mal by the throat. His back muscles clenched in tension. "Olivia is going nowhere, do you hear me? She stays with me." I had never heard his voice so low and frightening.

Scared Nate was going to lose all control and do something terrible, I ran over and tentatively touched his shoulder. "Nate, let him go. It's okay. Don't do this. Let him go."

Mal didn't move. He just stared into Nate's menacing grey eyes. "Nate, please, let him go," I cried out again, wrapping both hands around his bicep and tugging when he wouldn't move. Finally he released Mal and stepped back, but not before brutally shoving him away. Nate was breathing hard, his tense upper body jerking with every harsh inhalation. He turned, looking me the eyes. Once again, his dark grey irises were plagued by anguish and confusion that I simply didn't understand. Fisting his hands at his sides, without a word he turned his back to me and strode into his bedroom, slamming the door behind him.

I stood, mouth agape, wondering what the hell was going on. I seemed to be on a roller coaster ride in crazy town. My head was spinning.

"I think you'd better go," I said, turning to Mal.

"Can't you see? It's you that needs to go. He's already unstable. If he stays around you much longer, he'll lose it all. If he does, it will be on your head." He rubbed his throat and made his way to the suite's doors but stopped before he opened them. "If he loses this fight, Olivia, I will be holding you personally responsible."

***

THE REST OF the morning went by in a blur of packing and moving on. Nate remained quiet, the remnants of his fury still clinging to him. I tried talking to him, but Wes advised me to leave him be. He said Nate would work the incident out in his mind and come around when he was ready. I'd explained to Wes and Cassie what had transpired with Mal when Nate had snapped at them both over ridiculous things. Wes had been ready to go after Mal too, but Cassie calmed him down with a few blunt words. She was good for them. I could see that. They trusted and respected her, while she looked up to them like older brothers. I was kind of envious of how close she appeared to be with them.

The four of us were travelling together to Nate's property. Bernie, Nate's coach, was travelling separately with all their training equipment. Nate was driving with Wes riding shotgun. Cassie and I were in the back enjoying the expanding mountainous scenery around us.

"Are you okay?" she whispered.

I nodded and gulped down some water from my bottle. "I'm fine," I whispered back. "It's Nate I'm worried about."

Nate met my eyes through the rear-view mirror. It was only a brief glance, but it told me so much about how he was feeling. He was angry, confused and uncertain. I felt the same way. Despite our lack of conversation since the previous night, and even though the sex had been anything but gentle love making, I knew something had shifted between us. It unnerved me. We'd both been clear that acting on our desires was purely for sexual pleasure and nothing else. But as I sat there watching him drive, I thought of the way he'd reacted to Mal and how he'd been with me the night before. I realised it had been stupid to think we could enjoy each other's bodies and not forge some form of emotional connection. Those feelings, certainly from my perspective, had been there already. I'd been fooling myself thinking otherwise.

I pulled my eyes from him and stared out the

window. It was going to be hard being around him and knowing nothing beyond a physical connection would be possible between us.

***

I CLIMBED OUT of the car and looked around in awe. Nate's place was a tranquil, picture perfect, little slice of heaven hidden in the foothills of the mountains. It was lush and green, but I could also imagine it covered in snow during the winter months. Turning in a full circle, I took in the large, double fronted house resting at the foot of the long driveway. Beyond that were endless fields of trees and shrubbery. From where I stood, I could see the corner of a building poking out from behind a camouflage of foliage. I wondered if that was Nate's training den.

While Nate and Wes retrieved our belongings from the car, I strolled over to the house, running my fingers along the stonework. Despite my tendencies to design more contemporary structures and buildings, Nate's French home held a quaintness that I automatically felt drawn to.

I stepped over to a row of colourful rosebushes, in full bloom, that screened off a terrace beyond. The scent of the flowers was intoxicating as they fluttered in the breeze. Bees buzzed from bloom to bloom collecting pollen. The scene was all very enchanting.

"So, what do you think?" I spun around at the sound of Nate's voice close to my ear.

"Just... wow! It's stunning out here," I beamed. It truly was a beautiful location.

He looked around as though he were seeing it for

the first time. "It's not bad. I was lucky enough to purchase the land quite cheaply a few years back. I haven't really done anything to it yet. That's where you come in. I'll give you the guided tour later and show you what I hope to do."

***

NATE SET MY luggage down in my bedroom. It was just as I had imagined it would be from the outside; rustic wooden floors and furniture combined quaintly with a floral patterned wallpaper and pale yellow bedding. It wasn't a huge room, but it would suffice for my needs whilst I was there. I sat on the edge of the bed and ran my hand along the intricately carved footboard.

"The bathroom's next door. My room is across the hallway," Nate said stepping further into the room. He dropped down into a crouch in front of me, resting his hands on my knees. "You can set your stuff up in here, or there's a small room downstairs you can use as your office. It's entirely up to you—whatever you want to do. Make yourself at home."

"And what about you, what will your schedule be like while we're here?" I bit my lip, feeling suddenly aware that I would mostly be left to my own devices.

Nate tugged on my lip with his thumb, pulling it free of my grip. His finger skimmed along my chin, tracing the outline of my mouth. "I have to train… a lot," he stated softly, his eyes fixed on my mouth.

"Nate, is having me here going to be a problem for you?" I decided to ask.

"Why would you think that?"

I shrugged. "Mal."

Nate's eyes frosted over, becoming cold and distant. "Don't worry about him. He's scared I'm going to take my eyes off the prize and he'll lose a shit load of money." He jumped to his feet. "Unpack your stuff, then I'll meet you downstairs to show you around."

Lying back on the bed, I wondered how much of an influence Mal had been on Nate's career over the years. They didn't appear to be close, not even friendly. As Nate shut the door behind him, my phone began to ring in my jeans pocket. Too distracted by my thoughts I answered without checking the display.

"Liv? It's me."

"Adam?" I shot up. "What's wrong?"

I hadn't heard from him since our argument. My mind began racing with thoughts that something had happened to my parents or that I was being called back to the office when I wasn't yet ready to leave Nate. In that briefest of moments before he spoke again, my mind had conjured up so many terrifying scenarios.

"I…" I heard his deep breath in. "I wanted to check in to see how you're doing," he continued softly.

"Oh."

"Look, Liv, I need to apologise for how I left things with us before. It was wrong, and I'm sorry. I should never have let you go out there without making things right before you left."

I fell back onto the mattress again and stared up at the ceiling. I was relieved to hear his voice. Despite the tension surrounding our friendship when I left, Adam was my rock, always had been. However, I felt confused. For weeks I'd wanted to speak to him and talk things through. I'd imagined our conversation over and over. Now he was on the phone, wanting that discussion, but there were hundreds of miles between us. I didn't know how to respond to him.

"Liv, say something, please."

"I don't know what to say to you, Adam" I admitted.

"Tell me how you're getting on," he encouraged.

"There's not much to tell you. We only just arrived at Nate's property today. I haven't even seen the land he wants to build on yet."

"Today?" he asked, sounding surprised. "Where have you been? I thought you flew out days ago?"

I recounted my time in Monaco, leaving out the details of the previous night's bedroom antics.

"Are you sure you're okay, Liv? You don't sound like yourself," Adam said softly.

I played it off, insisting I was tired and overwhelmed by the trip so far. In some ways it was true. I was certainly overwhelmed by Nate and everything that surrounded him.

We ended the call with Adam apologising again and saying he would keep in contact. He said he couldn't bear to lose our friendship, to lose me. I dropped my phone on the bed and closed my eyes for a moment, trying to compartmentalise the crazy that had become my life. There was only so much madness one could handle at any given moment.

I awoke with a start, flailing an arm into the air when something touched my shoulder and getting a resounding smack when it connected.

"Fuck!"

"Oh my God, Nate, I'm sorry." I quickly sat up,

watching as Nate rubbed his eye.

"Your right arm's getting stronger," he chuckled.

"What were you doing sneaking up on me like that?" I held a hand over my pounding heart.

"I wasn't sneaking. I've been calling you for five minutes. You obviously couldn't hear me because of your snoring."

"I do not snore."

"Oh you do. I think you're going to need to come up with plans for a new house too, seeing as you've rocked the foundations of this one." His words and tone were playful but there was a sincerity burning deep in his eyes as though the statement had a double meaning.

"Funny!"

"Are you coming downstairs? Cass has cooked dinner."

I flung my legs over the side of the bed so I was sitting beside him. "She has? Does she usually do that?"

"Why else would she be here? I need a woman around to cook and clean for me."

"Male chauvinist pig!"

He laughed. "She enjoys doing it, but that's not why she's here, not entirely."

"I still think you're a pig," I grumbled.

"Oink, oink," he said, standing. "Be downstairs in five minutes or Wes will have eaten yours too." He kissed the tip of my nose and then left.

A few minutes later, I made my way downstairs with a broad grin on my face. It was good to see Nate in high spirits. My smile faded when I stepped into the large kitchen and saw the serious faces sitting around the table.

"This is bullshit, Mal." Nate stood at the end of the large oak surface, gripping the edge.

"Nate doesn't need anyone else, he has me." Bernie insisted, glaring at the man sitting opposite him. It was obvious that Mal had few, if any, supporters.

"This is business. You're losing focus, Nate. The fight is in a matter of weeks and you are nowhere near prepared. Royce here will work with Bernie to help get you back on track." Mal sat there looking smug in his charcoal grey suit. His eyes flicked to me as I stood in the doorway not wanting to interrupt.

"I do not need another trainer," Nate bellowed. "Bernie and I do things my way, you know this."

"Your way doesn't appear to be working anymore. Not since you became… distracted. Remember, I own your arse Nathan. Royce is staying, end of discussion."

"Own my arse? No, Mal, you helped me out at the beginning, got me my first fights."

"Preciscly, I got you to where you are. You would be nothing without me. Now for God's sake, get rid of the bitch and get back in the gym." He pushed away from the table to leave.

"What did you say?" Nate was facing off with Mal in an instant, his fists balled, ready to strike.

Wes and Cassie rushed over, pulling Nate back and yelling at him to calm down. Bernie forced his chair back roughly and stood beside the three of them, looking menacing. They were a team, unified against whatever Mal had planned. I stood motionless, shocked at what I was seeing… again.

"Was my warning to you back at the hotel not enough?" Nate said to Mal, staring him in the eye. His voice was menacingly quiet.

"You have to see she isn't good for you, well not your career. I'd have to test her out personally to see how good she was in other areas."

Nate's hand flexed, ready to strike, but Wes and Cassie were prepared and held his arms. Still in Mal's face, Nate said something so quietly that I couldn't hear what it was. Judging by the slight widening of Mal's eyes, I presumed Nate wasn't apologising. Nate turned away and marched across the room. On the way past, his eyes met mine briefly but he didn't stop. He needed space. If I were him, I would need to distance myself from Mal too.

I met Wes and Cassie's worried eyes across the expanse of the large room. It was clear from their drawn in brows and wide-eyed expressions that they had never seen Nate like this before. Rushing after him, I screamed his name repeatedly as he marched away from the house and into the trees.

"Nate!" I breathed heavily, finally catching up to him near a large wood and brick building. "Stop!"

"Go back to the house, Liv."

I moved in front of him, pressing my hand to his chest, stopping him from moving any further. "No. Talk to me."

He searched my eyes for long moments. His chest rose and fell with each deep breath as he struggled to get a handle on his rage. Slowly his anger dissipated.

"I can put up with his crap. I will even tolerate his demands of another trainer, but I won't let him talk about you like that, Liv. You deserve more respect than that."

I moved my palm to his cheek. "Ignore it. He

doesn't bother me. What you think and want is all that matters."

Nate sucked in a deep breath and rested his forehead against mine. "What I think is I want you," he whispered.

With just those seven words, the air surrounding us changed, igniting into a heavy cloud of desire, need and something deeper, something more elemental.

"I want you too," I replied.

Seconds later, Nate had tugged me through a large barn door, closing and locking it behind us. The air was thick with dust, the tiny specs illuminated by the moonlight filtering in through a few skylight windows.

Nate backed me up against a wall, pushing his pelvis against mine. My breath caught as he gripped my thigh and lifted it to his hip, holding it tight. All thoughts of Mal and what was happening back in the house disappeared. With warm lips, he covered my neck with kisses, taking a moment to savour the skin along my jaw. Finally, his lips crashed against mine for a brief but explosive kiss.

"Don't underestimate what you're doing to me, Liv," he growled, stroking his hand along my thigh, stopping to grip my backside.

"Ditto," I whispered through a shudder, when his hand moved forward, skimming across the denim covering my aching core. His other hand brushed against my breast.

Bringing his lips back to my ear he whispered huskily, "You're distracting, and a pain in the arse, but I don't think I'd be able to focus at all if you weren't here. Not now."

My head flew back to rest against the brick wall as I

soaked in the pleasure of his nimble fingers pinching my nipple through the fabric of my t-shirt.

"And you're an arrogant, moody bastard...." I let out a breathy cry when his fingers squeezed harder. "But I'm glad I'm here."

I felt his smile against my skin as he kissed along my jawline. "Ah, there she is, my feisty, little Jelly Bean." He hoisted me further up his body, encouraging me to wrap both legs around him.

"Oh, Nate," I playfully swooned as he began to move us both across the room. "You're so strong. However do you manage to hold me and my big, fat butt?"

"This," he said with a slap to my backside that made me yelp, "is not big and fat. It's fucking sexy as hell, just like the rest of you."

He began kissing me ruthlessly and lowered me onto something firm, yet padded. I looked up to see a punch bag hanging from a beam nearby. "This is your gym?" I asked, twisting my head to see what else was visible in the dim light.

Not to be distracted, Nate began removing my clothes. First my t-shirt was dragged up and over my body and flung over Nate's shoulder, followed quickly by my bra. "Yes, I was going to come in here to beat out my frustrations on the bag. I wasn't expecting this kind of workout though." I wriggled and gasped when he nibbled and sucked on the sensitive flesh of my breasts.

"You're working out?" My eyes rolled and my toes curled when he unzipped my jeans and pulled them down, following the waistband with his lips and tongue. The jeans, along with my knickers were discarded to the side as Nate kissed his way up my inner thigh. My breath caught and I began panting with anticipation when his tongue skimmed once, twice, three times through my needy centre.

"*We're* working out," he said, lifting his head and replacing his tongue with a finger. I lay there mesmerised by the glistening on his lips, the sight so erotic because I could barely see anything else. His finger slipped inside, swirling around in slow circles. My back arched off the mat, meeting his touch and begging for more.

"You want more?" he asked, kissing around a nipple.

"Yes… Fuck!" He guided a second finger inside, and with a merciless rhythm, he began pounding them into me until I was crying out his name, begging him to release the pent up tension. My body shook as wave after wave of pleasure finally washed through me.

When I managed to peel an eye open, Nate was staring down at me. The soft moonlight lit his eyes and I saw something soft in them that I dared not consider. It must have been a trick of the lighting.

"Beautiful," he murmured, reaching down to unbutton and push down his own jeans. A moment later, with his eyes locked on mine he pushed himself inside me. I clenched around him, savouring the sensations of his heat rubbing me so perfectly.

Burying his face into my neck, Nate began moving with slow gentle thrusts that felt sublime against my still quivering tissue. But I needed more.

"Harder, Nate." I begged, digging my nails into his shoulders. "I need more, I need to come again."

With haste, he began pumping and rotating his

hips, pushing harder and deeper, fighting to give me what I wanted whilst also searching for his own release. "Liv," he moaned deeply on a drawn out breath. That sound in itself would have made me climax if I hadn't just screamed out his name again as a starlit galaxy appeared behind my closed eyelids. Kneeling up abruptly, he cursed and pulled out, holding his cock in his palm as warm liquid spilled out over my stomach. He groaned a deep throaty noise and fell to his side, fighting to catch his breath.

"I can't believe I was so fucking careless," he chastised himself.

My eyes widened. I couldn't believe it either. I'd been so caught up in the pleasure of the moment; a condom hadn't even entered my mind. "Don't do it again," I grumbled and then wanted to slap myself. That statement assumed there would be an again. Even though we'd now had sex three times, there had been no discussions about any expectations—or feelings—beyond those moments of stolen pleasure.

"You're not mad?" He leaned up to look at me.

"If you tell me you're riddled in STDs, then I'll be fucking fuming and looking to cut off your dick in the most painful way possible. But, no, I'm not mad."

"Way to ruin the moment, Liv."

I rolled my eyes. "Way to put my life at risk, *Nate.*"

He shifted so he was lying right beside me, circling his fingers around a nipple. "I would never do anything to put your life at risk. In fact I will go out of my way to protect you." His eyes, begging for forgiveness, peered up into mine. "I'm sorry, okay? I'm clean, I promise. I got a clean bill of health during my medical before I flew out here."

"They test you for STDs in a pre-fight medical?" I asked incredulously.

Nate chuckled and reached forward to smooth my hair away from my eyes. "They do a full check-up, looking for possible drug use mainly." That made sense. His face grew serious. "I really am sorry, though. I should have been more responsible. Do you want me to take you to a doctor, just in case?"

I shook my head. "No, if you're clean we should be fine. I'm on the pill so we have no worries there. I mean it though, Nate. We can't forget again."

He nodded and looked at my belly. "I guess I should clean you up."

Five minutes later, we were cleaned up and dressed, and Nate was showing me around his gym.

"This place is amazing, Nate. I don't understand why you'd want to change it." With the lights on, I looked around the large open space, taking in all the equipment he had and the large cage tucked away in the far corner.

He moved in behind me and wrapped his arms around my middle. "This is adequate for Wes and me, but I want so much more from this whole place. I want a larger gym, accommodation, consulting rooms, dining facilities… I want to turn this place into a safe and inspiring training and rehabilitation facility for young people."

"Why specifically young people?" I asked.

"I have my reasons," he replied cryptically. Whatever the reason, I had a feeling it was related to his past, the past he refused to talk about.

"I guess we'd better go back and face the music," he said with a sigh, leading me back to the barn doors.

251

~CHAPTER SIXTEEN~

WESLEY WAS PACING THE KITCHEN floor when we re-entered. Mal was nowhere to be found. Cassie peered over from where she was washing dishes, and the new guy, Royce, sat appraising us quietly.

"Where the fuck have you been, Nate?" Wes asked, looking beyond pissed off.

"I needed to cool off." I left Nate's side and walked towards the table, noting the hostile energy in the room.

"I need to talk to you… in private," Wes said, already striding towards the hallway. Nate nodded and followed.

"This is all kinds of weird, huh?" Royce asked as I pulled out a seat at the table. He was older than Nate, maybe in his late-thirties, with short, cropped, dark hair that showed off several scars. From the shape of his obviously previously broken nose, I assumed he had once been a fighter himself. His body appeared to be that of a once committed athlete, still broad but not as muscular and toned as he would have previously been. With deep olive skin, and vivid blue eyes, he could be classed as handsome, in a rugged kind of way. He also carried himself with the same arrogance I'd seen from Nate and Wes.

"Um, yeah. I guess."

Several minutes passed as we sat in silence. Royce's eyes were on me the whole time, making me fidget and fiddle with the hem of my top. His assessment made me feel a little uncomfortable.

"He doesn't need anyone else here," Cassie blurted out, throwing a dish towel on the counter. I jumped. "Like Nate said, this is bullshit."

Unfazed by her outburst, Royce leaned back in his chair, cradling the back of his head in his hands.

"It's always good to freshen things up." He shrugged.

"Ugh, arrogant as well as ugly." Cassie picked up a knife from the drainer. "You know," she said, pointing the knife in his direction, "Nate is very particular about his training. He won't take kindly to having a stranger join the team, telling him what to do and when to do it. The only person he respects and will listen to is Bernie."

Royce sighed and closely watched the knife Cassie continued to point towards him. "I'm not here to make things difficult for Nate or for anyone. Far from it. I don't particularly agree with Mal and his reasons for me being here. But he's paying me well and a job's a job."

"Unbelievable!" Cassie threw the knife in a drawer

then walked out, muttering to herself.

"Well, that went well." Royce exhaled with a drawn out breath and sank lower into his chair.

"Were you expecting a warm welcome?" The tone in my voice was deliberately bitter. If Nate didn't want the guy there, neither did I.

"I guess not. I wasn't expecting to land in Antarctica though."

"Royce—"

"Roy... please, just Roy. I hate the name Royce," he said, laughing.

I scowled but continued. "Okay, *Roy*. Tell me why you're here then. What has Mal told you?"

He looked nervously towards the hallway before continuing in a quiet voice, "He said Nate was unstable, that he was losing his mind and not focusing on his training. He wanted me to come and keep an eye on him, said something about—and I quote, 'some bitch distracting him.' I presume he was talking about you?"

My cheeks heated as my eyes widened.

"Look," he continued, raising his hands up. "I'm not here to cause waves. I just want to do what I can to keep Mal happy and keep him paying me. I won't cause any problems."

Shaking my head sadly, I said, "You're here, that's already a big problem."

I continued grilling him for several more minutes, and the longer I talked with Roy, the easier I began to feel about him. Despite Mal's underhand reasons for him being there, Roy was simply trying to earn some money. I learned he had indeed once been a fighter but had never made it big like Nate had. A back injury in his early twenties meant he'd had to stop fighting. After a year of moping around with no income in his home country of Brazil, he connected with another fighter who was traveling to Europe for a fight. He was offered the chance to join their training camp and jumped at it. Realising he had nothing to return to in Brazil, he'd ended up staying, working from gym to gym finding jobs where he could.

"When Mal offered me this job and told me how much he would pay, I couldn't turn it down. This money will pay my bills for the next year, Olivia."

I sat there, staring at him while he talked, my chin resting on my palms. He had the most mesmerising accent. I tried to be faithful to Nate's feelings about Roy being there, but the longer we chatted, the more I found I liked the guy. He'd been dealt a rough hand and was only doing what he had to in order to survive. I even suspected that Nate could possibly learn something from him.

"Sorry, what was that?" I jerked up, realising he had been asking me a question.

"I said, how about you? How long have you and Nate been together?"

"Oh," I fumbled around for something to say. Despite our recent antics in the amazing sex arena, Nate had made it very clear there was never going to be an *us*.

I laughed it off. "Oh, we're not together. I'm just here as his architect."

Fucking lame, Liv.

"Yeah, that's right. She's just another employee." Turning abruptly at the sharp voice, I locked gazes with Nate.

"Nate... I...." He closed his eyes briefly and shook his head, stopping me from continuing. Then he looked at Roy.

"I don't want you here, Royce. I don't need you here, but Mal has put you in this position. If you are staying, and I'd prefer it if you didn't, you'll be in the small room at the back of the gym, away from the house. Away from *us*." He met my gaze then, his eyes burning with a deep rooted anger. The trouble was I wasn't sure if that anger was directed at Roy or me.

"Get your things and I'll take you down there." Nate tore his eyes away from me and strode out of the kitchen door without looking back. Roy grabbed a large bag and quickly followed after him.

"I'll catch you later, Olivia. It was nice meeting you," he shouted over his shoulder with a smile.

***

THE FOLLOWING WEEK was strained to say the least. Nate resented Roy's presence on his property with such passion that I wondered on more than one occasion if they would end up in a brawl. He always managed to rein in his anger, either by taking it out on a punch bag or by phoning Mal and letting loose with a string of expletives, reminding him he was capable of doing his own training. Nate did, after all, have Bernie and Wes there to train with and support him. I spent more time with Cassie, helping her around the house while the guys were training. I discovered she was a fantastic cook, utilising the Asian cuisine skills she'd learned growing up and adjusting them to support Nate's strict dietary requirements.

When Cassie was in the gym with the guys, I would take out my sketch books and wander around looking for ideas and inspiration. I discovered that at the rear of the property, at the end of a track that ran through one of the fields, there was a small river. It wasn't particularly wide or deep but it did offer the perfect spot to retreat to when I needed a moment of peace to myself. As the days moved on, I needed that space more and more.

Since the night of Roy's arrival, Nate had been distant with me. He'd kept his promise of showing me around and pointing out his visions for the property and what he wanted me to do for him, we ate meals together and had a couple of short exchanges when I'd needed to find out more about the local area and to discuss the progress of his plans, but other than that, Nate went out of his way to avoid me. I'd challenged him a few times, asking what his problem was and he would simply tell me he was there to prepare for his fight and I was there to design, nothing more, nothing less. Nate the attentive lover had been completely replaced by Nathan, the arrogant fighter.

The only glimmer of light on my otherwise dark horizon was that my relationship with Adam was getting back on track. He phoned me most days, regaling me with stories of the office. It was dull and boring stuff, yet it never failed to brighten my mood. Or maybe it was just hearing my best friend's voice that did that for me.

"What's up, Liv? You're quiet." Adam asked one bright afternoon. I'd spent the morning in a local town, and when I'd returned, Nate had been standing in the kitchen with Mal, Bernie, Roy and Honey. She had been standing far too close to him for my liking. Nate's back was to me so he hadn't seen me when I'd entered through the open kitchen door, but she had. Her bitchy smile grew wider as she murmured something to Nate and stepped in closer, placing her claws on his arm. The more I saw her, the more I suspected there had been, or maybe still was, something going on between them. Nate vehemently denied that was the case, but I wasn't so sure. Not able to stomach being in a room with both her and Mal, I'd turned on my heels and wandered down to *my spot*.

I picked up a stone chipping from the rock I was sitting on and threw it into the river, watching as the impact created ripples across the surface. "I don't know, Ad," I sighed. "I guess it's just different out here than I thought it would be."

"How are the drawings coming along?"

That was probably the only thing going well. With Nate being so withdrawn, I'd spent a lot of time travelling around, photographing and sketching the local architecture. Most days I would busy myself out on the property, doing all the technical stuff I was going to need to design the new facility, or I'd lock myself away with my Mac and add to the drawings that were slowly coming together. I was pleased with how they were looking and felt confident that I'd managed to meet Nate's brief whilst ensuring everything was in keeping with the area. It had been a tough task. I mean, how many large-scale sports shelters and rehabilitation centres did you find in the middle of the French countryside?

I smiled as I told him about the plans and what I'd learned of the area in the short time I'd been here.

"Is he treating you okay?"

"What? Where did that come from?" I was taken aback by the sudden change in subject.

"I want to know that you're being looked after okay. You're all alone over there, and I need to know he's not taking advantage."

Nate had taken advantage, and at the time I'd enjoyed it. But that had all changed. "Yes, I'm being looked after okay. No, he's not taking advantage of me. I hardly ever see him because he's training all the time."

"So why do you sound so down then? The Liv I know never lets anything get her down."

I kicked off my flip flops and dipped my toes in the water. "Adam, I'm fine, honestly. I just feel a little isolated out here…"

My eyes followed the path of a low flying bird and came into direct contact with Nate's deep grey, brooding stare. He was standing on the opposite bank watching me closely. He must have been out running because he was wearing grey sweatpants rather than the shorts he favoured in the gym. His white, sweat soaked t-shirt clung to every ridge of his fine physique. I immediately brightened at seeing him and smiled warmly. That smile faded when he simply nodded and continued jogging along the riverside path.

"Damn moody bastard," I muttered.

"Excuse me?"

"Oh God, not you, Ad." Sometimes I wished there was a brain-to-mouth filter app I could download, because my own inbuilt one didn't seem to work.

"Listen, I know things were awkward between us for a while, but I want you to know I meant what I said, Liv."

My head shook. "Ad—"

"No, before you start calling me names…" I relaxed slightly at his playful tone. "I do love you. Maybe it's just the whole female friend, overprotective, care for you thing, who knows. What I'm trying to say is that I'm here for you… as your best friend. If you need me, I'll be there."

"Thanks, Ad," I replied softly. "That means a lot." It was such a relief to have my best friend back.

I slowly ambled back to the house, contemplating whether I should see if Nate had returned to the gym. We needed to talk and sort things out because I wasn't sure how much more I could take of his cold shoulder.

Cassie was coming through the doors when I approached. She spotted me and smiled widely.

"Hey, how has your day been?" she asked, locking the door behind her. There was my answer. Nate obviously wasn't inside.

"Okay, I guess. Where's Nate?"

She joined me on the path and we walked together back towards the house. "I'm not sure. He went for a run and I haven't seen him since. I was supposed to be giving him a massage, but he didn't show. Royce really put him through his paces this morning."

"Oh? I take it they are getting along now then?"

Cassie laughed. "Oh my God, you should see them, Liv. It's like two school boys trying to outdo each other. They are definitely two hugely competitive male egos. I still don't like Royce—there is something about him I don't trust. But, he *is* getting Nate to train harder, so that can only be a good thing." Her smile dropped briefly. "I hate that this whole Roy situation is affecting Bernie too. The poor guy feels like he's been elbowed out the way. He has always been there for Nate, always pushing him and getting the best out of him. Even Bernie can't get through to him these days. Mal said bringing Roy on board was to help Nate. All it has really done is made him a moody, unapproachable arse." Her head shook sadly.

When we reached the house, I stopped Cassie from opening the door. "Cass, can I ask you something?"

"Sure. Of course you can."

We moved over and sat at the outdoor dining table, enjoying the last of the late afternoon sun. "What do you think is going on with Nate?"

"What do you mean?" she asked, pulling her sunglasses over her eyes and tilting her face towards the sky.

I needed a female opinion on what was going on, someone who would tell me straight if I was being paranoid, but I wasn't sure how much she knew about Nate and me. "I have to tell you something and then I need your take on it."

She lifted her glasses again and gave me her full attention. "Shoot."

I explained about the few times Nate and I had been together and how he made me feel. I didn't go into detail but told her how my feelings for him had been growing. "I'm not sure if it's connected or if it's just me, but he's been cold with me since Roy arrived," I finished.

Cassie leaned forward, resting her forearms on the table. "You love him," she said with a smirk.

"What? No… No I don't. How can I love him, I hardly know him?"

"You have feelings for him, though, right?" I nodded. "And if things had continued as they were, those feelings could have grown into love?"

"Maybe," I muttered.

"Liv, I honestly don't know what's going on with him. He hasn't said anything. He never does. When he has these moods, I mostly just let him get on with it. From what you've said, though, I'm pretty positive he has the same feelings for you. He just doesn't know how to deal with them." She stood, smiling down at me. "Give him time. When he's ready, he'll come back to you."

I thought about her words as she walked away. I had been so consumed by thoughts of why he'd closed off that I hadn't considered why I was so bothered. Then it hit me. Hard. Cassie wasn't wrong. To a certain extent I had fallen for Nate. Maybe not full blown, I-can't-live-without-you love, but there were definitely stronger feelings than just lust floating inside me. I was screwed. I needed to get Nate's plans finished and back on a plane home as soon as possible.

***

A FEW DAYS LATER, Nate was still quiet. I'd been working at my computer all morning and needed a break so I went for a wander. The doors of the barn were open, and I heard the grunts of someone repeatedly hitting the punch bag. Sneaking in quietly, I sat in a chair in the corner and watched. Bernie held the bag while Nate thundered punch after punch into the leather. This went on for several minutes with the punches becoming more and more aggressive with each swing. Nate looked volatile.

When Roy stepped out from the shadows and crossed over to a table I ran over.

"What's going on?" I asked as he poured a sachet of something into a sports bottle. "What's that?" I pointed to the drink.

Roy shook it. "Isotonic drink. We need to keep Nate's body hydrated."

That made sense with all the training he was doing. "What's up with him?" I nodded in Nate's direction where he continued to jab the bag, oblivious to my presence.

Roy shrugged. "He's just focused." He then walked away, taking the drink to Nate.

I sat and watched for a while longer, wincing when they climbed into the cage and started grappling. I began to see the raw power in Nate. When I'd witnessed him training in Monaco, I'd thought he'd been giving it his all. I had been so wrong. At one point, Wes had to jump in the cage and pull Nate from Roy when he tapped out from a painful and un-natural looking arm lock. When the two men began arguing over Nate's aggressiveness, I was unable to watch any more. Quietly, I left the barn and returned to my makeshift office. Something about Nate's demeanour was seriously worrying me.

~CHAPTER SEVENTEEN~

ANOTHER WEEK PASSED WITH NATE being…
professional with me. He wasn't rude, or dismissive, he
wasn't being anything. Every day he would be in the
barn working out and training with Bernie, Wes, Roy
and Cassie from sun up to sun down. Once a day I
would head in there for my own workout, training
alone or working with Cassie. I missed Nate. I missed
our banter. More importantly, I missed the way he
pushed me. I often thought back to that very first
training session we'd had together, how he had taken
me way beyond what I felt comfortable with but had
ended up igniting something within me. He hooked
me in early and became the driving force behind the
new woman I stared at every day in the mirror.

Tightening the laces on my Converse, I stepped out
into the balmy night time breeze. I'd spent the day in
my makeshift office with fans blowing on me from all

angles while I worked on the plans. It had been a scorching hot day with high temperatures and no daytime breeze to help cool things down. Regularly, I'd found my gaze drifting out the window, looking towards the barn and wondering what was happening inside, what Nate was doing. So, after yet another tense dinner, I'd grabbed my shoes, deciding I needed some air and space.

Wandering through the rows of grapevines, lit only by the glow of the moon, I appreciated the beauty of the area. It was so quiet and peaceful, the only sounds coming from the chattering of crickets calling out for a mate… or warning off the competition. I tugged a small bunch of grapes from a vine and began popping them into my mouth one by one. It seemed such a tragedy that so much of Nate's land would be spoiled by more buildings and concrete.

I was nearing the bank of the river when I heard a voice. Peering through the vines, I saw Roy leaning against my rock, talking on his phone. I should have turned and left him to his privacy, but something kept me rooted to the spot, fighting to hear his words on the breeze.

"Yes… we're on schedule… no, they have no idea…" A squawking noise startled me, sending me searching for the sound. My heart pounded as I spotted a nocturnal bird swoop low and scoop up something from the ground before flying off into the dark night sky once again. When I turned back to continue spying on Roy, he had shifted position, his voice now muffled and unintelligible. Suspicious, I was curious about who he was speaking to and what the other end of the conversation was. A quick peek around gave me no obvious cover to be able to get any closer. If I moved in, I would be seen for sure, and I didn't want Roy to know I'd been eavesdropping. Resigned to the fact I'd not be able to sate my inquisitive nature, I retreated further back into the vines, quietly making my way back to the house. I wasn't going to be able to enjoy some quiet time on my rock that night.

It was getting late by the time I made it back to the house. Knowing I had a busy day ahead of me, I decided to call it a night. I would crawl into bed and do some reading before falling asleep.

"Where have you been?"

I stumbled on the loose shingle path and whirled around, searching the blackness of the rear yard. Nate was sat at the table to my right sipping a glass of water.

"You scared the shit out of me," I replied stepping towards him.

"Where have you been?" he repeated, looking up at me as I approached.

"I went for a walk."

"You shouldn't be out walking alone in the dark," he chastised.

"What? Are you kidding? We're on your property, Nate, out in the middle of nowhere. What could possibly happen to me out here?"

"A lot could happen to you out there. Don't do it again."

I laughed once, a humourless, bitter sound. "And what do you care?"

"I care very much, that's the problem," he muttered, staring into my eyes, holding my gaze.

My pulse raced under the weight of his stare. I

didn't know what to say. I wanted to throw a jibe at him, something about indifference not being very caring, or maybe bitch about being unable to care for someone if you knew nothing about them and avoided them all the time. I didn't. I couldn't. My eyes were riveted on his, hypnotised by the glittering silver orbs fixed on me.

"That's the problem, Liv. I care too fucking much," he said again, shaking his head. "But there is nothing I can do about it." He sighed, sounding resigned.

"What the hell are you talking about?" I finally found my voice—my don't-mess-with-me-I'm-pissed-off voice—and pulled out the chair opposite. "You've acted like I'm your worst enemy these last two weeks."

"I know and I'm so fucking sorry. Having Royce thrust onto me really pissed me off, and then when you said… Look it doesn't matter. I know I've been a bastard, and I'm sorry. This fight is going to be the death of me, Liv. I feel so angry, so out of control." He leaned forward, resting his elbows on his knees and clutching his hands in front of him. He seemed so dejected, not the same vibrant man I'd come to know.

"Hey!" Moving in front of him, I dropped to my knees and took his hands in mine. "I can't imagine the pressure of preparing for something like this. It must be immense. But I'm here for you, Nate. I can help you. Let me help you," I implored.

Nate sucked in a deep breath, slowly exhaling it through his nose. Then he took me by surprise when he lifted me easily off the ground and pulled me onto his lap. "I've missed you," he said, his hoarse voice muffled as he nuzzled his face into my hair.

"And I've missed you." I wrapped my arms around

his neck and held him close, feeling some of his tension fading away.

"I meant it, Liv," he said after a few minutes of comforting silence. "Please don't go walking around by yourself. The property isn't secured. Anyone or anything could be out there." His grip on my waist tightened. "I don't know what I'd do if anything happened to you."

"Okay," I whispered, soothingly. At that moment, feeling him clinging to me as though he needed me to survive, I would have agreed to anything.

**

THINGS SLOWLY IMPROVED between us. Nate was still aggressive with his training, and I tried to stay away whenever he was with Roy because he would still end up snapping at me. When we had the chance to be alone though, he would relax. I began doing a training session with him every day, getting him to throw a few more of his fancy martial art moves into my sessions. He was happy to help, knowing I could use them as self-defence one day if needed. We also tried to spend some down time together each day, away from the barn and prying eyes. We would go for walks down to the river—the rock eventually became *our* place, not just mine—we would talk and joke, but it was all in the friend zone. Not once did Nate show any signs of wanting to rekindle the physical side of our friendship. Some days, that bothered me, especially if I'd caught sight of him wearing nothing but shorts and hand wraps, glistening with sweat, the longer strands of his hair slicked back. He was hot, there was no denying it.

I would be lying if I said I didn't want to experience the pleasure he had brought me again. But I was content with what we had.

Suddenly, there were only two weeks to the fight and everything became more hectic. Nate was inundated with interview and media requests, his training kicked up to a new level and there was a buzz around the place that had been noticeably absent before. To add to it all, I'd managed to put most of my focus on what I was there for and only had a few minor changes to make before the plans would be finished and submitted for approval.

I felt great, alive.

"What's the number one rule?" Nate asked as we circled each other. Everyone else had decided to take an afternoon off. Wes, Cassie and Bernie took the Cayenne and drove into town, feeling the need to socialise with people beyond the boundaries of Nate's land. I wasn't sure where Roy had gone, but he had taken another vehicle and gone off somewhere alone. Nate wanted to use the time to show me a few moves. That's why I was in his cage wearing a pair of short shorts, a tight fitting vest top and had training mitts tied to my hands.

I kept his gaze as I continued sidestepping not allowing him near me. "Keep my guard up." I lifted my hands into the defensive posture he had drilled into me.

"And the second?"

I jumped and quickly backed up when he lunged. "Always be prepared. Attackers are unpredictable, opportunistic."

"Good girl," he said with a smile.

"Nate?" I asked, risking a jab which he dodged.

"Yes?"

"I want to learn more of the stuff you do. You know, more of the grappling and holds."

He lunged again, this time managing to get hold of me and knocking me to the floor. "Is that so?"

I wriggled under his weight, trying to free myself of the hold he had me in. It was all very similar to that time in his apartment back home. "Yes," I breathed through my exertions. "I want to be the one capable of holding you down. Will you show me some holds?"

He sat back on his knees, allowing me to move. "And what is the fun in that?"

"The fun in that is me getting the upper hand for once." Moving to my knees, I mirrored his posture.

He grabbed my hands and placed them on the hard contours of his upper arms. Then with a firm yet measured grip, he circled his long, strong fingers around my biceps. "How about this? I want you to fight against me. Get me down and I'll show you something extra special."

"That's unfair." I pouted. "You are so much better than me. I don't have a hope in hell of getting you beneath me."

His lips pulled in, trying to contain a smile. "Isn't that my line?"

"What?"

"Nothing," he said smirking. "Are we going to do this or not?"

"Okay, but you better be fucking easy on me, Nate, or I swear to all that is holy, I *will* find some way to kick your arse."

He either thought that the most ridiculous thing he

had ever heard, or took pleasure in the idea of it actually happening. He started to chuckle. His laugh was infectious, causing me to laugh with him until my sides hurt.

"Okay, Rocky," he said, wiping his eyes. "Let's do this."

We repositioned on our knees, spreading them wider for extra stability, our hands gripping each other's upper arms.

"Okay, tell me when to st—" Before I could finish, Nate had me on my back. He kneed my legs out straight and gripped both of my hands in one of his. With the weight of his body covering mine, he had me immobilised and subdued within seconds.

"You play dirty," I grumbled, trying unsuccessfully to dislodge him.

"I'd like to," he whispered, looking down on me.

Staring up at him, I noticed his eyes had changed. Gone was the playful silver glint. In its place was deep, grey heat and a burning intensity.

I swallowed hard. "What?"

"Do you trust me, Liv?"

"Yes, but—" He silenced me with a finger over my lips.

"I want to do something I've been fantasising about for weeks," he said, moving up my body until he was straddling my chest. Taking my hands, he quickly loosened the ties of my gloves and then lifted me, carrying me towards the outer edge of the cage. I watched in horror—and heat—as Nate used the laces of my gloves to tie my hands to a pole.

"I like you in my cage," he whispered seductively, repositioning himself between my legs.

I wanted to ask him what he thought he was doing. I wanted to yell and scream at him to untie me, but I couldn't. The words were stuck in my throat along with the scream of pleasure I wanted to make when he bit a nipple through my sports bra. I tried protesting, I really did, but all that came out were whimpers and moans caused by his hot tongue and the feeling of his lips skimming over my heated flesh.

"I want to show you a new move," he said, pushing my t-shirt up and then shuffling back, nipping and licking his way over my stomach.

"Yeah? What move is that?" I panted, squirming beneath him.

When he reached my pelvis, a deep, gravely groan vibrated from his throat. Quickly, he removed my shorts and panties, trailing his tongue back up along my thigh, to the throbbing epicentre of my womanhood.

"It involves a bit of tugging..." His teeth latched on to my pulsing clit and gently tugged. I gasped, pulling on my restraints.

"Some pushing…" My leg muscles quivered when his tongue darted inside my warmth.

"And lots of movement." I almost came when his lips traced along the lips of my sex, leaving no millimetre untouched.

For a brief moment, he moved away. I whimpered immediately, missing the warmth of his mouth but it soon returned, kissing along the inside of my thigh. The scratch of his stubble on my overly sensitive flesh was harsh but added to the sensual feelings slowly consuming me.

As he made his way higher, I peered down, excited

by the erotic picture I knew I would find. Nate's eyes were on mine, feral and needy. His arms wrapped around my thighs, holding me firm while his tongue once again trailed along the seam of my sex. Gasping in pleasure, I could no longer keep my eyes open. My back arched and I surrendered to the sensations.

While I panted and moaned, Nate continued torturing me with just his mouth. His stubble burned against my thighs, but the silkiness of his hair skimming across my pelvis soothed. His deep, earthy scent permeated the air. My senses were overloaded. Being unable to move my arms and knowing he was using only a small part of his body to bring me such intense pleasure, it was the most erotic moment of my life. All too soon I was crying out his name. My back arched off the canvas and my legs began to quiver until they were cramping. The orgasm that rocked through me was so intense, I was left panting and unable to move a muscle. He had literally paralysed me with passion.

Nate moved up my body, trailing his lips along my flesh. He kissed my temple and the tip of my nose while he fumbled to untie the gloves. Free of my restraints, he pulled me up to straddle his lap, wrapping his arms firmly around my waist.

"I don't think I'm going to be able to train in here anymore," he said, placing a kiss on the tip of my nose. "I won't be able to concentrate."

"Oh?" My fingers trailed a line down his chest, starting in the dip at the bottom of his throat and moving down. I spent time tracing the tattoo covering his pectorals and looked him in the eye when he flinched at my touch. I wanted to ask him again what it symbolised, but the warning was there in the deepness of the grey, telling me not to go there yet. Resigned, I carried on moving downwards.

"Every time I'm in here, I'll be picturing you on the canvas squirming in pleasure and not Wes or Royce squirming in pain," he said, watching my fingers as they trailed along the waistband of his shorts. Suddenly he jumped up, taking me with him. It always amazed me how strong he was and how effortless he made picking me up seem.

"Nate? What's wrong?" I felt the confused crumpling of my forehead. I hoped to god he wasn't pulling away. I didn't think I could take it. Not again. I'd so easily submitted to his desires without thinking or questioning. It had been dangerous, with our history, but that's what he did to me. He stripped me of all rational thoughts and left me with nothing but the need for him.

He backed me up against the mesh of the cage, pinning my hips with his and holding my face with both hands. His eyes searched mine. "I can't go there with you," he whispered. "Not here. Not yet."

He must have seen the hurt in my eyes, because he continued, "I want to. God, do I want to. I have to hold myself back, though, Liv. These past few weeks have been fucked up and it's only going to get worse. The next time I make love to you, it will be without restraint, in a bed, with all the time in the world for me to savour every inch of your delicious body."

"Oh." I swallowed, picturing the scene.

He picked up my shorts and handed them to me. "We should get out of here before the others get back."

***

TIME WAS FLYING past and there was only one week left until the fight. Nate had kept to his promise of keeping his hands off me—much to my disappointment—but he was attentive in other ways. I began getting concerned about his mood shifts and pure aggression in the cage when he actually knocked Royce unconscious after another heated exchange. He was only out for a minute or two, but it scared the crap out of me how angry Nate could get. Warning signs were ringing out all around me, but I couldn't quite work out where the emergency was. And every evening, Nate would park the fury and sit quietly with me. We would talk, watch French TV with English subtitles or go for walks down to *our spot*. It seemed to be our one place of true comfort and tranquillity. Maybe it was the feeling that the running water could take the stresses of the day away with it. Maybe it was just the only place that we could really be alone.

I was drinking a cool glass of water in my makeshift office when Nate called me from the kitchen.

"One minute," I yelled back, shifting my phone to the other ear. "Sorry, Ad, Nate's calling. I better go and see what he wants."

"Are you sure you're okay?" Adam asked, tenderly. He was still concerned about me, even though I'd told him over and over that things were better.

"Adam, I'm fine. If you keep asking I swear I will kick your arse when I get home."

He chuckled. "Fighting talk huh? You've been around Nate too long."

"Noooo, I've always been like this. Feisty Liv,

remember?"

"No, I don't. You've been gone too long. I've forgotten what you look and act like."

I rolled my eyes. "Funny. I've got to go, Ad. But I'm fine, honestly. Stop worrying."

"Never," he muttered.

We said our goodbyes and I made my way into the kitchen. Nate stood near the door, waiting patiently. He pulled my denim jacket off a hook and held it out. "Come."

I took the garment from him, my brows drawn in. "Where are we going?"

"I need to get out of here for a while."

I shrugged into the jacket and pulled it around me, wondering where he planned on taking me.

"Are you not training today?" I asked, following him out into the backyard.

He pulled out a remote from his pocket and pressed a button. "Not today. I need a break. They are all driving me mad. They can't seem to grasp the fact I know exactly what I'm doing, or that I can handle my own schedule."

A door on the garage slowly opened, revealing a bright red, gleaming Ferrari sitting alongside the Cayenne. Nate hit the remote again and the car beeped to life.

"This is yours?" I gaped.

He smiled unapologetically and shrugged. "Boys and their toys and all that."

"But it's not a Porsche!" I laughed and with a shake of my head, eased into the passenger seat when Nate opened the door for me.

A few minutes later, we were speeding through the

dramatic French countryside. With the roof of the Ferarri down, the early morning sunshine beamed down on us as cooler air rushed over our heads. I took in the stunning scenery surrounding us—the miles and miles of unspoilt vineyards and fields with a backdrop of snow-covered mountaintops. I smiled at the occasional farmhouses and cottages that came into view and tried to commit them to memory so I could sketch them later.

Nate looked over, his eyes hidden behind mirrored aviators. He gave me a rare, untroubled and relaxed grin and increased the volume of the stereo. I continued watching the trees rush past, feeling the joy and lightness of the moment. When we hit a straight part of the road, Nate pushed his foot on the gas, sending the car speeding forward. I was forced back into my seat, squealing and laughing. Nate's face lit up into a broad grin when I shouted in joy and lifted my arms into the air, letting the air rush through my fingers. Closing my eyes, I tilted my head back to feel the sun on my face. It was the perfect moment, just the two of us, carefree and happy. I could almost forget there were even any stresses awaiting us when we returned.

Thirty minutes later, Nate pulled into a large, gravelled parking lot. Stepping out from the low car, I stretched and looked around. The area was unremarkable, with no clear indication of where we were or what we would be doing. The area was lined with tall evergreen bushes and smaller hedges. Nate rounded the car and stood behind me, wrapping his arms around my waist.

"Do you like water?" he asked, resting his chin on

my shoulder.

I turned in his arms, raising my hands to lift his glasses away from his eyes so I could search them with my own. "Water? What is this place, Nate? Where are we?"

He looked over my shoulder, and then pulled his eyes back to mine. "I used to come here when I was younger. We came here every year for our summer holidays."

I was startled by his willingness to suddenly impart information about his childhood. I didn't know what to say. He took my hand in his and started walking us towards a gap in the hedge.

"I haven't been since I was fifteen," he continued.

Beyond the hedge, I stopped walking; my eyes began darting in every direction. Laid out before us was a spectacular view of a white cliff face covered with green trees and bushes. However, what took my breath away was the wide expanse of river at the foot of the rocks. My eyes followed the path of the water until it curved around a bend and out of sight.

Sensing my wonder, Nate wrapped an arm around my shoulder. "Isn't it amazing?"

"I... Nate, it's beautiful."

Taking my hand again, he led us down a steep path, taking care that I didn't trip on the loose gravel.

"Have you ever been kayaking?" he asked when we reached the bottom.

Shaking my head, I looked at the bright yellow kayaks resting on the pebble beach. My palms began to sweat as I stepped closer to the water's edge.

"Nate!" I swallowed hard. "It looks really deep out there."

He chuckled. "Why does that bother you? Are you planning on falling in?"

"No! It's just…" I couldn't believe how nervous and vulnerable I felt about sitting in a fiberglass boat out on the open water.

He moved in front of me and cupped my cheek, tilting my head so I'd look at him. "I won't let anything happen to you. I'll be with you the whole time. We'll be doing this together. Okay?"

His eyes continued searching mine, waiting for my answer.

I sucked in a deep breath. "Okay."

Once again, I was dazzled by his full, megawatt smile before he leaned in to place a kiss on the tip of my nose. "You amaze me. You know that, JB?"

Twenty minutes later, Nate had helped me into a life jacket and situated me in the front seat of the kayak. I settled in, trying to get a feel for the paddle. I wondered how I'd ever get the hang of moving it through the water so we'd actually get anywhere.

"Ready?" Nate asked brightly from behind me.

"As I'll ever be."

We were pushed out onto the water and I instinctively held my paddle tighter, fearing I'd end up losing it.

"Relax, Liv. We're in no rush. We'll take it slowly until you get the hang of it." He continued to patiently explain to me the correct rhythm of moving the paddle through the water, and before I knew it, I was following his strokes as we glided along the river.

We slowly made our way down the canyon, with Nate pointing out areas of interest or wildlife. It was truly beautiful and serene being out on the water surrounded by nothing but cliffs and vegetation. It felt like we were the only two people on the planet.

When we hit an area of rapidly flowing water, I panicked, fearing we were going to capsize, and slammed my paddle into the water at the wrong angle. The move caused a big splash that ended up hitting Nate.

"You did that on purpose," he shouted, holding his paddle with one hand while wiping his eyes with the other. He chuckled then dropped a hand into the water to send a splash in my direction.

"Nate!" I yelled. "I can't believe you did that. You knew it was an accident!" I wasn't going to let him get away that. With a sly grin, I slammed the paddle on the water's surface again sending another flurry of water droplets over him.

"Oh, you wanna play, huh?"

Before I knew it, I was laughing hysterically as Nate and I splashed each other as the oblivious water continued carrying us along on our journey.

"Stop!" I screamed, fighting to catch my breath. "Stop." I leaned back so I could look at him. "Please stop."

Nate looked down on me with fond eyes and a broad smile. "Okay, JB, seeing as you asked so nicely, I'll stop. Do you want to rest up for a while? We can pull over somewhere if you want."

A few minutes later, we'd managed to navigate over into shallow water and pulled the kayak onto a secluded beach. With the sun now high in the sky, I removed my jacket, placing it on a rock to dry out before lying down on a small grass verge. Nate pulled off his hoodie, placing it next to my jacket before settling down next to me. I closed my eyes and sighed with contentment as the sun began to warm my chilled skin.

"This place is the last happy memory I have of my parents," Nate said quietly after a few moments of silence.

I peeled an eye open, shielding it from the sunlight with my hand. Nate was staring out at the water, throwing stones. His happy mood from minutes before had disappeared.

"Do you want to talk about it?"

He peered down at me with sad eyes, trying to decide if he wanted to talk or not.

"Like I said, we used to come here every year. My parents would rent a cottage and we'd spend our summers hiking, rock climbing, kayaking—you name it, we would do it." He covered his eyes with his sunglasses and looked out over the water again, remaining silent for a moment. "That was the compromise… or the illusion, to make them look good with their *friends*. Our parents were do-gooder's, Liv. Or liked to appear they were.... The trouble was that helping others became more important to them than Wes and I. The holiday once a year was their attempt at making up for the fact that the remaining fifty weeks of the year we hardly ever saw them."

He shifted onto his side and removed his glasses. Using his elbow to support himself, he rested his cheek in his palm and watched me. I could see his scattered thoughts and memories playing on his mind as his brow furrowed and his eyes clouded over and darkened. Mirroring his pose, I gave him an encouraging smile, letting him know he had my undivided attention.

"When we were little, we didn't really think anything of it. We were looked after by various nannies and babysitters. To us, it was the norm. Then, as we grew older, we became more aware of our lack of parental support. They were never at school events, never once sat down to go through homework with us, and if we dared question it, we would be punished.

"When I was fifteen, they started talking about wanting to travel to other countries to do their *helping work*." He said the last with such contempt and hatred, his whole body was shaking with his anger. Reaching over, I placed a reassuring hand on his arm and encouraged him to continue. I didn't want him to hurt, I hated seeing him so upset, but it was obvious he had been holding on to his feelings for too long. Now was the time to cut open the wound and let everything drain free.

Nate looked at my hand and stared at it as he continued. "By that point, I had started rebelling against them. I guess it was a way of trying to get even a tiny bit of their attention, even if it was for a tongue lashing or worse." I stiffened, understanding what he was implying. He gave me a small, sad smile and reached over to tuck a lock of wind-blown hair behind my ear. "I began sneaking out of the house whenever they went off to yet another meeting. That was how I met Bernie. He'd caught me trying to steal alcohol from a local store one day and gave me an ultimatum. He said I either had to join him to learn focus and respect or he would go to my parents and the police. I was more scared of what my parents might do than I was of the police or anything Bernie might do, so I agreed to go with him. He took me to this gym and made me work: cleaning things, taking out the rubbish, stuff like that. He also started showing me how to train, how to focus my anger and frustration into a controlled physical workout. I quickly became addicted. It was there I was first introduced to MMA.

"After my sixteenth birthday, my parents informed us they were selling the house moving to South America. They expected Wesley and me to go off and finish our education in some boarding school somewhere. They had it all planned out for us, even down to the courses we would take and what jobs we would eventually go into." He scoffed at the memory. "When I told them I had no intention of doing what they wanted, that I would be staying to work in the gym and studying to become a personal trainer, we had a massive argument. They told me I was stupid, calling me a worthless dunce who would never make anything of himself, so I packed a bag and left home without looking back. Four months later, they packed Wes off to some boarding school in Oxfordshire and left."

His eyes were glassy as he continued staring, unseeing into mine.

The loud call of a bird overhead snapped him back to the present. He blinked once, refocusing his gaze.

"I'm sorry!" he murmured, sitting up and pulling his features back into an unreadable mask. "I didn't mean to burden you with my dull history."

I scrambled up onto my knees next to him. I could read him so well now that I knew if I didn't say or do something he would withdraw from me again. We had come so far, and I understood the significance of him opening up to me. I wasn't about to let him take a step back.

"Nate, you haven't burdened me with anything. I'm glad you told me." I touched his face, stroking my fingertips along the sharp contours of his jaw. His hand flew to mine, holding my palm against his skin.

"I've never told anybody that before," he murmured softly.

I blinked in surprise. "Never?"

"Never. You must have figured out by now that I'm a very private person. It isn't anybody's business that Wes and I were the least of our parent's worries, that we were nothing but an inconvenient burden to them."

I bit my lip and searched his eyes, my heart breaking for the lost boy who felt so unloved.

"Liv, don't look at me like that," he whispered. "I don't want your pity."

Straddling his lap, I placed both palms on his face, ensuring he looked me directly in the eyes. "I don't pity you, Nate. I'm just trying to understand how that must have felt, what you must have gone through." I shook my head in disbelief. "My parents may be eccentric, but I know they love me and will do whatever they need to for me. They will always be there for me. I cannot imagine what it would be like if anything happened to them and they weren't around anymore."

Sadness briefly flashed across his face but was soon replaced with softness. "When we're done here and go back home, I'd like to meet them," he stated, pulling my hands from his face and clasping them over his chest.

"Oh? Why's that? So you can see where the

weirdness comes from?" I smirked, trying to lighten the mood.

"No, so I can thank them," he replied, all serious.

"Huh?"

"I want to thank them for bringing such a bright light into this world. You have illuminated my dull life, Liv." He leaned in and placed a soft kiss on my lips. My eyes fluttered closed and I sighed.

"After…" He paused momentarily. "Before you, everything was mechanical and monotonous," he whispered against my lips.

"You've made my life interesting too, Golden boy." I giggled, feeling his fingers tighten around my waist.

"Interesting, huh?" In typical Nate style, he flipped us easily so I was on my back. He loomed over me, playfully narrowing his eyes. "How interesting?"

"Nate!" I warned, seeing the mischievous smirk on his face. "Don't you dare."

I tried wriggling away, but he had me pinned with his hips and legs.

"Nate! No! Please!" I screeched when he began to run his fingers along my sides, tickling me mercilessly. "Nate!" I couldn't breathe through my laughter.

Suddenly his lips were on mine, crashing down with a passionate force that left me breathless for an entirely different reason. I wiggled and squirmed under his weight, this time trying desperately to get as close to him as possible. Trailing my hands around his back, I grabbed the hem of his T-shirt and yanked it up until Nate had to break the kiss to allow the shirt over his head. As soon as it was free, he connected our lips again, groaning when I ran my fingertips along his skin. A hand worked its way underneath the hem of my t-shirt and up to my breast. With a gentleness that was in stark contrast to his demanding lips, he cupped me, softly squeezing, assessing the weight in his palm. All the sensations of his touch combined with the sounds and smells of nature around us, it was all too much. I moaned into his mouth and fumbled around for the zip on his jeans. I needed him. Right there.

He pulled back, breathing heavily. "Liv, we need to stop before we end up getting arrested for public indecency."

I lifted my head and quickly peered around. "We're in the middle of nowhere, Nate. No one will see."

He smiled down at me with fondness and more than a little desire. "As tempting as that sounds, we can't risk it." At that moment, loud splashing broke the peacefulness of our surroundings. Looking along the river, a group of five kayaks filled with teenagers rounded the bend, heading in our direction. Nate collapsed on me as we burst into laughter.

"Come on, JB, I think we'd better get out of here."

~CHAPTER EIGHTEEN~

Sucking in a deep, calming breath, I rubbed my sweaty palms along my thighs. This was it. This would be the make or break morning for Nate's French facility… and for me to prove to Adam's dad that I could cut it in his company. I had never felt so nervous in my life.

Cassie was driving me into Grasse to meet with a local architect who would be taking over from me to see Nate's building project through to completion. As a Brit, there was only so far I could take the project, and without the relevant French licences, or being part of the relevant governing body, I had to give over my plans and hope someone else would approve them.

"Nervous?" she asked, looking over at me with a smile.

I bobbed my head and continued staring out the window. If I said anything, I thought I might be sick.

Nate had wanted to attend, in fact he was severely pissed off that he couldn't, but duty called and he'd had to stay home to train. Later, he would be meeting with a journalist and photographer from some men's fitness magazine. It was times like this that I had to take a step back and appreciate who Nate was. On a day to day basis, to me he was just Nate, part time personal trainer, business owner, fitness freak, friend and my occasional lover. To the world, he was Nathan Oakes, superstar. King of the cage.

Slowly, the scenery around us changed. Areas became less fields, more houses until we were driving through larger towns. I took it all in. In some ways, each one was just another town, not so dissimilar to home. In other ways, the air around us seemed to vibrate with culture and uniqueness. On more than one occasion, I had to stop myself from screaming for Cassie to stop the car so I could whip out my phone to snap a few photos.

Eventually the GPS navigated us through the streets of Grasse into a small business development of modern, low-rise, nondescript buildings. Had it not been for the stunning backdrop of mountains in the far distance, I might have been disappointed by the lack of character the brick buildings offered.

We pushed through the doors welcoming us into the offices of Monsieur Perryn Rondeau. At least I presumed it was a welcome message that the bronze placard was displaying. My concept of the French language was definitely of the 'I have no idea' variety. That is why Cassie had accompanied me. Not only was she an excellent masseuse, a fantastic fighter and trainer – that detail had surprised me when I'd learned of her amateur fighting record – and generally lovely lady, she was also fluent in French.

"Ready for this?" she asked, as we waited to be greeted by the receptionist.

I took a deep breath. "Yes. Let's hope all my research has paid off and everything in here," I held up the cylinder containing Nate's plans, "is okay. I know Nate is keen to get everything agreed so he can move forward with the project."

Cassie gave a brief smile and then spoke to the receptionist. My eyes darted back and forth between the two as I tried to work out what they were saying. It was useless though, I really didn't have a clue. A few minutes later, we were shown into an office and a short, plump man with a balding head stood to great us. Cassie held out her hand, introducing herself, and then gestured towards me.

"Madame," the guy, who I presumed was Monsieur Rondaeu, indicated for me to take a seat at a small conference table tucked into the corner of his office. I sat and looked around the room, analysing and appraising the artwork on the walls. Each piece was an architectural drawing beside what looked like a photograph or painting of the finished building. Some were beautiful, others had me wondering what I could have done better.

"Liv?"

I blinked in Cassie's direction and then heat shot into my cheeks when I realised I'd zoned out of the conversation I hadn't been able to understand anyway. I cleared my throat. "Sorry?" I gave Monsieur Rondaeu an apologetic smile.

"Monsieur Rondaeu would like to see the plans."

"Oh, right, sorry." With shaky hands, I fumbled with the cardboard cylinder until, eventually, the papers spilled out onto the table. With the papers laid out neatly, I stood tall and took a deep breath. I couldn't believe how ridiculously nervous I was. In reality, the meeting should have been fairly straight forward. I'd hand over the plans and Rondaeu would do the rest. I was just anxious that everything went smoothly for Nate.

We spent the next thirty minutes looking over the plans, with Cassie translating queries and discussions for us. When we spilled back out into the car park, my shoulders slumped as I exhaled a deep breath.

"Thank God that is over. I don't think I've ever felt so nervous," I said.

She laughed. "At one point in there I thought you might pass out on me."

"I thought I was definitely going to pass out," I grumbled.

"You did great, Liv. Monsieur Rondeau seemed impressed with your plans, for a woman."

"What?" I shot around, slamming my hands on my hips. "For a woman? What the fuck? A woman is not capable of being creative in this field? I bet he thought I was Nate's PA, sent to present on his behalf. That's what the funny looks were for, weren't they? He didn't believe I'd done them, did he? Well fuck that."

Cassie held a hand over her stomach as she laughed. "Yes, he was shocked, Liv, but I don't think he saw you as the pretty assistant. Your integrity remains intact."

"Well that's all right then," I grumbled, striding towards the car. "So we are all good?"

She held up the remote to unlock the car. "We're all good. He said everything is fine and Nate should be able to start building in a few months."

I tucked myself into the car, smiling. Mission accomplished.

***

FAME, IT WAS a whole new ball game. I was fast learning that being rich and famous wasn't all it was cracked up to be. With only two days to go until the fight, we had packed up our stuff and returned to the splendour, glamour and luxury of Monaco. I immediately missed the peacefulness and solitude of the countryside. The Monaco we had left behind weeks before was not the same place we returned to. Apparently, Nate's fight was a huge deal. All around there were posters, billboards and flyers, all publicising the highly anticipated rematch between Damián 'Dark Destroyer' Sanchez and Nathan 'Golden Boy' Oakes. The place was buzzing with MMA fever and everyone wanted to be a part of it.

After only six hours of being back, I'd learned it would be nearly impossible for Nate to go outside of the hotel without security. I'd begged him to go for a walk with me as night fell and the walls of the giant suite seemed to hem me in. I missed our evening stroll down to our rock and had already begun to feel claustrophobic. We hadn't even made it beyond the hotel lobby before loyal fans were clamouring for his attention.

Autograph books, napkins, photos and even a voluptuous chest—I was glad he politely declined that one—were all pushed in Nate's direction with the demand he sign them. I found myself being pushed further and further back until I could no longer see him in the throng of people hotel security was having trouble containing. In the end, I gave up and strolled into the bar. At least there I could sip on a sparkling water and watch in amusement the circus taking place in our regal surroundings.

I caught the bartender's attention and ordered my drink, propping myself up on a bar stool. Pulling my phone out of my pocket, I checked for messages. There was a long, drawn out voicemail from my mum which I couldn't help but listen to. She was as crazy and eccentric as ever, telling me about the latest plant she had purchased. I did get a tear in my eye though, when she said she couldn't wait for me to return home, how proud she was of me and how she hoped I'd learned a lot, but she wanted me home. She missed me. I swiped the tear away and scrolled to my text messages. There was one from Adam.

Still worried about you. Wish I was there. Miss you.

I sent a quick reply telling him to stop being so silly. I was fine and would be home soon. Nate still had a crowd around him, so I opened my browser, deciding I'd do a little bit of research on what I should expect from the fight. I'd seen boxing matches on TV, and had caught glimpses of the fights they'd shown on the screens at Golden Oakes when I first started going, but I had never really watched an MMA fight before. It seemed like a lifetime ago that I had scoffed at the manliness of the men tumbling around on the gym TV screen. Having witnessed first-hand what Nate was capable of, my view of the sport had somewhat changed and I was eagerly anticipating the fight. Pulling up a site detailing this latest contest, I began reading about the apparent feud between Nate and Sanchez. It explained how Sanchez had not taken his previous defeat well and was determined to win this time. There was a small article alluding to the fact that this was some sort of personal grudge match for Sanchez. The details as to why were unclear, but it had something to do with the death of his father. I remembered the incident outside the club when a reporter had mentioned something similar and wondered how Sanchez's father was mixed up in all of this.

Wondering if he knew anything about the story, I lifted my gaze, and instead of finding Nate, I noticed an unknown man watching me. The next thing I knew, I was blinded by a bright, white light. And then another, and another.

"That is her… Miss Buchanan, I have a few questions. What is your relationship with Nathan Oakes?"

"Miss Buchanan, is it true that Nate had a breakdown during his training camp?"

"What are your thoughts on Sanchez's allegations?"

"Is it true Mr. Oakes plans to build an illegal, underground fighting arena?"

My eyes darted around the small bar area as more lights began flashing and more reporters joined the foray.

"Miss Buchanan…"

"Olivia…"

My breathing became laboured and my heart hammered a relentless frenzy in my chest. I began backing away, desperate to distance myself from the piranhas looking to get to Nate through me. My head shook frantically as I moved backwards.

"No comment," I managed to croak. "I have no comment."

When the backs of my knees brushed a chair, I lost my balance, falling backwards and landing hard on the unforgiving tiled flooring.

"Get the fuck away from her," Nate bellowed, rushing into the room and knocking a reporter out of his way. Without another word, he scooped me up into his arms and rushed out of the room. The shouts and camera flashes continued, following us until the doors of the elevator closed behind us. I rested my head against Nate's shoulder, trying in vain to control my breathing. It had been an intense experience, one I had no desire to ever repeat. Yet I knew, whilst I was around Nate— especially while he was so high profile, we wouldn't be able to escape the fans or paparazzi.

Lowering me to my feet, he held my face in his palms, searching my eyes. "I'm sorry. I'm so fucking sorry. I should never have let you be alone." His voice sounded strangled with fear and regret.

"It's not your fault. I was forced back. I was fine until they cornered me in the bar. Should they have even been in there?" I replied softly.

Unable to break eye contact, Nate shook his head. "No, security should have been able to stop them getting in," he breathed, inching in closer.

The elevator slowly ascended towards our floor but

we barely noticed. It was like we were stuck in the moment, paralysed by the emotions raging through us. Nate's hand skimmed around my neck and buried into my hair. "I need to kiss you," he said, edging his face towards mine.

The moment the warmth of his lips touched mine, my eyes closed and I sagged against him. The adrenaline of the scene downstairs drained away, leaving me powerless to resist. Not that I wanted to. His hand sank into my hair and gripped whilst his body leaned into mine, restraining me against the wall while his lips moved across mine, firm, insistent and beseeching.

The elevator doors opened on our floor. Without breaking the kiss, Nate walked us the few steps across the hallway to our suite, fumbling with the swipe card until the door finally swung open. Inside, we stumbled until my back hit the wall. My heart pounded with the overwhelming need for Nate consuming me. He twisted his other hand into my hair and deepened our kiss, exploring the caverns of my mouth as if he needed to commit everything to memory. His posture shifted as he groaned a low, sexy sound from the back of his throat.

Breaking the kiss, he lifted me off my feet, wrapping my legs around his waist. He kept his forehead resting against mine, our eyes locked, as he silently walked us into his bedroom. Tenderly, he laid me back on his bed. We hadn't spoken a word, but we didn't need to. The raw magnetism between us said everything, as did the unified pounding of our hearts.

With slow, sensual ease, Nate removed my clothing then stood staring down on my body. He'd seen me naked before, but this time, with the look of hunger and wonder in his eyes, I felt more exposed than ever.

"You are so fucking beautiful, Liv," he said quietly, removing his own clothes.

"What, even my big fat butt?" I laughed.

"Especially your butt," he said climbing on to the bed. "From the moment I first saw you, I knew there was something about you. I tried to deny it, I tried to fight it but it was inevitable. We were meant to end up right here, right now."

I sighed in pleasure as he stretched out along me, feathering kisses along my neck and collar bone. Fisting the sheets beneath me, I felt powerless against his advances as slowly, he coaxed my body and mind into a frenzy with soft lips and gentle fingers.

Moving above me, he supported his weight on his forearms and looked down, bright grey, intense eyes searching mine. "I want you, Liv. All of you. Just me and you."

I swallowed hard, knowing what he was asking for. The power of his gaze spoke of his longing. Staring into the deepest recesses of his beautiful eyes, I debated the moment. We'd spoken about using protection, but I trusted that he was clean. He had, after all, been through several pre-fight check-ups. With a nod, I shifted position, allowing him to settle in between my thighs, and with his eyes burning into mine, he slowly sank himself inside my body until there was no distance between us, no gap. We were one. I was him and he was me. Together. Perfect. Feeling overwhelmed by the moment, I sucked in a deep breath, filling my lungs with air and slowly exhaling. Nate was tender, passionate, generous and caring as he moved inside me, never once breaking the connection of our eyes. He wasn't fucking, not this time, this time we were making love. We were laying our hearts on the line and hoping the other person scooped it up and cherished it. At least, I hoped that's what it was because I was lost; lost to the moment, lost to the pleasure, lost to him.

His movements were strong and in control, keeping a regular, slow and sensual rhythm. My orgasm crept up on me, washing over me with such power it stole my breath. I could do no more than gasp and hold on, soaking in the feelings, as the tremors rippled through my body. Nate sucked in a deep breath, his mouth opening without words as he thrust into me one last powerful time, trying to bury himself inside as deep as possible before dropping his forehead to mine and stilling over me.

"Olivia Buchanan, I fucking love you," he whispered, and my heart stopped beating, replaced with a million butterflies taking flight in my chest. *I love you too*. I wanted to say the words back, but my throat was too clogged with emotion.

We continued staring into each other's eyes, wonder and awe evident in his gaze as much as I could feel in mine. In that profound moment of pleasure, I knew my life would never be the same again. Nate had taken me mind, body and soul. It was the moment I knew I'd lost. I could no longer deny my feelings. Whether he knew it or not, Nate had won my heart

.

~CHAPTERNINETEEN~

I AWOKE WITH A SMILE. Even knowing what lay ahead of us over the next few days, I couldn't shift the memories of the previous night from my mind. There was no way of telling what it meant for Nate and me, only time could determine that. In my heart though, I knew I loved him. I wanted to be by his side, to support him through his struggles, the expansion of his businesses, to watch as my designs became his reality and to see what he would make of the opportunities he was creating. I wanted it all. But I knew that it would all have to wait. Beating Sanchez had to be his focus.

Beside me, Nate shifted in the bed, moving closer and throwing an arm over my body. I giggled when he mumbled something in his sleep and relaxed. It felt good to know he seemed to need me as much as I needed him.

My smile faded when my fingers ran across the outline of the tattoo on his chest. We hadn't spoken any more of his revelations the day we'd been kayaking. I knew he'd tried to brush the impact of his childhood off, making out that he was unaffected by the cruel acts of his parents, but I was livid for him. How anybody could abandon their own children was beyond me. Still, he had come through it all. He was strong, confident and successful in everything he did. In many ways, I wished his parents could see what a fine man he had turned into. I was proud of him, even if his own flesh and blood hadn't been.

I remained cuddled against his body, enjoying the image in front of me and the feel of his warm skin against my cheek. I'd been here before, watching him sleep and enjoying the view. This felt different. This time it felt deeper, like I had some new-found connection to him. Awake, he consumed me with his power and masculinity. In slumber, he cloaked me with peace and calmness.

Nate's eyes fluttered open. "Hi." He smiled a sleepy grin.

"Hi yourself." I returned his smile. "How are you feeling?"

"Waking up next to you? Never better."

I sighed, happy and content, as his lips trailed kisses along my shoulder. "You're wrong you know," he whispered in my ear, trailing a finger over the confused furrow of my brow. "You won! I'm the one who lost."

Realising I'd spoken my thoughts aloud the previous evening, I buried my face in his shoulder, embarrassed.

"Hey," he murmured, tilting my chin to look at

him. "Nothing to get embarrassed about, JB. It was the sweetest thing I've ever heard." He pressed a kiss to my forehead and then swung his legs out of the bed. He sat there for a moment, his shoulders slumped and his head dropped. "Liv, what happened last night... I need you to know that it meant *everything* to me... I'm just... With my past, I'm... I'm not sure where we go from here." Pulling himself to his feet, he turned to face me. "Tell me where we go from here."

Scrambling across the covers, I jumped out of bed and wrapped my arms around his waist. Looking into his eyes, I said, "We go wherever we damn well like, Mr. Oakes, because you're the ultimate. You are the *golden boy* and I want to be with you." The tension in his body disappeared in an instant as he laughed heartily.

He drew me in close and encased me in his strong arms. "I love you, Olivia Buchanan."

"And I love you too, Nathan Oakes." This time the words flew from my lips freely and proudly.

***

MEDIA CONFERENCES, INTERVIEWS... *weigh ins*, they were full of gossip mongers looking for their next juicy tidbit to twist and turn into a wonderfully fabricated story. They were all an act, a carefully choreographed role play designed to heighten emotions and give the journalists something to report. Or at least that's how it seemed. I knew it was how Nate felt.

"What do they prove?" he'd grumbled during our short journey to the casino where the fight would be taking place the following day. We were going in for his official weigh in. "Fuck all, that's what. As far as I'm concerned, our hands and feet should do the talking during the fight. It shouldn't matter what I say in front of a bunch of idiots who are only there because they are told to be and not for the love of the sport. This shit should be done behind closed doors."

I sank back into the leather seat of the Cayenne and let him have his rant. I knew some journalists had a genuine passion and reported the facts, but many, like the ones who had hounded me the night before, didn't. I wondered if joining him today had been such a good idea. If any one of those men or women sitting in the audience said anything Nate didn't like, I had no doubt he would fly off the handle. My being there made that much more likely.

The auditorium was packed when I snuck in the back with Cassie. We'd been warned by Nate's PR people that it would be best to stay low key and unnoticed. The incident in the hotel had spread like wildfire, with articles talking about forbidden love, fights with journalists, drug abuse on Nate's part—yeah, that one made us laugh seeing as his pre-fight test had been clear—among other things, popping up all over the net. Cassie assured me it was all part and parcel of the media hype. Nate needed to stayed focused and not let the attention get to him.

We crept along the outside wall, staying in the shadows, making sure we still had a good view of the stage. Cassie explained what the process was and what I could expect. It all felt so surreal. The room was loud, with journalists, sponsors, promotions people and fans all fighting to be heard over one another. There was a buzz in the room that was difficult not to get caught up in.

A gentleman in his early forties stepped on the stage along with a few other official looking people. They spoke amongst themselves for a few minutes before the main guy stepped forward holding a microphone branded with the main fight sponsor's logo. The flash of camera lights grew insistent and the noise in the room lifted to almost unbearable levels when he welcomed the challenger, "Damián 'the Dark Destroyer' Sanchez" on to the stage. It was the first time I'd seen Sanchez in person. He had a similar stature to Nate, tall, lean and totally ripped. If it wasn't for his darker, South American skin tone, he could have been mistaken for Nate from a distance. They had the same dark hair, cropped short on the sides, and the same gait that immediately commanded respect.

I watched on in surprise as he stripped down to just a small pair of black briefs before climbing on to a large scale set up in the centre of the stage. I didn't like how the few women in the audience screamed. If they screamed like that for Sanchez, they would be going frantic over Nate. I selfishly wanted that vision of him wearing next to nothing reserved for my eyes only.

They concluded Sanchez's weigh in, announcing his weight to the crowd. Then the guy with the mic introduced Nate. "Ladies and gentlemen, your champion, the one you're dying to see. Nathan 'Golden Boy' Oaaaaakes!" The place erupted. Flash bulbs went off like a merciless electrical storm lighting a dark night sky. As Nate made his way to the stage, people reached out to shake his hand and called his name. Women screamed, telling him how much they loved and wanted him. *He's all mine bitches.* I sagged against the wall trying to grasp the reality of the situation. The cool, focused man walking onto the stage was mine… all mine. The room suddenly felt like a furnace and I wasn't sure if it was my reaction to Nate stripping down or if the room had actually become hotter from all the activity.

I fanned my face frantically, causing Cassie to laugh and nudge me in the shoulder. It was announced that Nate too had weighed in at two hundred pounds. There really was nothing between the two contenders as far as weight went. I stood up tall again, standing on my tip-toes to get a better view when Nate and Sanchez squared off to each other. I'd never seen such venom from Nate before. There were lots of hateful glares on both sides, and even a few pushes, before Bernie was pulling Nate away and someone from Sanchez's team pulled him back too. Being new to the whole scene, I wasn't sure if it was all for show or if they genuinely detested each other that much. I figured it would certainly make for an interesting fight the next night.

The compere guy approached Sanchez with his microphone, yelling over the noise of the crowd. "Damián, you've had two flawless bouts since your last fight with Nathan, how confident are you that you will beat him this time?"

"I *know* I am going to beat him," Sanchez replied with a strong Brazilian accent.

"There have been a lot of allegations that this is more than just a title rematch for you. What are your thoughts?"

Sanchez glared evilly at Nate. "This is definitely a

grudge match. I'm looking for revenge." Without another word, he stepped away and into the crowd of his team.

The compere moved over to Nate, looking a little bewildered. "Nathan, how do you feel about coming out of retirement? Has your time away impacted on your fighting at all?" Nate looked less than impressed with the question and replied with a mediocre answer about working flat out with Bernie and his new trainer who had both worked him to his limits and prepared him for the fight of his life.

"What are your thoughts on this grudge Sanchez has?"

Nate narrowed his eyes on his opponent. "I don't have a clue what he is talking about. He needs to keep his mouth shut and do his talking on the canvas tomorrow evening."

***

I SPENT THE rest of the evening hanging out with Cassie and reading in my room. Nate attended more interviews and a photo shoot, and by the time he got back, he was so wound up and frustrated he went to the hotel gym to work it out in there. I hadn't dared even say anything to him because the look in his eyes frightened me. I just wanted the fight to be over with so we could try to work out how we moved forward as a couple.

The next morning when I opened my eyes, I felt groggy and nervous, not happy and content as I had been the previous day. Nate, Wes, Cassie, Bernie and Roy had left early for whatever pre-fight stuff they had to do. I was left in our suite with the instructions to be dressed and ready for the car that would pick me up in the evening to take me to the casino.

I decided to eat breakfast alone out on the terrace. My hope was that the morning sun and sea breeze would help ease the churning sensation I had in my stomach. Something was amiss, but I couldn't put my finger on what it was. Yes, I was nervous for the fight—Nate was deliberately putting himself on the receiving end of someone's fist. But I knew it wasn't just that. He was a well-trained martial artist who could defend himself and counter with a deadly blow. So why did I feel so worried?

***

By NOON, I was restless beyond belief. I felt cocooned in the suite, unable to go out for a walk for fear I might be recognised by any number of journalists or fans. Since my face had been plastered all over the internet for the previous two days, it wasn't worth the risk of another run in with anyone this close to the event. I tried watching TV, but the only English channels were either sports or news. The news was full of doom and gloom and the sports ones full of pre-fight build up. Neither helped my mood. I'd tried watching a movie but having to try to concentrate on the subtitles and watch the film at the same time just annoyed me. I turned it off and threw the remote on the bed in a huff.

I checked my phone for the millionth time, hoping to have received a message or something from Nate. There was just a text from my mum wishing him good luck and saying she had booked the fight on pay per view. I had to laugh. Unless it was a gardening show, mum never watched TV. I could just imagine her and dad sitting down to watch the fight. Mum would be watching through her fingers, shaking every time a punch or kick was landed, and dad would be mumbling about what the point of it all was.

With nothing else to do and no one to talk to, I grabbed my ereader and sunglasses and settled myself on one of the sun loungers on the terrace. It was a nice, warm, sunny day and I hoped the sea breeze would help ease my nerves and agitation. After reading and re-reading the same page over and over as my mind whirled a million miles an hour, I made one last attempt at understanding what I was looking at. The uneasy, nervous feeling I'd had all day would not disappear.

Finally, I absorbed the words on the page and moved to the next when my phone rang.

The screen showed me the handsome profile picture of my best friend, smiling with me at the last Ashworth-Moore Christmas party. "Adam!" I chirped, hitting the button to accept the call.

"Hi, Liv. How's it going?" The distinct sound of concern was missing; in fact, I could hear a faint smile in his voice.

I grinned. "It's going. I'm so glad you called, I missed your voice."

"Yeah?"

"Yeah. Things are kind of crazy around here right now, and I'm all on my own. I needed to hear a friendly voice. How is everything with you?"

"It's great now."

I pushed to my feet and walked towards the railing, staring out over the marina. "Oh? Why, what's happened?"

"I'm about to meet up with a gorgeous girl. I haven't seen her for a while."

"That's great, Ad. Are you going anywhere nice?"

He chuckled. "She's staying in some swank hotel. I'm meeting her there."

I smiled. Adam deserved to be happy. "Anyone I know?"

The door opened and closed behind me. "You could say that."

I swung around and gasped. "You're here?" I dropped my phone on to a lounger and ran across the terrace, throwing my arms around his waist. "Oh my God, you really are here. It is so good to see you!"

Adam tentatively wrapped his arms around me and then tugged me in close. "It's good to see you too, princess."

"What are you doing here?" I asked, tipping my head back to look at him. He was a sight for sore eyes. Having not seen him for over eight weeks, I suddenly realised how much I'd missed him.

"I was worried about you," he said, tucking a strand of hair behind my ear.

"I kept telling you, I'm fine."

"So why did you look like you were about slit your wrists?"

I pulled away, reclaiming my seat. "I did not look like I was about to do away with myself. Jeez, Ad, dramatic much?"

Pulling out the chair next to mine, Adam sat, appraising me.

"Would you stop looking at me like that. You're freaking me out," I grumbled.

"You look different," he said softly.

I stared down at my hands. "I feel different."

"So, are you and Nate... you know... together?"

"Honestly? I think so. I hope so. But, it's all so new, and with the fight and Nate being hounded by the press... I don't know, everything just seems so screwed up right now," I admitted as my lower lip quivered.

Adam took my hand and squeezed. "Liv, you know my feelings. I meant every word I said before you left. But first and foremost you are my best friend. I'm here because I'm concerned about you, and I want to make sure you are okay. So, tell me everything. Let me help you."

For the first time in a long, long time, I cried. Having Adam with me brought out so many emotions I'd been trying desperately to repress. The last six week had been a journey of so many ups and downs and it wasn't even over yet. As I wept into my palms, Adam jumped from his seat and pulled me into his warm, comforting, familiar embrace.

"Shhh," he cooed, brushing his lips across my forehead and running his hands down my back. "Tell me what's going on, Liv."

I sniffled and moved away, swiping at my wet eyes with the back of my hand. As my head lifted, movement inside the suite caught my attention, a shadow moved away quickly. Hoping Nate was back, I ran past Adam and yanked the French doors open. The room inside was still except for the click of the main suite door. I ran to that and pulled it open, but the hall outside was empty. Whoever had been in the room had managed to get in the elevator immediately and was gone.

Closing the door slowly, I walked back into the main room. Adam stood just inside the terrace doors, watching me carefully.

"Someone was in here," I said quietly.

"Who?" he asked, sounding concerned.

"I don't know. I didn't see." I suddenly realized how things could have looked between Adam and me. I closed my eyes and shook my head. As if things weren't crazy enough as they were, I now had to worry that someone had got the wrong impression. And what if that someone had been Nate?

Adam crossed his arms over his chest. "Liv, I think you need to fill me in. Something's going on here. I've never seen you so nervy."

Sinking down on to one of the plush sofas, I began regaling Adam with the soap opera that had been my life since leaving London.

"Wow," he said when I was finished.

"The joys of being connected to the rich and famous, huh?"

Adam joined me on the couch, looking a little shell shocked. "I wish I'd been able to come sooner."

"Why? There's nothing you can do. This is all part of Nate's life. This is who he is," I replied with a shrug.

"You really like him?"

I looked him in the eye when I told him, "I love him, Ad."

He nodded, and to my relief, he seemed accepting, if a little resigned. "Okay. I'll say no more on that matter. I just hope he doesn't hurt you, Liv, because so help me God, MMA fighter or not, I will kill him if he does."

I gave him a small, grateful smile and decided to change the subject. My best friend was with me and I wanted to hear all of his news.

~CHAPTER TWENTY~

"STOP FIDGETING, YOU LOOK BEAUTIFUL," Adam told me for the umpteenth time since leaving the hotel.

I gazed down my body at the tiny black dress that had mysteriously appeared in my wardrobe, along with a note saying *'wear me tonight'*. "I'm not sure. Don't you think it's a bit too short and tight for my voluptuous figure?" I tugged on the hem hoping it would give me more coverage, but all that did was expose more cleavage than I felt comfortable with.

Adam stopped in front of me and placed his hands on my shoulders, holding me firmly in place so he could look me dead in the eyes. "You. Look. Beautiful. You have an amazing body, and yes, the dress probably is too short. But I'm a hot blooded male who appreciates the finer things in life, so I won't grumble." He smirked and my eyes rolled at his comment. Suddenly, Adam's gaze darted over my shoulder. His brows pulled together as he narrowed his eyes. "Or maybe I will." I followed his gaze and noticed a group of men staring at my legs.

"Well, I guess we'd better take our seats then, before you start your grumbling," I joked, wrapping my arm through his.

Earlier in the day I'd arranged for Adam to join me ringside. I'd been feeling uncomfortable about attending on my own, so having him accompany me was perfect. As promised, there had been a car waiting for us outside the hotel that whisked us through the busy streets to the exclusive casino resort the fight was being staged in. When we stepped out of the car, I felt like a celebrity A-lister. Camera flashes went off around us as fans and photographers alike each fought for a photo opportunity.

Walking into the casino lobby, I finally understood just how big of a deal these things were. Huddled in little groups, drinking champagne and chatting, were stars of stage and screen as well as a big named musician and several well-known sports stars. Wide-eyed and more than a little intimidated, I'd grabbed two glasses of champagne from a passing waiter and nudged Adam into a quieter corner. I stood awkwardly, pulling at and fussing with my dress, feeling out of place against the glamour surrounding us. Adam simply wrapped an arm around me and laughed, telling me it was all part of the lifestyle of the rich and famous. I pouted and told him that I wasn't rich or famous. Then I'd looked up and seen the huge banners of Nate hanging from the ceiling, swaying in the air conditioned breeze. I'd gulped, realising that being involved with Nate meant being involved with events like this. It was a part of *his* world.

The arena was as I expected yet a total surprise all at the same time. I knew MMA fights were popular, and I'd had an idea there would be a lot of people there, but as we stepped through the door, the deafening noise of chanting fans, whistles and pounding music was almost unbearable. The room was dark, save for the coloured laser lights darting around and the spotlights centring on the monstrous cage in the centre.

The buzz was already at fever pitch from the few undercard fights that had already taken place. When I learned that Wes had won his fight with a TKO in the first round, I screamed and flung my arms around Adam, kissing his cheek in joy. He'd stiffened at first but then laughed with me and hugged me back. It was hard not to get caught up in the atmosphere, and as my glass of champagne began to mellow me out, I soaked up the vibe and began to enjoy myself.

During another undercard fight between two bantamweights, a gargantuan of a man with buzzed hair, wearing a crisp black suit, dark grey shirt, black tie and a barely visible earpiece, came over.

"Miss Buchanan, would you come with me please," he said.

I looked at Adam, who looked at Colossus and then back at me and shrugged.

"Where are we going," I shouted, grabbing my bag as I stood.

"Mr Oakes would like to see you," he replied and began striding off in front of me. I shot a *what-the-hell?* look at Adam and quickly followed behind. A minute later, we were navigating through corridors littered with people, some in sportswear, others in suits. They all looked at me curiously before continuing with their phone calls or conversations.

Eventually we stopped outside a closed door and Colossus knocked. The door slowly opened, revealing Nate sitting on a massage bench. He was already prepared for the fight, with his hands and ankles bandaged with blue wraps. His torso was bare and already glistened with a sheen of sweat, and he wore nothing but his black silk shorts. The tattoos covering his body were more prominent than I'd ever seen them, rippling with each movement he made.

Bernie stood behind him, reeling off directions and advice, but Nate just sat there, his head and shoulders slumped forward as he looked at the ground between his spread thighs. My throat closed up at the sad, lonely image sitting before me. I had expected him to be pumped up and raring to go.

Cassie appeared from behind the door and gave me a hug. "He needs you, Liv," she said with a weak smile and called over to Bernie. Bernie looked up and, seeing me in the doorway, whispered something to Nate then quietly left, closing the door behind them. Nate and I had been left alone.

"Hi," I said, stepping further into the room. His head shot up, his eyes probing mine as I inched closer.

"You wanted to see me?" I asked, stepping in front of him.

"Tell me you're mine," he growled, piercing me with dark eyes.

"I'm yours," I said without hesitation. "What's this about, Nate?" I took a further tentative step forward, his look unnerving me.

"You said you'd fought, Liv. You said I'd won. That no matter what you were mine."

Searching his eyes, I saw vulnerability in him I hadn't seen before. "You have. I am."

Suddenly he winced, his eyes looked pained. "Nate, what's wrong?" The feeling of unease I'd felt all morning began to resurface.

He shook his head. "Nothing, I'm fine. Liv, if that's true, tell me, what is *he* doing here?"

My brows pulled in with confusion. "Who?"

"Him," he roared, waving an arm in the general direction of the arena.

Suddenly it made sense. "If you're talking about Adam, he was worried about me. He wanted to be here to support me. And you."

Nate looked down and rubbed at his temple, battling with his own thoughts.

"Nate, I promise, you won. There is nothing between Adam and me. I love you," I said desperately, needing him to understand.

The table shook as Nate jumped off, sending it scooting back several inches. "I saw you, Liv," he hissed getting into my face. "I came back to surprise you. I wanted a moment of fucking peace in this crazy day to enjoy some quiet time with you."

"There was nothing to see," I said, pleading. "Why are you being like this?"

"He was fucking kissing you, Liv. He was all over you." His voice broke as he closed his eyes. "He was touching you."

"Nate, no!" I flung myself forward, determined to show him I was his. "It wasn't like that, I promise. Please understand," I begged.

315

"He had his lips on you," he whispered.

"He was just comforting me. I was crying for *you*, Nate. I was overwhelmed by what I feel for *you*, about everything I've been through during this trip. He was being my friend. He knows I love *you*."

He paused, his hand lifting but stopping before it touched me.

"You were crying?" he finally asked sadly and rubbed his thumb along my cheek. "Because of me?" I bit my lip and looked away. The pain and regret in his eyes was killing me. "Fuck! Liv, I'm so sorry." His arms wrapped around me instantaneously. Hugging me tight to his chest, he buried his nose in my hair.

"I have never been scared of anything in my life. Even when I left home not knowing where I was going or what I would do, I never felt fear. But seeing you in another man's arms, Liv, I was absolutely fucking terrified."

Sagging against the warmth of his skin, I buried my face into his neck and circled my arms around his waist. "I never wanted this, Nate. I had no intentions of falling for anyone. I was career focused and love was not an option. But you... you drew me in. How could I not end up falling for you?"

I breathed him in, savouring his unique scent, feeling immediately at ease. It was like he had become my strength. Without him, I was comfortable and had survived. In his arms, I felt indestructible. He gave me strength, peace and a sense of belonging. I belonged to him.

Our moment of peace and contentment was broken by the sound of the door opening and footsteps crossing the tiled floor.

"Sorry to break this up, you two lovebirds, but Nate needs to get ready." Bernie laughed, strolling over to Nate to check his wrist and ankle wraps.

"I guess I better get back to my seat," I whispered backing away.

Nate kept his eyes on me until I was at the door. "Remember, Liv, I've already fought and won." I smiled and mothed *I love you* as I backed out.

Back in the auditorium, I dropped into my seat and took another look around the room. Every seat was now occupied and the growing anticipation of the crowd had reached a whole new level. Suddenly, nothing felt real. Looking around the hundreds of people that believed in Nate and were there to support him was intimidating as much as it was pleasing. But fear began to slither through my veins once again. I couldn't help but hope the optimism and faith of all these people was founded because I was suddenly terrified for Nate. I had a sinking feeling in my gut that I wasn't sure was just down to nerves.

By the time the compere had climbed into the cage, the room had roared to life. While everyone else was chanting and calling out Nate's name, I wanted to run and beg him not to fight. The ominous feeling that had hounded me all day now totally consumed me. Totally oblivious to my inner fears, the room around me had become a hive of activity. Fans eagerly called for the main fight of the evening, while the security presence on all doors and along the main walkway through the crowd doubled. The lights went completely out and there was a moment of utter silence, the calm before the storm. Suddenly, a thumping dance track filled the room while strobe and laser lights danced. It should

317

have been an exciting time. Instead, I feared every moment.

After being introduced, Sanchez appeared at the top of the main walkway and slowly made his way down. I felt physically ill watching him bouncing around, lifting his hands in the air and fist bumping fans as though he'd already won.

When Nate's name rang out around the arena, the noise of the crowd became unbearable. I should have been revelling in the excitement for him, joining in the cheering for him, but I couldn't. My heart was in my throat as my palms grew clammy with nerves and my pulse quickened. He walked along that pathway with the posture of a fully focused athlete, but I could see the emptiness and pain in his eyes and the nervous twitch in his arm. He didn't want to be out there just as much as I didn't want him to be.

"Oh God, Nate, why are you doing this?" I whispered to myself. Something in his eyes sent a knife to my heart.

He climbed into the octagon and stood near the side, moving his gum shield around in his mouth and rocking his head from side to side. Roy and Bernie stood behind him on the other side of the mesh, shouting out tactics and instructions. Nate didn't appear to be listening. His stony, almost black stare was focused on Sanchez. He didn't bounce around like his opponent nor did he react when Sanchez tried squaring up to him. Nate simply stared him in the eye, giving nothing away. In that moment, Sanchez's whole demeanour changed. Gone was the arrogance of his entrance. Now, he was fully focused, studying Nate and looking for any sign of weakness. The looks exchanged between the two sent shivers down my spine. I wrapped my arms around myself and shifted closer to Adam. I hoped the heat from his body would warm me up. I also hoped being close to my best friend could help ease the terror that was beginning to consume me.

A nervous energy seemed to sweep through the crowd as the octagon cleared, leaving just Nate, Sanchez and the referee. My breath caught when they touched gloves and the fight began. They were tentative at first, both fighters moving around the octagon, pushing out the occasional testing arm or sweeping a cautious leg. One minute they were almost dancing, the next, Sanchez had moved in throwing a hard right hand that caught Nate's chin and sent his head cracking back. Nate shook off the punch and countered by putting all of his weight into a punch that had Sanchez dropping to the canvas. The crowd roared, thrilled by the barbaric sport playing out in front of them. I shifted in closer to Adam, just resisting the urge to bury my face into his chest so I couldn't watch. Nate followed Sanchez down on to the cage floor, pinning him with his legs. His fists rained punch after punch down on his opponent. The crowd thundered, chanting Nate's name over and over as he claimed his place as the dominant fighter.

Yet still, I couldn't shift the ominous feeling.

Four minutes into the first round, Nate had taken Sanchez down several times, but he hadn't managed to pull off a knock out move or a hold that made Sanchez tap out. The audience grew restless. They wanted blood.

As Nate's speed and aggressiveness increased, so

did his sloppiness. Just before the horn sounded to signal the end of the first round, Sanchez caught Nate with another iron fist. My breath caught when Nate's face bounced backwards. His eyes were closed and his face was pinched in a mix of pain and blankness. Sanchez caught him again, this time with a kick to the side that sent Nate stumbling back a few paces. The crowd, now at fever pitch, were shouting, weaving and bobbing along with the fighters, yelling at Nate to pull it back together. Sanchez was getting back in to the match.

I breathed a huge sigh of relief when the horn bellowed out across the room and the fighting stopped temporarily. I would say Nate had won that round but he'd been letting Sanchez in. The fighters moved to their separate corners where tactics were discussed, tired muscles were cooled and hydration replenished. I watched Nate's corner intently, silently sending him all my love and my belief that he had this.

Adam wrapped his arm around my shoulders, whispering his own encouragement for my man. He knew me well and could tell how nervous I was. While Nate gulped down a drink, Bernie gestured wildly with his hands, no doubt yelling at him for getting too sloppy. He didn't respond to Bernie nor did he seem to acknowledge him in any way.

My concern hit an all-time high when Nate's stony expression focused on me for a brief moment from across the cage. His breathing was harsh from his exertions. Sweat coated his taught, tanned skin, but he was tense. Too tense.

Soon the horn was blaring out across the arena again, and both fighters returned to the centre. It became apparent that my worry over Nate's well-being was not unfounded. Something was definitely not right. His kicks and punches grew sloppy and slow. People all around began shouting for him to lift his guard when his arms hung limply by his sides. Sanchez soon had the better of him, ploughing him with sickening knee strikes and punches. A harsh right hook caught Nate on the chin and he went tumbling to the canvas. Sanchez was on him immediately. Locking his legs around Nate's body, and his arms around his neck, he held tight, not offering any mercy.

I screamed and jumped to my feet.

"Tap out, Nate! Tap out!" I yelled over and over, but he wouldn't move. He didn't fight back. Sanchez tightened his hold and still Nate remained motionless.

Something was very, very wrong.

I continued screaming, begging Nate to tap out as the referee ran in and pushed Sanchez away, declaring the fight over. My begging wails continued as paramedics were urgently ushered in to the octagon and to an unmoving Nate. My terror-filled wails didn't stop when Adam pulled me into his arms as Nate was rushed past us on a stretcher. They only eased up when I collapsed against Adam, sobbing like I had never sobbed before.

~CHAPTER TWENTY-ONE~

TIME, SOMETIMES WE WISHED IT would hurry up because we had somewhere wonderful to be, or had something exciting to do. Other times we wanted it to stop so we could remain in a happy moment. We would savour it, relish in it, capturing the memory like we would a photograph, as something we never wanted to forget. Then there were the occasions we wanted to go back in time so we could prevent something terrible from happening. I stared at the big, black, carved hands on the huge clock hanging on the wall and wished we could turn them back a couple of hours.

If I could go back in time, I would have tried to stop Nate from leaving his dressing room for the fight. I would have told him over and over how much I loved him. I would have never left his side. If I'd only been able to stop him from stepping into the octagon with Sanchez, then I wouldn't have been sitting by his side now, terrified beyond belief. But the thing with time is that it doesn't stop. You can't turn it back. All you can do is go with the steady tick tock of that second hand as it paces out our lives, controlling and mocking us.

My heart hammered in my chest as I stepped up to Nate's still body lying on the bench. He looked pale, his face pinched into a hint of a grimace. A lump had formed above his left eyebrow, the flesh in the centre of it torn and brutal looking. A young guy, who had been tending to Nate's wounds and monitoring him, stepped away, giving me the room to move in close. Taking his hand between mine, I squeezed gently, hoping for a reaction. "Nate, come on, sexy, open your eyes for me." The desperate tone of my voice echoed through the room as my shaking hands held his tightly, waiting for any movement. When he didn't respond, my heart sank a little further. *Why won't he wake up?*

Having pulled myself together, I'd dodged through the mayhem of stunned fans, inquisitive journalists and security personnel to find Nate. He had been stretchered out to his dressing room where a team of medics were watching and monitoring him closely. I begged them over and over to take Nate to the hospital, to do something. The reply was simple; there was no need because he was breathing and responding on his own. It was only a matter of time before he came round. I couldn't believe what I was hearing. One of the doctors was talking animatedly to Mal in a quiet, darkened corner, and I couldn't help but wonder if Mal was part of the reason why Nate was still there and not being whisked away in a speeding ambulance.

I hated him. After everything he had put Nate through before the fight, I felt like he was now endangering Nate's life by insisting the medics treat him there. In reality, I didn't know if it was anything to do with him, but I felt he was to blame for this somehow.

I felt torn. I couldn't move Nate myself, and everybody else trusted that the doctors knew what they were doing. All I could do was sit tight and pray those ticking second hands were not a countdown to something I wouldn't dare contemplate. I'd only just got him, there was no way I could handle losing him.

I startled when a body appeared in my peripheral vision and looked up into the warm, smiling eyes of the other medic treating Nate.

"Excuse me, mademoiselle, let me try this." The guy, whose name badge introduced him as Esra, moved up beside Nate, and I took a step back. He pulled a small bottle out of his pocket and hesitated a moment, cocking his head to the side as he searched for any signs of awareness from Nate. I looked at him in confusion until he twisted the lid off the bottle. "Smelling salts," he clarified, lifting the lid and wafting the small bottle beneath Nate's nostrils.

Watching with bated breath, I gasped when Nate's chest suddenly expanded with a deep inhalation of breath. His chest rose and fell sharply a few times before, finally, his eyes began to flicker open.

"Oh my God, Nate!" I cried, gripping his hand tightly as confused, unfocused eyes blinked up at the ceiling. In reality, he'd only been unconscious for a matter of minutes, but it felt like hours, days even. Every emotion ran through me while I stared at Nate: fear for what had happened, joy that he was coming round, anger that he'd been left this way and nobody seemed to care… it went on and on.

I found myself being shoved out of the way by Esra and the other medic who finally seemed to be concerned about Nate's wellbeing. Reluctantly, I moved off to the side, plastering myself against the wall to give them space. As the adrenalin in my system slowly began to recede with each second that passed, I began to feel as though I too might pass out any minute. My palms were sweating more than they ever had before. I had to clasp my hands together in a vain attempt at controlling the shakes, and my legs felt as though every muscle had been removed. Any moment now, they would give out, and I'd be a crumpled, emotional heap on the floor.

As Nate's alertness slowly improved, he was monitored closely until finally he was able to clearly formulate responses to their questions. With tears in my eyes, I stayed back, watching the man I loved come back to me.

The quiet order of the room was soon disrupted by the sound of Wes's voice bellowing down the corridor. "Get out of the fucking way," he yelled. Along with, "He's my goddamned brother." It was the first time I'd ever heard emotion in Wes's voice. He was usually so jovial and fun spirited. Nothing ever seemed to faze him. Until now.

The door swung open and Wes came barrelling in, looking angry yet terrified. Dressed in black track pants adorned with sponsorship logos and a plain black T-shirt, he looked just like most of the other people milling around behind the scenes of the big arena. But the graze above his right eyebrow, now pulled taut by the widening of his eyes, showed Wes had been through a battle of his own. Ignoring everybody else in the room, Wes hurried to Nate's side, stopping just inches from him. He was breathing heavily, his shoulders rising and falling with each attempt to control his emotions.

"What the fuck happened out there?" Despite his hard words, Wes's voice broke as he addressed his brother.

Nate blinked and looked at Wes. His features were still cloudy, confused by his ordeal. "I... I'm not sure," Nate stuttered, trying to sit up. The doctor by his side gently pushed on his shoulder to get him to lie still, while he yet again checked his vitals.

"You scared the shit out of me. I didn't know what the fuck was happening. I was stuck in the press room doing an interview with a know-it-all bitch when all hell broke loose outside the door. I would have been here sooner, Nate. If I'd have known, I would have been here for you." The panic Wes had been consumed by left his tightly-strung body. He dropped back onto a nearby chair, burying his face in his hands, visibly shaking.

"Hey Wes, it's okay. I'm okay." Nate glared at the doctor, daring him to say anything as he awkwardly pulled his weakened body to a sitting position, his legs dangling over the side of the bench. "Wes, look at me." His voice was soft, yet commanding, despite his fragile state.

I was still shaking as I stood against the wall, watching the two brothers interact. I knew what Nate had told me of their past, but the two of them had always seemed like chalk and cheese, like they simply tolerated each other because they were of the same blood. However, witnessing the two of them now, it was clear their occasional arguments and incessant bickering were nothing more than typical sibling interactions. They were as close as two brothers could possibly be. It hit me that Wes actually idolised his brother. Why else would he have ended up following Nate's footsteps into the world of MMA? Wes respected Nate, that much was evident, and I now appreciated why. Not only was Nate his older brother, he was also like his dad, best friend and favourite uncle all rolled into one.

Wes lifted his eyes to meet Nate's. For a moment, neither of them spoke. They communicated with a language only the two brothers could understand. Finally, Wes sighed, his voice soft when he said, "They said you weren't waking up, Nate. I thought... I thought I'd lost you." I could see it on his face, his absolute terror that he could have lost his brother, the one person in his life he had always been able to rely on.

Nate moved forward on the bench but thought better of trying to stand when he seemed to sway. He closed his eyes briefly and shook his head, as though trying to shake away the disorientation. "Well, as you can see, you had no such luck. I'm still here, albeit with a massive headache." His face screwed up, seeming to consider why that was the case.

"So what happened out there?" Wes asked again, sniffing and blinking rapidly as if trying to hold back tears.

Nate frowned. "I don't know. One minute I was in full control, I had him. The next... I don't know. I felt disorientated and then… nothing. I can't remember anything."

I watched on quietly as the doctors continued to check on Nate while he chatted quietly to Wes. I was contemplating leaving them to their privacy when Nate realised I was there. The moment his eyes met mine, his lips pulled up into a smile that stole my breath. It wasn't full like the friendly grins I was used to; it was almost shy and vulnerable. I'd seen it on him twice before: once when we'd been kayaking, the second time just the night before, after I'd told him I loved him. On both of those occasions, he'd dropped his defences and opened up to me, letting me see the real man behind the macho mask.

Returning Nate's smile, and grateful that he seemed to be okay, I took a step forward. Without warning, the door swung open again and a dark presence filled the doorway. The head of every person in the room shot up, looking towards the visitor. The air suddenly felt oppressive, and goosebumps prickled along my skin as Damián Sanchez strolled in. Dressed in a black, well-tailored suit and a crisp, white shirt, it would have been easy to dismiss him as a well-mannered, cultured sophisticate… until you looked at his face. His evil grin and the menacing darkness of his eyes proved he was anything but a refined gentleman.

"So you're awake then… what a shame."

I gasped, horrified he could say such a thing.

Wes was out of his seat and standing beside Nate in an instant, crossing his arms over his chest. To most people, he would have seemed intimidating, but next to Nate and Sanchez he looked small and unimposing.

Sanchez chuckled and moved to stand in front of

Nate, ignoring the eyes of every person in the room. "Call off your puppy, Oakes. Does he think he's going to piss on me or something?"

Wes growled and took a step towards Sanchez, clenching his fists. Nate shot out an arm, holding his brother back. "What do you want, Damián? You got your win." I watched Nate closely. Knowing he'd lost the fight would be killing him. Not understanding what happened would be fucking with his mind. During all the mayhem that had happened prior to the fight, Nate had been resolute in his determination to win. For Nate it wasn't a matter of bragging rights, or the money, it was about proving to himself and everybody else that he was strong: strong in body, strong in mind. To lose would show a level of weakness, and Nate never wanted to appear weak. I now knew that was because of his upbringing, because of wanting to prove to his absent parents that he was worthy of something.

Sanchez clasped his hands in front of him. "You're right, I did win… so why do I still feel cheated?"

Everyone stood around watching, waiting, not knowing what to do or what to say. The animosity between the two was palpable, and I feared that even in Nate's weakened condition, he would still allow Sanchez to rile him to the point of wanting to fight back. Mal was still in the corner, cowering away, not saying or doing anything. I wanted to scream and shout at him, to yell at him to protect his guy, but he just stood there with wide, uneasy eyes. The medics stood a few feet behind Nate, also looking uneasy and unsure. Wes was glowering at Sanchez, his hands in permanent fists by his side. I knew if an argument erupted between these fighters, the other people in the room wouldn't be able to stop them from turning it physical. All mayhem would break loose.

Swallowing the lump of fear in my throat, I took a tentative step towards the men, hoping I might be able to be the voice of reason if push came to shove. *Don't be so stupid Liv, they aren't going to listen to you.*

Nate's eyes were dark and narrowed as he continued to glare at his opponent. "I don't know what you're talking about. So why don't you get the fuck out of my dressing room." He spoke calmly and slowly, but the deathly undertone to his voice sent shivers down my spine.

Ignoring Nate's words, Sanchez continued, "I feel cheated because beating you, bringing you down, was supposed to make me feel good. It was supposed to be my payback. But you just laid there. Where's the satisfaction in that?"

"Payback for what?" Nate snarled.

"My father's death."

Nate blinked a few times, stunned and then began laughing. "Seriously? This shit again? What the fuck are you talking about?"

Sanchez shifted his body, moving into a position that said *I'm calm* while also stating *Don't fucking mess with me.*

"Are you sitting comfortably? I want to tell you a story. Then we'll see if you are still laughing." The ice in Sanchez's voice turned the air chilly. I feared whatever he was about to say would not be a friendly fairy tale. "What do you remember about your parents?"

Wes brushed off Nate's hand and stood toe to toe

with Sanchez. "They have nothing to do with you," he growled.

"That is where you are wrong, little boy." Sanchez laughed without humour, glaring at Wes.

I continued to move slowly around the outside edge of the room until I was standing a few feet behind Nate. I wanted this all to stop. Nate had only just woken up and hadn't yet been given the all clear from the doctor. Having this kind of altercation so soon would not be assisting his recovery. I felt a momentary relief when a security guard entered the room, but whilst things between the fighters were only verbal, he was happy enough to stand and watch how things played out, not getting involved.

"It has everything to do with me," Sanchez seethed. "My father is no longer with me because of your parents."

Wes growled and stepped further forward, nudging Sanchez with his chest, but Nate's deep voice prevented him from taking things any further.

"Stop with the bullshit, Damián, and spit out what it is you have to say." I kept my eyes trained on Nate, terrified that this was all too much for him. He looked tired and weary, and I could see more bruising colouring his face. It was obvious he'd been in a battle, and it appeared it was not over yet.

Sanchez's eyes were as black as coal as he looked between the brothers. "Your parents weren't quite the wonderful, humanitarian diplomats you believed them to be."

"Don't say another fucking word about them," Nate snarled.

Sanchez's eyes flicked to Nate's then to Wes' before

the corner of his lips pulled up into an evil curve. "They were involved in some crooked deals back in Brazil, got themselves caught up with the wrong people. Those people wrongly ordered the execution of my father for the death of your parents and the young lady they were with." With my eyes still firmly fixed on Nate, I noticed the very second his body went rigid, every one of his muscles tensing.

"Was your father responsible for the deaths of my parents and my fiancée?" Nate asked slowly, menacingly. I gasped as my hand flew to my mouth. His fiancée?

"It was a fucking accident. Your parents' car was speeding, he didn't stand a chance. He was in the wrong place at the wrong time. Because of your family, I lost *everything*, and now I plan to take everything from you. Winning the fight was just the start. Your precious facility is—"

"You son of a…" Wes didn't finish his sentence; he was on Sanchez before anyone had time to blink. As the room turned into chaos with the two brawling men on the floor and security trying to stop it, Nate sat there. He was completely still, staring at the spot Sanchez had just occupied.

Approaching Nate, I placed a gentle hand on his arm. "Nate, are you okay?" I asked hesitantly. I didn't know what to say, what to feel. He'd never told me anything about a fiancée before. During our conversations, Nate had always made out he wasn't interested in relationships. I tried to recall any conversations we'd had about his past girlfriends and realised that he'd always dodged that topic, concentrating on where he was with present romantic relations, or the lack thereof. I wondered what she'd been like and how long they had been together. And Brazil? What was she doing in Brazil with his parents?

Security managed to pull Wes and Sanchez apart and dragged them out of the room yelling and swearing at each other. Mal and Bernie followed, obviously wanting to help discharge the erupting tensions. A stunned looking doctor took nervous steps towards Nate, saying he needed to check on him. He quickly busied himself asking Nate questions, which he simply nodded or grunted his responses to. After a few minutes, the doctor seemed content that Nate had suffered no major injuries or damage from the fight, and after warning us to call for a doctor if anything should change, he exited the room as quickly as he could.

Finally alone, I sat next to Nate and reached for his hand. Whatever his reasons for not telling me about his fiancée, now was not the right time to dwell on it. He was obviously hurting, and I needed to support him. His hands were still covered by blue wraps so I slowly began to unwind one, freeing him of the confining tapes. He watched me closely, almost mesmerised by the gentle unfurling of the material. With one removed, I immediately took the other hand and uncovered it too. He still hadn't spoken when I took both hands in mine and gave them a gentle, reassuring squeeze. The silence felt almost oppressive, heavy with Nate's sorrow and unspoken questions. Questions I doubted there were answers to.

"Liv, get me out of here. I have to get out of here," he said wearily, tilting his head to look me in the eye.

With a feeble smile, I nodded and jumped off the

bench. I wasn't happy about taking him away, I still felt he needed medical attention, but right then, my priority was doing whatever Nate needed. I grabbed his clothes and helped him get changed. Without a backward glance, we ducked out of the room and made our way to a rear exit, careful to avoid any lurking reporters or fans.

"What about Wes, Cassie and Bernie?" I asked, as we pushed our way out to where our car was parked. Surprised at our arrival, the driver jumped out and opened the rear door for us.

"The car can come back for them. I just need to be alone, away from here." In the car, Nate dropped his head back against the head rest and closed his eyes. As we weaved through the streets of Monaco I studied Nate's profile, illuminated intermittently by the glow of streetlights. He looked like he was in pain, not a physical pain, but hurt from an emotional blow that I simply could not comprehend. My throat constricted around the lump of emotion that formed there when I thought about whatever sorrow Nate was feeling and about what I could have lost tonight in that ring.

Shifting across the seat, I rested my head on his shoulder and wrapped an arm across his chest. Now wasn't the time to discuss his past and what he hadn't told me. I knew he'd need time. I could give him that. In the meantime, I would show him with my actions that I was there for him if he needed me.

As I snuggled in closer and held him tightly, Nate wrapped an arm around me and buried his nose in my hair. I smiled, feeling the tenderness of his arm stroking along mine. I took my comfort from Nate taking his from me. Despite the evening's revelations, we were a team now, and I had every intention of keeping it that way.

~CHAPTER TWENTY-TWO~

BACK IN OUR HOTEL SUITE, I kicked the door closed behind us and helped Nate through into his bedroom. He was weak and kept an arm around me as though he needed my support to be able to stand. There also seemed to be a blankness in his eyes that I wasn't sure came solely from the fight or the revelations after it. Easing him onto the bed, I pulled his shoes off and helped him out of his clothes before encouraging him to lay back. He needed time to rest. His body needed to heal and his mind to process his thoughts.

"Don't leave," he whispered, grabbing my wrist when I turned to go.

"You need to rest, Nate," I said, trying to keep the emotional quiver out of my voice.

"Liv, don't leave me, please. I need you." Looking into the hurt and aching depths of his beautiful eyes, I knew I would never leave him. I couldn't.

Nodding, I kicked off my own shoes and crawled onto the bed with him. His arms immediately wrapped around me and hugged me tight, like he never wanted to let me go.

After a short silence, Nate shifted on the bed and turned to his side so we were face to face. His eyes burned with an intensity I'd never seen before as he stared into mine, searching, or pleading maybe. He grabbed my hand and entwined our fingers together. "Her name was Louise. I met—"

I shook my head. "Nate, you don't need to explain. I don't need to know."

He brought our conjoined hands up to rest over my lips. "Shh, I want to tell you this. I should have told you before. I don't know why I didn't. Instead I acted like a fucking idiot and kept running away." He frowned then kissed my fingers and returned our hands to the bed.

"I was an angry nineteen-year-old when I met her. Bernie had helped me channel most of my anger into training but occasionally it would still escape. On my birthday, I felt the familiar feelings of betrayal and anger towards my parents and the gym hadn't been enough. I'd had too many beers and wanted blood. I was about to get into it with some guy over something silly when this girl, this blonde-haired angel, walked up to me and flashed me her dazzling smile." My stomach churned at the way his face lit up thinking about her.

"She took the bottle I was holding, and I just let her. I was mesmerised. She had me under some sort of spell. The guy I'd been about to rip into was jeering, but I ignored him and followed her smile as she beckoned me out of the bar, out of danger. Outside, she'd laughed and said something about not wanting her clean floors getting sticky with beer and blood. She was the owner's daughter and had been watching me growing increasingly agitated all night. She asked if I wanted to walk it off with her. Before I knew it, we'd been walking for hours and I'd opened up to her about everything. She was so easy to talk to and didn't judge me. A bit like you."

He looked into my eyes for a brief moment and then fell to his back, staring up at the ceiling. "We shared numbers that night, and within a week, I'd taken her out on our first date. Within six months, despite our young age, I knew I needed her. She grounded me, stopped me flying into rages when I thought of my parents. By this point, I'd already had a few pro fights and was starting to make a name for myself. I wanted to make things between us permanent. I couldn't risk her running away from me too, so I asked her to marry me. I honestly didn't think she would say yes, but to my astonishment, she did— on the proviso that we go to Brazil to see my parents. She thought I needed to talk to them to try to either rebuild a relationship with them or to be able to put everything behind me and move on with my life without the bitterness." He grunted a disgusted laugh. "I would have done anything for her, so I agreed. Being diplomats, it wasn't difficult to find out where they were, so I used the winnings from my fights and booked the tickets."

He swallowed deeply and turned to face me again. The pain in his eyes broke my heart, but I remained quiet, giving him the time to get his words out.

"When we got there, I contacted them and we

arranged to meet for a meal. The meal was awkward, just as I expected it would be. They hadn't changed a bit. They chastised me for my career choice, saying I would never amount to anything. They said at least I had done something right by choosing Louise, but until I could prove myself with a worthy career they were disappointed in me, even more so because Wes had chosen to follow my lead.

After the meal, they were driving us back to our hotel and I knew that would be the last time I would ever see them. Unless they could accept me for who and what I was, I wanted nothing to do with them. As we drove along, they continued berating me from the front of the car as Lou watched me sympathetically and kept mouthing 'I'm so sorry.' I knew she felt guilty for making me go. The funny thing was, despite their ridicule, it felt like I had been unburdened. I'd had my chance to say my piece and was ready to move on.

We were about five minutes from the hotel when a motorcycle appeared alongside the car. They were paps. Somehow they had caught wind of me being there and who I was connected to. My dad tried to lose them but they just kept following, incessantly snapping photos. My parents were yelling, blaming me and Louise was silently sobbing next to me, gripping my hand tightly. She was terrified." A harsh shudder travelled the length of his body and I realised he was fighting to hold back tears.

"I heard a loud bang, almost like a gunshot, and then everything went black."

I tensed up by Nate's side, feeling sick for what he was about to say. He shifted on his side again looking at me with red rimmed, dark, shadowed eyes. "I woke up in a hospital, aching all over, with my head bandaged up. As I came round, I remembered being in the car. I freaked out, begging the doctors and nurses to tell me where Lou was. They told me there had been an accident and my parents, along with Louise had... they'd died on impact.... They said they couldn't understand how I'd managed to escape with only a cut to my head and concussion."

Automatically, my eyes trained on to the scar above his left eyebrow. I'd always assumed he'd gained it through a fight. I tugged my hand free and lifted a trembling finger to the silver scar and lightly traced over it. "Is that how you got this?" I asked, my voice shaking.

Nate nodded and laughed bitterly. "Yeah, tell me how that's fair. The most beautiful, selfless person in the world loses her life whilst I got away with a stupid scratch." He closed his eyes in pain and shook his head.

I understood now. His reluctance to let me get close, his extreme reaction to reporters, the apparent disinterest in women and standoffish ways, he was just protecting himself. I'd never been through anything like that, but I could guarantee that if I'd lost someone that meant everything to me, I sure as hell would never get over it and allow someone else in. But he had. He had let *me* in. He'd told me he loved me. Or maybe he didn't love me like I'd fallen in love with him.

Not knowing what else to say, I simply whispered, "I'm sorry you went through that."

Suddenly, Nate twisted so I was on my back and he was leaning over me. He stared down at me as I blinked up at him in surprise. "I'm sorry I didn't tell you the full story. I buried it all many years ago because it hurt too much." I swallowed hard and nodded. "Liv, I thought I would never be able to feel anything ever again, never mind love someone else. I need you to understand how much you mean to me. You came in to my life when it had flatlined. Nothing mattered. I was just going through the motions, existing. To everyone else, I was Nathan Oakes, the successful fighter and business owner. They didn't know what was underneath and I didn't want them to. Somehow you managed to see beyond all of that and wormed your way into my soul. I never thought I'd find love after Louise, but I was wrong, so wrong. I love you. God, I love you so much."

"I love you too," I sobbed, pulling him down on top of me and crashing my lips against his.

The kiss grew in intensity, an outpouring of both our emotions. Nate's hands had wrapped around me so he was hugging me tightly to his body, and my hands sank into his hair so I could hold him to me. When I moaned, he took full advantage and sneaked past my lips to tease my tongue with his. I could feel the firmness of his arousal pushing against my thigh as he pulled me in closer. I wrapped my leg around his back and arched into him. And then, as though I'd been drenched with icy cold water, I remembered him lying unresponsive on that dressing room bench. I gasped and pushed him off me.

"Nate, no," I panted, trying to calm my ragged breath. "You need to rest. The fight."

He groaned and rolled onto his back. "I'm okay," he mumbled.

"No, you're not. You were knocked out and need

341

to rest," I protested, stretching out beside him and wrapping an arm over his body. His chest made a deep rumbling sound as he grumbled something. I lifted my head and raised a brow. "Do I need to beat you up too?" He burst out laughing and pulled me back against his chest.

"No, JB, you don't need to beat me up. Just lay here with me." That, I could do. I settled my head into the crook of his neck and sucked in a deep breath. His rich scent immediately eased away some of my worries. Cuddling in close, I listened to Nate breathing, and as soon as the sound had evened out and I heard the faint sound of a gentle snore, I closed my eyes and joined him in sleep.

***

I AWOKE WITH a start, my heart beating frantically and trying to keep up with my heightened emotions. *Of course, it was just a dream,* I reasoned, placing one hand over my chest as the other one shakily clawed through my hair. Twisting my head to the side, I took comfort from the fact that Nate was, indeed lying beside me. The images I still had in my mind of him sprawled out unconscious on the floor of a cage while Sanchez laughed evilly, declaring his victory, and everyone cheered him and no one went to help Nate were all too real.

Moving onto my side, I watched him closely for a few minutes, reassuring myself that he was breathing. His chest was rising and falling gently and his slightly parted, beautifully kissable lips vibrated minutely with his relaxed, soft breaths. Curling one arm under my head, I gently traced the patterns of his tattoos with my other hand. The scroll of writing across his right pec now made perfect sense. '*What the heart has once owned and had, it shall never lose.*' Once again, my heart hurt for the losses he'd suffered through his life. It made me appreciate Wes, Cassie and Bernie even more. These were people he trusted. They were loyal and cared a great deal for him.

A quick glance at the alarm clock told me it was almost two in the morning. I'd only been asleep for an hour or so, yet I felt strangely energised with everything spinning around in my head. I couldn't stop thinking about the heartache Nate had been through over the years. I thought back to a conversation we'd had when we'd first been in Monaco, when I'd been pissed off that he wouldn't talk to me and blaming him for not opening up to me. Now I knew why. If I'd been trying to build bridges with my estranged parents only to have them reject me again, and then be the sole survivor of a crash that took the lives of not only those parents but the love of my life as well, I think I would have probably tried to bury those feelings too. And now to find out your opponent's father had been responsible… I shook my head at that thought. That kind of pain must be excruciating.

The minutes crept by slowly as I cuddled against Nate, lost in my thoughts and feelings, wondering how he would be when he woke and everything crashed down on him. I wanted to be there for him, to erase the pain and heartache. I couldn't help but be afraid that he would retreat into himself and pull away from me. No, I wouldn't let that happen. He'd told me he loved me, and God, did I love him back. I would be his support, whether he wanted it or not. He didn't need to struggle through a life of fog clouding everything anymore. I would be his place of comfort, so he could embrace and deal with his feelings. He didn't realise it, but he had given me the same. He'd become my safe place. Through Nate, I'd learned so much about the real person underneath my tough exterior. With him, I had finally opened myself to accepting love. Before him, I'd always used the excuse that I was simply career focused and had no time for love. The reality was I'd been afraid. Nate had somehow, without even trying, made me fight through my own barriers to allow him into my heart.

I stroked my fingers along the stubble on his jaw as I remembered our times together: the fun side of him—when he'd laughed, and joked, and teased me; the serious businessman, watching me intently while I presented drawings and ideas to him; and the relentless trainer who had seen more in me than I had ever imagined. I smiled as I remembered those initial training sessions with him. He had been so brutal, pushing me until I felt sick and shouted at him. Then there were the times we were intimate together. Nate had been such a skilled lover, bringing me to pleasure with such ease. But, even then, there had been so much more than physical gratification between us.

Voices outside the door caught my attention. The sounds grew louder until a loud thud and Wes's angry voice echoed around the suite, making me jump. I strained to hear what he was shouting about and noticed another voice—a male voice—and then all went silent. I wanted to know what was going on and who the other person was, but my need to stay with

Nate was greater.

Nate groaned from beside me and shifted on the bed, hugging me tight into his chest. "Tell him to shut the fuck up," he grumbled.

Lifting my eyes to meet Nate's, a look of pain and confusion clouded his handsome face as he blinked at me in the glimmer of moonlight spilling into the room through the windows.

"Hi!"

"Hi, yourself," I whispered back, fighting the urge to fling myself on him and smother him with kisses.

"What's going on?" he asked.

I frowned. "I don't know."

Suddenly, there were more voices in the other room all pleading with Wes to calm down. "No, he needs to know this shit. Now," Wes bellowed. The door flew open, drenching us with bright light from the living room before the lights in our room flicked on. Nate and I hissed in unison as I buried my face into his chest, trying to block out the glare.

"Wes, what the fuck are you doing here? Do you know what time it is?" Nate barked, shifting in the bed so he could sit up but keep me planted into his side.

"Yes, I know what fucking time it is." I peered up to see Wes pacing just inside the doorway. I could see Bernie and Cassie standing just beyond him and there was someone else there just out of view.

"Mind telling me why you felt the need to barge in here and wake us up?" Nate glared at his brother.

Wes stopped pacing and levelled rage-filled eyes on Nate. His chest was heaving, and I could tell he was barely containing his anger. "We trusted those bastards. *YOU* trusted those bastards."

345

Under my touch, Nate bristled, his muscles tensing. "What are you talking about?"

"Mal and Roy, we trusted them, the fucking cheating scumbags. I'm gonna fucking kill them." He turned to storm out of the room but Bernie placed a hand on his chest, forcing him to stop.

On the bed, Nate moved me to the side and jumped to his feet. "Wesley you better tell me what the fuck is going on."

The tension in the room was at astronomical levels. Cassie and Bernie stood in silence with wide, concerned eyes. Wes was shaking with rage. Dragging my knees up to my chest, I hugged them tightly, watching Nate move over to the group, standing strong with his legs spread wide and his arms crossed over his chest.

"What happened to you during the fight?" Wes asked Nate, finally calming enough to speak. "You were winning. You had that bastard."

Nate shook his head. "I don't know. Everything was going to plan and then... nothing. I can't remember."

"You know why?" Wes seethed, his anger reigniting.

"Why?"

"They fucking drugged you, Nate. They were all in it together."

"What?" Nate and I gasped in unison.

I watched on with wide, scared eyes as Nate's body went rigid. Cassie and Bernie rushed to Nate's side. They were all talking over each other, telling Nate that Roy and Mal had been conspiring with Sanchez. Sanchez wanted the guaranteed win and Nate's humiliation. Mal wanted the financial gain of a certain win and would win more from betting on the outsider, Sanchez. Roy was the link between them and the one that made it all happen.

"How do you know all this?" Nate finally bellowed, shutting everyone up.

"That'll be because of me," the other mysterious person lurking outside said as he stepped into the room.

"Adam?"

"What's he doing here?" Nate growled.

Adam's eyes flicked to me with a small smile and then looked back at Nate. His back straightened, sensing Nate's hostility. "It's good to see you again, Mr. Oakes." Nate narrowed his eyes, but before he could say anything, Adam continued. "After the fight, I was wandering around out the back waiting for Liv. I didn't know what was going on or if she'd need me."

"She doesn't need you. She has me now," Nate cut in, and I couldn't help the little smile that pulled on my lips at his possessiveness.

"Yeah, I get that," Adam continued quickly. "Anyway, I was stood outside a room I thought was yours. The door was open a crack and there were voices inside. I assumed it was all of you until I recognised Sanchez's unmistakable accent. I don't know why I listened, but something just felt off about the conversation. I caught a bit of what they were saying and realised it was all underhand. I think maybe you need to hear it for yourself." He fumbled in his pocket and produced his phone, tapping on the screen for a second before the faint sounds of voices filled the room through the phone's speakers. Everyone froze as we listened to voices of the three men arguing about the fight. Apparently, Nate should have only been slipped enough of whatever he had been given to make him lax and sloppy. Sanchez had still wanted it to look like he'd wiped the floor with Nate. They'd argued over the fact that Roy must have given him too much, and Mal was panicking that they would get caught.

Nate's wide eyes were locked on Wesley's as we all listened, a silent communication being made between them even as the truth rang out.

As the recording finished, everyone remained quiet for a moment, stunned into silence by what we'd heard. Eventually, Nate turned to Adam and lifted his hand. "Thank you. Would you mind sending the audio to me?"

"Of course." Adam said, shaking Nate's hand. "What are you going to do with it?"

Finally coming to my senses, I scrambled off the bed and ran over to Nate, wrapping my arms around his waist. He slipped an arm around my shoulders and pulled me in. "I'm not sure yet, but those fucking idiots will not get away with making a fool out of me."

Adam nodded in understanding then looked at me. "You alright, Liv?"

Nate tensed so I gave him a reassuring squeeze. "I will be when I know this one is okay," I said with a smile, trying to ease some of the tension in the room.

"I'm fine, JB," Nate said placing a kiss on the top of my head.

Adam smiled sadly. "Look after her, man. She deserves the best." With that he backed off towards the door. "I'm gonna head off to my room. Let me know if you need anything else."

Just before he left, Nate called his name.

"Yeah?"

"Thank you. And I promise I'll treat her like a princess." Adam nodded and left, closing the door to the suite behind him.

"What do we do now?" Wes said in a calmer tone.

"Right now, we do nothing. Right now, you lot can fuck off so I can get back to bed. We can deal with this tomorrow."

Taking the hint, the three of them left, leaving me and Nate alone.

"What are you going to do?" I asked Nate as we walked back to bed in a tight embrace.

"Right now, I'm going to strip you out of those clothes and bury myself in you so we can forget about everything but you and me."

~CHAPTER TWENTY-THREE~

One Week Later

IT WAS MONDAY MORNING AND we'd been back in the UK for a few days. I'd spent the first two days at Nate's place because he kept pleading that he needed me to watch over him. I'd rolled my eyes but given in anyway. How could I refuse? I wanted to be with him as much as he wanted to be with me. He didn't *need* me to watch over him at all, he was just manipulating my caring personality to lure me in. As if he needed to do that. The day after the fight he'd been thoroughly checked over by more medics, ones Nate hired himself, and they deemed there was no lasting damage caused by the fight or the drugs. They'd taken another sample from him and Nate planned on using the results as part of any evidence he used against Mal,

Roy and Sanchez.

He wouldn't tell me what he planned to do, and I think, in part, that was because he honestly didn't know. His pride wanted to rip them apart and call them out for what they had done. The private Nate, the one who liked to keep everything close to his chest, was probably hoping to deal with everything quietly and behind closed doors. Me, I wanted him to drag those bastards through every damn court possible.

I'd never trusted Mal, not from the moment he'd laid his hostile gaze on me in Monaco. And Sanchez, well he was just an arrogant arse with an unwarranted vendetta. I still wasn't quite clear what the whole deal was with his dad and the deaths of Nate's parents and fiancée, but I was pretty sure it would all eventually become clear.

But Roy, now he was a completely different ball game. He had totally played me. I'd trusted him. I'd believed he had Nate's best interests at heart all along. I just wished I'd been able to pick up that something wasn't right a little sooner. I mean, Nate changed whenever Roy trained with him. Even the others had commented on how aggressive he became. We'd all just assumed it was because he detested the fact that Roy was there. In reality, Roy had been slipping stuff in Nate's drinks all along. I still felt sick whenever I thought about what that could have done to him.

I had every faith in Nate that he would do the right thing. He had a team of lawyers and MMA officials he was consulting with and knew that, whatever the outcome, it would be the right one.

Pulling in to a parking space outside the offices of

Ashworth-Moore, I looked towards the front entrance. It felt strange being back. I'd always thought I was a confident go-getter before. Now I realised I had been nothing but an inexperienced newbie. Heading back to work for my first day in over six weeks, I realised that the last time I walked out of those doors I was nothing but a girl. I was returning a woman, a career focused woman. But I now had a wonderful man by my side who completed me. My time with Nate in France had taught me so much. I'd picked up so much insight into French architecture and planning laws that I hoped I would be able to use to my advantage. In fact I planned on approaching Mr. Ashworth to present my proposal of having a branch of the company devoted to foreign planning. I loved the thought of being able to do more designing in France, it was a truly beautiful country, and I understood why Nate wanted his new facilities there.

Taking a deep breath, I stepped through the doors. As soon as the first click of my new heels echoed around the reception area, Trish was on her feet and rounding the desk. "Oh my God, look at you," she gushed as she engulfed me in a bear hug. "You look amazing. How was France? How was Mr. Oakes? What was his place like? What was Monaco like? I've always wanted to go."

I giggled dragging myself from her hold and wrapping an arm through hers, encouraging her to walk with me. "First off, thanks. I *feel* amazing." And I did. The mixture of healthy eating, exercise and some French sun had done wonders for me. I had toned muscles, my skin glowed and for the first time ever, my hair had a constant shine. It was all down to Nate.

When we got to the stairs that would lead me to my floor, I stepped away from Trish, answering the rest of her rapid fire questions. "France was amazing. Mr. Oakes was amazing." I grinned and she raised a questioning brow. "His place is beautiful and tranquil. I actually didn't want to leave. Monaco was just as you see on television and well worth a visit if you get the chance."

As I turned to walk up the stairs, she stopped me. "Back the heck up there missy. What do you mean Mr. Oakes was amazing? Something you're not telling me?"

I shot her a beaming grin. "A lady never tells."

I heard her huff of frustration as I ran up the stairs laughing. I still had a grin on my face when I entered my office and dropped my bag in the bottom drawer of my desk before switching my computer on. It booted up and then… nothing. That little black cursor sat there not moving, not flashing, giving me the royal, *'welcome back bitch.'*

"You've got to be kidding me," I said, scowling at the screen. Nothing changed.

"Problem, Liv?" Adam asked, standing in my doorway with a grin on his face.

"Don't tell me," I said, slapping my finger down on the mouse button repeatedly. "We have network problems, and Gary is working on it as we speak?"

He laughed and moved further in to the room, settling down in one of the seats opposite my desk. "How did you know?"

"Oh, lucky guess." I gestured wildly with my hands in the air.

He chuckled again before his face dropped and he

stared into his lap for a moment. When he looked up, I was startled by the sadness in his usually sparkly eyes. "Please tell me he's looking after you well," he said, wistfully.

My irritation with the computer forgotten, I sat back in my chair and smiled. "He's wonderful, Ad. He is so loving and challenging, and annoying and frustrating. He's perfect for me." We both laughed at that. It was the truth. Nate really was perfect for me in every way.

"I'm glad to hear it, because if I ever hear he treats you as less than the princess you are, he'll have me to answer to."

"Okay, Ad, I'll let him know." I said with a smile.

Adam pushed to his feet and nodded with a grin. "Good, make sure you do because my best friend deserves nothing but the best." I smiled with affection. I loved Adam, just not in the same, all-consuming way I did Nate.

"Oh, and my dad wanted to see you when you got in. You shouldn't keep the old man waiting." His brows shot to his hairline in mock horror as he made his way to the door. "I'm glad you're back, Liv. It hasn't been the same around here without you."

When he left, I stared at the empty doorway for a minute before remembering I was needed somewhere. I rushed across the office space to the larger, executive offices at the far end of the building. I paused in front of Robert Ashworth's door with my hand ready to knock. What if he was pulling me in to tell me I'd let the company down, that he'd heard about my inappropriate and unprofessional relationship with my client and therefore he had to let me go? I loved my job. I didn't want to lose it.

"Come in, Olivia," came the deep, booming voice of the company chairman.

Steeling myself to receive my fate, I pushed through the door and plastered on a fake smile as I approached Mr. Ashworth's desk. As usual, his expression was unreadable and gave nothing away while I sat nervously in one of his expensive leather chairs.

"Welcome back," he said, steepling his hands in front of him on the desk.

"Thank you, it's good to be back."

"I'm sure you're wondering why I've called you in." The lack of intonation in his voice or expression on his face was unnerving.

"Yes," I said, trying, and failing, to sound confident.

He stood from his desk and shocked the hell out of me by coming around to my side and resting against the edge of the desk. I stared up at him with wide eyes.

"I just wanted to congratulate you on a job well done in France, Olivia. Mr. Oakes has expressed his deepest gratitude for our allowing you to accompany him over there and for once again exceeding his expectations with the plans for his new facilities." I felt the corners of my lips twitch with the desire to beam at him. I couldn't become complacent though, with Mr. Ashworth there was usually a but. "I have also been contacted by Monsieur Rondaeu, who was extremely impressed by your talent and professionalism. He has proposed that we form a partnership for UK expats or holiday home owners wishing to build or otherwise renovate their French properties. And Olivia, once we have the agreements in place, I would like you to head that up. In fact, I'd like you to expand us further into European countries."

I nearly choked. "Come again?"

For the first time ever, as far as I was aware, Robert Ashworth's eyes softened and he grinned. "You heard me. You have done exceptionally well since you joined us here. I know it hasn't always been easy for you, but I see a bright future for you in this business. I want to tie you in with us so we don't lose you to someone else."

"Wow, thank you. I don't know what to say." I honestly didn't. For the first time ever, someone had left me totally speechless.

After promising Mr. Ashworth I would at least consider his proposal – oh who was I kidding, of course I'd accept as soon as any paperwork was placed in front of me – I flounced back to my office and immediately dialled Nate's number.

He answered on the third ring. "Hey sexy, how's your first day back?"

"Oh, the same old. Got called into the chairman's office and was offered a promotion to head up a new European design section." All my intentions of remaining cool, calm and collected evaporated when I let out the loudest, girly squeal ever.

Nate laughed. "That's fantastic, JB. I'm so proud of you."

Warmth spread through my body hearing him say that. I still hadn't gotten used to any praise coming from him. Our relationship was still so new, but it was blossoming every day, and every day I fell deeper and deeper in love with him.

"Listen, I've got a meeting with my lawyers. You're still coming to the gym after work though, right?"

"Oh yes!" I said with far too much enthusiasm. "Tonight, Mr. Oakes, I am going to take you down."

"I'll look forward to it, JB," he said and chortled before hanging up.

Flopping back in my chair, I stared up at the spotlights in the ceiling with the biggest grin on my face. Oh, how things had changed, and all because one skinny, plastic Barbie-bitch couldn't keep her cruel and snarky comments to herself. I owed her a ginormous jam donut and a fully loaded chocolate and caramel latte.

~CHAPTER TWENTY-FOUR~

Eighteen Months later

THE PLACE WAS THE SAME but different. The same loud and raucous crowd chanted Nate's name over and over. The giant cage in the centre of the room looked just as big and imposing as before, but not quite so intimidating and scary. The overly loud music that threatened to pierce my eardrums added to the excitable ambience of the fancy Monaco casino.

Last time we sat in these seats, I had been a bundle of nerves. A deep, dark feeling of dread had consumed me, paralysing me with fear about what Nate was about to do.

Today, I couldn't wait.

Adam again sat to my right, trying in vain to contain my excitement. It had got to the point that he almost had to restrain me from leaping up and hollering out Nate's name as only his number one fan could.

"Liv, calm the fuck down," he grumbled, slapping his palm on my knee as it bounced like a space hopper on speed.

I slapped his hand away and narrowed my eyes on my best friend. "I will not *calm the fuck down,* Adam. Do you know what all this means?" I shrieked and grabbed a fistful of his t-shirt.

Adam grinned at my over exuberance and pulled my hand away. "Yes, princess, you might have told me once or twice."

It meant that Nathan Oakes was about to take to the cage again to beat the crap out of Damián Sanchez. And this time he was going to win.

After his defeat to Sanchez, the rumour mill had worked overtime making Nate out to be some kind of drug-dependent cheater. Not only had it damaged his reputation in MMA, Golden Oakes and GO had suffered as well. That was until Nate's lawyer—with the help of Adam's recording—exposed the truth about the Mal, Roy, Sanchez debacle. Despite the fact they were each suitably punished for their actions and Nate was cleared of any wrong doing, he still felt the need to have one last fight to regain his title and his credibility. Personally, I thought it was all about his ego. He didn't want to retire on a loss. I told him time and time again that it didn't matter. His loyal fans and I loved him and respected him regardless. He was determined though, especially when Sanchez had somehow managed to not get kicked out of the sport as most people had expected he would.

So, with the help of only those he trusted implicitly—Bernie, Cassie, Wes and me—he trained like a dog so he could have a rematch. He wanted revenge in the only way he knew how to get it, in the Octagon.

Sanchez, being the fucking idiot he was, rose to the rematch challenge. Despite finding out it had in fact been Sanchez's drunken father who had caused the accident that killed Nate's parents and Louise, Sanchez still held the Oakes brothers responsible for the fact his father had then been taken out too. It would appear that Sanchez didn't want to accept that his father had in fact been the one involved in crooked deals and had been executed for losing over one million dollars' worth of cocaine. His respect for his father was so intense that it was easier for him to lay blame everywhere but where it should have been.

I let go of Adam's t-shirt and turned in my seat as a rush of activity in the cage set the crowd into overdrive. Just like I remembered from last time, there was suddenly a larger security presence in the arena and the music had definitely become louder and obnoxiously more techno. It was crowd pumping music. And it was working. All around me, men bellowed *'kick his ass Golden Boy'* and *'Oakes, Oakes, Oakes.'* Those chants made me grin like a loon. The sexual suggestions being yelled by the ladies, not so much. I got it, I did. He was hot as hell, and no pre-menopausal lady could be unaffected by his looks and charm. But he was mine, and I had become very territorial. Until a little over eighteen months ago, I'd planned on being married to my career. One set of intriguing grey eyes was all it took to obliterate that idea.

The cage announcer moved to the centre of the stage and pulled the microphone to his lips. The adrenalin that had been trickling through my veins suddenly ramped up tenfold into a tidal surge. My palms were sweating, my knees bouncing uncontrollably—Adam gave up trying to pin them down—and my heart was pounding to the frantic beat of the music.

"Ladies and gentlemen, the moment you have all been waiting for…"

Unconsciously, I grabbed Adam's arm and squeezed hard, keeping my eyes trained on the door and, ignoring Adam's cries of pain. I was just too excited to see my man.

"…Let's hear it for your golden boy, Nathan Oaaaaaakes."

"Oh My God!" I shrieked, jumping out of my seat and clapping loudly. It took everything in me to stop from jumping up and down like an overly excited five-year-old. Then the music hit me. The song had changed to Nate's entrance music, a song I instantly recognised, 'Wiggle' by Jason Derulo. It had kind of become my anthem since meeting Nate. A smile tugged at my lips, even though I narrowed my eyes and pursed my lips in mock annoyance at the handsome man slowly making his way along the walkway. People were yelling his name and shouting words of encouragement, but he blanked them out, focusing on keeping his muscles warm and supple. And me.

As he neared, his eyes were fixed on mine, his focus now on me and me alone. I swallowed hard when he stopped a mere inch in front of me, much to the surprise of the officials walking along with him.

"This song, really?" I croaked, failing miserably at trying to stay composed when his body and eyes were burning so fiercely into me.

His head tilted as though listening to the music for the first time before his face lit up into a dazzling smile.

Much to the delight of his audience—well the male members of it anyway—he snaked his arms around my body and tugged me in tight. "It's for you. It's all for you." He growled against my ear before smothering my lips with his in a kiss that had my knees trembling and my heart practically jumping from my chest in an attempt to throw itself at him.

All around us, people were whistling and catcalling, but I barely heard. In that moment, it could have been just the two of us.

All too soon, he pulled away, but not before sliding his hands down to my backside and giving a cheeky squeeze. I yelped and looked frantically around me, flushed with embarrassment, as he laughed and backed away towards the entrance into the cage.

The next few minutes went by in a blur while I tried to calm my racing heart and shaking hands that had nothing to do with nerves anymore. Adam sat beside me, laughing the whole time. Bastard. It was safe to say he'd moved past his apparent romantic love for me and had reacquainted himself with the older emotion of loving me as a friend. It had been a huge relief when he'd reverted back to his old ways with me, although I suspected there was someone else I needed to thank for that—a petite, yet fiery, masseuse to be precise. Not that either of them would admit it, but I'd seen the lust filled gazes they'd been shooting at each other lately. I couldn't be happier for my two closest friends if things were working out for them. Adam needed a challenge, and Cassie certainly provided him with one.

With my senses finally returned to near normal levels, I focused on the cage and the men now in it. The fighters were being introduced; their stats, fighting records and disciplines being announced to their adoring fans. I noticed the posture of the two men as they stood facing each other. Sanchez was glaring at Nate, but he seemed different than before. There was a definite uneasiness to the way he held himself, almost as if his shaking arms and legs were masking his fear. I knew why when I studied Nate. He stood taller, prouder, and definitely had the edge over Sanchez with his physique. His arms, chorded with thick veins, tensed into fists ready to strike. Strong leg muscles rippled with his eagerness to get started. His usually sparkly silver-grey eyes were dark and dangerous. They bored into Sanchez with the intention of destroying his opponent.

He was sexy as hell.

The horn sounded, echoing throughout the arena, drawing spectators to their feet whilst others cupped their mouths and shouted tactical ideas. Without the feeling of dread settling over me, it was a buzz like no other. And knowing that one of the guys in the cage was mine, well it set my heart on fire with pride and possession.

Nate and Sanchez touched gloves, and then, like they had previously, they spent about a minute circling the cage, testing, judging each other. They threw out half-hearted punches to either gauge reaction or open up a defence. Whatever they were doing, the crowd were getting restless, wanting more action.

"Take him out, Golden."

"Oakes, Oakes, Oakes."

"Kill the fucker, Nate."

They were just some of the chants ringing out around the arena yet the two men were still moving around tentatively.

Without warning, Sanchez lashed out, striking Nate with a full-powered punch to the jaw that had his head cracking to the side. Startled by the sudden hit, Nate's guard momentarily dropped and Sanchez used it to his advantage, swinging with a left hook and following up with a fierce knee to the stomach. Unable to keep his balance, Nate toppled to his knees with Sanchez following him to the canvas.

Suddenly my excitement and jubilation were gone as sickening memories of the previous fight returned. All I could see was Nate's lifeless body lying prone on the cage floor.

Turning in my seat, I buried my head in Adam's shoulder, not wanting to look. I couldn't see him lose again. I couldn't watch while Sanchez choked the life out of him and laughed.

Suddenly the cheers became fever pitched and I could sense the crowd all jumping to their feet.

No, no, no, not again.

Adam wrapped an arm around my shoulder and drew me in. "Liv, you need to see this," he yelled in my ear to be heard above the over-exuberant crowd.

My head shook. "I can't. I can't see it again." Grabbing a fistful of his t-shirt, I held tight hoping his comfort would protect me from whatever Nate was going through in the cage.

The crowd grew louder.

"Liv, you *really* need to watch this." With a gentle force, Adam pushed me away and made me face the cage.

"Knock him out, Nate."

"Kill the bastard."

I was shocked to find the person who had jumped to their feet and was yelling at Nate to, *"finish him,"* was me.

Nate had somehow managed to regain the upper hand and had Sanchez in a prone position, grappling on the floor. I knew that ground work was where he was strongest and could do most damage.

He must have heard my yells over the scream of the crowds, heard my voice encouraging him. His lips pulled into a sly grin before he began pounding Sanchez with a series of punches so fast I could barely see each individual movement, they all blurred into one. Sanchez tried to defend, rocking this way and that, trying to knock Nate from him. But Nate was stronger, more powerful, and before I could tell what was happening, he'd locked his arms around Sanchez's neck.

I held my breath, waiting to see what would happen next. Nate was breathing heavily, his back glistened with sweat from his exertions, but still he kept his hold. Each of his strong muscles tensed and stretched as he fought to contain Sanchez's attempts to escape.

My breath exploded as a sob when Sanchez's hand flew out to his side and slapped the canvas three times.

Nate's whole body sagged with relief as his hold on

Sanchez eased and he stepped away. Around us, the crowd went wild, but all I could see was Nate. My Nate. My champion.

"Ladies and gentlemen, at three minutes and thirty-two seconds of round one, your winner by submission, your golden boy, Naaaaathan Oaaaakes." Nate's hand was tugged into the air as the cage announcer declared him the winner. Bernie and Wes rushed into the cage, slapping his back and yelling their praise while, all around, people were screaming his name.

I stood motionless.

There was no yelling. There were no fans. It was just Nate and me. Silent tears of happiness streamed down my face as a mixture of relief, pride and overwhelming love for this man, this fighter, consumed me.

Nate's gaze finally locked on to mine, his lips pulling up into a blinding grin. My knees felt weak, they were barely holding me upright. Nate gave me strength though. With his smile, he gave me everything. Swiping away the tears, I returned his smile, hoping he could see how proud I was of him. How much I loved him.

Our peaceful connection was broken by a compere approaching Nate with a microphone. "Nate, congratulations! How does it feel to be world champion again?"

Nate kept his eyes locked on mine as he answered. "It's incredible."

"It sure was. Your fans were worried there for a while that we might have been having a repeat of your last fight. Do you have anything to say to them?"

Nate's eyes clouded and narrowed but still he kept

them trained on me. "That was never going to happen. Sanchez needed to be taught a thing or two. I've done that tonight."

"We'll you certainly pulled it out of the bag when you needed to. I have to say, you looked good out here tonight. What was different this time round?"

"I finally realised what had been missing from my training routine." He nodded in my direction, still keeping our gazes locked. "I found the missing piece and was prepared to fight for it."

He wasn't the only one. I hadn't realised until I met Nate that something had been missing from my life. I'd been so determined to stay focused on my career and to impress my bosses, I'd lost sight of the possibility that there might be something just as rewarding as a satisfying job. I'd lost sight of love. In Nate, I too had found my missing piece. I'd initially thought I had to fight my feelings for him, that love had no place in my life or even in his. But in the end, I'd been prepared to fight *for* him and not *against* him.

As Nate climbed down from the cage and made his way to me, I felt an overwhelming sense of completeness. Tugging me into his arms, he captured my lips in a kiss that was both possessive and passionate. It was a kiss of victory. We'd both fought. We'd both won.

~EPILOGUE~

Nate

I STOOD RESTING AGAINST THE wooden door frame of my new, custom-built gym. Across the room from me was the most beautiful sight in the world. It wasn't the gritty, contemporary look of my new gym or the bare, brick walls that were decorated with various posters that had my attention. The large skylight windows that allowed vast amounts of sunlight in to brighten the room were special to me, but not as much as the person responsible for them was. No, the sight that had me reeling, like I'd been pummelled for ten long rounds, was the brown-haired beauty currently standing mesmerised by the latest decoration to have been hung on the wall. My belt. Or more specifically, my championship winning belt.

I'd been watching her for the past five minutes as she simply stood and stared, her lips twitching and pulling up into a beaming smile. Fuck, that smile. That was the sucker punch, every time. No matter what I was feeling or going through, with that simple smile, Liv could pull me out of whatever mood I was in. There had been many occasions where she'd rescued me from the rage that often crept over me when I'd been thinking of my parents. Other times, I'd felt pissed because yet another flake had come on to me, thinking their perky, fake tits would entice me into their bed. Fuck that! I neither wanted nor needed insincere people in my life. I wanted genuine, loyal people, those that saw me for who I was. And she did. Liv didn't care that I was in the public eye because of my love for a sport. She embraced my sport because I loved it, and she wanted to share in that passion with me. She also didn't care that I had a fat bank account and could give her anything she wanted. And I would, if she would only let me. However, she never did. She never asked for anything other than my love and respect, and I was happy to be allowed to shower her with both.

I couldn't tell you precisely what it was about Olivia Buchanan that first drew me to her. Maybe it was that initial vulnerability I'd seen in her eyes as she'd tried to seem cool on the treadmill at my gym, Golden Oakes. Maybe it was the overwhelming need to protect her I'd felt when she'd fallen off the thing, stumbling over her own footing. It could have been the way my body had reacted to seeing her inquisitive eyes peeking into my private training room. There had been something refreshing about her quiet intrigue. Most of the women I trained—and a lot of the men too—were simply prepared to pay the hefty price for my time so they could brag that they'd been trained by *the* Nathan Oakes. It wasn't because of what I could truly teach them but because of who I was.

Liv's feisty attitude had definitely been part of my attraction to her too. I'd loved how she persistently challenged me and fired back with her sassy comments. It had been refreshing to have someone stand up to me without the artful bravado of the fighting world.

Pushing myself away from the doorframe of my new French gym and treatment rooms, I strolled across the room to my very sweet, very sexy, Jelly Bean—JB. I wrapped my arms around her waist. God, I loved this woman. From the very beginning, when I first propositioned her to train with me, she'd had a vivacity and inner beauty that simply radiated from her very being.

Tugging her against me, I stroked one hand underneath her perfect tits and ran my nose along the soft skin of her neck, breathing her in deeply. She always smelled delicious, like fresh berries. "What are you staring at" I asked, already knowing the answer. Even if I hadn't been watching her, I would have known. She'd not been able to lose the proud look since Sanchez tapped out during the fight the night before. It had definitely been worth putting off retirement again to fight him just to see the look of love and adoration on her face. I'd do it again, over and over, if I could guarantee she'd never lose that expression for me.

My lips followed the path my nose had and her

whole body shivered under my caress. "You know what I'm looking at." Her smile widened as she tilted her head to the side, a silent request for more. She always wanted more.

"Bernie's photo?" I feigned outrage.

She turned in my arms and slapped me on the chest. "No, you idiot. I was staring at your belt. It's kind of awe inspiring."

"Awe inspiring huh?" She was the awe inspiring one. On a daily basis she managed to surprise me. She had a definite talent for drawing—buildings, objects, scenery, it didn't matter. It was all so detailed and beautiful. Olivia was a true artist. Yet the real beauty of it was that she just couldn't see how good she was. She never saw herself as better than anyone else, or put others down. Well, unless they were skinny, blonde bitches making inappropriate comments. Then she'd quite happily verbalise her opinions. Both made me love her even more.

"Yes, awe-inspiring. You, Nathan Oakes, are most definitely awe-inspiring." She ran a finger along the small cut above my right eye. Along with a slight bruise on my right cheek, it was the only evidence I'd been in the cage the night before, a stark contrast to the bruising and swelling I'd come out with the last time, when… No, not going there. Those fucking arseholes got their just deserts for what they did to me. Well, apart from Sanchez who'd managed to weasel his way out of any wrong doing. We'd all born witness to his threats, but it hadn't been enough for the officials. So I'd made him pay in the best way possible, humiliation in front of hundreds of thousands of people across the globe.

"You know what is awe-inspiring?" I asked, my voice sounding a little more choked than I'd intended. That's what she did to me. She brought out a level of emotion I'd long forgotten existed.

Lifting her chin with my fingers so she would look me in the eye, I continued, "You."

Before she had a chance to reply and refute my claim, I grabbed her hand and started walking. "Come for a walk with me." I needed to take her down to our special spot before the evening's guests started arriving.

Out in the courtyard, caterers rushed around putting finishing touches to the tables and decorations. Tonight was the official opening of the GO Sports & Leisure Training and Rehabilitation Centre. My centre. My dream. A place I was immensely proud of.

I knew if it hadn't been for Bernie taking me in and pulling me from a probable life of crime, I wouldn't be where I was today. I'd probably be in the slammer... or worse. Bernie had taught me about myself and about focusing my energies in the right way. When I had the opportunity to purchase this piece of land, I'd known what I intended to do with it. I wanted to give back and help others in an area that had given me my only real happy childhood memories.

For years, the place had remained in its disused, vineyard state, providing me with a place to crash and train when I needed peace and solitude but not living up to my hopes for it. Despite my intentions, I'd not been able to truly appreciate the land and what it could offer. It wasn't until I came across the talents of Olivia Buchanan that I finally had a vision for the place. It was like she lit something in me. Suddenly, everything came into focus and I knew what I wanted. Just as she had done with the UK plans for GO, Liv had blown me away with her ideas and drawings. I'd never be able to thank her enough for making my dreams a reality. I would certainly try though.

We walked in silence along the landscaped path towards the river, to *our* place. The path led from the courtyard, where the gym and treatment rooms were located. It twisted around an accommodation block that housed ten bedrooms, each with en-suite facilities. It continued past four separate bungalows and the restaurant. Set back, away from everything, was my renovated house. Liv had been determined that the old building not be knocked down. She'd loved the rustic, old French charm of it and convinced me to simply extend and update. She had been right; the new, old home was awesome, especially when Liv was with me.

Finally, our rock came into view, and I led Liv over to it. Evening was turning into dusk. The river, darkened by the muted navy and gold sky, gently flowed past, reflecting the trees and rock faces lining both banks. From behind us, the soft sounds of laughter and music carried on the warm evening breeze. We didn't have long. We'd need to get back to our guests so I could proudly show off Liv's creation. This night was as much hers as it was mine, and I'd invited all her friends and family out to celebrate with us. I hoped we'd be celebrating more than the opening though.

Liv took her spot on the rock, and I settled in behind her, pulling her against my chest. She sighed in contentment.

"This view never gets old," she said, wriggling to

373

find a comfortable spot.

"No, it doesn't," I replied, craning my neck so I could see her profile. I much preferred the view of Liv to the river.

"I'm so proud of you, Nate. What you have done with this place… what you'll be doing for so many people, it's noble. You should be knighted or something."

I chuckled at her ridiculous statement. I was simply providing facilities to those who needed a helping hand or a starting point. If anyone was proud, it was me. Of Liv. She had worked so hard to make a name for herself and was steadily building the new European section of Ashworth-Moore that she'd been asked to head up. She now had several people working under her and continued to build their client base abroad. My JB was going places.

"I don't know about that, JB, but I'm happy to be your *Sir* anytime. All you need to do is ask." I nipped her earlobe.

"Hmm, let me think about that… Please, Sir Oakes, let me worship at your feet. I've been a naughty girl, I need spanking… yeah I think not." My chest jerked against her back with laughter.

"Oh, I don't know, it doesn't sound like such a bad idea."

"Pfft. Not happening, Oakes. No knighthood for you."

We sat in comfortable silence, in our spot, enjoying the rapidly changing landscape as the last of the sun disappeared and stars began to twinkle above us. We would need to get back to the party soon, but before we did, I had one very important thing I needed to ask.

Reaching into the inside pocket of my black suit jacket, I pulled out the small circle of platinum I'd been hiding and held it in my fist. This was the moment. After months and months of preparing, this was my final fight, the fight of my life. I had no idea if I would be celebrating my win and taking home the prize though.

My hand shook slightly as I moved it in front of Liv, keeping it fisted. She looked down, her brows pulling together with a cute confused expression, but she didn't say anything.

"JB, you know I'm a man of few words, so I'm just gonna ask this outright." Slowly I stretched out my fingers, revealing the platinum and diamond engagement ring. "Will you marry me?"

Her head cocked to the side before she lifted the ring from my palm and looked it over, studying it intently. My breathing stopped. I'm pretty sure my heart did too. Did she not like it? Maybe I'd misread the signs that this was what she wanted too.

For several moments she simply held the ring aloft, checking it from this angle and that. Then she slipped it on the ring finger of her left hand. "Yes," was her easy and simple reply.

"Yes?"

"Yes, Nate. I'll marry you. I didn't need Mount Everest on my finger though, as beautiful as it is. I would have said yes if you'd given me the ring pull from a can of coke."

I let out my breath and chuckled. Marriage proposal acceptance, Olivia Buchanan style. "Thank you," I said, turning her head so I could kiss her.

"You're welcome," she mumbled through our kiss.

I smiled against her lips.

"I love you, Olivia Buchanan."

"And I love you, Nathan Oakes. My champion."

~ABOUT THE AUTHOR~

E.J. Shortall was born and raised in London, England where she currently still lives with her teenage son.

Having worked in education for the better part of 12 years, EJ decided a change was needed and, following a moment of inspiration, she decided to put pen to paper and start writing her first novel. Not content with just the one, she continued with book two and hopes to write many more.

She has always enjoyed reading, but found it was mostly just a holiday extravagance. Then she discovered a certain worldwide best seller, and that was it she was hooked. Reading quickly became an obsession and she couldn't devour books fast enough. The books on her shelves and reading device range from sweet, Young Adult romances, to smouldering erotic encounters.

Aside from reading and writing, EJ also enjoys amateur photography and cake decorating.

"I'm on one amazing roller coaster ride at the moment, meeting new and wonderful people, discovering new music gems to integrate into my stories, and learning so many new skills. I can't wait to see where this journey takes me."

To find out more about E.J. and her other titles, visit her:

Email: ejshortallauthor@gmail.com
Newsletter: http://bit.ly/ejshortallnews
Website: www.ejshortallauthor.com
Facebook: www.facebook.com/e.j.shortallauthor
Twitter: twitter.com/EJShortall

~ALSO BY E.J. SHORTALL~

Silver Lining (Silver series book one)

Amber Merchant had it all. Living with and engaged to her teenage sweetheart, a nice house and the job of her dreams. Not anymore!

Following a devastating revelation from her Fiancé, Amber finds herself single once again and moving on. To protect herself she vows to stay away from men and guard her wounded heart.

During an evening out to celebrate her newly single life, a chance encounter with a tall, dark and handsome stranger leaves Amber's head reeling. Intrigued by her draw to him but scared for her heart she flees.

Craig Silver, twenty nine year old CEO, is the last person Amber needs in her life. Battling his own demons, Craig is content on a life of meaningless affairs, one night stands and no commitments.

At first it seems their attraction is mutual… until she runs.

When fate intervenes and their paths cross again, Craig refuses to take no for an answer. Encouraging Amber to take a chance on a single date he sets them on a path of love, lust, truth and deception.

http://mybook.to/SilverLining

Silver Dove (Silver series book two)

Full of romance, intrigue, emotion and passion, Silver Dove is the concluding part to Craig and Amber's story that began in Silver Lining.

After the chaos of their early relationship and with their history of broken pasts behind them, Craig and Amber prepare to say 'I Do' on their Happy Ever After.

Life rarely runs to plan though.

Amber has fought long and hard to bury her fears and become a stronger person, but when old feelings resurface and tragedy strikes, it takes an intervention from Craig to prove her doubts are unfounded and to believe in love and hope.

Just when they think they are at a point where they can be happy and move forward together, the pair find themselves fighting obstacles and difficulties that will truly test the strength of their bond.

Can Amber gather the strength to fight against the forces trying to destroy her? Will Craig keep his promises of remaining truthful? As a couple are they tough enough to battle through these turbulent times and emerge stronger than ever?

http://mybook.to/SilverDove